DAUGHTERS
of
SHANDONG

DAUGHTERS
of
SHANDONG

EVE J. CHUNG

BERKLEY
New York

BERKLEY
An imprint of Penguin Random House LLC
penguinrandomhouse.com

Copyright © 2024 by Eve J. Chung
Penguin Random House supports copyright. Copyright fuels creativity, encourages diverse voices, promotes free speech, and creates a vibrant culture. Thank you for buying an authorized edition of this book and for complying with copyright laws by not reproducing, scanning, or distributing any part of it in any form without permission. You are supporting writers and allowing Penguin Random House to continue to publish books for every reader.

BERKLEY and the BERKLEY & B colophon are registered trademarks of
Penguin Random House LLC.

Map by David Lindroth

Export Edition ISBN: 9780593817407

Library of Congress Cataloging-in-Publication Data
Names: Chung, Eve J. author.
Title: Daughters of Shandong / Eve J. Chung.
Description: New York : Berkley, 2024.
Identifiers: LCCN 2023036908 (print) | LCCN 2023036909 (ebook) |
ISBN 9780593640531 (hardcover) | ISBN 9780593640555 (ebook)
Subjects: LCGFT: Historical fiction. | Novels.
Classification: LCC PS3603.H85334 D38 2024 (print) |
LCC PS3603.H85334 (ebook) | DDC 813/.6--dc23/eng/20231106
LC record available at https://lccn.loc.gov/2023036908
LC ebook record available at https://lccn.loc.gov/2023036909

Printed in the United States of America
1st Printing

Book design by Daniel Brount

This is a work of fiction. Names, characters, places, and incidents either are the product of the author's imagination or are used fictitiously, and any resemblance to actual persons, living or dead, business establishments, events, or locales is entirely coincidental.

To my grandmother, and to my children, who never got to meet her. It is my hope that through this story, they can understand her strength, and appreciate what a phenomenal person she was.

DAUGHTERS
of
SHANDONG

When I recall my birthplace, Zhucheng, Shandong, I think first of our *shiheyuan*, the traditional courtyard home that I grew up in. Within the white walls that housed my family for generations, I smell my mother's cooking and hear my sisters sing.

Zhucheng today is famous for dinosaurs, but back then their skeletons slept, undiscovered beneath fertile farmland. As a child, I tumbled through fields, dancing ignorantly above these giants. I leaped along our town's outer wall, chipped away by time, a stone mouth with jagged teeth. Though bombs left our landscape pockmarked, we endured. We regrew and we rebuilt.

Peace was slippery, quick inhalations between violent tides. When war came again, we held our breath as it dragged us into its ebb and flow. It swallowed our people. It claimed our homes.

The China I knew ached, and the hometown I knew bled.

Yet still, I close my eyes and see curving rivers and wildflower fields. Soft clouds caress stalwart mountains. Our temples stand, defiant and holy.

I carry that land in my blood, in my bones, and in my memories. From across the sea, I draw strength. In my present, I feel warmth. Most important, I choose to remember love. Wherever I am in this world, I remain as I was, and always will be—the wheat that bursts through Shandong soil, and the Northern flowers that bloom in snow.

Zhucheng, Shandong

1

HEIRLESS

Nai Nai said whores weren't allowed in the house, so she kicked Mom out, slamming the wooden door shut with a clatter that startled the birds. We didn't know where my sister Di was, but Three and I sat beside Mom as she leaned against the courtyard wall of our *shiheyuan*, hands red and chapped from washing dishes. "Don't worry," she said to us. "She'll calm down when your father comes home." Nai Nai was a small, thin lady with ebony hair, birdlike hands, and dainty bound feet. Yet, even as she tottered in her small silk slippers, she had the presence of a warlord and a tongue like a whip. I was eleven, and old enough to know that no one could calm her after such a rage, not even her first and favorite son.

It was fall, and dried leaves swirled in the chilly wind, skimming yellow grass that swayed gently. Luckily, the harvest was finished and most of the workers had gone home. Mom didn't want reports of this shameful spectacle to make the rounds—the peasants hated Nai Nai as much as they loved gossip, and this story would have spread like a wildfire. We lived in rural Zhucheng, a small town where my family reigned. For generations, our men had excelled in imperial exams, earning prestigious government positions and building an empire through renting land and running businesses. Our palatial *siheyuan*, with its gleaming orange tiles and wooden latticed panels, was an ostentatious testament to our wealth. Magnificent stone lions framed the entrance of the courtyard, which was large enough for a lotus pond full of shimmering koi. They swam in circles lazily, eyes globular, and gulped at two-year-old Three as she peered into the water.

Nai Nai had a nose for lies and could almost always tell when a secret lurked inside her walls. Still, Mom had been hiding her pregnancy for weeks. "It will be a boy this time. I can feel it, Li-Hai," she said to me repeatedly, as though her anxious mutterings could manifest a son. As soon as I was born, I was a disappointment. When Second Sister arrived one year later, she was a failure. Father wistfully named her Li-Di, since *di* meant "younger brother." Then Third Sister came along, a catastrophe so horrific that she got only a number: Three.

Three girls rattled the Angs enough for Nai Nai to take drastic measures. Though she watched every coin like it was a fragment of her soul, she decided to trade an ounce of gold for a glimpse into the future. Together, she and Mom went to a famous fortune-teller in a neighboring town and asked if a male heir was forthcoming. Mom wrote down the date and time of her birth as he examined the lines on her palm, reading it like it was a map of her life. Handing Mom an amber amulet for protection, he declared solemnly that Mom would not have a son until she turned thirty-six.

Mom was only in her late twenties then, but Nai Nai came home giddy, delighted that an heir would arrive eventually. She ordered my parents to sleep in separate rooms and forbade them from having intercourse until Mom's thirty-sixth birthday. Lauding herself for her ingenuity, she boasted, "This will save us the expense of raising additional daughters!" After all, girls were nothing more than wives for other people's sons.

Father obeyed and set up his own bedroom, but he told Nai Nai that fortune-tellers were a scam. "We make our own fate," he insisted, a feeble protest that she ignored. At night, Nai Nai remained a vigilant guard, monitoring the hallway with bizarre frequency. Despite her enthusiasm, even the fiercest dragon succumbs to slumber. A few months later, Mom became pregnant for the fourth time.

"Don't tell anyone," Mom whispered to me, and continued her chores as though nothing had changed. Every morning, she woke up at four a.m. to cook breakfast for about eighty workers who lived on and tilled our land. They began work at dawn, so Mom had to grind flour by lamplight. She was a fantastic cook, and made buns and dumplings like they were art. With deft hands, she could roll dough thin like paper for butterfly wontons, knead fluffy, airy dessert bun clouds, and pull springy, chewy bread that rose like soldiers saluting in the steamer.

Despite our wealth, Nai Nai watched the pantry with military precision. Every evening, she weighed the flour to make sure that Mom wasn't being too generous to the workers. The food was never enough, so Mom snuck extra helpings where she could. Through practice, she learned to spin white lies that squeaked under Nai Nai's shrewd radar. Once, Mom made pork buns for a worker's sick child and told Nai Nai the meat was gone because it had spoiled. She passed extra noodles to everyone, and then claimed that mice had broken into the pantry. The workers appreciated Mom and understood the gravity of these risks, because they had a saying: "Wild dogs are dangerous, and ghosts are scary, but nothing is more terrifying than Madame Ang," my Nai Nai.

Nai Nai could have hired servants to help Mom with her tasks, but she considered frugality a pillar in sustaining the Ang fortune. Also, she detested Mom—first, for marrying her son, and second, for having large feet. My parents had been betrothed as infants, and Mom's family, the Daos in Rizhao, were *biao* cousins of the Angs. *Biao* cousins had different surnames and, at that time, could marry one another, but *tang* cousins, who shared the same surname and family tomb, were akin to siblings.

The Daos owned the majority of the ships in Rizhao's waters and prospered through maritime trade. A wealthy girl like Mom should have had properly bound feet, and my Lao Lao had tried to bind them—she had wrapped Mom's feet early on, insisting that a happy husband was worth the agony of broken bones. In Lao Lao's world of silk and porcelain, the freedom to walk was an acceptable price to pay for a man's affection. The *Kuomintang*, the Nationalist government, however, had banned foot-binding, and their campaigns against it grew increasingly aggressive. After a few years, Lao Lao grudgingly cut Mom's bindings. The damage, however, was irreversible. For the rest of her life Mom hobbled, her feet having been molded flat on the bottom with a pronounced arch at the top.

Nai Nai, meanwhile, had remained defiant before the Nationalist prohibition. She was proud of her three-inch lotuses, and no government lackey could scare her into relinquishing thousands of years of tradition. "Large feet are for peasants," Nai Nai said with disdain when seventeen-year-old Mom arrived for the wedding. "If you aren't a proper lady, you might as well be useful!"

I wished that young Mom had heeded that red flag and fled back to Rizhao, begging her parents for another match. Instead, she went ahead with the ceremony, cutting ties with the Daos—a bride's mother used to throw a bucket of water out the front door after the wedding to symbolize that her daughter, like the water, could never return.

Salivating, Mom told me that her parents sent crates of crabs for that banquet, which ended up being her last special meal. In our *shiheyuan*, Mom was not allowed to eat crab, because Nai Nai reserved delicacies for the men. Instead, Mom had to crack open the shells and pluck the soft flesh into bowls for Father and Yei Yei. She might have snuck a bite here or there, but it was a great change from her childhood of abundance to her married life, taking a quick morsel while hunched over a counter, with one eye on the door. In her own house, my mother was a thief of minuscule riches, eating these stolen tidbits not only for the taste but for the evocation of childhood memories, the only luxury that she could keep for herself.

On the morning of our eviction, Mom had been in the kitchen poaching eggs for Nai Nai's breakfast. As she filled the sink with water, the smell of dirty dishes triggered a bout of nausea and she vomited. Sirens went off in Nai Nai's head, and she launched her accusations like cannonballs. "You're pregnant, aren't you?" she cried, upending the remainder of her soup, white threads of egg sloshing all over the table. Mom should have lied, but she was too sick to think straight and crumbled under Nai Nai's glare. She nodded.

Grabbing Three, I dove underneath the table as Nai Nai began yanking bowls from the cabinets. Angry Nai Nai didn't care about wasting money, which meant she didn't care about anything. Screaming, she hurled the bowls at Mom, who covered her head as they shattered like ceramic bombs against the wall. Sharp shards scattered across the floor as Three shook in my arms—she knew better than to cry when Nai Nai was in a mood. "My son would never disobey me!" Nai Nai shrieked, her aim worsening with her mounting fury. "You must have had an affair. Tell me who it is. Is it one of the workers? Whoever it is, I'll find out!"

Her tirade lasted at least ten minutes and ended with "Whores go to hell!" and the three of us outside without our jackets. As I wrapped my hands around my bare arms, I wondered what Nai Nai would have done if the fortune-teller had said that Mom would never have an heir. Would she have killed her? Sold her? It was hard to say. I'd lived with Nai Nai all my life, and I wanted to believe that there was a limit to her cruelty. However, the old lady continued to surprise me.

From across the koi pond, my cousin Chiao stepped into the courtyard, clutching a toy sword in his sausage fingers. "Auntie! Hi, Auntie!" he yelled, skipping toward us, his round belly bobbing. "Look what Yei Yei brought me! Hai, wanna play bandits and warlords? You have to be the bandit since you don't have a sword."

Before I could reply that bandits had swords too, Mom said, "Chiao, run inside and get some warm clothing for Hai and Three. It's getting colder now that the sun is setting. When you are back, you and Hai can play."

"Okay!" Chiao agreed cheerfully, not bothering to ask why we were stuck outside. Within our *shiheyuan*, Chiao was in his own bubble of favor, and it did not occur to him that we were being punished. After all, he was the coveted son of Father's younger brother, Jian, and the only grandson in my generation. He got the best of everything—including crab! Nai Nai gave him crisp fried dough for breakfast and slabs of soft braised pork belly for lunch. Yei Yei said only boys got gifts, and he returned from Qingdao with trinkets for Chiao, while Di and I watched, empty-handed.

Girls were lucky to be housed. We were lucky to be raised. We were lucky to be fed.

I was jealous of Chiao, but I knew that only men could worship our ancestors at the family tomb; only Chiao could provide for Nai Nai and Yei Yei, and my own parents, in the afterlife. Di and I were taught to pray for Chiao's success, and I did, because Mom's welfare in the spirit realm would depend on him one day. *Zhong nan qing nu*, an idiom that meant "Value men and belittle women," was embedded in my understanding of our world.

It was almost sunset when Father came home, a leather bag on his shoulder, Mom frantic at the gate. Three and I waited outside as Father went to find Nai Nai and confess his complicity in the betrayal, his wife trailing small in his shadow. Mom said that once upon a time, Father loved her; I was just too young to remember it. Maybe it was true, but I saw my parents as a land animal and a sea animal chained together, forced to remain on the water's edge—each surviving but neither thriving. When they were younger, Father supposedly snuck Mom pork hock stew from the kitchen and brought her flowers from the field. He changed after he went to study literature at university in Qingdao, shortly before the Japanese invasion. To escape the Japanese bombs, we temporarily moved farther north, to Weihaiwei, a former British territory on Shandong's coast, while Father remained in school. His education transformed him into a man who spoke in proverbs and dwelled in the realm of poetry. After the war, he returned to a wife who knew only cooking and farming. Once surrounded by inspirational teachers and like-minded scholars, at home he found himself in a vacuum of silence, which gradually filled with his resentment. Filial piety, however, required him to produce an heir. His misery—and hers—was irrelevant.

Father opened the door, and Three and I entered the kitchen to find Mom sweeping up the broken bowls. Nai Nai sat red-faced at the table, simmering. "Six more years! All I asked you to do was wait six more years! Now there will be another useless mouth to feed!"

"You can't take the fortune-teller so seriously," Father said quietly. "It could be a boy."

Nai Nai was unmollified, but she couldn't stay mad at her son. Instead, she focused her ire on Mom, blaming her for being a temptress. "I told you not to fight fate, but you didn't listen," Nai Nai said angrily. "Your arrogance has invited misfortune, and your daughter will be a blight on our household!"

That evening, while Father ate the dinner that Mom had cooked, Mom had to kneel on the floor—Nai Nai's favorite punishment to mete out. I grew up watching my mother on her knees, sometimes for an entire evening, for minor transgressions, like spilling soup. Solemnly, I looked at her, but she would not meet my gaze. Small, shiny teardrops fell from her eyes like pearls, shattering as they hit the tile. *I hope that when I grow up, I can have a son*, I thought, seeing my own future in her helpless form.

Life was unfair, but Mom said that it could always be worse. "Be grateful," she told me. "At least you were born to a good family. You will likely marry a rich man and have a comfortable life." I dreaded marriage, but it was as unavoidable as death. If I was lucky, maybe I would pair with a man with a kind mother—or a dead one.

2

THREE SISTERS

In July 1948, Mom went into labor with the summer heat hanging over her and with Nai Nai complaining bitterly beside her. A baby cried, and Nai Nai let out an anguished wail. Fourth Sister had arrived, and she was an abomination. Father didn't bother to name her, so Mom called her Li-Lan, with *lan* meaning "orchid."

For the next month, Mom was in confinement, a period of postpartum rest during which she had to stay indoors and refrain from bathing. To bring on Mom's milk, Aunt Ji, Chiao's mother, secretly prepared pork hock stewed with peanuts, omitting the soy sauce to prevent scarring and dark spots. Aunt Ji's feet were even larger than Mom's, but she had birthed a prince, and therefore could be a queen. The two women, however, had a tender relationship. Nai Nai was still angry at Mom, so Aunt Ji told her the meat was for Chiao. When in doubt, we blamed everything on our treasured heir, whose affable smile was our best defense.

While Mom recovered, we girls were supposed to cover her tasks. Di, however, was always hiding. Her greatest talent was picking the right place to be at the right time. When chores were handed out, she would disappear. When goods were handed out, she would reappear, as if by magic. She got away with it because she was just another girl among a bunch of girls. If I complained, Mom would say that I was being petty—I was the oldest, after all, and it was natural for me to work more and care for my younger siblings and cousins. I resented Di's laziness, but my bitterness didn't matter—Di was always in her own world and seemed happiest when left alone.

Generally, I was in charge of minding Three. If there was anyone more disappointed than Nai Nai by Lan's birth, it was she. She was despondent to have to share Mom's attention, and she grudgingly accepted me as a substitute. "Get used to it, Three," I told her. "Hopefully, Lan will not be as annoying as Di, but regardless, she's here to stay."

It was a blazing hot day, so I took Three to the river, hoping that a cool wade would cheer her up. Our family owned a large portion of the riverbank and planted sweet potatoes there each year. By the end of the harvest season, we had heavy sacks bursting at the seams with chewy deep orange sweet potato strips that would last well beyond the cold season.

I carried Three on my hip, while Chiao and his younger sister, Pei, gamboled along the road beside us. Heart-shaped sweet potato leaves kissed our shins, and the smells of incense and paper burning saturated the air, an ominous reminder that it was Ghost Month, a time when the gates of the underworld would open and the barrier between us and the spirit realm would become porous. "Remember," I said to my cousins, "we have to keep this trip a secret." Mom was superstitious and would be furious if she knew we'd gone to the river while ghosts were out—apoplectic if she knew baby Three was with us. What if a vindictive spirit caused an accident?

I was only a little afraid of ghosts, but was terrified by the aggressive sun that beat down overhead. Mom couldn't expect us to avoid the river during the hottest month! We sweat so much that our clothing stuck to our backs and chests, and we were excited for the relief that the cool water would offer. Three clung to me as we walked along the bank, the river burbling as it tickled the reeds, which in turn sighed contentedly.

Earlier that day, Chiao and I had gone to the watermelon fields, searching for bounty with deep yellow patches. Together, we had knocked on swollen green globes, listening for crisp, juicy flesh, and lugged our chosen sacrifice back. When we found a place to sit, I unpacked slices from my bag and the four of us sank our teeth into summer, pink juice dribbling from our chins to stain the sand.

"Wash up," I commanded my cousins, after sticking the rinds in the soil around the sweet potato plants.

Hollering like monkeys, Chiao and Pei charged into the shallows, sending waterfowl honking and flapping. After splashing their faces clean, they waded through the reeds, searching for frogs. *"Ribbit, ribbit,"* Chiao croaked between giggles. I took off Three's clothes and my shoes and held her hand as we stepped in.

The water swirled around our legs, sending a chill that shivered down my spine and spread through the rest of my body like wind in my veins. Three looked up at me, her face still pink, and smiled a wide, toothy grin. Her hair hung in wisps, almost a light brown in color, clinging to her sweaty forehead. She began to stomp her small feet, splashing and muddying the water. Though she was now a big sister too, I couldn't help but marvel at how small she was—her tiny fingers seemed swallowed in mine as I held on to her tightly.

"Hey, I caught one!" Chiao exclaimed, holding up his cupped hands triumphantly, as though he had found a gold nugget. He leaped through the water in long, splashing strides, clouds of sand blooming with each step. "Want to see a frog?" he asked Three.

Three peered at his muddy hands curiously as he uncupped them like an oyster opening to reveal a pearl. A speckled brown river frog stared back at us and blinked its clear, slimy eyelids. I recoiled, but Three cocked her head and reached out to touch it. Suddenly, like a spring, the frog bounced from Chiao's hands and landed with a sticky splat on my arm. Startled, I let go of Three's hand and she stumbled back, falling rigidly like a wooden plank into the water. Time slowed down as I saw her submerged with her eyes wide-open in terror, sand billowing around her.

Grabbing her quickly under her arms, I yanked her out, sputtering and screaming. *Mom is going to kill me*, I thought as I pressed her tightly against my chest so she couldn't see how scared I was. Three wailed, the water from her body soaking my shirt.

"It's okay, Three," I said in as cheerful a voice as I could muster, rubbing her small back. "It's just a bit of water!" When I was able to shake the fear from my face, I pushed her back and wiped her eyes. "That wasn't so bad, was it?"

"Sorry, Three," said Chiao, with Pei behind him. "I didn't mean for it to scare you!"

Three coughed loudly, accusingly, and gave us all a sour look. "Please don't tell Mom," I pleaded, hoping that she wouldn't have the vocabulary to do so.

The sun dried us quickly as we made our way home for lunch, Chiao and Pei chattering about how hungry they were. In the kitchen, Mom had bags under her eyes, but her hair was tucked into a neat bun and her clothes were clean. Lan was tied to her back, a shock of black hair sticking out over her shoulder. With her stubby nose and beady black eyes, Lan looked like a naughty ghoul in disguise. Wearily, Mom removed a pot from the stove and didn't ask where we had gone. She was probably just happy to have had Three occupied and Chiao and Pei out of the way. No one mentioned the river. Sighing with relief, I grabbed my chopsticks to pull noodles into bowls for everyone.

A few days passed and I thought nothing more of the incident until, one evening, Three came down with a fever. Even though it was summer, Mom covered her with thick blankets, hoping that the warmth would help her body fight against the illness.

Mom said that the cold made you weak, and water allowed the cold to sink into your bones. I started to feel uneasy. Could the fall into the river have cooled Three and lowered her defenses? Three was listless, and instead of clinging to Mom or me, she remained quiet—too quiet. When I picked her up, her head drooped and she closed her eyes, as though she were going to take a nap. She began to cough, weakly but persistently. Mom gave her herbal medications, which helped briefly, but Three never healed. Days blended into weeks, and the cough remained.

I still didn't tell Mom about the river, and neither did Chiao or Pei—although they did not have the same sense of responsibility that I did. I was the oldest, and I should have kept everyone safe. The secret burned in my belly, but when I tried to speak it, my words turned to ash; I couldn't find the courage. Mom urged me to take breaks and rest while caring for Three, but I only bit my lip and shook my head. Unaware of the guilt that ate away from inside me, she praised me for being such a caring older sister.

In my mind, I replayed Three's fall repeatedly. That frog must have been a ghost—one that had been hiding in the reeds, waiting to cause mischief. I should have known better than to go to the river during Ghost Month. We should have spent the day burning paper money and incense instead. I should have protected Three, but I had led her to danger. *I should have never taken her. I should have never taken her.* This became the macabre mantra that I recited to myself day and night as Three seemed to shrink before our eyes.

We realized that Three had tuberculosis, which was especially contagious in the warm, wet summer air. To prevent the rest of the family from getting sick, we stayed isolated in a room—just Mom, me, Three, and Lan. Mom had told me and Di to go with Chiao's family, but I had refused. This was not because of my guilt; rather, it was because I knew my place, and it was with Mom—I could never let her go through this alone. My aunt left food outside our door, and Chiao and Pei would sometimes slip me notes with jokes and drawings. I was never a comedian, but I tried my best to boost Three's spirits, singing her songs and reciting children's rhymes. Like the herbal medicine, my cheer helped a bit, but its effects began to wane.

Three fought us over the medicine less, too weak to resist. The herbal concoctions, however, seemed to make no impact at all. She came to a point where she stopped eating solid food. Little Three, who used to rival Chiao in her gluttony, turned down her favorite dishes; we offered yams, sweet sticky rice, and dumplings, with no success. "Please eat," I begged. "Just a little bit." Mom held slices of moist sesame oil chicken to her lips, but she only shook her head and closed her eyes. She was dying.

Mom had faced many hardships in her life, but I seldom saw her cry. I knew that she had begged Father and Nai Nai to take Three to a doctor, to no avail. One night, while Lan and Three lay sleeping, Mom and I left the room together. Perhaps she thought that my company would help her case. Perhaps she thought that it would lend her strength.

In the living room, Nai Nai was seated on her favorite chair, a beautiful piece of solid, polished mahogany that had come from Mom's dowry. Yei Yei was away on business, and Father was seated across the table, on a matching chair from that furniture set. Glass lanterns cast a warm glow on their faces as shadows danced along the walls.

Mom entered with her hands folded and her jaw clenched. Nai Nai raised her eyebrow when she saw us, and Mom sank to her knees, bringing her hands together in prayer. "Please," she said. "Mother, Xiao-Long, Three is very sick. She needs a doctor."

Father's face softened with sympathy, but in the dim light he still looked imposing. I felt more like his subject than his child. He replied, "Chiang-Yue, we just talked about this yesterday. Tuberculosis can take a long time to heal, and you must be patient. Our daughters have been sicker than this before, and you've always worried, but they've always gotten better."

I held my breath to keep from speaking out. He was wrong. He knew nothing of Three's medical history, having barely paid attention to her since her birth. How could he speak so confidently when he was so ignorant?

"She will die," Mom said, her voice choking. "She is dying. There are lesions on her body and she won't eat. I am begging you, call the doctor! Or let me take her to the doctor. I know there is a treatment for tuberculosis, and she needs it. Please, save her!" She inclined her head and bowed, touching her forehead to the ground, and I followed suit, kowtowing before them like they were an emperor and empress dowager, for in our world that was what they were.

Nai Nai ran her fingers along the dragon and phoenix carvings on her armrest, as if bored by a lackluster performance. "You are supposed to be in quarantine," she said, irate. "Do you want the rest of us to get sick too? Get out of here before you spread it further!" Gold bracelets on her wrists clinked as she waved us away.

Mom started weeping and said in a small and desperate voice, "I am here because my daughter needs me to be. Please. You can punish me as much as you wish. Just have mercy on Three." Seeing Mom cry sent fissures through my heart, and hot tears began streaming down my own cheeks.

"You don't work," Nai Nai said, pointing to Mom as though she were accusing her of a crime. Her nails were long and manicured, unlike Mom's, which always had to be kept short or else they would interfere with her chores. "You have no understanding of the value of money. A doctor costs *money*. And tuberculosis treatment is expensive. You can't even imagine how expensive it is. We don't waste that money on a girl child."

Mom broke down and sobbed, bowing again with such vigor that her head thumped loudly as it hit the floor. "She's going to die," she repeated. "She's only two."

I glanced at Father pleadingly, but he only sat there, avoiding eye contact as though we were two strangers asking for charity. The living room was opulent, with antique brush paintings, quartz and amber carvings, and German crystal glasses on display in cabinets. We were in a cage made of riches; though Mom and I could admire them, they were not ours. Inside, we were trapped, helpless as I envisioned my sister floating away.

As the candles flickered, I wiped my eyes, frustrated that we had to convince them that Three's life was worth at least as much as any of these trinkets. My sister's value was in her bubbly laugh and her small hugs. It was in the way she marveled at horses and chased dragonflies, the way she brought me my shoes every morning and kissed me before she napped. Her value was an amalgamation of intangible, priceless little things, yet all Father and Nai Nai could see was numbers. To them, a daughter was only debt.

Shifting slightly in her chair, Nai Nai cleared her throat and said, "If Three is actually as sick as you say she is, then you are negligent for leaving her side. What Three needs is a mother who is present and dedicated, not money thrown out the door."

Father might as well have been a statue. Though Nai Nai was nasty, I was angrier at his stoic silence. Three was his daughter. How could he ignore our despair? Whenever he came home, Three ran to greet him at the door. Her first word had been *"baba,"* and I knew that she loved him. Yet, in the past weeks, he hadn't visited her once. I was so angry, but I wasn't allowed to speak. *It's not her fault that she's a girl*, I wanted to scream. If Chiao was sick, the Angs would have sold their *shibeyuan* to pay for his cure. I knew life wasn't fair, but I didn't think it was this cruel.

Beside me, Mom was shaking so hard that her teeth rattled. "Three is a skeleton now! If you come see her, you will know. I have done everything that I can, and it is not enough!"

"It is irrelevant," answered Nai Nai. "She is one of four. You have three other daughters. What comes to pass is the will of the Gods."

"Please!" Mom cried.

"Enough!" Nai Nai thundered, losing her patience. She stood up on her tiny feet, gripping the arms of the chair for stability.

Father leaned over and gently took Mom by her elbow, raising her to a standing position. "It is enough, Chiang-Yue," he said, afraid that we would upset Nai Nai further. "You should go back and care for Three. She needs you." To me he said, "Hai, support your mother. Be good and help her care for your sisters." He reached out for Mom's hand, but she grabbed mine instead, and squeezed it so hard that I almost yelped. She was borrowing my strength now, but I didn't have any to give. I was even more powerless than she was, even lower ranking in our family hierarchy.

As we retreated, Nai Nai had to have the last word. "I warned you not to taunt fate, didn't I?" she said. "You already had three girls when I told you to wait for a son. Instead, you tried to defy destiny. Since you added another daughter, the Gods must take one away. You have no one to blame but yourself." Her ominous words seemed to echo as we walked down the hallway, each step heavy with sorrow. As I held Mom's arm tightly, I was convinced that a demon had stolen my grandmother's flesh and impersonated her in our living room. How else could she be so evil?

"No more crying," Mom whispered to me when we entered our dark room. She lay down and pulled Three into her arms. "It will only make your sister more stressed." I wiped my eyes, but I knew that Mom was speaking to herself.

The next day, Three stopped drinking and wouldn't give in, no matter how much we coaxed her to. All we could do was keep her company. Mom wrapped her up in Lan's blankets, swaddling her tightly as though she were a newborn, rocking her and singing lullabies softly. She was a mere husk, so small that she didn't weigh much more than Lan. Three left this world cradled in Mom's arms, with nothing but a melody to ease her pain.

When Three stopped breathing, Mom said quietly, "Do not let tears touch her." Gently, she laid her down on the bed, placing her head on a pillow as though she were sleeping. "The dead cannot know our grief, or else it binds them to this world. She needs to pass on to a new life. A better life."

I burst into tears, keeping my hands on my face to make sure no tear fell where it shouldn't. "I'm so sorry, Mama," I said. "I took Three out during Ghost Month. I took her to the river, and she fell into the water and was chilled and became weak from it. If that hadn't happened, maybe she would have survived."

I braced myself for Mom's anger, but she only reached out and pulled me into a tight embrace. "Of course not," she said. "It is not your fault." She paused before continuing bitterly. "It was the will of the Gods." Although she said that, I knew that Mom forgave me because she was too busy blaming herself.

Three was buried in our family grave, in a small plot with other children who had died in infancy. There was no funeral, but Mom, Di, and I wore white and burned incense to bid her soul farewell. We made an offering to the Guang-Yin Bodhisattva, praying that she would protect Three and guide her to her next life. I scanned the sky, looking for any sign to reassure me that Three would be all right, but there was no message in the cotton clouds that could comfort me. As smoke rose and the incense turned to ash, Mom said out loud to the Buddha, "For two years, I raised her. For two years, I loved her. Forever, I will mourn her."

Mom's grief became its own illness, but instead of eating away at her body it ate away at her soul. There are some moments in life that we replay in our minds and hearts, fantasizing about different outcomes, regretting choices made and weighing how much they led to the results that we called "destiny." Three's death—or, rather, the illness leading up to her death—is a sequence that I have envisaged hundreds of ways. For Mom, it must have been thousands. She must have thought back to and analyzed every step, misstep, and non-step in the preceding months, only to come to the same conclusion—that she had failed as a mother.

After we left quarantine, Di and I shared a bedroom again, but

I couldn't even look at Di. She hadn't adored Three like I had, and could not understand what Mom and I had endured. I resented her for not isolating in quarantine with us. I resented her for not joining us as we knelt before Nai Nai. And most of all, I resented her for not sharing our blame, our regret, and our grief.

3

A LIST OF ENEMIES

Winters in Shandong were long and harsh, especially inland, where sheets of snow blanketed the landscape by December. As autumn fled, gales of wind descended upon us from the mountains, howling outside our windows and rattling our doors with their fury. At night I lay in my bed, a *kang* that had space underneath it to burn coal for warmth, and I listened to the wailing of a land that longed for the reprieve of spring.

Fat snowflakes fell early that year, at first lightly like little dancers descending onto a stage, and then heavily in clumps. We bundled Lan in so many layers that she could barely move, and after our chores were done, we played in the snow. Chiao was getting much stronger than me, and he packed snowballs so hard that I accused him of hiding ice in them. When we got too cold, we ran inside and sat in front of the fire, drinking warm soup with sticky rice balls, *tangyuan*, which we chewed until our teeth and lips were stained black with sesame paste.

We didn't know that only a few hundred kilometers away, half a million soldiers were about to be slaughtered.

The Chinese Civil War, which had resumed shortly after the Japanese withdrawal in 1945, appeared to be coming to an end. This was not a cause for celebration, because we were on the wrong side of it. I was shielded from the severity of the situation, because news trickled down to me from Mom, who got only snippets from Father. He had compared the Nationalists to a phoenix that braved the Japanese with broken wings after decades of fighting warlords and Communists. Years ago, he was confident that they had risen from the ashes of World War II to lead China anew.

The Communist Party, however, had emerged from the same war with renewed vigor. Bolstered by the rural poor and by weaponry that Soviet forces had confiscated from the Japanese, their coalition of ragtag volunteers had grown to be a unified behemoth. Foreign aid allowed Chiang Kai-Shek to cling to the urban areas, but the countryside was slowly and surely turning red. As the Communist tide advanced, Jinan, the capital of Shandong, became the first major city to fall. Father's phoenix, which had previously struggled to fly, was now struggling even to stand.

"We got a letter from my dad!" Chiao yelled, running into the courtyard so quickly that he slipped on a patch of ice and landed on his back. He bounced up as though he were made of rubber and brushed the snow off his pants. "We're fighting the Communists in Xuzhou!"

Chiao's father, my uncle Jian, was a colonel in the Nationalist army. It was December, and we hadn't seen him for half a year. Still, I continued building a snow fort, unbothered by the news. After all, I was a Shandong child. Our people were known to be fighters, whether as soldiers, mercenaries, bandits, or bar brawlers. We had lived through so much violence and war that we saw conflict as akin to the forces of nature—something beyond our control that we simply had to endure and adapt to.

"Is Uncle Jian okay?" I asked. Aside from his safety, I saw no reason to fret over Xuzhou, which was in a neighboring province. I didn't realize that the battleground had moved south because we had already lost the North. Chiang Kai-Shek had ordered that Shandong be abandoned, and the withdrawal of troops was nearly complete.

"There's too much snow!" Chiao cried. "Our air force can't fly, and our soldiers are defecting by the thousands! And there are spies everywhere!" In his hand, Chiao held a toy pistol. More than anything else, what he wanted was to be like his father. "I wish I could be there too. When I grow up, I'm going to fly planes. Or ride tanks!" Holding up his gun, he made popping noises and pretended to take a hit in his shoulder before diving behind my fort. He was only ten, and though lives were at stake, neither of us understood the danger that loomed ahead.

The fight for Xuzhou, with nearly six hundred thousand troops on both sides, ended up being one of the largest battles in the entire world in the twentieth century. Besieged in the dead of winter, the starving Nationalist troops began to eat their horses. In early January, the Communists launched a final offensive, sending our soldiers scattering southward, cementing Communist control over Northern China.

One frigid morning, I was with Mom in the kitchen, preserving root vegetables, with big clay jars on the tables and the smell of vinegar potent in the air. In the morning silence, a soft knock on the door startled me like a shotgun. Someone called, "Miss," for Mom. Mom quickly wiped her hands on her apron, her brow furrowed since we were not expecting anyone.

As she opened the door, the winter wind swirled its way in

gleefully, blowing flour into the air like fine snow. Three of our long-term workers—Mr. Hu, Mr. Zhang, and Mr. Wang—stood before her. I had known them all my life; Mr. Zhang had been with the Angs for decades. Mom said that he reminded her of her father, and she often gave him extra food or special items. Most recently, she had slipped him a bit of white flower oil for his inflamed arthritic fingers. "Please come inside," Mom said. "It's so cold!" She ushered them in hurriedly and they bowed, wiping the snow off their boots. I shivered as I closed the door behind them.

Something was wrong. Normally, the workers greeted Mom boisterously and warmly, laughing and joking with one another despite the hard day ahead of them. Their silence was louder than any alarm could be.

Mom cleared her throat and asked, "Have you eaten yet?"

"Yes, we have," Mr. Wang insisted, the other two nodding in agreement. "Thank you. We are very full."

Mom reached for a basket of freshly steamed *mantou* that she had made that morning and she handed one to each man anyway. "I'll get tea," she said, scurrying for some cups, snapping her fingers at me to indicate that I should help her.

"No, thank you, miss," Mr. Wang said, tucking his *mantou* in his pocket. "We cannot stay long. And if anyone asks, we were here to talk about adding work hours for spring."

Mom paused, having never heard such a request before. She gestured at me for the tea anyway, so I went to boil some water, making as little noise as possible so I could hear the men's low voices.

"Miss," said Mr. Hu, who was the man whose sick son Mom had given pork buns to, "you must leave town. The Communists are coming for you."

Mom froze, as did I, my arm extended toward the kettle. "What do you mean, Mr. Hu?"

"Did you know Shandong is under Communist control now?" Mr. Hu asked, his hands clasped together tightly, anxiously. Beside him, Mr. Wang shifted back and forth.

"Yes, I know the Nationalist army has left," Mom said, hesitant. She didn't want to seem stupid, but that was all the information that she had. "They will be back, though. The Communists can't possibly hold the North." From what we knew, the Communists were not organized—they were like bandits, appearing occasionally, never lingering, because they feared Nationalist persecution. I couldn't imagine what their government would be like, and I had overheard Yei Yei say that they would not be unified for long. He was convinced that they would splinter into factions, like warlords, and nothing would change.

Mr. Wang's dark eyes were solemn as he said, "That might be true eventually, but there are Communist cadres in Zhucheng now. They are asking people about the landowners and the wealthy families, so they can make a list of enemies. The Angs are already on it!"

"Why would we be their enemies?" Mom asked. "Is it because of Jian?" I was just as confused as she was. Why should the Communists want to fight us? We weren't competing with them for power. Wouldn't they want to focus their efforts on conquering the rest of the country? Shouldn't they worry about capturing Chiang Kai-Shek?

Unnerved, Mr. Hu added, more bluntly, "The Communists want a revolution. They are killing all the landowners so they can redistribute everything. They are coming for you, and they will not be merciful. You need to take your children and leave as soon as possible!"

I had never seen our workers as agitated, aggressive, as they were in their warning. They looked at us urgently, as though we should drop our vegetables and pack our bags immediately.

Mr. Wang lowered his voice, his face so taut that creases formed in his dry red skin. "They will torture you at best, kill you at worst!"

Mom gasped, alarmed. We were isolated in our *shiheyuan*, but the men's eyes were like telescopes, bridging the distance between us and rest of the countryside. Their words sounded extreme, but it was clear that they had witnessed something horrible. Yet I didn't think the Communists could kill every landowner in China . . . but we also didn't think that they could win this war. Underestimating them seemed to be our greatest downfall—along with the corruption and incompetence that Yei Yei said was poisoning the Nationalists from within.

"Where can we go?" Mom asked, her face pale as she wondered aloud. "If the Communists control Shandong, is there any city here that would be safe?"

Mr. Hu shook his head, his expression softening to one of pity, and said, "I don't know. Maybe Qingdao, since it is still under Kuomintang control. It is larger, and people won't recognize you easily. Here, every person and animal knows the Ang family—and where you live."

Mr. Zhang added, "You need to get out before the cadres see your faces and can recognize you. Please, miss. I know it's not easy to leave, but you will have no life to live otherwise." The other two men nodded fervently in agreement.

"You need to be quick!" Mr. Hu insisted.

"Leave during the day," said Mr. Zhang. "Not at night, or you will draw suspicion."

"You must act like you know nothing, suspect nothing," said

Mr. Wang. "Don't look nervous. Act as though you are leaving on a simple shopping or trading trip."

My head was spinning as the men all started talking at once, pushing their suggestions. Our family was so large—how could we possibly leave Zhucheng unnoticed? If the Communists caught us on the road, would we be punished for trying to run?

Mom held up her hands as though she were surrendering. "All right, I understand. Thank you for thinking of us and for warning me. However, I cannot do anything until I discuss it with my husband and father-in-law." Mom bowed to the three men to show her gratitude. Both of us knew that none of them liked Father or Yei Yei, and that they notoriously hated Nai Nai, but they cared enough about Mom that they were willing to spare the Angs on her behalf.

Mr. Zhang's face broke into a sad, tender smile. "You don't need to thank us," he said gently. "It is the right thing to do. I've known you since you married into this family as a young girl. I could not live in good conscience if I stood by and allowed you to be murdered."

Mom's lip trembled. Touched, she understood that the three of them were taking an enormous risk in warning her. She gathered three empty sacks and said to me loudly, "Hai, fill these bags with fresh *mantou* to thank these three men for agreeing to fix the stables once the snow eases up." Turning back to them, she said, "Thank you for taking on these extra hours. I know it's hard, especially when it's so cold."

I tied the bags, the *mantou* still warm, so that the men could tuck them under their coats for extra heat on their way home. Mom also grabbed a few jars of pickled cabbage and boiled eggs and bags of dried yams and pushed them into the men's arms, even as they protested. They bowed their heads before opening the door, another blast of icy wind heralding their departure.

As soon as they left, Mom rushed to tell Father what she had heard. Yei Yei and Father were home in Zhucheng because Shandong University, where they worked respectively as a comptroller and a professor, was closed for the winter holidays. That evening, my parents and grandparents stayed up late discussing the workers' warning. Di and I crouched in the cold, dark hallway, elbowing each other for room as we listened with our ears pressed against the door.

"Everyone has a price," said Yei Yei, confidently. "No matter what the Communists say about equality and eliminating class, they can still be bought. Just think about the 'taxes' that we give to the warlords. With the right bribe, they'll leave us alone."

Nai Nai's sharp voice chimed in. "It's probably a ploy. The workers want us to flee so they can steal from us while we are gone." Nai Nai rarely spoke to any of the peasants and she assumed that most of them were thieves in waiting. Their friendship with Mom made her distrust them even more. "We can't be too gullible. They are manipulative people, after all."

"We've all heard about the denunciation rallies, though," said Father, concerned. "The Communists are inciting peasants to kill landowners. North of here, there have been hundreds, if not thousands, of brutal murders already. I heard a landlord was tied up and burned alive! Mao wants a massive land reform, and the easiest way to accomplish that is to eliminate us all."

So Mr. Hu was right, I thought, and I shivered as I wondered how it felt to be set ablaze. Would that happen to us too if we stayed? A sharp finger poked into my rib cage.

"Sis!" Di whispered. "Is it really true? Did you know that?"

I was still mad at Di because earlier we were supposed to help Mom wash dishes but she had disappeared as usual, leaving me alone with a full sink. "Of course I knew that!" I snapped as quietly as I could. "Everyone knows that."

"Why is Yei Yei being so stubborn, then?" Di asked, unbothered by my irritation.

I shushed her, pressing my ear harder against the door to hear Yei Yei's argument.

"Once the Communists rule all of China they won't care about the peasants. I've seen it so many times," said Yei Yei. "Revolutionaries, rebels—they are all idealists. Power changes everyone. Power is an iron mold—it reshapes anyone and everyone into the same thing. The Communists are no different. They will rise, they will rule, and they will want what every ruler wants—more power, more money."

"But we are also Kuomintang," Father emphasized. "Shandong University is government funded. They will consider us political enemies too!"

"Party lines change all the time," said Yei Yei dismissively. "Shandong has had more rulers than a witch has moles. We'll just put our heads down and smile and tell them what they want to hear. In all likelihood, the regime will change again in a few years."

"The Nationalists can still win," said Nai Nai hopefully. "The war is not over yet. We still have armies in the South."

"The war is not over, but the scales have already been tipped too far," Father replied bitterly. He rarely raised his voice at his parents, but he was getting frustrated. "We've lost several generals, and hundreds of thousands of men. Maybe we can hold the Yangtze River, but it will be months before Chiang Kai-Shek can claw his way back to Shandong. Until then, we must be careful. We should heed the workers' warning and leave!"

"And go where? And when?" Nai Nai's voice grew shrill as she exclaimed, "And what about the New Year? We cannot leave before honoring our ancestors. That is certain to bring about bad luck!"

Father said somberly, "War does not stop for the New Year."

I jumped as Di's nail dug into my side again. "Stop poking me!" I hissed.

Di was hotheaded and rarely afraid, but the prospect of missing New Year's Eve dinner sent her into a panic. "Surely even the Communists celebrate New Year?" she whispered. "Everyone goes home for the New Year!"

Shaking my head, I said, "Uncle Jian probably won't come home either. Chiao says that the Nationalists are preparing to defend Nanjing at all costs." Now that this war was having tangible impacts on our lives, I regretted my nonchalance back in December.

In the room, I heard Father sigh with exasperation. "I agree that we can probably bribe them eventually, but there is too much momentum now. They will want to make an example of us to satisfy their supporters. We should escape while we can. The Communists have not yet organized themselves to administer Shandong. They don't have the infrastructure to monitor roads. There is a window of opportunity that we would be foolish to ignore. We can always come home when it's safer."

"Not if the workers and the Communists steal our property!" Nai Nai cried. "What is the point of saving life if there is no livelihood? We are only living to die another day."

"Every day of life is living to die another day," Mom said, so quietly that we could barely hear her.

Nai Nai huffed. "What do you know? Insolent girl. Go kneel." I could hear Mom's knees bang against the wooden floor—even though this entire discussion was happening because she had warned them of the danger!

"Rise," Yei Yei said absently, the only one who could counter Nai Nai's orders. "Now is not the time for us to fight each other. However, I will say that if I have to die, I prefer to die proudly in my home, not as a pauper on the street."

"Let's stop talking of death," Father said, irritated. "No one has to die. We just need to be cautious."

Distress permeated Yei Yei's voice as he said, "If we abandon our home, we will lose it for sure."

"Especially if it is a scam," Nai Nai added.

"I don't think the workers would lie to Chiang-Yue," Father argued gravely.

"Then Chiang-Yue should stay behind!" Nai Nai countered. "If the workers love her so much, then they won't hurt her anyway. Maybe she can use her good relations to convince them to leave our property alone."

I dug a finger into my ear, wondering if I had heard correctly. *Did Nai Nai just suggest leaving Mom here in Zhucheng, alone?* In the dark, Di's large eyes were like black mirrors reflecting the dim light that filtered through the space between the door and its frame. I couldn't tell if she was as shocked and worried as I was or if she was still thinking about the New Year dinner. Our workers would never hurt Mom, but Father's agitation reminded me of the three men trembling and nervous in our kitchen. What did Father know that we didn't? If Father was so scared, he couldn't possibly leave his wife behind. Right?

Nai Nai's proposal hung in the air like a vulture waiting to land.

Slowly, Yei Yei said, "This is a good solution. Chiang-Yue can persuade the workers to preserve our property. Xiao-Long and the rest of the family will come with us to Qingdao. After the initial fervor dies down, or maybe even when the Nationalists retake the

North, we will all come back. We can be prudent without sacrificing everything we have."

"Chiang-Yue can also light incense for our ancestors during the New Year," Nai Nai added, relieved. "The Qingdao house is cramped, and she and the girls will have more space here, with the *shiheyuan* to themselves."

Di and I looked at each other, crouched awkwardly in our eavesdropping positions. So they wanted to leave all of us? Given the choice, I would stay with Mom anyway. To me, safety wasn't Qingdao, or any other city. Safety was Mom. Still, I was offended that Nai Nai wanted to ditch me. *Come on, Father,* I thought. *Tell Nai Nai she's wrong!*

"Yes," Yei Yei agreed, sounding calmer. "In Qingdao we have no land to farm, and limited food. We will only be there temporarily, and Chiang-Yue can keep us updated about our home. She can write to us when it is safe to return to Zhucheng."

I wished that I could see their faces and read their expressions. It was agonizing waiting to hear Father's thoughts. I knew Mom wouldn't argue—she couldn't argue. Mom was a wife who had failed the Angs, bringing them debt instead of continuity. If she couldn't birth their heir, at least she could protect their wealth.

"Chiang-Yue, are you willing to stay here alone?" Father asked. Though it sounded like a question, I knew that it was an expectation.

There was a long pause, and I pressed my ear against the door, ready to catch every word that would fall from Mom's lips.

"I can stay behind," Mom said slowly. "As long as our older daughters go to Qingdao. Lan is too little to leave me, but at least take Hai and Di. I need to know that they are safe."

Before Father could reply, Nai Nai interjected, "Who will take care of them in Qingdao? We will be busy. If you aren't there, we can't possibly have two more children. There will already be Chiao and Pei, and the house is small!"

Taking Nai Nai's cue, Father replied, "The Communists are after landowners, not little girls. After they purge the men, they will move on. It will only be a few months of separation, and then we will be together again."

Though I had hoped for another response, Father's failure to fight for us was characteristic, and the disappointment I felt was as familiar as a broken-in pair of shoes. I was unaware, however, of the consequences that would spiral from that evening's fateful discussion. Nai Nai's words were the shovels that dug our graves. Yei Yei's agreement sealed our coffins. But ultimately it was Father's acquiescence that would bury us in darkness.

Over the next few days, Nai Nai became a military commander, directing family members on what to pack, what to leave, and what to burn. All of our valuables—any jewelry, gold, and artifacts—were carefully stowed in wagons and the car. Nai Nai made Mom and Aunt Ji maneuver items like puzzle pieces to make sure that every nook and cranny in the trunk was filled.

I said a tearful goodbye to Chiao and Pei, who hugged me. Chiao whispered, "Later, when we go, do me a favor and fart on Di's face when she's sleeping. It's cold, so if you take off your pants, you can actually see the fart! So she will wake up to a cloud—of fart! A fart cloud! Promise me you will do it, and tell me about it when we come back?"

I laughed through my tears, thinking how much I would miss him. I waved as he and Pei ran back to Aunt Ji, Chiao turning to make a gesture with his hand to show a giant fart coming out of his butt.

Father bade us farewell and told us to be obedient. He and Mom shared a formal and cold goodbye while Nai Nai called him impatiently to help her into her carriage.

After the family departed, I retreated into the warm kitchen with Di, noticing how unusually empty it looked. I began to open the cabinets one by one, finding them barren. Di, alarmed, checked the pantry. By the time Mom came in with Lan on her hip, we had found a few jars of pickled vegetables and twelve bags of flour. "Is this all they left us?" I asked Mom, dismayed.

Mom surveyed the kitchen, which looked like it had been ransacked. "Father left us a tael of gold," she said, opening her hand to reveal a gleaming coin with a circle in the center.

"We can't eat gold," Di wailed, scanning the kitchen for any tidbit that we might have missed. "I'm so hungry. At least we can sell it to buy some real food!"

Mom shook her head. "No, this we need to save." She tucked the precious tael inside her shirt, in her undergarments, close to her heart.

"So we just eat *mantou* and pancakes all winter?" Di asked as I tried to mentally convert the flour to bread and estimate the number of days it could sustain us for.

"We will manage" was all Mom said. As she lined up the jars on the table, I could tell from her expression of concentration that she too was adding, dividing, and determining when we would need to panic. "We may have much bigger problems to deal with," she added absently. "Now, help me clean up." I grabbed a rag and started wiping down the tables as Di pouted, took the broom, and swept feebly, as though she were painting a delicate picture on the floor.

4

LIONS AT THE GATE

With the family gone, the courtyard was stagnant, quiet, and lonely. My footprints looked forlorn on the snowy ground, which normally would have been trodden by circles of small feet, long dashes of big feet, markers of a full and lively home. Di was more independent than I was, and she was unbothered by the isolation.

She had just turned eleven and had only solitary hobbies: daydreaming and collecting trading cards of famous singers. For Di, people on paper and imaginary conversations were more interesting than me. Her aloofness amplified the impact of my cousins' absence as I wandered alone through the empty rooms, bored and ignored. Meanwhile, Di tucked herself into various corners of the house, holding her cards like a fan and pretending that they were her captive audience. It was hard to see her, but I could hear her crooning in a deep voice that Mom said was stolen from a past life—like it belonged to an older woman, one who had loved, lost, and yearned.

Di lived in love songs, and unlike me, she wanted to marry

early so she could leave the Angs. While I was obedient, accepting our parents as they were and making the best of it, Di hated being second-class to Chiao and boiled with resentment at any slight, whether real or perceived. I shared her frustration sometimes, but I still never wanted to marry. Why would I want to follow in Mom's footsteps and spend the rest of my life on my knees? No matter how bad the Angs were, surely we would be worse off at the mercy of our husbands' mothers!

The main thing that Di and I had in common was that we both hated Nai Nai and were glad that she was gone. Finally, Mom was allowed to have some peace. She tried to help us with our studies, but she struggled because Di and I were already ahead of her in every subject. We had been homeschooled by tutors who visited twice a week, but with Father gone, our teachers would not return after winter break. Di rejoiced at the extended vacation, but I was worried about falling behind. I already struggled to keep up with Chiao, who had access to more lessons and subjects than both Di and me combined. In the stretches of silence following Father's farewell, Di danced with her singers and I practiced my calligraphy and writing. The flowing ink offered a modicum of relief; preparing to return to normal was the only way I could reassure myself that sooner or later, we would.

Within a week of the Angs' departure, however, we were startled by the sounds of many voices outside in our fields. They were agitated and varied in pitch, like the calls of strange birds. It was unusual for so many people to be out during these cold months. Our windows were closed with wooden shutters, and we hurriedly put on our coats and opened them to look outside. A group of men and women was marching toward our *shibeyuan*.

Slamming the shutters closed, Mom moved quickly toward the door. "Watch the baby," she said.

I looked at Di, who held my gaze and said, "Don't worry. I'll stay with Lan." Nodding, I dashed after Mom.

Outside, the sun was bright and the sky cerulean, but the wind was so cold that I thought it would peel the skin off my face. As the group neared, I saw that some of them wore caps with a single red star—the logo of the Communist Party. Several were armed with guns and clubs.

A young man stepped forward, greeting us. His large eyes were covered by thick eyebrows, and shaggy hair framed his angular face like a mane. Two of his front teeth were missing. "I am Comrade Kang Wen-Ming," he said. The word for "comrade," *tongzhi*, meant "same will," or "same purpose." "I am looking for the Angs, Ang Hong-Bu and Ang Xiao-Long." The crowd behind him buzzed with excitement, like caged dogs ready to hunt.

"They are away on business," Mom told him. "They should be back in a few weeks." Members of the crowd muttered at her response, postulating that the men had fled. Clenching my fist, I hoped that they would trust Mom and turn away. Even though Father had said that the Communists wouldn't harm little girls, their weapons made me nervous.

"Where for business?" Comrade Kang asked, ignoring the chatter behind him.

"The city," Mom replied, and then added, "Qingdao."

"What business does he have in Qingdao?" Comrade Kang pressed.

Mom smiled. She was so calm and composed, as though they were just neighbors talking about the weather. I wondered if the crowd could sense the fear that roiled inside me. Would our weakness make them more aggressive? Mom said, "I wish I knew, but my husband does not discuss business with me. I take care of the home only."

Comrade Kang's eyes scanned the long walls of our *shibeyuan*. "A beautiful home indeed." His expression intensified as he added, "A grand landowner's home, built off the sweat and blood of peasant slaves."

Mom opened her mouth, but no words came out, like she was a koi gaping. We had been menaced by warlords and bandits before, and we had always responded with bribes. Now, however, there was nothing to give—the single gold tael might have fended off a mercenary, but not a group. My mind raced as I thought about what else we had to offer. Our bags of flour? The fish in our frozen pond? The stone lions at the gate?

"Zhucheng is liberated now," a scrawny man next to Comrade Kang said. "That means you landlords will no longer be allowed to oppress the people of China!"

There was scattered applause behind him, and I surveyed the crowd, realizing that some of the people there were our long-term workers. In the center, I saw Mr. Zhang, who had come to our house. I couldn't believe it! In his knobby hands, swollen from arthritis, he clutched a rifle. How could he stand alongside our aggressors? I thought he was Mom's friend!

"Our first mission in our liberated China is land reform," said Comrade Kang. "Everyone, every peasant, shall have their own lot on which to grow food." He gestured to our house and the land around it and said, "This now belongs to us all." Behind him, those with weapons brandished them threateningly.

Mom glanced from rifle to rifle, avoiding the eyes of their angry bearers, and said only, "I need to wait for my husband. He will be back in a few weeks. Perhaps you can speak with him when he returns."

"Of course," said Comrade Kang. "We will be sure to find him. In the meantime, you must leave. We are confiscating this property for the people of China, and it will be distributed fairly to our brothers and sisters."

Mom's face twitched, betraying her alarm. "Get out? Of our house?" She viewed the snowy landscape and looked back at the shuttered windows on the room where Di and Lan were waiting. Turning back to Comrade Kang, she asked, "Where should we go? It's winter and so cold, and I have three daughters!"

"My youngest sister is only an infant," I added, my words escorted by little clouds as my warm breath mixed with the freezing air. Kicking us out would be a death sentence at this time of year!

A cadre in the back stepped forward, his face twisted in anger. He was clean-shaven, with large eyes, handsome except for the hate in his eyes. "And how many peasants have gone through winter cold and starving, their children dying because they were too poor to afford real food and medicine? Now you rich pigs will finally learn the meaning of justice!"

The crowd behind him started angrily shouting insults that I had never heard before.

"Bourgeois scoundrels!"

"Social parasites!"

"Enemy of the people!"

Mom and I cowered, backing away as their voices escalated and blended together incoherently. In a flash, a cadre zoomed forward and jabbed Mom in the stomach with the butt of his rifle. She crumpled forward, her cries drowned out by the roar of the crowd as they raised their arms, collectively rising like monsters rearing. I threw myself in front of her, screaming, bracing myself for the impact of their weapons. "Stop!" I shrieked with such force that I thought the inside of my throat would tear. "Don't hurt my mom! She didn't do anything wrong! Stop!"

A deafening gunshot pierced the air and everyone ducked.

Mom's arm flew over my shoulders, and we fell to the ground together, knocking the breath from my lungs.

"Leave her alone!" yelled a familiar voice. Everyone looked toward the center of the crowd. It was Mr. Zhang, his rifle pointed upward. He ran forward and stood between Mom and our aggressors, his stance wide, holding the rifle so tightly that his hands trembled. The faint minty scent of white flower oil emanated from his fingers. "This woman is no more a landowner than any of you. She is a miserable wife, abused by the Ang family and as oppressed as any peasant. Maybe more so, because she lives with her oppressors!"

Mom and I huddled together, the snow seeping through our pants and stinging our knees. Swallowing, I tried to ease the tightness in my throat and calm the storm brewing inside me. I was livid, indignant, as these strangers whispered to one another about Mr. Zhang's words. They didn't even know Mom, yet they were ready to beat her. If Mr. Zhang hadn't intervened, would they have beaten me too?

One by one, others in the crowd began to speak on our behalf. "Old Zhang is right," another worker said. "The Angs treat her like a servant. She is awake before us workers, cooking breakfast before sunrise!"

"She works hard too!" someone else added. "We cannot blame her for her husband's crimes!"

Comrade Kang held up his hand as more workers began to vouch for Mom. "She will not be punished," he assured them. "But the property must be confiscated. The Angs are to leave immediately."

Shaken, Mom rose and said, "I will leave, but I have two daughters inside. Please allow me to get them, and we will go together."

"You may take your daughters," Comrade Kang allowed, "but nothing else!"

"I understand," said Mom. "Come, Hai. We must get your sisters dressed and ready."

I grabbed Mom's arm, looking over my shoulder at the crowd, which still seemed hungry for vengeance. Our eviction was a mere appetizer, and they would not leave until they could at least savor our shame as we vacated.

"Leave the door open," Comrade Kang commanded.

Mom complied. They couldn't see much through the doorway anyway, and the windows were still shuttered. Lowering her voice as we entered the kitchen, Mom whispered one word to me: "Flour."

I understood, and as we passed the pantry, I lifted three bags of flour and braced them against my hip. They were heavy, easily five kilograms each. Mom was stronger and grabbed four. In Mom's bedroom, Di sat clutching Lan in her lap. She was frightened at first, but she was quickly relieved to see us. She couldn't have heard all of the dialogue, but she had heard the gunshot for sure. "Mom, Sis, what is happening?"

Lan squirmed out of Di's lap, slid onto the floor, and crawled toward Mom.

"I don't have time to explain," Mom said gently, putting down the flour so that she could lift Lan. "We need to leave immediately. Go to your room and put on every piece of clothing that you have. It doesn't matter if it's uncomfortable. I want every layer on."

"But why—" Di began, but then saw the flour and stopped. She could tell something awful was going on, and she let her questions drop.

Mom handed Di one flour bag and said, "Go to the pantry and

take two more sacks. Tie one to your belly, another to your back, and one more behind your butt. And be quick!"

I didn't need Mom to repeat the orders to me, and I hurried to undress myself. Taking one of the long strips of cloth used to carry Lan, I wrapped the three bags around myself. They were heavy, but we would need this sustenance. What were we going to do about the cold, though? Perhaps the flour and the layers of clothing could insulate us, but we would die without shelter.

"Hurry up!" Comrade Kang bellowed from outside.

Mom threw open Father's closet and added a few of his thick winter garments over herself. In my frenzy, I piled on whatever could fit me, tearing a shirt in the process. Eleven layers of shirts and eight pairs of pants later, I frantically rolled up undergarments and socks to stuff into my sleeves. On my bed, my favorite cloth doll stared at me, pleading with me to take her too. "I can't," I said remorsefully. "I have too much to carry already."

Mom yanked open her nightstand drawer and flung the lid off her wooden jewelry box, which contained only two items. One was a jade bangle given to her by Lao Lao on her wedding day; she slipped this on her wrist, tucking her sleeves over it carefully. The jade was of the finest quality, a deep green like moss—the greener the jade, the more potent its protective qualities. If there was any time when we needed this bangle's powers, it was now.

Mom's second item was a ruby ring, gifted by Father after she had told him that she was pregnant with me—she never got any more jewelry after my birth. After undoing my braid, Mom slipped the ring on a lock of hair at the nape of my neck, then rebraided it so that the ring was snug and hidden. The entire time, I listened for the sound of footsteps, certain that the impatient cadres would charge in and catch us. Would they kill us for taking our jewelry? Would they punish us for hiding the flour?

Di returned, waddling like a stuffed duck. Scanning the room, Mom pulled a silk blanket from the bed and wrapped it around Lan, tucking the corners in. "Let's go," she said, "before they suspect what we have done."

The three of us walked stiffly out the door, blinking as the sun hit our eyes. Slowly, we stepped past the lion statues that had been erected as charms to protect the family. A childish part of me expected them to come to life and devour our aggressors one by one, but they remained still, impotent. *Like Father*, I thought. *The Communists are after landowners, not little girls.* Had he been lying when he said that?

As we exited, Comrade Kang commanded the cadres to search our house. "Leave nothing unturned!" He thought that Father and Yei Yei were hiding inside. Eight cadres stomped through our courtyard, chatting as though they were completing a daily chore, not stripping us of our home.

Mr. Zhang said, "At least let them take some food; she's a mother with three children!"

Annoyed, Comrade Kang held up his hand to halt his team. "You may take some provisions," he agreed stingily.

I was already struggling with the weight of the flour, but I braced myself as Mom handed Lan to me. Relieved of her, Mom walked rather gracefully back into the kitchen—she had spent her life constantly carrying small children while working, and twenty kilograms of flour was comparable to a well-fed toddler. A few minutes later, she came out, wincing and hobbling with a jar of pickled vegetables and with two bags of flour wedged under each of her arms.

Even with the cold, my skin was slick with sweat that oozed from my anxious pores. Surely the crowd knew we had items beneath our coats. Surely a cadre would pat us down. Surely we would get in trouble!

"Let me help you," Mr. Zhang said, deliberately avoiding any honorific title as he grabbed the jar and the flour. "Come to my house. We can figure out next steps from there."

"Thank you," Mom said, taking Lan from me as we shuffled gingerly through the snow. As we departed, members of the crowd booed, and jeered that Mr. Zhang was a brainwashed slave. I felt embarrassed for doubting him earlier, and I understood now that he had come with the sole purpose of protecting us.

When we were out of sight, Mr. Zhang said, "Now give me some of the other bags of flour that you have, so I can help you carry them."

Mom began to deny at first, and then she sighed and said, "How did you know we had other bags?"

Mr. Zhang smiled. "You have smuggled items out of that house to give to us workers so many times over the past years. Did you really think I would believe that the queen of hiding would leave her own home and bring nothing?"

I felt proud of Mom, not only for her kindness to the workers in the past, but also for her calm head and quick thinking so that we made it out with our most essential possessions.

Eager for relief, Di struggled and stuck her hands under her shirts, but realized that she could not remove the flour because she had tied it on so tightly. Mom and I had the same problem—unless we took off all of our clothing, there would be no way to dislodge the bags.

"If you can carry Lan," Mom said, "that would be enough. We can manage."

Mr. Zhang nodded and lifted Lan onto his shoulders.

Up ahead on the main road, there was a mule-pulled wagon and Mr. Wang, who had accompanied Mr. Zhang weeks ago.

"Thank goodness they didn't kill you," Mr. Wang remarked, relieved, as he hopped down from the driver's bench. "Other landowners have been beaten to death outside their homes!"

I shuddered, imagining the blows that might have rained down on us if Mr. Zhang hadn't fired his gun. *The Communists are after landowners, not little girls.* Father's words echoed again as I tried to clear my head. My legs were aching from trying to keep my balance through the snow with the weight of my contraband. "Thank you for your help," Mom said again, breathing hard from exertion. "Thank you both for your kindness."

"Don't thank us yet," Mr. Wang said grimly. "Hurry into the wagon. Let's get you out of here."

Groaning, we relied on a strong push from Mr. Wang and Mr. Zhang to climb up. The two men jumped into the front and Mom kept her arms wrapped around us like a hen with her wings over her chicks. I leaned against her, still in disbelief, as we jostled forward on the road, the occasional braying from the mule puncturing the silence.

Back at our house, the Communists were probably combing through our belongings, opening the closets, and searching under every *kang* bed for Father and Yei Yei. How would Comrade Kang react when he realized that the house was empty? I couldn't help but think of my doll in her faded yellow dress—I didn't play with her anymore, but she had been my favorite toy when I was younger. It was silly to dwell on losing her, but I was anguished as I imagined cadres throwing her into the fire. At the very least, maybe they could redistribute her to another child.

On Mom's lap, Lan smiled happily, unaware that our lives had been upended. She enjoyed the wagon ride, blissfully warm in her layers of clothing.

5

THE SHED

Mr. Zhang's home was simple, with dirt floors, a thatched roof, paper windows, and a shared latrine in the back. It was barely big enough to accommodate him and his wife, let alone Mom and us girls. Beside it, there was a shed, made of wood and insulated with bales of hay, for housing livestock during the winter.

"I am sorry I do not have more to offer you," Mr. Zhang said, embarrassed as he opened the shed door. Inside, there were a donkey, several chickens, and a small brown dog that barked at our arrival. The ground was littered with their dung, feathers, and bits of hay, and it reeked so badly that I could taste the fetid air in my mouth. Unnerved by our presence, the donkey snorted its displeasure and the chickens clucked anxiously. I fought the urge to gag as I stepped in, wondering where we were going to sleep.

Mom smiled and said, "You have saved our lives more than once now, Mr. Zhang. A debt accumulated on top of a debt—we have only gratitude." As disgusting as it was, the shed would at least shelter us from the wind and snow; without its walls, we would freeze to death.

"I will try to bring you some more food," Mr. Zhang said, leaving the door propped open. A hen scraped the ground with its claw, pecking for bugs.

Maybe if I closed my eyes, I would wake up in my warm *kang* bed, and find that this morning had been a terrible dream. Though I was exhausted, I was too nervous to rest.

As if reading my mind, Mom said, "Don't be scared, girls. I just need to write to your father, so he knows to come and take us to Qingdao. We'll have to stay here for a few days, but it's temporary." She took off most of her layers and folded them neatly despite our messy surroundings.

"Do you think Nai Nai and Yei Yei will be angry at us for losing the house?" I asked as I untied my bags of flour.

"Probably." Mom sighed. "But what could we have done? There were too many cadres, and they had guns."

Di bristled and said, "If they were so concerned, then they all should have stayed to defend our home! Who are they to criticize us when they are safe in Qingdao, preparing for a New Year's feast?"

My stomach rumbled at the thought of this extravagant dinner, which would normally feature an animal that swims, an animal that flies, and an animal that walks the earth. In my hungry mind, a parade of poultry, pork, and seafood danced, until Nai Nai's stern face brought it to a screeching halt. She would probably ban us from the dinner table for failing to protect our property. Even worse, she would make Mom kneel for days.

"It will be fine, Di," said Mom, trying to keep us calm. "If we can get a message out quickly, we can probably be in Qingdao before the New Year. Hai, go ask Mr. Zhang for some paper."

Remembering that Mr. Zhang was illiterate, she changed her mind and said, "Ask him where we can buy paper and ink. We will need to sell this flour to get money first."

"Sell the flour!" Di and I exclaimed together. We had lugged those sacks all this way, our bodies aching, but they couldn't be worth much.

"What about a piece of jewelry?" I asked, touching my braid where the ruby ring was hidden. Unraveling my long black hair, I pulled it out and handed it to Mom, who tucked it into her pocket.

"We don't know what the future holds," said Mom warily. "We may need to flee again, and we have only our feet to carry us. Flour is heavy, and hard to bring. Jewelry is light. Cash is light."

At home, Mom never handled money, because Nai Nai didn't trust her. Food came from our land, and anything else was bought by Father on Nai Nai's orders. None of us understood the concept of inflation, so when Mr. Zhang told Mom that the yuan was worthless now, she was confused.

"I need cash," she said as though he were the one who did not comprehend. "I need to send a message to Qingdao."

Mr. Zhang patiently explained, "The Nationalist government is too poor—they have been printing money without stopping, and that's why the money is meaningless." According to Mr. Zhang, the Chinese yuan was worth three million times less than it had been a decade ago. In the cities, people were trampling one another to withdraw their savings from the banks. "You are better off using your flour to barter," Mr. Zhang continued. "A piece of flatbread is easily worth tens of Chinese dollars now!"

Yet another reality of the war that we were unprepared for. Using his limited connections, Mr. Zhang still managed to help Mom mail a letter to Yei Yei's house at Shandong University. Returning to Zhucheng now would be dangerous, but our family could hire someone to pick us up. Though Mom put on an optimistic face, I could see her insecurity from the quiver in her lips when she smiled, and the wringing of her fingers when she spoke. It made me apprehensive, but I couldn't let her know. I wondered if the carfare would cost more than tuberculosis treatment, and whether it would surpass the monetary threshold that the Angs had set for our lives. *There are four of us here,* I thought. *Surely the balance will be in our favor?*

Word spread that we were staying with Mr. Zhang, and other former workers came bearing anything they could spare to help us. Now we were the ones being offered flour, warm buns, dried vegetables and fruits, and even some pork jerky.

After a few days, Mr. Zhang built us a small, rickety platform to sleep on—just four bricks and some planks of wood, but at least we would be above the animal droppings. We swept the shed thoroughly every morning and evening, and gradually, the air became tolerable. At night we huddled together, squeezed under the same blankets for warmth. Each morning I awoke, disappointed to find myself still in the shed, the crowing rooster mocking me as my nightmare continued.

Two weeks went by with no word from our family, and then the Lunar New Year was upon us—our most important holiday and a boisterous celebration. Normally, Mom prepared days in advance, grinding wheat and marinating meat to ensure that New Year's Eve cooking, which started well before sunrise, flowed as smoothly as a well-conducted symphony.

Shooing chickens from our platform, Mom joked, "How nice. I can relax, since I won't be so busy cooking this year."

Di pouted as she pulled feathers off our blankets. "I wonder what Father and Nai Nai are eating."

"Probably nothing, since they don't have Mom to cook for

them," I teased. Mom laughed so loudly that she startled the chickens, which flapped frantically, sending dust and hay into the air. The dog wagged its tail at the commotion, and I felt a little lighter knowing that I was able to bring Mom some joy.

"Whatever they eat, I hope they choke," Di said quietly. Mom closed her eyes. I wasn't sure if she hadn't heard her or if she simply pretended not to. Such ill words required admonishment, but Mom was too tired to respond. Our noses ran like faucets, and the cold was debilitating.

As we shivered in the North, Chiang Kai-Shek trembled in the South. We heard our neighbors say that the astounding humiliation of his forces in Xuzhou had prompted Nationalist leadership in Nanjing to call for his resignation. On February 1, 1949, Chiang bitterly announced his retirement.

In the days that followed, I went each morning to the main road, sometimes with Di, and watched the horizon, hoping to see our family car. Even after a lifetime of neglect and repeated disappointment, I still held my father on a pedestal. Back in our *shiheyuan*, we had always looked forward to his return from the university, and treasured any shred of attention that he was willing to spare—a kind word, a pat on the head, anything to acknowledge our existence. Despite his weaknesses, I maintained faith in him. Though Three lay buried in the frozen ground, I stared at that road, expecting Father, waiting as the wind whipped my face. Each afternoon, I hung my head, trudging back to the shed with wet shoes and numb toes.

The help from neighbors was growing sparse as everyone tried to conserve what they had for the rest of the winter. One evening, Di whispered to me, "Father will probably just get a new wife. One that has better luck popping out sons."

That same suspicion lurked in my own pool of dark thoughts,

where I imagined our family in Qingdao ripping up the letter that we had sent. Maybe Father already had a mistress at the university, ready to take Mom's place; it was not uncommon for men to keep their wives at home and indulge in affairs at work. Women were disposable. Girls were disposable. Even the horses had gone to Qingdao with Father, while we were left behind.

"Mom says that he will come to get us, and I trust Mom," I said, trying to be brave. It was the best that I could muster, because I was afraid too.

Instead of Father's car, we saw new faces as Communist cadres entered and lingered in Zucheng. They wore military-style tunics with pockets at the chest and sides, and cloth peaked caps. Fervently, they shared their ideology through speeches in our town square and announced their plans for a liberated China. Despite hailing a class-free society, they had divided us all into new classes. There were the gentry, landlords, and business owners, all of whom were class enemies. Then there were peasants, with the most favored class being the poor peasants—landless people who tilled soil and turned over crops to landlords for rent. They were the majority population in China, and the force that had propelled Mao Ze-Dong and his cadres to victory.

I knew little about Mao, no more than I knew about warlords outside our region. I might have heard him mentioned here and there since he had risen to become the leader of the Communist Party, but my family considered him a thug and had not expected him to survive the Long March or endure past the second war with Japan. To everyone's astonishment, Mao grew from a snake to a dragon, returning from the caves of Yan'an with a vengeance. Father had read some of his earlier writings and said that Mao had a taste for blood. Now that he was the new god of red China, blood was going to rain. My family was going to drown.

The cadres went after almost everyone bearing the Ang name. News traveled from mouth to mouth, and we were appalled to learn that members of our family were beaten, tortured, and executed, while others died by suicide. In more temperate areas, closer to the sea, so-called reactionaries were burned or buried alive. Yei Yei's brother was bound and thrown into a ditch, screaming until he was suffocated by the dirt shoveled over him. Little by little, handful by handful, the once-powerful Ang family was chipped away until only a scattered few remained. Mom said that she was thankful that Yei Yei and Father escaped, because they surely would have been killed. We didn't think about ourselves. *The Communists are after landowners, not little girls.*

Many of our former workers knew that we were staying with Mr. Zhang. Fairly quickly, the Communists knew too. We hadn't thought to run. They had already taken our home, our land, and our dignity—we were squatting in a shed, smelling shit and eating scraps. Moreover, their quarrel was with the Ang family, and as Di and I had been told over and over again, girls didn't count; in our family tree, only Chiao's name had been written for our generation. *The Communists are after landowners, not little girls.*

Mr. Zhang's dog was the first to alert us to their arrival, barking incessantly by the shed door. It was early and we were all inside, nibbling on stale buns for breakfast. We rushed to dress, and came out to find Mr. Zhang speaking firmly but gently to a group of four cadres, all armed with rifles. The cadres looked surprised when they saw us. By then, we were as ragtag as any poor peasants; we hadn't bathed since we had left our *shibeyuan*, and we were covered in dirt, straw, and animal hair. The corners of our mouths were dry and cracking from lack of nutrition, and we had all grown thin, Mom especially so.

"You must be Mrs. Ang," said one of the cadres, the shortest in the group. "I am Comrade Lao Shin-Yi. We are looking for your husband and your father-in-law." Comrade Lao seemed to be in his twenties. His face was smooth and youthful, and his teeth were white, with a smattering of black decay on the edges.

"My husband is in Qingdao," Mom replied, keeping Di and me behind her. "I have not heard from him at all and do not know when he will return."

"You are lying!" another lanky cadre accused. "Tell us where he is!"

"I promise you that all I know is that he is in Qingdao," Mom said politely. "Would I be here, alone with my three girls, living with livestock, if I knew where my husband was?"

"That's what I've been trying to tell you," added Mr. Zhang. "Mrs. Ang and her daughters were abandoned by the rest of the family. They don't know any more than you or I do!"

I knew that he was trying to help us, but the word "abandoned" lodged in my chest. This was the first time anyone had admitted intentionality behind our circumstances. *We haven't been abandoned*, I reassured myself shakily. *Father is just late. Qingdao is far, and the mail service is slow. Any day now, he will arrive.*

The cadres peered into the shed, and at that time our donkey friend chose to help us out by letting out some steaming hunks of poop, which fell with a splat on the floor, as if to affirm that we were living in a shithole.

Disgusted, the cadres turned to one another and conversed in low voices, pointing to me and Di. Finally, Comrade Lao said, "The Ang family needs to be held accountable for its crimes." He looked at Mom with her sunken cheeks. "Show me your hands."

Confused but obedient, Mom took her hands out of her pockets. He grabbed them and examined closely, running a finger across the hard calluses on both her left and right palms and fingers. He was like a fortune-teller, except instead of predicting her future he was reading her past.

"These are thick, old calluses," he concluded, seeming impressed. "Years and years of work." He turned to me and Di, gesturing for us to show our palms too.

My mouth filled with saliva, and I swallowed nervously. Di and I stood side by side and stuck out our hands as though we had misbehaved and punishment was due. Comrade Lao performed the same test, running his fingers along our palms, which were comparatively soft. He noticed that I had a bump on my middle finger, at the first joint near the fingertip, a callus from how I held my pens when I wrote. He pressed on it. "Your family is truly privileged if even a daughter can write. Are you the eldest?"

"Yes," I replied hesitantly. *Don't be scared*, I told myself. *The Communists are after landowners, not little girls.*

He nodded and signaled to the other three cadres. "You will come with us, then," he said. My stomach sank as the cadres stepped forward, their eyes dark and emotionless.

"No!" Mom screamed, running between me and the cadres. "Please, no. Please don't take her!" Lan began to wail on her back, startled by Mom's cries.

Paralyzed with fear, I could only look at Mom like the child that I was, expecting her to save me. I had no idea where they would take me or what they would do. They might as well have been spirits from the underworld, ready to drag me away from the people I loved and the life that I knew.

Mr. Zhang rushed to grab Mom's arm and hold her back. "Please stop, miss," he said, forgetting to drop the title. His face was white as he tried to calm her. "Please. You will only make it worse."

"Take me!" Mom cried, ignoring Mr. Zhang's plea. She lunged

forward, trying to break from his grasp. "Please take me. I represent my husband! I represent the family!"

Two of the cadres raised their rifles slowly. Comrade Lao held up a hand, signaling for them to lower their weapons. He said to Mom, "I had heard already that the heir to the Ang family treated his wife miserably, and I see from your hands that you are no more than a slave. The old traditions allow wives to be treated like farm animals to abuse at will. Our revolution will free the oppressed. We are not here to punish victims of the previous system."

"But my daughter is no more responsible for my husband's actions than I am," Mom pleaded as Mr. Zhang's fingers dug into her thin arms. "She is a child! She has no choice in anything!" I turned toward Mom, but Comrade Lao grabbed my shoulders.

One of his compatriots took a rope and looped it around my neck as though I were a horse or an ox. It was scratchy against my skin, and he tugged on it to steer me toward him. With his hand still clamped on me, Comrade Lao said, "With the men gone, she is now the heir to the Ang family here in Zhucheng."

I couldn't believe my ears. "But I'm a girl," I whispered, confused. In my shock, I could only echo words that I had heard Nai Nai say. "I'm a mouth to feed and a dowry to pay. I am not an Ang."

"A girl cannot be an heir!" Mom exclaimed. "She will marry and leave the family; she is not an Ang! She is not one of us! The only Ang here is me! Take me!"

"There is a limit to our patience," Comrade Lao warned. "We will return her once judgment has been made. If you are so concerned for your daughter's welfare, bring us your husband and have him stand trial before the people, as he deserves."

My legs wobbled but I dared not fall, because I was certain that the rope around my neck would become a noose. The horror in Mom's eyes drained any courage that remained in me. She was the person I depended on for comfort when I was scared, and if she was terrified, then I was truly lost. "Father said they won't hurt girls," I managed to utter, holding in tears. "I'll be okay." Though I could say it out loud, I couldn't assuage myself as I recalled the demise of the Angs in the countryside. What punishment did the cadres have in store for my father? Would they take any mercy on me, standing in his place?

"Please bring her back" was all Mom could say, her voice breaking. "Please," she begged the cadres. "I've already lost a daughter; losing another will kill me. Please don't hurt her. She's only thirteen!"

Comrade Lao glanced at my pink cloth shoes and my stained red jacket and said, "Thirteen? I thought she was younger. She looks small. Like I said, bring us your husband. If you help him evade justice, then your daughter will pay the price." Without any further remarks, he led me away. The rope chafed as I craned my head back and saw Mom, who looked just like she had when Nai Nai refused to pay for Three's medical care—heartbroken, helpless, and hating herself. Though she had stopped struggling, Mr. Zhang maintained his grip on her arm, as though she were an arrow that would shoot forward if he let go. Beside them, to my surprise, Di covered her face with her hands and wept, her tears accompanied by loud, shaking sobs that I had never heard from her before.

6

DINNER PARTY

The cadres and I plodded along the wet path, my knees weak, with Comrade Lao beside me and the others guarding my front and back. Most of the stores were just opening and vendors wiped their signs, pausing to stare as we passed. Occasionally I recognized someone, but they averted their gaze, as though I could sully them by association. Shutters banged open as strangers poked their heads out, speculating out loud about my fate.

"Do you think they'll really hurt her?" a peasant woman asked her husband, thinking I couldn't hear. "She's so young. They can't be too harsh. The ground is too frozen to bury anyone anyway!"

My eye twitched and Comrade Lao cleared his throat. "No one is going to bury you," he said. "At least, I don't think so. What's your name?"

His paltry reassurance scared me even more than the peasant woman's musing. *He doesn't think so?* Was burying me actually a possibility? The last thing that I wanted to do was talk to him, but my survival likely depended on his whims. "Ang Mu-Yen," I lied. Somehow, I felt like he would have less power over me if he didn't know who I really was. "Mu-Yen."

Comrade Lao greeted a man who carried a bundle of rope on his back, before saying, "I know you are in a difficult position, but I don't want you to think of us as the enemy. You are young, and your generation will drive this movement." His face seemed softer than it had been before, more empathetic, the stern creases in his brow having melted away.

Still, I stared back at him incredulously. "Then why are you trying to hurt me?" I asked, disturbed that he was expecting conversation while I was in such a humiliating situation.

Comrade Lao blinked indignantly, as though I had insulted him. "I am not trying to hurt you. There must be accountability for your family's crimes, but that is different." Leaning closer to me, he said, "Think of it this way. When a child misbehaves, a parent must beat them to teach them, right? You're a Shandong girl. Surely you've been beaten by your elders before?"

Uncertain about his point, I nodded slowly; corporal punishment was common.

He smiled. "All good parents discipline their children. Punishment is not given out of hate, but out of love—to make the child a better person. We, the Communists, are like your mother and father, wanting only the best for you and all of China's brothers and sisters." I could tell he was proud of this analogy, but I didn't know what to say. The Communists were not my parents. Comrade Lao was not my father! From his twisted logic, it sounded like I was about to receive a spanking. My intuition, however, screamed that it would be worse.

"Let me share some words from Mao Ze-Dong," he continued patiently, like a prophet. "You must know Comrade Mao by now, right? If you do not, then let this be your first lesson. Mao said, 'If we have shortcomings, we are not afraid to have them pointed out and criticized, because we serve the people.' Everyone, even us cadres, needs to reflect and self-criticize, and think about how we can improve. Young people like you can be reeducated. You are already taking a step in the right direction by living with Mr. Zhang. I see potential in you, but you must atone in order to move forward."

Instead of feeling better, I was only more confused. Mao was irrelevant to me. All I knew was that the Communists had taken my home. The Communists had hit my mom. And now a Communist was walking me like a dog on a leash while another parroted a lecture that made little sense. Proceeding with his monologue, Comrade Lao said, "You will understand when you are older. When all Chinese people can stand proudly on their feet, our country will do the same. We are entering the age of a liberated China. A strong China. No more opium. No more colonies. It is an exciting time to be young and alive!"

My legs wobbled as we climbed up a hill, reaching a familiar field where I used to come to play. On the other side was a line of trees, a sparse forest that eventually met the river. If I were to follow that river trail for about forty-five minutes, I would reach the riverbank where I had taken Three, where my family planted yams every year. In the spring, this field would be filled with wildflowers of every color, and it would be fragrant from the blossoms and the smell of clean, wet earth. I used to run here with my cousins, picking flowers and stringing them together to make necklaces and hair wreaths. Together, we rolled down the hill, laughing as grass and petals clung to our clothing.

I wondered where Chiao and Pei were. I imagined them somewhere warm and cozy, their bellies full, as they laughed together, played together. Did they even think of me, and where I was? How I was? Could they possibly imagine that I would be standing here, my neck red and raw from the rope chafing at it?

Wildflower Field was now covered with snow that had been trampled so much that it was packed against the ground like ice. A bunch of desks, maybe ten, were arranged in a semicircle. Small and identical, they looked like they had been taken from a school. Some people were seated at the desks, while a large crowd of at least one hundred gathered behind.

I gasped as a cadre yanked my hands behind my back and crossed my wrists, tying them, then tying again at my elbows. Nearby, three men and two women were similarly tied, their eyes shifting anxiously from the crowd to the cadres. I recognized one couple with the surname Lin—also landowners in Zhucheng. They did not seem to recognize me; the few times that I had met them, they were visiting Father and our greeting was just a formality. Had these five people also been evicted? I was by far the most disheveled, so perhaps they hadn't been, or perhaps they had found friends with better lodging to share.

Another cadre, who was well muscled, with a square jaw and thin lips, asked Comrade Lao, "Is that the last one?" *That*. Not "she," like a person, but "that," like an animal or an object.

"Yes, Comrade Cheng," Comrade Lao replied. "Eldest daughter of the Ang family."

Comrade Cheng, annoyed, regarded me and said, "We will find your father and grandfather. They can leave Zhucheng, but they cannot escape the revolution." He looked older than Comrade Lao, and he exuded confidence and authority as he walked to the front of the semicircle to address the crowd.

When Comrade Cheng was out of earshot, Comrade Lao whispered to me, "Your father is a bad man. He is a criminal. Open your ears and your heart and listen to the people who have suffered under him. I hope that will open your eyes so that you can see why we must unite and dismantle the old system."

With no gloves or mittens, my bare hands were already numb from the cold, so much so that I could no longer feel the itchy rope against them. *My father has done bad things,* I thought. *Is he a bad man?* I couldn't say that. I had been taught to be loyal to my family and grateful to my parents, who had raised me. It was Mom who cared for me, but the money to do so came from Father. That counted for something. His money had ensured that I had clothes to wear, food to eat, and a place to sleep. He hadn't let me die.

A thought flashed into my head: *He is letting you die now.* I recalled that long night of debate after the workers had first warned us. It was Yei Yei who had wanted to stay, and Father who had pushed to leave. I didn't understand at the time, but looking back, I realized that Father must have known what would happen. He abandoned us, knowing that the Communists were coming, knowing that the Nationalist army had surrendered—he left us with nothing but some flour and a single gold coin. No guns to defend ourselves, no horses or even a donkey upon which to flee. How was that not a death sentence amid this war?

Comrade Cheng's booming voice interrupted my thoughts. "Workers, friends, comrades—the liberated!" He paused as the people cheered, their warm breath rising like an ominous fog. "We have struggled together, fought together, and overcome together. The Nationalist forces have fled with their tails between their legs. As Comrade Mao has said, all reactionaries are paper tigers. In appearance, the reactionaries are terrifying, but in reality, they are not so powerful. Just look at them now!"

The butt of a rifle jabbed against my back as the cadres pushed us forward and ordered us to kneel. Mr. Lin lost his balance as he bent his knee, and a cadre promptly barked at him to right himself and punched him in the face. Shaken, Mr. Lin settled like the rest of us, blood trickling from his nose. The six of us were in a line, with me at the very end on the left side, facing the crowd, which craved retribution.

In the first rows there were a few of my family's workers, but for the most part, I did not know anyone. Yet it was as though they knew me. Their faces were twisted in hatred as they glared at me, as though I had personally injured each and every one of them. Despite the fact that I was wearing several layers of pants, my skin felt bare against the icy ground as the wetness seeped through.

Comrade Lao reached over me and hung a large, thick cardboard sign around my neck. I peered downward and read it: "Oppressor; reactionary; enemy of the people."

Comrade Cheng commanded the crowd with a charisma that I had never seen before, his words an opiate that kept them entranced. Holding his hand toward us, he said, "It is the people who will carry this revolution, and it is the people who will judge your crimes. You kneel before them today because you have spent hundreds of years riding on their backs. Taxing the poor so that they work like slaves to till your land, yet starve because you steal the fruit of their labor from their mouths. Despite your struggle to keep us on our knees, we have risen to build a just society! And now we embark together on a new people's democratic dictatorship. An alliance of the working class and the peasantry!"

The crowd, including our former workers, roared in approval, clapping their hands fervently and whistling. Comrade Cheng waited for them to settle down before continuing. "And now the time has come for you to answer for your crimes. The people will speak their bitterness, and judgment will be made."

As he stepped away, members of the crowd began to curse, a

cacophony of complaints that rose to a crescendo. There were so many people shouting together that it was hard to pick out individual insults, but a few rang loud and clear:

"Evil gentry scum!"

"Bloodsucking landlords!"

"Arrogant thieves!"

"Oppressors! Bullies!"

A wet clump of dirt smacked the side of my face. People scooped up handfuls of snow mixed with rocks and started pelting us with gusto. The dull, wet thud of impact reminded me of a snowball fight, but instead of hearing the squeals of children playing, I heard the agonized screams of frightened adults. Every muscle in my body was rigid, paralyzed as each of their cries resonated within me, and suddenly I realized that the cries were my own. "I'm not a landlord! I'm a girl!" I screamed as freezing slush dripped from my forehead into my mouth. Snow and dirt hit my chest like hammers, pummeling the breath from my lungs. "Stop! I'm not a landlord!"

"Pigs!" a woman cried, shaking her fist at us. "Selfish, greedy pigs!"

"I'm not a pig! I'm a girl!" I shrieked to deaf ears. Father had been wrong when he said they wouldn't hurt me. He didn't care. He only wanted to save himself.

Venomously, the crowd yelled grievances against specific families—the Lins, the Wus, the Zhaos, and my family, the Angs. "Ang family cowards!" a worker of ours shouted. "My father slaved all his life for you with no complaints, and you paid him so little that he died early because he couldn't afford a doctor!"

"Ang family, you are all Kuomintang bootlickers!"

"Ang family! You never gave us enough food! We worked from sunrise to sunset, eating measly little meals while you sat on your asses and stuffed your faces!"

"Ang Li-Hai, your grandmother is evil!" I looked up, shocked to hear my name. Another one of our long-term workers stormed angrily to the front of the crowd. "Your father is evil! Your family is evil! Evil, reactionary, Nationalist-loving bastards!"

With my head up, a muddy fistful of snow hit me straight in the eye, and the grit stung as it seeped between my eyelids. What could I say? In my panicked mind, scenes from the past flashed before me—Nai Nai examining the scale, chiding Mom for a kilogram of flour lost. *Careless!* she had screamed. *Wasteful!* Father and Yei Yei discussing the crop share paid for rent. *Fifty percent is common. Fifty percent is fair.*

Of course the workers were hungry. Of course they were angry. Of course they wanted us dead. "I'm sorry," I whispered, though no one could hear me. "I'm sorry about the food. I'm sorry about Nai Nai. I'm sorry about my family." *I'm sorry that I never did more to help!*

Through my blurry vision, I saw someone restrain the worker who had named me, and pull him backward. My knees and ankles felt like they were being crushed underneath my own body weight, the pain like a blade being shoved behind my kneecaps. The cold had spread into my hip joints and they burned, the awkward position of my arms now excruciating.

Mrs. Lin screamed as bright red blood splattered on the dirty snow. Someone had thrown a stone at Mr. Lin's head, leaving a nasty gash across his eyebrow. People cheered as another rock whistled by, missing him narrowly. The Communist cadres stood with their arms folded; they looked satisfied, as though the frenzied energy from the crowd nourished them. I wished that I could take a stone myself and bash it across their faces. They said Father was evil, but what did that make them?

A good parent, of course, I heard Comrade Lao's awful voice say. Disgusted, I tried to shake his words from my head, but his smirking face was all I could see. Beside me, Mrs. Lin cried, snot running from her nose. She had been struck in the face several times too now, her cheek a fleshy pulp. With a groan, her husband fell face-first into a puddle of blood.

"Get up!" a cadre yelled, running over. Another cadre came to yank Mr. Lin back to a kneeling position, but he was no longer able to support himself. He was older, and the ice around him was bright red and slushy. The cadres leaned him against his wife, but the two of them toppled over pathetically.

"Leave them," Comrade Cheng commanded. The two cadres stepped back, and the Lins lay together, Mrs. Lin weeping, Mr. Lin silent, eyes squeezed shut. I looked at his lips, hoping to see his breath, but with Mrs. Lin heaving so, I could not discern hers from what might have been his. *He's dead. They've killed him, and soon they'll kill me too.*

Comrade Cheng turned to face us and announced, "As a result of your crimes against the people of Zhucheng, it has been determined that you landlords will be stripped of all your land, property, and personal belongings."

The crowd cheered and shouted praises for the cadres. "Long live the Communist Party! Long live Mao Ze-Dong! All power to the peasant associations!"

Blood dripped from the rope that had rubbed off skin from my wrists. Of us six, I was the only one with no life-threatening wounds. I knew that it wasn't luck that shielded me; it was Mom's kindness. In the crowd there were several who knew her and likely restrained or redirected the fury of their compatriots. I was caught in a tug-of-war of karma between the sins of my father and the good deeds of my mother. Would her altruism be enough to save me? Terror gripped me like a vise, threatening to squeeze the breath from my body. *The ground is too frozen to bury us.*

Comrade Cheng gestured for Comrade Lao to come, and the two of them stood before me, their shadows blocking the sun overhead. "Ang daughter," said Comrade Cheng. "Your father is a liar. A cowardly member of the gentry, a filthy landlord, a reactionary, and an oppressor of the people. By allowing him to hide, you are complicit in his crimes. Where is he?"

My heart battered, fighting to escape from my chest. Throat dry, my voice cracked as I spoke. "All we know is that he is in Qingdao. My mother already told you this. He left for Qingdao on business, and we don't know when he will return."

"You are lying," Comrade Cheng accused. "We searched your family home in Qingdao, and it was empty."

Impossible. "That can't be," I said. "My father wouldn't have left Qingdao without telling us." *Comrade Cheng must be lying.* Did the Communists even know where Yei Yei's house was?

"Don't play dumb," Comrade Cheng retorted with a sneer. "When we searched your home in Zhucheng, it was empty as well. No valuables, no food. Nobody leaves for a business trip and cleans out their house like that. Unless your mother took all the valuables and hid them?"

"No, of course not," I replied quickly. "My mother and I had only a few minutes to dress and leave. We walked away with my sisters and the clothing on our backs. Everyone that day saw us. We carried nothing out!" In our hands, anyway, except the few provisions that Comrade Kang had permitted us to go back for.

"Then you knew that they were going to flee." Comrade Cheng pounced. "If the house was so empty while you were living there, then you all knew that they were not coming back. Now tell us where they are. Your father and your grandfather need to face the people, who deserve justice!"

"My father did not tell us what his plans were," I said, shrinking as he loomed above me like an executioner. "I am telling the truth. He only said that he was going to Qingdao." *And if he's not there, where else could he possibly be?*

"So your whole family leaves for Qingdao, takes everything in the house, and you ask nothing? Admit that they were fleeing!" His anger was augmented by his growing frustration, his eyes like black flames.

I wasn't sure what to say, but I desperately wanted him to stop. Would admitting that my father fled create more problems for us? Or would they leave us alone? "I . . . I don't know," I said. Like a thunderclap, Comrade Cheng slapped my face so hard that I almost lost my balance.

"Lying little bitch!" He stood over me, his stance wide and hand raised, ready to strike again. "Now, I'll give you one more chance to tell the truth. Where are your father and grandfather?"

"I don't know," I stuttered, terrified and bracing myself for another blow. "I really don't know. My mom doesn't know; my sister doesn't know; none of us know!"

He slapped me again, harder this time; I thought my jaw would crack. I tasted blood from the force of my cheek smashing against my teeth. "How can you not know?" he roared, his hot breath against my face. "How can you see people in your house pack their belongings—it must have taken days—how can you see and claim to know nothing?" He slapped me again, with the back side of his hand this time to preserve his palm.

Comrade Lao stepped forward. "Comrade, I think she may be telling the truth. She seemed to be genuinely surprised when you said their house in Qingdao was empty."

Comrade Cheng snapped, "Do not pity the snakelike scoundrel!" He slapped me again and I fell over, my shoulder hitting the ice. Some in the crowd were repeating and yelling "Snakelike scoundrel" at me. "Confess!" Comrade Cheng said. "Confess! Your disgusting landlord father fled. Your grandfather fled. They fled because they are guilty! They are Nationalist traitors! They think they can escape the revolution, but we will come for them. Confess what other sins you have committed to oppress the people of Zhucheng!" Each sentence ended with a blow, peasants hooting in satisfaction as I lost count of the number of times he hit me.

"Comrade Cheng, she is young," said Comrade Lao, hesitating as he spoke. Despite the Communists' claiming to have no rank, it was clear that Comrade Cheng was his superior. "Mao said the revolutionary camp must be expanded and embrace all who are willing to join the revolutionary cause. She can break the influence of her family and come to the Party."

"Not if she cannot admit her own failings first," said Comrade Cheng firmly. "Confess!" He dragged me upright like he was grabbing a rabbit by the scruff of its neck, only to knock me back down, my nose smashing against the ice.

My vision blurred. Blood was pooling in my mouth, but I could only let it dribble out for fear that spitting it would be seen as a slight. "I don't know what else I can say," I sputtered, eyes watering from the pain, tears running down my inflamed cheeks.

"Admit that your family has profited off the backs of workers for generations!" Comrade Cheng shouted, his face only a few centimeters from my own as he held me upright by my collar.

I swallowed blood before I could coherently say, "My family has profited off the backs of workers for generations."

"Admit that your family collaborated with the reactionaries! Admit that your father is Nationalist scum!" I was crying in full force now, sniveling and hiccuping, feeling like a traitor as Comrade Cheng fed me these words.

"We collaborated with the reactionaries. My father is Nationalist . . . My father is a professor!" I blurted, struggling to speak through my sobs. I thought about Uncle Jian, who was a Nationalist colonel. Did they know that? If they did, was it something I should be admitting myself to avoid further abuse? Did Uncle Jian also count for my crimes? I couldn't think straight. I was too tired, too cold, and too hungry from weeks of rationing, shivering so much that I had to concentrate to keep my teeth from chattering.

"The university is a cesspool of gentry parasites," Comrade Cheng spat. "It is a propaganda machine to keep the lawless in power. Your father is not just scum; he is among the lords of scum supporting the oppressive feudal system."

Another searing, stinging slap hit me so hard that I thought my neck would disconnect. I hadn't said anything! Or maybe it was because I hadn't said what he wanted me to say?

"Admit that you helped your evil father escape!" Comrade Cheng roared. "Admit it!" Suddenly he reached into his belt for his knife, which gleamed as he pulled it out, the steel hanging threateningly over my head.

As the sunlight reflecting off the blade blinded me, I screamed, barely coherent. "I didn't do anything! My mom didn't do anything. My sisters didn't do anything. We can't control my father or my grandfather. We cannot question them! We have no power. We are girls! They didn't want us because we are girls! They left us behind because we are girls!" I hated myself for cowering before him and squealing like a frightened pig, but I was too weak to be brave, too scared to be strong.

Comrade Cheng was panting from the exertion of hitting me, and he lowered the blade and stepped back, a horrible smile on his face. "There it is," he said, as though he had wrenched a prize from my lips. "The despicable Kuomintang scum abandoned his own family. The gentry are the ones propping up useless patriarchal traditions. It is these traditions that we will bury as we liberate our nation!" He grabbed my braid and yanked it so hard that my head fell back, exposing my throat for him to slash. *Has Three already gone to her next life, or will she be waiting for me? If she's there, maybe death won't be so scary.*

With one swift motion he cut off my braid, strands of wet, dirty hair falling into my face. I fell forward again, onto the ice, as he threw my braid beside me like a vanquished snake. My clothes were drenched and the cold was drawing the life out of my body, the light within me dimming. I was shivering so badly that I was squirming into the snow like a burrowing worm. More than anything else, I just wanted to close my eyes. My heartbeat slowed to a sluggish drumming. I heard the engine of Father's car, loud at first, and then distant as he drove away.

Comrade Lao pulled me back onto my knees, but my head was so heavy, it flopped like a doll's. "Let this be your second lesson," he said gently. "We are fighting against the harmful customs and beliefs that Confucius inflicted upon the masses. We are liberating not only the peasants and the workers, but also people like you who have been oppressed by tradition."

My head still spun from the blows, and I could not digest what he was saying. He was telling me that they were here to liberate me, yet I had just been beaten so hard that I could feel my face swell even in the cold. *It's not out of hate. It's out of love.*

Comrade Cheng looked at me disdainfully and said, "You are not beyond hope. But you need to cast off the shackles of tradition and shed the influence of the gentry." He looked at Comrade Lao and said, "This one is done." I was soaked, freezing, my bloody mouth tasting of metal as they moved on to the remaining three, interrogating each of them. I didn't realize that they were actually being lenient with me. The two men from the Zhao family were landlords and gentry like Father. After a brutal beating, Comrade Cheng sentenced them to death and Comrade Lao shot them in the head with his pistol. I had never seen an execution, but by then I was so numb, and drifting in and out of consciousness, that I flinched only slightly when I heard the first gunshot. Something in me must have turned off, because the second gunshot didn't even register.

The remaining woman, Mrs. Wu, was a widow; her husband had been murdered when they were evicted from their home. According to her interrogation, she was a writer affiliated with the university. She was sentenced to be reeducated and marry one of the Communist cadres, whoever was willing to take her with her broken nose and split lip.

Long after Comrade Cheng had finished his inquisitions, Mrs. Wu and I continued to kneel, the Lins and Zhaos splayed beside us, blood and brains streaked in the snow. *What will happen to their bodies? Who will give them a funeral?*

The Communists left us there until late afternoon, allowing for turnover in the crowd so that people could take shifts hurling insults and whatever items they chose to throw at us. My arms and wrists had gone so numb that when they finally untied me, it felt like knives were slicing along my veins as the blood came rushing back into my hands. "Leave the signs," Comrade Cheng commanded. They wanted everyone who passed us to know our shame—as if being covered in dirt, mud, and blood was not enough.

By then I had been kneeling for over six hours. As soon as I stood, I fell, and crawled on my knees and elbows because I wanted to leave so badly. No one touched Mr. and Mrs. Lin, who still lay facedown in the ice, or the two Zhaos. *The ground is too frozen to bury them anyway.* I pushed myself back up, shaking, desperate to return to my mom.

I staggered down the hill, bracing myself with my arms out for balance. Someone called my name. "Li-Hai! Li-Hai!" *It must be one of the cadres.* I was too afraid to turn and look, but I also lacked the strength to run. Snow crunched beneath boots as two men caught up to me, and I almost cried with relief to see that they were Mr. Hu and a younger man.

They slung their arms around me, lifting me like a strong tide. I opened my mouth, and Mr. Hu said, "You are safe with us. We will take you back to Mr. Zhang's. Do not say anything. Everyone is watching, and everyone is listening."

"We need to carry her," the young man said. "We will move too slowly otherwise."

Mr. Hu nodded. "Yes. We need to get her somewhere warm as soon as possible."

My head swam as Mr. Hu pulled me into his arms and hurried down the hill, away from the field that used to hold so much beauty. Mao infamously said, "A revolution is not a dinner party, or writing an essay, or painting a picture, or doing embroidery; it cannot be so refined, so leisurely and gentle, so temperate, kind, courteous, restrained, and magnanimous. A revolution is an insurrection, an act of violence by which one class overthrows another." He had been irrelevant before. I would remember him now. I would always remember him. Remember them. In the dark of night, when other children saw monsters, I would see Comrade Kang and Comrade Lao, panting, smiling, screaming.

It took what seemed like hours for us to reach the shed as they took turns carrying me. I kept my eyes on the ground, as I still wore the shaming sign around my neck, stained red by my blood.

We arrived at dusk, and I could see that Mom was waiting outside the shed, staring anxiously at the road. When she saw me, she let out a cry and ran madly, grabbing me from the young man's arms so hard that I screamed and fell. My whole body throbbed, yet I still couldn't feel my fingers.

"Thank the Gods! Thank the Gods you are alive!" she sobbed, clutching me as though I might float away. "I'm sorry I couldn't stop them. I'm sorry that it was you and not me." She turned toward Mr. Hu, bowed deeply while holding me, and said, "Thank you for bringing her back. Thank you, thank you. I can never repay you."

"You don't need to thank us," Mr. Hu said gravely. "I only wish we could have done more."

"You already took a great risk coming back with her," Mom said, tears in her eyes as she lifted the sign gingerly off of my neck.

The young man said, "Sometimes we need to take risks to do what is right." I realized then that the young man was Mr. Hu's son—the sick one whom Mom had given the meat buns to. He had grown significantly; no longer a child, he was broad and taller than his father, a seed that had sprouted into a beanstalk.

By then Di had come out with Lan on her back. "Thank the Gods you are home!"

"I'm so sorry," Mom repeated, crying and rocking me like I was an infant, which aggravated my injuries. "I'm so sorry, Hai. It should have been me."

"It shouldn't have been any of us," said Di quietly.

"It's not your fault, Mama," I said, my voice hoarse and weak. "It's okay. I survived. I'll be okay now."

Mom examined me, appalled by my swollen face and raw arms. "What did they do to you? Who was it? Was it the men who took you?"

I shook my head, broke down, and cried loudly, like a toddler, with my sisters, Mr. Hu, and his son watching. "It was everyone, Mama. Everyone. It wasn't just the Communists; it was the people. Some of our old workers too. They said that we are evil, reactionaries, oppressors—too many bad things to count."

What I wanted to ask her was, *Did Father and Yei Yei hurt so many people that our Ang family deserves to be punished by the revolution? Do I deserve to wear this sign and to receive the hatred and disdain of everyone in Zhucheng? Did we deserve to lose our home and live in this shed?*

"Come," Mom said. "Mr. Zhang said we can bring you by the fire in his house and warm you up." She took my hands, and it felt as though I were wearing thick gloves—my fingertips were white, waxy, and hard.

Upon seeing me, Mrs. Zhang wrapped a wool blanket around my shoulders and ushered me before the fire. Gently, she lowered me into a chair while Mr. Zhang brought boiled water, which Mom held for me to sip. They took off my shoes, and I wiggled my toes. I could move them, but couldn't feel them. Mom examined my hands and feet and said, "It's frostbite, not severe. We'll warm you up slowly." Tenderly, Mom wiped my cut hair and my face with a warm towel, wringing the dirt into a basin. I was so filthy that several times she had to empty and refill the basin with a mix of boiled water and soap.

As the warmth slowly seeped into my body, I felt like I had been drugged. My eyelids drooped heavily and I closed them, drifting off to sleep. Every other second, Mom shook me awake, and I wanted to swat her away. I was just so tired. I imagined I was lying down in a warm river, allowing its current to carry me away—far away from the Communists, far away from Zhucheng, far away from Shandong, from China, from the world.

I opened my eyes and saw Mom's worried face staring straight into mine. Smiling weakly, I said, "I'm just going to sleep. Don't worry. I'll be okay."

She nodded, her face fraught with tension, but she said calmly, "I will be here. I won't leave."

I closed my eyes again. Mr. Zhang and Mom talked, but it sounded like water trickling and burbling. Like the sound of the river near Wildflower Field, where we had taken Three to play.

7

EGG

For days I avoided going outside, despite the darkness and the smell in the shed. It wasn't just out of shame for my face, which looked like a sloppy mosaic of red and purple bruises. More than that, it was because of the potential embarrassment of running into anyone who had been at the rally or who had seen me as the Hus carried me home with that awful sign around my neck. Mom had thrown the sign in the fire, but I felt like the words were tattooed on my forehead; anywhere I went, people would know who I was and that I deserved punishment. The thought of meeting cadres, who often strolled through residential areas to banter with peasants, was enough to keep me glued to our wooden platform.

The swelling in my cheeks subsided and the bruises faded to a greenish yellow, but it took weeks for my face to look normal again. Although I recovered the use of my hands, my knees were damaged and my mind would never be the same. Eventually I could walk, but from then on, my knees ached whenever I was cold, and always before it rained.

Gently but firmly, Mom flung open the shed doors and made me face daylight again. She said that humans are like plants and we need to feel the sun on our skin. The name of her hometown, Rizhao, literally means "sunshine." "In darkness, you don't know which way is up and which way is down," she said. "Let's change your clothes and fix your hair. Short cuts seem to be the fashion in the cities anyway." She was trying to console me, but my missing braid was like a phantom. I was so accustomed to flipping it out of the way or hunching a shoulder up to prevent it from falling forward. In older Chinese tradition, cutting hair was a mark of disgrace. With dull scissors, Mom snipped away, shreds of my dignity drifting to the ground as the steel blades scraped against each other.

Mr. and Mrs. Zhang helped as much as they could, but even they were becoming afraid of the repercussions of associating with us. The cadres had been kind to Mr. Zhang and the other peasants, to the point that the people echoed Comrade Lao and said that the Communists were like their fathers and mothers, caring for their well-being. It seemed like it was only me and my family who continued to live in fear, glancing over our shoulders and tossing and turning at night, uncertain what the next day would bring.

I told Mom what Comrade Cheng had said about our family home in Qingdao. "Do you think it's true?" I asked her. "Do you think they went somewhere else and just didn't tell us?"

Mom answered, "I don't know. It might have been a bluff because the cadres wanted to know whether you were telling the truth or not. Or it could be true. Maybe Father wrote to us and the letter was intercepted. Everything is so messy now. We don't even know if your father received our letter."

As winter waned, the Communists exerted tighter control in the region, restricting travel to prevent class enemies and Nationalist sympathizers from trying to flee. Getting a letter or a message anywhere was impossible unless it was with a cadre.

"Do you think Father is trying to find us?" I asked.

Mom looked up at me, scanning my face with her eyes, noting where the bruises still lingered. Without hesitating, she said, "No."

I was surprised by her answer. She was usually quick to defend Father and offer an excuse or an explanation on his behalf, even if she herself didn't believe it.

Mom continued, saying, "No one is coming for us. Except the Communists."

I stiffened at the thought, my breath caught in the bottom of my lungs. Mom put a warm, strong hand on my shoulder and squeezed it gently. "Hai," she said, "I am haunted by regret that I didn't take you away earlier. And I cannot trust that this is the end of it. There are too many things that I don't know—that I can't know. I don't know where your father is. I don't know if we will ever see him again. I don't know what will happen in Zhucheng once the snow melts. I don't know how much longer Mr. and Mrs. Zhang can let us stay here. But I do know one thing. I know that we need to leave here."

I let out my breath, and inhaled again, finally. "When?" I asked.

"Once the snow thaws, and you are strong enough to walk for longer, we will go. The sooner the better. I suspect that the Communists will not leave us alone until your father and grandfather are found, and we both know that the two of them will not be coming back here. Not for a long time. Maybe not ever."

"Where are we going to go? Qingdao?"

Mom nodded. "Qingdao is the only place we can go. Maybe your father will be there. Any rural area will be like Zhucheng—there will be rallies, and the populations are small. People will wonder where we came from, and it won't be hard for them to figure it out. In Qingdao, we will be just a few of many ants—it will be easier for us to hide who we are."

For the first time in months, I felt more excited than afraid. Joyous even. I didn't know what the journey would be like, but in the unknown there is hope. How would we even get to Qingdao? We had no car, no horse. Nobody around us except the cadres had vehicles, and the workers could not spare any animals for our journey—and anyway, if they helped us escape, they would surely be punished. "Mom," I asked, "how are we going to get out?"

Mom said what she always said. "We will find a way."

As the days passed, I willed my body to heal as quickly as it could, walking every day to test myself. I never ventured up the hill toward Wildflower Field anymore but would go the opposite way, toward the mountains.

One day, I pushed myself farther along my new route and saw Di sitting on a stone, basking in the sun like a turtle trying to absorb its warmth. I almost called out her name, but then I noticed that she had something small and brown in her hands. Quickly I crouched down on my elbows and knees, keeping my eyes on her like an awkward predator. Unaware of my presence, she knocked the brown thing against the stone gently on both sides and carefully peeled something off the top. It was an egg!

Di peeled a piece of shell from the opposite side of the egg, then drew the opening to her mouth and sucked on it. My jaw dropped as I watched her slurp and gulp, licking her lips in satisfaction. After noisily making sure that she got every drop, she discarded the empty shell, still a clean brown globe, on the ground behind her.

"Di!" I yelled, standing up and waving my arms to get her attention.

Startled, she jumped up to her feet. "Sis!" she said nonchalantly, greeting me. There was still a bit of egg yolk in the corner of her mouth.

"Where did you get that egg?" I asked.

Di started to deny, but then guessed that I must have been watching her and admitted, "From the chickens in the shed."

I had assumed that she was doing odd jobs for food and I was shocked to hear that the egg was the Zhangs'. "Di!" I exclaimed. "We are supposed to give those eggs to Mrs. Zhang! How could you steal them?" I knew she was hungry; we all were. But the Zhangs had shown us so much kindness, and it was so ungrateful of her to take advantage of them.

Di rolled her eyes at me and said, "Mrs. Zhang doesn't notice. In any case, we are starving. And they will be getting our land in the land reform anyway, so the least they can do is spare a few eggs. Call it a last rent payment."

She didn't seem embarrassed or remorseful at all—if anything, her tone was defensive. "It's not just the theft itself that is bad," I said, "but that you didn't think to share any of it with us." Months ago, the idea of eating a raw egg out of its shell would have been revolting to me, but in the present day, any egg was a good egg. I thought about how she had so expertly cracked and drained it. "Is this the first time that you've done this?"

"None of your business," Di snapped, getting angry.

"It *is* my business," I insisted. "If Mrs. Zhang wants to kick us out, of course it is my business! What if she suspects us of stealing? She could report us to the cadres!"

"She's not going to know," Di said. "It's winter, and the hens are probably old. All chickens produce less with age. I didn't take many anyway."

Didn't take many? That confirmed that she had indeed done this before. In the mornings, we opened the shed doors for light and swept the shed clean, carefully collecting any eggs and bringing them to Mrs. Zhang. I wondered how many times Di had snuck one, or maybe more, in her pocket, and come to this field to eat like an outlaw. "We are all hungry, Di!" I exploded. "We are all sick of eating buns and flatbread! You aren't the only one who is having a hard time, but you're the only one being selfish!"

"Selfish?" Di exclaimed incredulously. "We don't need to be hungry. I saw Mom put that jewelry away. Why doesn't she just sell it for some real food? What are we going to do with that jewelry when we are all dead from starvation? We have all that flour too, which Mom is rationing beyond reason!"

I couldn't believe Di was so shortsighted. "Are you stupid?" I yelled back. "Is your pig brain so tiny that you don't understand that we have no source of income? The jewelry is for emergencies. We need to save, and we need to be careful—do you not understand that? We need that to last as long as we can until—" I stopped. We always said, *until Father comes to get us*, or *until we are reunited with our family*.

"Until what?" Di demanded, reading my thoughts. "Father is not coming. We need to adapt, and that's what I'm doing. I'm adapting."

"No," I said, seething. "Adapting is what we do as a family. Together. What you are doing is stealing, and only for yourself."

"So if I stole an egg for Mom it would be okay?" asked Di. "Or for Lan, because she's a baby? Should I just let myself die because I'm neither ranked senior nor an infant?"

"You don't need to steal from the Zhangs to live," I emphasized, frustrated. "Spring is coming. There are rabbits in the mountains that we can learn to catch, and wild vegetables that we can pick. Winter is hard but it is temporary. We could have gotten through it without disrespecting those who have been kind to us!"

"Fine," Di said. "Take your stupid egg!" She leaned and grabbed the eggshell and threw it into my face, then bolted as fast as she could into the forest. She turned back and yelled, "You stupid mama's baby! Ugly frog face!"

I was livid, but even when I was at my healthiest Di with her long legs was faster than me. With my knees still weak, I could never hope to catch her, especially running through the bumpy trail toward home. Arguing with Di was futile and always left me angrier than if I had ignored her in the first place. Even if I was only one year her senior, she was supposed to listen to me—but she rarely did. It was true that if she had stolen the egg for Lan, I would have been less upset, since at least the theft would have been altruistic. But what was the point of hypotheticals? She had not stolen the egg for Lan; she stole it for herself.

I picked the bits of eggshell from my face and wiped off the slime with my hand. Checking to see if anyone was watching, I licked these broken brown fragments and sucked on my fingers, hoping to get any bit of nourishment that remained. Though no one saw, I was ashamed of how pathetic I had become.

Feeling like a thief, I slunk back to the shed, debating whether or not to tell Mom about the egg. On one hand, I wanted her to reprimand Di. On the other, I also knew that Mom had enough to worry about without having to go kowtow to the Zhangs for her daughter's transgressions. When I approached the shed, though, Mom was busy talking to Mr. Zhang outside his house, their voices hushed. Momentarily I forgot my outrage, quickening my pace so I could catch their conversation.

"I've spoken to all of them," said Mr. Zhang. "You need a travel permit to go anywhere now. The cadres have taken over most of the towns and have checkpoints everywhere. They are monitoring the roads for class enemies."

Noticing me approaching, Mom waved absently and then crossed her arms in frustration. "The cadres here will never give us authorization to leave!"

Nodding in agreement, Mr. Zhang said, "Of course not. The Ang family is too prominent in Zhucheng, and the Party loses face if people know that the men escaped. The cadres will keep you here until your husband returns. If they give up on him, it only means that you and your daughters will face the full punishment that they've been saving for Mr. Ang."

I winced, remembering that Comrade Lao had designated me as the family heir. I didn't want to wait around for another rally or additional persecution for being my father's daughter. Even if my knees were still sore, we needed to leave—as soon as possible. "How important is this travel permit?" I asked. "Could we pretend that we just lost ours if asked?"

From the grave expression on Mr. Zhang's face, it was clear the answer was no. "If you have no permit, the cadres will arrest you!" he exclaimed. "When they find out you are an Ang and that you escaped Zhucheng, they will probably execute you!"

Mom swallowed, wrapping her arm around my shoulder. "We have no choice, though," she said. "If we stay here, we might be killed anyway!"

I was no fortune-teller, but even I could see that our future in Zhucheng was likely limited to two paths: death like the Lins and the Zhaos, or forced marriage to a cadre, like Mrs. Wu. "We have to try," I said quietly. "We can't just sit here. What does this permit even look like?"

Mom smiled, encouraged. "I've never seen one, but it's only paper and ink. If the Communists won't issue one for us, maybe we can make one ourselves?"

Mr. Zhang hesitated, uncertain that our plan was viable. "They are not complicated documents, but there is a red authorization stamp. Many cadres are like me and can't read, but we all know to look for that stamp. Without it, cadres will know your documents are fake and you will be punished!"

Undeterred, Mom turned to me and said resolutely, "You have always been good at calligraphy, right, Hai?"

"Yes," I answered slowly, confused by her optimism. I wasn't just good at calligraphy and writing—I excelled at them, loved them. The telltale callus on my finger was proof of all the practice, but no amount of fine writing could mimic an authorization stamp. "From what Mr. Zhang is saying, it sounds like the stamp is more important than the actual words, though!"

"Don't worry about that," Mom said, excited. "I have an idea. It's a little crazy, but I think it will work! Let's see how much flour we have. We'll need to do some bartering."

8

SOAP AND INK

With a stack of flatbread delivered with kind words, Mom got some paper and borrowed a brush pen and black ink. This entire winter, Mom had been trading flour for small items, like sewing supplies, and even a pair of thick socks for Lan. By the end of March we were down to only four bags—and had to give up one more for a bottle of red ink. I held that precious glass bottle in my hands, visualizing the piles of buns, the bowls of noodles, and the tower of flatbread that were now within its vibrant crimson liquid.

"So, what's your crazy plan?" I asked Mom as I proceeded to write, *Official Travel Permit. Authorization to depart Zhucheng and enter Qingdao, Shandong Province.* I didn't know what language to use, and this sentence was my best guess.

"We're going to make a stamp," replied Mom. "I bartered for a block of soap, and we can use a hair pin to carve it."

I almost dropped my brush. "That *is* a crazy idea," I said, impressed. "But it's also an ingenious one!"

Beaming, Mom said, "I'm glad you agree. Because you are the one who's going to do the carving!"

With Mom standing watch, I sat hunched outside in the light, trembling as I pinched the metal hairpin firmly in my sore fingers. Mom had assumed that my calligraphy skills would somehow make me a deft carver. "No one's coming, right?" I asked anxiously every five minutes.

"Don't worry," she replied. "I'll warn you. Just focus on carving. The soap is getting thin. We can't afford to keep cutting it!" Whenever I made a mistake, we had to slice the soap block to give me a clean slate. I was getting better each time, but the pressure of Mom's expectations made my hands sweat and the hairpin slip. Curls of soap fell as I meticulously chiseled, *Zhucheng Chinese Communist Party*. Another guess, another gamble.

Using a rag, I rubbed the red ink onto our makeshift stamp; then I placed it gently on the paper and pressed while Mom held her breath. I lifted it and marveled. That red stamp was the kiss of legitimacy that we needed. Some characters were slightly crooked, but the permit looked authentic—to our eyes, anyway.

Over the next few days, Mrs. Zhang, relieved that we were preparing to leave, let us use her kitchen. Mom instructed Di and me to make as much flatbread as we could in preparation for our journey. Di, however, had never been good at cooking—her flatbread dough was so sticky and lumpy that it ended up being a waste of flour to have her help. Exasperated, Mom dismissed her and she bounded off to the fields. *Probably to go eat some secret eggs*, I thought bitterly. I didn't want her bad company in the small kitchen anyway. My knuckles and finger joints ached as I kneaded the dough, my turbulent thoughts dwelling morbidly on each and every potential danger ahead of us.

One morning, Mom handed Lan to me to care for while she

ran a few final errands for our journey. She never left for long, because Lan was still nursing, but that day was an exception. In the afternoon, feeling wary that Mom had not come home, I nibbled on some flatbread and gave Lan a piece to chew on. Like a bandit, Di showed up for lunch and gobbled down her portion, barely chewing before she wiped her mouth with the back of her hand and jumped away.

"Have you seen or heard from Mom?" I asked.

"No," Di replied over her shoulder, already back out the door.

"Can you take Lan with you?" I yelled after her, hoping that she would babysit so I could make flatbread more efficiently. "Di! Di! Take Lan with you?"

But Di was already out of earshot, or perhaps was just pretending she didn't hear me. Lan looked at me with sad eyes—she needed milk, but I had none to give her. Every minute that passed transformed into a new fear. What if Mom tripped and broke her leg? What if Mom got trampled by a horse? What if Mom was arrested by the cadres?

Dusk fell and I stacked the last of my flatbread, leaving a small pile for the Zhangs, to thank them. Di sauntered home as the sunset sky turned amber, and I told her coldly that Mom was still out. "That's odd," Di remarked. "It's getting dark. I'm sure she will be back soon, though. We can't do anything but wait anyway." Shrugging, Di retreated into the shed. "Call me if you need help," she offered limply. I rolled my eyes, thinking about how I had asked her to take Lan and she had bounded away like a pony with no reins. Did she not care about Mom? Did she not understand the gravity of losing her?

I waited outside, eyes on the road, holding Lan, who had begun to howl. So many times I had stared ahead at the path, hoping to see Father. Now that I had given up on him, I found myself here again, praying that my only remaining parent would return. *Please come back, Mom. I'm sorry for every bad thing I did, and for all the trouble I caused. Whatever you do, please don't leave us too.* Lan's mournful expression began to change into an accusatory one as she looked at me and repeated, "Mama, Mama," over and over again.

"I don't know where she is either," I said, bouncing her on my hip. "Trust me—I wish she was here too." In the darkness of my thoughts, I succumbed to my worst fear. *Mom abandoned us.* She was smart enough to know that the three of us would drag her down, especially a baby like Lan, whom we all had to carry. Now she had the fake permit and a plan. There was no reason to stay. *Mom loves us,* I thought, trying to reassure myself, but despair needled at me, and a voice inside me whispered, *We are all a burden. She's better off without us.*

Lan bawled, pausing only to inhale so she could scream anew, prompting neighbors to come check on us. When I told them we were waiting for Mom, who hadn't come back, their reaction was like Di's. They expressed sympathy and offered reassurance that she was probably just running late, but ultimately they returned to their own warm homes. Mom's absence was not their problem, and in this time of inquisition, people did better minding their own business—especially when it came to class enemies like us. Lan clutched my shirt, her tears soaking my chest.

"Please don't cry," I begged, almost in tears myself. "We might not even have a mom anymore. No one wants us." Nai Nai's words echoed in my head, and I added absently, my voice low, "We're just useless mouths to feed."

The shed door creaked open as Di came back out. "We're not useless," she said, standing next to us.

I looked at her and couldn't help but say, "You could hear me say that so quietly but you didn't hear me yelling for you to take Lan?"

"I don't know what you're talking about," Di said, my question slipping off her back like water off a duck's feathers. "Stop your wallowing. Come inside so that the neighbors don't beat Lan to death to get her to shut up. Besides," she added, "if something really happened to Mom, then we all need you to be well rested."

I sighed and accepted that Di was right. Lan's wails had subsided, and she was beginning to fall asleep from crying so much. As we turned to go inside, I spotted a silvery figure in the distance, illuminated by the moonlight. Peering ahead into the dark, I could make out a woman pushing a Chinese-style wheelbarrow, a flat wooden platform with a protruding wooden wheel, shoulder straps, and handles.

"Mom!" Di and I both yelled. Lan startled to alertness again and resumed screaming with gusto as though I had kidnapped her.

Running to take Lan, who then clawed savagely at her breasts, Mom whispered, "Into the shed! We cannot draw so much attention to ourselves. Hai, take the wheelbarrow."

I grabbed the wheelbarrow and steered it through the door, careful not to hit the donkey, who would kick me in retaliation. I felt my way to some flatbread that I had bundled tightly in a blanket to prevent the chickens from getting it, and I handed it to Mom clumsily.

"I'm so sorry I'm late," she said, peeling off her clothing so that Lan could nurse. She must not have had anything to eat all day. Chewing loudly, she explained through mouthfuls, "I didn't think it would take me so long. I went to see Mr. Hu so he could help me get a map—I didn't want to get one myself, because I was afraid that it would make it obvious that we were leaving. Mr. Hu got a good one with a lot of detail, and I'll show it to you tomorrow in the light. I should have come home after that, but I was afraid I would run out of time. I went to get our wheelbarrow."

"Our wheelbarrow?" Di repeated, confused.

"Yes," said Mom. "This is our wheelbarrow. It is from our property."

"You went back home?" I asked, surprised. "How?"

Mom replied, "Mr. Hu took me there with his mule and cart. Not all the way, but close enough. I didn't want him to risk taking me back, because if we got caught, the cadres would punish us both." Mom paused, her voice growing heavier. "Cadres live in our house now."

"What?" Di and I exclaimed together.

Hatred bubbled within me as I imagined Comrade Cheng and Comrade Lao eating meals at our kitchen table and sleeping in our warm *kang* beds—and pawing through the remainder of our belongings and judging us for how we had lived. I would rather have had my doll burned in the fire than given to one of their children.

Mom continued, not wanting to dwell on the loss of our home. "I still know our land. I went to the shed where we keep the bigger equipment for the harvest. I found our wheelbarrow quickly, but then I saw a cadre on the road. I got too nervous to take it in broad daylight, so I decided to hide in the shed until it was dark. I figured then everyone would be cold and go inside for dinner and I could walk back without being noticed. I'm so sorry to have worried you."

"It's okay, Mom," I said sheepishly, embarrassed for doubting her. "For a second, I thought that you had abandoned us too."

Mom laughed. "Abandon you? Why would I abandon you all? Where would I go? There is nowhere in this world, in this life, worth going to without my daughters," she said, grabbing my hand in the dark. We hugged each other, and I even hugged Di, forgetting about how upset I had been with her earlier.

"Rest as much as you can," said Mom. "We need to go as soon as possible, before word spreads. I trust Mr. Hu, but who knows who might have seen me or overheard any of our conversations? Tomorrow, as soon as it's light enough to see, we will leave."

9

LUCKY

Early the next morning, we packed all of our flatbread, wrapped in clean clothing, and a few canteens of water and the remainder of our personal belongings. We had so little that it all fit easily in the wheelbarrow, along with a compass from Mr. Hu and some boiled eggs from Mrs. Zhang. The dawn sky blushed, casting a soft pink light on the map as I opened it. Old creases lined the paper, which was faded from the repeated touch of travelers before us. Mr. Zhang knew the roads well, and I added his advice in notes in the margins. It was about one hundred fifty kilometers to Qingdao; there was no bridge across Jiaozhou Bay, so we had to go all the way around the coast. That would be the easy part, since we could follow the beach, with the ocean on our right. The challenge lay in navigating the small country lanes without getting lost—we wanted to avoid the main roads, which would have more checkpoints.

Closing the door to the shed, we waved to the donkey, who blinked and chewed his hay. The chickens were similarly unaffected by our departure. Mr. Zhang's dog, however, whined when he saw us packing. We had spent a lot of time with the dog, especially on the colder nights, when he would scratch the door to come into the shed. In the weeks after the rally, he lay beside me, the only company that I could accept as I lay motionless on the wooden platform. When we had asked Mr. Zhang about his name, he said it was just "Dog." He had only one, so he didn't need to differentiate. Dog was a mountain mutt, with wiry brown fur and pointed ears, a broad chest and short, muscular legs. He learned commands without being formally trained and could even catch rats and rabbits. I was going to miss him dearly.

Mom got on her knees and bowed to Mr. and Mrs. Zhang to express her gratitude for their kindness and the risks that they had taken. If asked about our departure, they would say that after deep self-reflection they realized they could not be affiliated with class enemies and had kicked us out into the streets. I prayed that no harm would come to them as a result of their goodwill toward us.

Lan rode on Mom's back and Di walked beside her, while I pushed the wheelbarrow, looping its straps onto my shoulders. It was heavy, but Mr. Zhang had oiled the wheel and it rolled smoothly—much better than the night before.

As we ambled away, we heard footsteps trotting behind us. It was Dog!

"Go," I commanded, forcing a harsh tone. We had stolen so many of the Zhangs' eggs; we certainly couldn't steal their dog too. "Go back home!"

"Don't worry about him," said Mr. Zhang, waving his hand. "He'll get bored or hungry and he will turn back."

So off we went, with Dog escorting us through the town's mostly empty streets.

Mr. Zhang was right about many things, but he was wrong

about Dog. Dog did not turn back, even as we passed the crumbling stone gate of Zhucheng and the limits of the village. Dog did not turn back as we cut into the fields, away from the main road. Dog stayed with us even as we stopped by a tranquil silver creek to rest and eat flatbread. He drank some water and lay down beside us, panting happily, and jumped back on his paws when we were ready to continue.

We walked slowly, since the wheelbarrow was heavy and the small roads were uneven. Occasionally the wheel got stuck in a hole, and the three of us had to throw our weight against the wheelbarrow to send it bouncing out with a jerk, our belongings flipping into the air. The straps distributed the load along my shoulders and back, but my palms chafed from directing the handles over the bumpy ground. When Di and I switched, weeping blisters had erupted along my shoulders and hands. Learning from my own mistake, I took some rags and wrapped them around Di's palms for protection.

Mid-April had arrived, but though the snow was gone, the air was still cold. Winter jasmine, the flowers that welcome spring, had burst defiantly along the road, radiant yellow petals like droplets of light. The landscape was mostly deforested, but in a few areas the locals had planted cherry trees, their shy blossoms peeking out from green buds. In the breeze, they shivered as though they were underdressed for their game of hide-and-seek. I focused on their beauty, hoping to draw any joy that could sustain my body, which felt like it was on the verge of breaking. Though I had tried to prepare, the walks I had taken in Zhucheng were woefully insufficient. Even with our sluggish pace, the journey was shin splintering, spine shattering. Mom never complained, but her gait became more lopsided as she began to limp from pain, wincing with each step.

By the time we found a place to settle for the evening, Di looked ready to burst into tears. Our water was gone and our throats were dry, but we didn't have the willpower to search for a stream. Together we pushed the wheelbarrow off the path and settled between some shrubs with long, willowy branches that we could hide behind. My feet were throbbing, and my shoes were so worn that I could feel every pebble and twig against my soles. Mom collapsed on the damp earth, eyes closed as she was momentarily overwhelmed by exhaustion. I lay on the ground, hoping in vain that I could absorb the soil's water through my skin and slake my thirst.

When we could summon up the energy, we gathered some sticks and laid our blankets down on top of them, improvising bedding for the night. Dog still had not turned back.

"I guess he is our dog now," said Di.

I should have felt guilty, but I couldn't help but rejoice at this unexpected gift. Leaning against Dog, I closed my eyes, feeling safer with his presence.

Mom broke off a piece of flatbread and tossed it to him. "At least you aren't a useless mouth to feed," she said. "You can warn us if someone is coming."

"He can catch rabbits too," I added.

"That's true," said Mom. "You are probably more useful than all of us if you can get meat!"

Since Dog was now part of our family, we had to give him a proper name. "Our family finally has a son," Di joked. We couldn't call him Little Brother, because that was essentially Di's name. So we settled on the name Lucky, because there is a Chinese saying that goes, *With dogs come luck—go lai fu*—which we hoped to invoke with Dog's new name.

"Do you like your new name?" I asked. "Will you be a good dog and bring us luck?" The newly named Lucky wagged his tail and settled with his head on my lap.

In the morning, the pale sunlight filtering through my eyelids drew me from slumber, but waking up was its own nightmare. I felt as though I had gotten into a fight with Mr. Zhang's donkey, and lost. My body screamed as though I had been kicked repeatedly in my sleep and then run over by jagged wagon wheels. As I forced myself to rise, there was a chorus of popping from my joints as my muscles resisted every movement. Mom and Di were also miserable, and Mom's feet were so swollen that they bulged from her shoes. Only Lan seemed refreshed, having slept warmly, curled up in a nest of our clothing in the wheelbarrow.

Undeterred, Mom unfolded the map and examined it. "I'm pretty sure we are somewhere along here," she said, pointing between two villages that I had never heard of. "I think we probably walked about ten kilometers yesterday. We need to do more today."

"My legs are killing me," Di whined, massaging her calves.

"Have some flatbread," Mom replied stoically. "We need to walk again, faster and for longer if possible. We can take breaks, but we cannot lag. There are dangers on the road, so the sooner we can get off of it, the better."

"I'll carry Lan," I offered, seeing Mom rub her lower back. It wasn't safe to put Lan in the wheelbarrow, especially with the bumpy terrain. "You need a break too, Mom."

Mom smiled gratefully. "I will carry Lan for our first shift, and then we can switch."

Like donkeys, we plodded slowly along the paths, occasionally getting onto the main streets when the side roads disappeared. The big roads allowed us to beg for water and check where we were, since there would be an occasional sign or other travelers. Qingdao was such a major city that almost anyone could point us in the right direction. We passed a few small towns, which Mom matched with the names on our map to keep our bearings, while the compass reassured us that we were moving eastward.

Whenever we saw cadres in uniform I froze, even though they ignored us, assuming that we were ordinary villagers. There were others like us with wheelbarrows, farmers who carried tools, fertilizer, and bags full of seeds. Wheat fields around us had sprouted and in a few months would become golden blond. Here in the North wheat grew like a weed, erupting from the ground every spring and standing tall and proud by early summer. As we passed these young plants, I longed to lie down and let them grow around me, over me, shielding me from the grueling kilometers ahead.

Early in the morning on our fourth day of walking, two cadres on sleek brown horses stopped us on the road. I had carried Lan for the past hour, and she felt like a boulder on my back. As the cadres trotted toward us I contemplated running, but Mom stood firm. With Lan's extra weight and my weak knees, I doubted that my body could withstand the impact of a sprint anyway.

"Good morning," said one of the cadres, dismounting swiftly from his horse. His leather boots were high quality, with silver buckles, but dusty from the road. "Where are you going?"

"To Qingdao," Mom replied, adjusting the wheelbarrow straps on her shoulders. "With my daughters."

The cadre raised his eyebrow, his hand tight on the horse's reins. "That's quite far. What business do you have there?"

"My husband's employer is selling tea," Mom explained. "We stayed with my mother-in-law to help her during the winter, and now we are going back home."

"What is your surname?" asked the cadre who was still mounted.

His horse had slender legs and a shiny coat, so elegant that it looked out of place on this bleak little road. Perhaps it was a prized animal confiscated from a landlord somewhere.

"Zhang," Mom answered. She was so quick to come up with these responses, like she was sparring with words, blocking each attempt of her opponent to uncover the truth.

"Do you have a travel permit?" the one standing before us asked.

I forced myself to smile because I was scared then. *They're going to know. They'll send us back. They're on horses—there is no way we can outrun them!* Sensing my anxiety, Lucky placed himself between me and the cadres, his ears back and his tail out straight. His stance made both horses nervous, the whites of their eyes showing as they stared at him.

Reaching into her front pocket, Mom plucked out the forged travel permit and handed it over. What had I written? *Zhucheng Communist Party*? Should I have written *Communist Party* without specifying the city?

The cadre unfolded the paper and examined it, and then passed it up to his partner, who nodded. "Where did you come from?" asked the one on the horse.

Relief coursed through me as I realized that they were illiterate—our hometown was written so clearly on the paper.

"Zhucheng," Mom replied.

"That's also quite far! Are you just traveling by foot?"

Laughing, Mom said, "Of course! How else would we go? We don't have money for horses!" Three disheveled women and a baby. Instead of a wagon we had a wheelbarrow; instead of a Pekingese, we had a mountain mutt. There was no way they would suspect that we were associated with gentry or landlords.

"Go ahead," said the first cadre, grabbing his horse's saddle and swinging his leg easily over it. "Take the main road—it's a lot faster." He pointed to a juncture where we could pass onto it.

"Thank you," said Mom as I grinned and glanced at Di, who hadn't seemed nervous at all. "I was looking for it—we got a bit lost."

"You are welcome!" Both cadres smiled warmly and waved to us as they continued on their path. "Travel safely!"

10

JIAOZHOU BAY

With the spring came weeds and small plants that we could eat. *Jicai*, a wild vegetable, sprouted all along the sides of one of the paths that we came across. We plucked it by the handful, roots and all in our haste, and piled our leafy bounty onto our wheelbarrow to wash when we reached a river. Neither Di nor I loved vegetables, and traditionally we never ate them raw and cold. However, a long winter with only the occasional pickled cabbage or piece of salted meat whetted our appetite for the fragrant, juicy crunch of fresh-picked *jicai*, which tasted like the essence of spring—and hope—in a mouthful.

    I had worn through my shoes completely after more than a week of walking, so Mom took some rags and wrapped my feet. Pain became our constant companion, radiating from our fingers as we clutched the wheelbarrow handles, and through our hips, down our legs, and into every toe. Blood seeped through our shoes—or rags, in my case—and oozed out of wounds on our shoulders where the wheelbarrow straps had taken off our skin. Despite Mom's aspirations, we had to slow our pace—but we didn't stop. Each day, we were like dutiful soldiers, marching toward our goal, the walk itself our battle.

At my worst times, I reminded myself that no matter how much my legs burned, it was better than the searing pain from my knees digging into the ice at Wildflower Field. Whenever I wanted to open my mouth and tell Mom I was tired, I thought about Comrade Cheng and found it within me to take just one more step. Step by step, breath by breath, we made our way out of the rugged mountain terrain, through fields, and finally to the sea.

Before we saw the ocean, Mom could smell it. She breathed deeply, as though she were inhaling a faint perfume, a scent that she wanted to absorb into her being. It was Mom who told me that memories are often embedded in smells, and through our noses we can unlock things long forgotten.

"What does it smell like?" I asked her.

"Home," she replied, smiling. She looked radiant, the happiest that I had seen her in a long time, despite the welts on her shoulders and the wounds on her feet. I wasn't sure if by "home" she meant that we were closer to our home in Qingdao, or to possibly finding my father—or if she meant her childhood home by the sea. I didn't ask her. I wanted to let her continue that moment, to savor the sweet euphoria of making it this far.

As we got closer to the sea, I detected a hint of salt in the air. There in the horizon, we saw it—Jiaozhou Bay, a glittering aquamarine expanse, like an infinite roll of shining blue silk undulating in the wind. Di's mouth fell open into a smile so wide that I could count her teeth. As we marveled at the magnificence of the ocean,

I had a newfound appreciation for my namesake—my name, Hai, means "ocean," and until now I had never understood just how precious it was to Mom.

Along the bay, the towns were bigger, and there were more cadres. We had to present our travel permit three more times. I grew better at keeping my composure, and Mom made her same standard responses. As with the first pair of cadres, I suspected that none of these road guards were literate. They saw the big red stamp and waved us through, even offering helpful suggestions on which roads to take.

Mao had told his followers, "We Communists are like seeds and the people are like the soil. Wherever we go, we must unite with the people, take root, and blossom among them." Perhaps this was the kindness that the Zhangs and other peasants were referring to. As we met more cadres on the roads through the countryside and by the sea, I found it hard to believe that these were the same Communists who had evicted us, slaughtered my family members, and nearly killed me.

One cadre, a thin man with a round face and large eyes, saw the rags on my feet and stopped us. With a soft smile, he bundled some straw and grass to stabilize my rag shoes. "I had to do this all the time when I was a boy," he told me as he tied straw straps around my ankles. He reached into his pocket and took out a few bills—Communist Party printed notes—and gave them to Mom. "Buy something nice for the girls to eat," he said. We had no idea how much they were worth, but we were grateful to get any money at all, and thanked him profusely.

I thought Mom would save the money, but that night we went to a market with the bills in hand. "Let's see what we can afford," Mom said, eyes twinkling. There were some small food stands out in the open, where each vendor usually specialized in one or a few items, advertised in bold writing on colorful wooden signs. Mom parked us, wheelbarrow and all, at a small table with red stools and went to talk to a potbellied vendor with gray hair.

Just the aroma was intoxicating, and I felt drunk as I perched on my seat. These outdoor markets often were dirty because of the food waste and lack of coordinated cleanup, but my hungry nose could pick out only the nice smells—of fried garlic, stewed meat, dried shrimp, and freshly chopped scallions. The satisfying sizzle of onions tossed in smoking-hot oil tickled my ears, and I had to keep my mouth clamped shut to prevent myself from drooling.

Mom plopped down between Di and me, beaming. "We've made it so far, and who knows what lies ahead? No matter what happens, let's at least have some enjoyment." What she didn't say, but I understood, was that we still didn't know if we would make it to Qingdao. If the Communists discovered that our travel permit was fake, then it would be not only the end of our journey, but also the end of our lives. We might as well have something to savor before then!

The vendor came to our table with a big, steaming bowl of fish soup. It was made with a whole fish, a type of sea bream, the soup thick and creamy from the protein in the bones and skin. Potato starch noodles, a few clams, seaweed knots, chunks of ginger, and thick slices of scallion were also in the mix. With a clatter, he set out some small bowls, spoons, and chopsticks. It had been a while since we'd had clean utensils to eat with. Picking the dirt from my fingernails, I wiped my hands as best I could on my pants and brandished my chopsticks like a weapon.

Together, we launched ourselves into this feast. Mom scooped out the fish eyes and gave one to Di and one to me. She took out the brain and fed it to Lan, then sucked on the skull to get any remnants. We peeled off strips of fish skin and slurped them up with the noodles, stuffing our mouths with juicy white hunks of meat. Starved for fat, we swallowed every single drop and morsel, even chewing on the ginger to get as much of the broth as we could. There was no conversation, just pure dedication to the food in front of us. We ate noisily, tossing bones and other scraps to Lucky, who crunched through them eagerly.

The vendor came to us again, and at first I thought he was going to chide us for eating like barbarians. Instead, he held a plate of steaming fried smelt, which he set down before us. "A gift," he said, smiling at Di and me, who were hunched over, our mouths so full that when we said thank you it was completely unintelligible. Mom elbowed us and we swallowed quickly, then exclaimed our "Thank you" again so loudly that Lucky jumped. We grabbed the hot fish by their tails, burning our fingers and then our tongues as we sank our teeth into their bellies bursting with nutty, crispy roe.

We were thin then, and our full stomachs bulged like little globes. Though we were still filthy and now reeked of fish and garlic, we were in bliss! Every bowl was licked so clean that it looked like it had been washed, the meal itself a beacon of light in a time of darkness.

At night we slept like logs, comatose and satisfied until late the next morning, when we woke up far behind our usual schedule. Though our bodies hurt and we groaned as we rose, our spirits were high, recharged by the kindness of strangers and an evening of abandon.

11

CHECKPOINT

Hour by hour, day by day, we'd completed our circle around the bay and were moving southward to Qingdao. As we inched closer to the city, the Chinese Communist Party inched closer to victory. We heard from other peasants that the People's Liberation Army had crossed the Yangtze River on April twentieth, and in a matter of days they captured Nanjing. Firecrackers popped as cadres joyfully announced that the PLA had climbed the Presidential Palace and torn down the Nationalist flag, mounting the Communist Party's red and yellow banner over Nanjing.

We had been walking for two weeks, and we'd finally reached a point where there were no longer any small country roads. There was only the big, wide main road to Qingdao, with rickshaws, wagons, horses, and even a few cars and trucks knocking dust in our faces as they barreled past us. The road was getting more crowded with displaced people from the countryside. Some families had only a few pieces of luggage, while others traveled with wagons packed with household furniture precariously balanced and reinforced with rope, moving slowly like snails with shells too large for their bodies.

Qingdao was not yet under Communist control, but every road leading to it was. Though cadres denied these rumors, we heard that the only force keeping the PLA from attacking was the American navy, which was still docked in Qingdao's harbor.

There were checkpoints everywhere along the road as cadres searched for class enemies, randomly stopping people on their way to the city. Those who did not have the right paperwork were sent back in the opposite direction if they were lucky; people were also being arrested and put into military trucks. I had no idea where the trucks were going, but I was terrified of joining them. I avoided making eye contact, nervous and sweating, praying that the cadres would aim for the cars and horses and let us pass.

Mom, on the other hand, had so much faith in our travel permit that she seemed confident, almost cheerful—as though she had the real thing nestled in her pocket.

"Madam," said a voice. I looked up and saw a cadre gesturing at us. His face was marked with hundreds of little scars, likely from smallpox, and his nose was crooked, as though it had been broken. My heart leaped into my throat as he walked over to us. Beside me, Di seemed bored, annoyed even, at the interruption. I envied her nonchalance at every checkpoint, wishing that I could borrow some of her composure. Instead, I felt like the household furniture on those wagons that we saw—except instead of rope, it was thread that was holding me together. In the presence of the cadres, a mere pull or twist would send me crashing down.

By then, we had met so many cadres who had been sympathetic and helpful to us. However, as soon as I saw that four-pocket uniform my vision would cloud and I would find myself again at

Wildflower Field. I remembered the cadre who fixed my shoes and gave us money, and the cadre who had smiled at us and offered directions, but all those little acts of kindness could not tip the scale against what Comrade Cheng and Comrade Lao had done. I would always be afraid of the cadres. No matter what they did or said, there was an inner voice that reminded me that their words or actions were all based on a lie—the kindness was not for Ang Li-Hai, but for the peasant girl whose toes stuck out of her rag shoes and who was covered in dirt, with a wheelbarrow in her hands and a mountain mutt trailing behind her.

"Travel authorization?" the cadre demanded.

Without blinking, Mom reached into her pocket and gave him the paper. By then it was worn from being handled so much.

Examining it, the cadre said, "Huh. Zhucheng?"

With that one word, any remaining shred of confidence I had disintegrated. This cadre was unlike the rest—this cadre could read. The ground beneath me felt like it was sinking, and I had to brace myself to avoid tumbling forward.

Mom and Di looked fine and calm, Di's long braid moving slightly as a cool spring breeze blew across the road. That same wind blew my short hair into my eyes, and the hair on the back of my neck rose from the chill. I wondered if they were just braver than I was, or if they simply had not put two and two together to realize that a literate cadre could actually understand what I had written and recognize where it might be wrong.

"Comrade Lao!" he called. "Come here!"

I grabbed Mom's arm now, my legs about to give. *Not him. Not Comrade Lao!* How did he find us? He must have traveled by car, deduced that we would eventually come to this road, and waited here with his fellow cadres until someone spotted us. My saliva tasted metallic, like it was tinged with blood. Was I bleeding? Swallowing,

I tried to reassure myself. *I'm fine. My mouth is fine. Hold it together!* Desperately, I tried to remember from the cadres' speeches what Mao had said. *A revolution is not a dinner party.* My eyes darted to the green military trucks that were parked in a row. *All reactionaries are paper tigers.* They were going to throw us all in one of those and take us back to Zhucheng with signs hung around our necks. *Reactionary. Oppressor. Enemy of the People.*

From the other side of the road, an older man we did not recognize walked over. "What is it?" he asked. As he stood next to the smallpox-scarred cadre, I realized that a different Comrade Lao had been called, one in his late fifties, with yellow teeth, deep wrinkles, and a chin full of white stubble. He was not the Comrade Lao who had felt the callus on my finger and assisted Comrade Cheng in Wildflower Field, but somehow my mind could not escape that place. I was holding on to Mom so tightly that she started to discreetly pry my fingers loose. *We serve the people. Take root and blossom.*

"Where is Zhucheng?" the first cadre asked.

"Oh, far," Older Comrade Lao replied. "At least one hundred kilometers, maybe two hundred! It's beyond the bay!"

"Ah, I guess that's why," said the first cadre. "The office there must do things differently." He handed the authorization back to Mom and said, "Sorry. A lot of the rural offices don't know the standards yet. They just make up their own rules!" He and Older Comrade Lao laughed. "Have a good day, and walk carefully. There will be more cars and horses on this route, and they are fast."

"Yes, thank you, Comrade," said Mom, gratefully tucking the permit back into her pocket.

We'd begun walking away, the wheelbarrow rumbling, when we heard Older Comrade Lao's voice yell, "Wait!"

Stopping again, we turned cautiously toward him.

"You should put that dog on a rope when you get into the city. It's not the countryside. You can't just have your animals loose willy-nilly!"

"Yes, of course," said Mom, smiling. "Thank you for your kind advice!"

"You are welcome!" Older Comrade Lao called cheerfully. "Safe travels!"

With that, we had passed through the last checkpoint on the way to Qingdao. I should have been elated, but I felt the opposite—bile gurgled in my throat, and I was ready to vomit. Shaking, I could barely keep my grip on the wheelbarrow handles. My body managed to resist until we were out of sight of the checkpoint, and then my legs finally did what they had been threatening to do—they collapsed underneath me and I tumbled to the ground, my cheek slamming onto the dry yellow dirt. Whatever had been holding me together had come undone, and I lay immobile, in pieces on the road, buried beneath snow that was falling only in my mind. It was going to suffocate me.

"Hai!" Mom called, falling to her knees and trying to support my head. Within me the floodgates opened and I started to cry, sob, my entire body racked with grief. I could barely breathe, my tears like tidal waves pulling me underwater. Sounds were muffled but I could hear Mom asking me if I was okay. Invisible hands had snaked around my throat, blocking any words from coming out of my mouth.

When I managed to talk, all I could utter was "I can't breathe."

Mom hushed me, while Di grabbed a blanket and draped it around my shoulders. The two of them wrapped me up and guided me to sit against the wheelbarrow as Mom rearranged our clothing to make a cushion. Together, they lifted me and laid me down so that I was curled up with my knees against my chest, the canteens of water beside me.

"It's okay," Mom said gently. "We are almost there. Just hang on for a little bit longer."

Tears continued to stream down my face as I struggled to inhale. *How could I fall apart when we are so close?* I was the oldest, and I was supposed to be strong. If anyone should have ridden in the wheelbarrow it was Lan or Di, not me. I was supposed to help Mom, who already carried so much, and I hated to be another drain on them all.

Mom carried Lan on her back and pushed me in the wheelbarrow, while Di walked beside her and Lucky behind Di. I felt every bump and dip in the road, no matter how slight, yet the swaying of the wheelbarrow was strangely soothing—like I could finally let myself go.

Step by step, just as we had done the entire journey from Zhucheng, we made our way to the city gates of Qingdao. Other travelers passed our slow-moving group, but we continued in silence. Mom's face was unrelenting and determined, her eyes focused on those stalwart stone walls, unwavering. She looked like a warrior who was about to overtake a city—not for the Nationalists, not for the Communists, but for herself and her daughters.

"Look," she said as the gates of Qingdao finally loomed over us. "Have you seen anything more beautiful than that?"

Di and I craned our necks up. The ancient wall curved outward, a towering semicircle with an imposing pagoda serving as its sentry. Two entrances framed the sides, and the road split in two as traffic veered in either direction. It must have been years, possibly decades, since these stones had been scrubbed, and vibrant moss creeped along the bottom and sides of the wall. Most of the slabs held strong, but there were several pockets where the stones had crumbled with age.

Mom swung toward the left, to the rusty iron gates that were wide-open like metal arms. To me, they looked like the mighty gates of heaven. *Beautiful.*

The bright blue sky above us was blocked out as we passed under the arch of the city entrance. A short tunnel, and then there was light again. I closed my eyes and let out a long breath as though it were air that I had been holding in for all these past months. I opened my eyes and looked at Mom.

She was covered in dust from the road, cut through by streaks of sweat running down her face, yet she glowed. We had arrived, and she was victorious.

Qingdao, Shandong

12

WORD OF MOUTH

After entering the city, we stopped to rest and eat flatbread as I recovered from my loss of nerves. Mom had visited Qingdao only a handful of times, and Di and I had never been. Even though we were still in the same province, in the same country, the sheer change in size and the strange-looking buildings made me feel like I was in a foreign land. The feature that stood out to me most was the noise. We sat together in an alley and could hear the constant squeaking of wagon wheels, clopping of horse hooves, and patter of rickshaw pullers. Everyone seemed to interact by shouting, regardless of whether they were arguing about traffic or having a friendly conversation about the weather.

All around us, people with carts, sacks, and suitcases lingered with no place to go. Many of them looked better kept and had more belongings than we did, but there were also beggars, including children who had clearly been homeless for a long time—their feet were black and their clothing in tatters, their skin cracked and dry from constant exposure to the wind and sun. Even the street vendors looked ragged, imploring and yelling at people to buy from them. Qingdao had already suffered from poverty, but now there were thousands of additional indigents who had been displaced by the Civil War.

Occasionally, the Catholic church set up stations to hand out bread and porridge, but it was a ruthless mess. Everyone pushed one another to make their way to these tables, disregarding those who slipped and shrieked and were trampled. Mom kept us away from these crowds, knowing that we were small and likely would get injured or killed. After all the food was claimed, she took us to beg, head bowed, for any scraps that could be spared.

Di, Lan, and I slept on the streets our first few nights, but Mom was too afraid to close her eyes. Human trafficking was endemic in the region, and the chaos of war had made it rampant. With Lucky beside her, she stood guard, and dozed for a few hours after I woke up, at sunrise. As daylight washed over the city, the huddled, hungry masses roused. However, there were also people who slept late into the afternoon. Some of them were sick. Others were drunk. But several of them were actually dead. These corpses were often naked—sad living souls had stripped them of their clothes and anything else of value. Mom whispered a Buddhist prayer whenever she saw them but didn't bother to cover our eyes. At that point, if she tried to shield us from the ugliness of the world, we would only spend our days in darkness.

Along each street, new arrivals combed through their fellow indigents, searching the city for lost relatives. It was a random and desperate network of people saying, *I am from this family—have you seen anyone from my family? No? Well, I'll be in this street. If you meet anyone else from my family, please tell them where to find me.* Mom followed suit, asking everyone she met whether they knew anyone from the Ang family or the Dao family.

Mom's parents had a house in an area called Dabaodao. Even though the Daos' massive shipping fleet was based in Rizhao, no business could ignore Qingdao's trading port, so they had bought a base for business operations during the first decade of the German occupation. Germany had seized the city as a protectorate in 1898 and divided it between Europeans, who lived in the Villa District, and the wealthy Chinese, who lived in Dabaodao. The Germans painstakingly modeled the Villa District after their own hometowns, with German street names and with parks full of trees reminiscent of their native forests.

By the time Yei Yei moved to Qingdao, the segregation was no longer strict, and wealthy Chinese could live anywhere. In 1924, the German military barracks in the Villa District became the Qingdao campus for Shandong University. Since Yei Yei was the comptroller in charge of the university's curriculum, the government gave him a house on campus commensurate with the prestige of his position.

Mom felt uneasy in the Villa because it was so foreign and, in her mind, indecent. Following the end of World War II, Qingdao had welcomed the American marines and sailors who were stationed there to disarm the Japanese, support Chiang Kai-Shek, and counter the influence of the Soviet Union. Given their sordid history of imperialism, Mom associated Westerners with dance clubs and brothels. From what she told us, we imagined that at night, immodest women with powder-white faces and bright red lips roamed the Villa streets like hungry ghosts. This discomfort, however, could not compete with our hunger. We had run out of provisions, and our search for relatives was urgent.

Hand in hand, we entered the Villa, only to find that Shandong University had closed; the American marines had a billet on campus, but that was largely deserted—most of the foreigners had evacuated. From the staff at restaurants nearby, we learned that classes had been suspended, and the professors had fled south to Nationalist-controlled cities. After months of silence and Comrade Cheng's words, we weren't surprised that the Angs were gone. Still, I felt bitter. How could they have left Qingdao without telling us? I recalled a grainy photo that I had seen of Shanghai. Was our family there, strolling happily in its cosmopolitan streets?

Our empty stomachs prevented us from wallowing for too long, as Mom redirected our efforts to finding her own family. With no map, we wandered until we found Dabaodao, which had a mix of Chinese and European architecture. It was dirtier than the Villa, with narrower streets and crowded buildings, and signs almost exclusively in Chinese. Like assassins we spread out, targeting everyone on the street for information about the Dao family. We spoke to hundreds of people, until our voices were hoarse, with no luck.

Finally, Mom saw a man who was wearing a white coat and holding several packages, and she stopped him as he entered a pharmacy. "Excuse me, please. Do you know anyone with the surname Dao?" She had guessed that he was a pharmacist and by virtue of his profession might know the people in the neighborhood.

"Yes," he answered. Though his tone was polite, he sounded rushed. "I know a Dao Chiang-Sen, who lives a few streets away from here."

Mom's face lit up with excitement. "That's my younger brother!" she exclaimed. "Is he here, living in Qingdao?"

The man leaned against the door of the pharmacy and shifted the weight of his packages. "I don't know how long he will be here," he said, "but I saw him only a few weeks ago. He comes to my pharmacy regularly whenever he is in Qingdao—he's been a loyal customer for a long time."

"Do you know where I can find him?" Mom asked. "I married and left my parents over ten years ago and don't remember their address in Qingdao."

The pharmacist looked suspiciously at Mom, and then at us, his stance indicating that he did not want us to enter his store. With disdain, he noticed Lucky, who had remained unleashed despite the cadre's warning. I could tell that the man was wondering how a son of the wealthy Dao family could be affiliated with, let alone related to, a smelly group of street rats like us. "I cannot give out information like that," he replied curtly.

"Please," Mom pleaded. "My daughters and I are alone. My husband is gone and we have no income and no food. We need relatives who can help us get off these streets. It's dangerous, and my youngest is not even a year old!"

The pharmacist's gaze fell on Lan, who sneezed loudly before laying her head against Mom's shoulder. Sighing, he said, "I don't know his address anyway, but you can try going to Jianing Road and asking around for him there." He pointed farther away, where the main street split into several alleys. "There might not be a street sign, so you can ask around again when you are closer." As Mom bowed and thanked him, he closed his door, relieved that we had left his storefront.

The residential area of Dabaodao was neat and uniform, with apartment complexes in cozy grid patterns. Jianing Road was full of *liyuan* houses constructed by the Germans and unique to Qingdao—white buildings that had red-orange triangular roofs and were connected by inner alleys and courtyards. Several families shared these spaces, creating tight-knit communities.

Mom took us walking up and down the alleys, asking everyone we met for her younger brother. Faster than expected, we found an older lady who knew him and, unlike the pharmacist, had no qualms about pinpointing exactly where he lived. "Mr. Dao lives on the first floor in that unit," she said, gesturing to the *liyuan* house across the street. Her face was wrinkled but her hair was still dark, and it stuck out from underneath a floppy floral bonnet. Flower patterns covered her shirt and pants, an explosion of colors that oddly complemented one another. In one hand, she held a broom. Inching closer, she held up her index finger and warned, "You don't want to go there right now—he has tuberculosis."

"What?" Mom exclaimed, alarmed. "How do you know?"

The old lady sniffed and replied, "I know everything. I've lived on this block for over forty years! My parents were workers here when the Germans first arrived. I know everyone who has passed through here and everything that happens here. Who are you, anyway?" she asked, staring at each of us, so close that her nose almost touched ours.

"I am Mr. Dao's older sister," Mom said, leaning back for space.

"Ah," said the old lady, scooting forward. She was wary, her eyes darting from the crusty rags on my feet to Lan, who slept on Mom's back, covered in so much dust that she looked like a clay doll. With the intensity of her glare, it was almost like the woman was taking photos with her mind. "I am Mr. Ding's wife. Your brother came here only a few weeks ago, but I know your family. Are you also coming from Rizhao?"

"Yes," Mom lied. In case the cadres came looking for us, she didn't want anyone to know that we had traveled from Zhucheng.

"How are things there?" Mrs. Ding asked, more curious than concerned. Before we could open our mouths she answered her own question, saying, "Probably terrible, from how you all look.

Have the Communists started the land reform?" She eyed our nearly empty wheelbarrow and followed with "Where is your husband? Are you alone?"

"It's a complicated situation," said Mom, determined to avoid divulging anything about what had happened to us. "We are so grateful to have run into someone as knowledgeable as yourself, but my daughters are tired and we need to see my brother." She grabbed Di's hand and gestured for me to roll the wheelbarrow forward. "We hope to see you again soon."

"Oh, you will," Mrs. Ding assured us cheerfully. "I am always here!" Her tone was kind, but I couldn't help but feel threatened. After what had happened in Zhucheng we wanted to be discreet, to blend in and be left alone. It was unnerving, thinking that we had just arrived and there was already a pair of inquisitive eyes watching out for us, and a pair of loose lips ready to report our activities to anyone with an ear and a few minutes of time.

We said goodbye to Mrs. Ding, and felt her gaze on our backs as we made our way to what was supposedly my uncle's house. In the courtyard, there were several laundry lines pinned with plain clothing that was faded from being washed so many times. Two bicycles leaned against the back wall, locked together with a long, rusty chain that had been threaded through both wheels of each. Along the side walls there were large potted plants that drooped from lack of water. A red diamond with the character for luck, *fu*, hung upside down on the door of the first unit. Mom approached and knocked loudly. As we waited, Di went back and shut the courtyard entrance for privacy, waving again politely to Mrs. Ding.

It took several minutes and some more knocking for a man who looked older than Mom to open the door. He wore a black cotton shirt and pants that were too large for his slender frame; I noticed that he had no belt, and he had clipped the side of his pants with a clothespin. There was no question that he was related to Mom—in his face I saw hers in a more masculine form, with high cheekbones, wide-set brows, and a thin nose. His skin was sallow, and there were bags under his large eyes. A sparse beard covered his chin. "Can I help you?"

Mom threw her arms up in the air and squealed in delight, sounding like a young girl again. "It is you! Thank the Gods it is you! Thank the Gods we found the right house!"

His eyes widened in recognition and he smiled, revealing a gold tooth. "Big Sister?"

Mom nodded, laughing, and reached out to pull him into an embrace. Despite his haggard appearance, we knew that he was five years younger than she was. "It has been so long, little Sen! Girls"—she turned to us—"greet your uncle Sen!"

"Hello, Uncle Sen," Di and I said together. I wondered if Mrs. Ding was right about him having tuberculosis. I maintained a distance, worried that Mom's quick hug was enough for it to infect her.

"I am happy to see you in Qingdao," Uncle Sen began, choosing his words carefully. "But if you are here, that must mean that you fled from Zhucheng?" Like the pharmacist's and Mrs. Ding's, his eyes went straight to my filthy rag shoes and Lucky, who was chewing on his own rump.

"Yes," Mom responded, the gravity of what we had suffered sapping the joy from her reunion. "The past few months have been terrible, and the journey here exhausting. I can tell you the details later, but, needless to say, we cannot go back to our home. Not for a very long time, at least."

Uncle Sen nodded in understanding, and said, "It was a nightmare in Rizhao too." When he saw Mom's face twist in fear he quickly added, "Mother and Father are alive and decently well. I told them to come to Qingdao, but Father is too weak to make the journey and Mother does not want to leave him. When I can build up our home here again, I will send a car for them. For now, the Communists will leave them alone."

"How are you so sure?" Mom asked, worried. "We also thought the cadres would spare us, but we were wrong. Were you forced to endure a denunciation rally?"

"Heavens no," Uncle Sen said with a shudder. "I saw a few, though. They were nasty, bloody spectacles. We've been having financial troubles for some time—I don't know how much you know about that, but it ended up being a blessing. By the time the Communists came to Rizhao they had bigger heads to hang." Uncle Sen peered past Mom at the courtyard door, which was closed. He looked up at the windows of the units above, and the apartments across, and saw that a few were open. "I can tell you more later. This may sound strange," Uncle Sen added hesitantly, "but your husband wrote to us in Rizhao."

A lump rose in my throat as Mom gasped. From her expression I could tell she was expecting good news. "Is my husband in Qingdao still?" Mom asked hopefully.

"No," Uncle Sen replied, shaking his head, glancing nervously again at the open windows. "Sorry to disappoint you, but it's a long story. Have you eaten yet?"

"We have eaten only a bit," Mom began, eager for more details about Father. "Not much."

Following custom, Uncle Sen should have invited us enthusiastically into his home for snacks or even a meal. Instead, he shifted uncomfortably. Lowering his voice to a hoarse whisper, he said, "Big Sis, I am recovering from tuberculosis. I don't want to get you or your daughters sick. I'm much better than I was before, but I worry that I'm still contagious."

Di and I both took a step back as he cleared phlegm from his throat, but Mom remained rooted to the ground. "We've survived tuberculosis," Mom said, unfazed. "Last year. And honestly, if you say that my husband is not in Qingdao, then we have nowhere else to go. We've been sleeping in alleys for the past ten days. It has been hard for us, especially my daughters." Mom thought mainly about us, but I knew it was hardest on her—she kept watch each evening but still rose each day to beg for food and search for relatives.

As Uncle Sen wiped his nose, I remembered that Di had not been exposed to tuberculosis. I opened my mouth to object, but I realized that Mom was right. Where else could we go? The streets were ridden with both disease and crime. Sheltering with a sick relative was still safer than being in the open with other desperate, hungry people.

"Come in, then," said Uncle Sen warmly. "You are welcome in my home. Just take your belongings. You can leave the wheelbarrow out here—no one in this neighborhood has use for a bumpkin's tool. The dog stays out here too," he added. "I can't promise that no one will eat him, though. Times are hard and he looks well fed." He laughed loudly, coughing between his chuckles, when he saw the horrified expression on my face.

I whispered to Lucky that we would be back, and I pushed him under the wheelbarrow, telling him to hide and to avoid any strangers. We followed Uncle Sen into his apartment, removing our shoes. When I reached down to undo the knots in the straps securing the rags, the cloth was so worn that a light pull from my fingers broke them.

The apartment windows were made of glass, and the light shone through beautifully, illuminating a set of carved furniture in the living room. It was similar to the set we had back in Zhucheng, but the wood appeared older and thirsty for varnish. Uncle Sen's home was an odd mix of wealth and destitution; the apartment furnishings were expensive, but the walls and shelves were bare.

"I will make tea," Uncle Sen said. "Why don't you all wash up? The water is actually working now, so you are in luck. The bathroom is over there."

He pointed to a small room that had a metal basin with a spout and a handle. Mom went in first, while Di and I stood outside, curious. She plugged a stopper into the sink, and when she lifted the handle, water gushed forth from the spout. We gasped, amazed. Back in Zhucheng, we had to get water from the well, which was itself an improvement on having to trudge to the river. I remembered Father lauding the water system in Qingdao as a marvel of engineering. Hearing his description of a modern faucet paled in comparison with seeing it with my own eyes.

One by one, we rinsed the dirt and dust from our faces, our hair, and our hands. There was a drain in the floor, so Mom found a pitcher and made us wash our bodies too. Lan screamed as Mom scrubbed her, furious to be woken up from her nap. The freezing water sent goose bumps flaring across my arms and legs, but it felt wonderful as it ran down to my feet and spun down the drain, removing the traces of the journey from our skin. Bathing helped put some distance between us and Zhucheng, as though we could erase some of the shame that had marked us.

After drying ourselves, we picked out our cleanest clothes and met Uncle Sen in the living room. He handed us each a steaming cup of golden brown oolong tea. "This tea is from holy Lao Mountain," he bragged, the warmth of the porcelain seeping into my fingers. This fragrant tea was one of the few luxuries left in the Dao home. We learned that prior to the Communists' arrival, Mom's father, my Lao Yei, had funneled the family's fortune into his opium pipe, smoking away Uncle Sen's future. As the Dao empire crumbled, Lao Yei lay in a drug-induced haze, a prison of his own making. By the time the Communists arrived, public anger against them was subdued. More important, their wealth had been in ships and boats—not land—and that meant that the Daos were businessmen, not landlords, who were the primary targets of the rural uprisings. Cadres confiscated the Daos' remaining assets but spared their lives and allowed Uncle Sen to leave.

As we sipped our tea, Mom grew impatient, sitting on the edge of her seat and tapping her foot. "Now, about your husband's letter," Uncle Sen began, leaning back against his chair, the hot vapor from his tea rising. With his cup up close to his lips, he looked like a dragon with smoke coming out of his nose. "If what he said in his letter is true, then he and the rest of the Angs are in Taiwan."

"Taiwan!" Mom, Di, and I exclaimed together.

"What is he doing there?" Mom asked, confused. Taiwan was as exotic and unfamiliar to us as Germany or Japan. It was so far south and separated by sea—it might as well have been another country. What were Shandong men, who had grown up on wheat and winter, doing on this tropical island off the coast of Fujian?

Uncle Sen reached for a folded piece of paper that was on the table beside his chair. "I took this with me when I left Rizhao. I laughed at myself then, thinking that there was no way that I would see you, but maybe it was a sixth sense that made me do it." He handed Mom the letter, which was written on thick, high-quality stationery as white as a pearl. "Xiao-Long asked us to make sure you got this letter, which he addressed to you. I guess he couldn't reach you in Zhucheng and thought that you might try to find us instead."

Mom took the fine paper, which crinkled as she unfolded it

hastily. Di and I leaned over her shoulder to read the contents, and she did not push us away. We deserved to know too.

"*Dear Chiang-Yue,*" the letter began, "*I hope that this letter finds you, and I am sorry that I cannot tell you this in person. We will not be able to return to Zhucheng anytime soon. Shortly after our arrival in Qingdao, we received word from Jian urging us to flee the North, not southward to Shanghai, but by boat to Taiwan.*"

Uncle Jian, Chiao's father, was the black sheep in a family steeped in academia. In his childhood he had been a troublemaker, spending more time outside of the classroom, being punished for bad behavior, than seated at his desk. He used to say that he hated reading, he hated math, and most of all he hated studying. To Yei Yei, the Ang identity was inseparable from their scholarly lineage, and he pressured both of his sons to pursue prominent positions at universities. Father followed dutifully in their designated path, while his brother rebelled.

Despite Yei Yei's pleas and threats, Uncle Jian enlisted in the army, enrolling in Huang Pu Military Academy, the most prestigious training facility for soldiers under the Nationalist government. Founded by Sun Yat-Sen and funded by the Soviet Union, Huang Pu produced many military commanders for both the Nationalists and the Communists. While Uncle Jian trained at Huang Pu, one of his classmates was none other than Chiang Ching-Kuo, first son of Generalissimo Chiang Kai-Shek.

While Father was tucked away safely in Qingdao during World War II, Uncle Jian was on the front lines fighting the Japanese, building relationships with fellow soldiers who would later lead the Nationalist army. His prowess on the battlefield and his keen strategic mind propelled him up the military ladder, and he became a colonel shortly after Japan's surrender. His position and his personal friendship with Chiang Ching-Kuo afforded him access to confidential information that Chiang Kai-Shek withheld from almost all other Nationalist authorities.

According to Father's letter, Uncle Jian knew back in 1948 that Taiwan was being prepared as a point of retreat. Chiang Kai-Shek had secretly ordered that treasures from the Palace Museum be shipped to Taipei, along with all of the gold deposits stored in the Central Bank, about four million taels. There were few, if any, written records of these commands, but Chiang Ching-Kuo had told Uncle Jian about them, and he had realized that even the Generalissimo was losing faith. The Nationalists were going to lose the mainland.

Uncle Jian warned Yei Yei and Father that soon there would be no more passage by sea from Qingdao to Taipei, and he had pushed them to leave as soon as possible. He had reports from every major battle and could see from the numbers alone that the Nationalists could not recover from their losses. Foreseeing an exodus of mainlanders in the wake of a Communist victory, he suggested that the family head to Taipei early and establish themselves before the island was overwhelmed by newcomers. With his connections, he could get them all safe passage and authorization to travel.

As Shandong University's administrators discussed moving to Shanghai, Yei Yei broke from his colleagues and leaped for the lifeline secured by his black sheep son, whose words had become gold, his insider information priceless. Within a few days, the entire family was at the harbor, boarding one of the last boats leaving directly from Shandong.

Father claimed that there hadn't been enough time to go back for us but that he had tried to send a letter to our *shiheyuan*. It was unclear if it had been lost by the mail service or intercepted by the

Communists—perhaps that was how Comrade Cheng had known that our Qingdao house was empty. Regardless, we never got it, and why or how was irrelevant. Father's written words couldn't have fed us, sheltered us, or protected us from the people they left us to. When he said he'd had no time, I heard that he'd had no will. The journey back to Shandong was too dangerous for the precious first son of a prestigious family, the risk unacceptable for the lives of women and girls.

Mom sat with the weight of Father's words, absorbing the contents of his letter.

"I'm sorry, Big Sis," Uncle Sen said, his eyes cast on his sacred tea, which was not divine enough to alleviate our hunger. There was no food in his kitchen, and he himself had been living off of tea, medicinal herbs, and noodle soup from street stands. "Your husband won't be coming back here. Not for a long time, anyway."

Mom's cup was empty, the pattern of the tea leaves settled on the bottom as confusing as our future was uncertain. Lifting her head, she said, "Little Sen, we need a place to stay. We need to be safe. We need shelter, and we have nowhere else to go. We won't take any food or money from you, but we would be grateful for the favor of sharing your space. I know we are many, but we fled Zhucheng with nothing more than what was on our backs and in that wheelbarrow."

Without hesitation, Uncle Sen said, "You don't need to ask me like a beggar. We are family. There is another room, which you and the girls can stay in. There is no bed, but we can put some blankets and towels on the floor. I will help you as much as I can, but I also don't have much." He pointed to all of the empty shelves and said, "I've been selling items to survive, but everything has gone to my tuberculosis treatment. I'm not strong enough to work yet, but I will find employment in Qingdao when I can."

"I will look for work too," said Mom, optimistically.

"It's a mess here," Uncle Sen warned. "Tens of thousands of jobs were lost when all the foreigners fled. Rickshaw drivers have no business, and factories have been shut down. The Americans are mostly gone, so even the prostitutes are unemployed. Everyone everywhere is looking for work."

Mom had never had a job or earned a salary in her life, but she had worked for Nai Nai under conditions that were more abusive than many types of employment. She was not afraid of hard work, nor did she consider herself above any task. "I will try my best," she responded. "As long as we have shelter, my girls and I can manage the rest."

13

MATCHBOX SHOES

Uncle Sen had told us he was recovering from tuberculosis, but it soon became evident that his health was not improving. He spent most of the day in bed, exhausted and sometimes feverish, hacking so loudly that it woke us up at night. When he was well, he was good company, except for his constant jokes about slaughtering Lucky and serving him for dinner. He said to me, "It's different in the city than in the countryside. Here only rich people have dogs. When the Communist army comes to Qingdao, they'll take you first for flaunting your wealth with your fat little pet."

Lucky was not fat by any means, but Uncle Sen had a point. Dogs in the city were generally fluffy decorations, not working dogs like the peasants in Zhucheng had. Lucky was no lapdog, though, and he held his own—not only by hunting rats like a cat, but also by eating garbage like a goat. In the past, there had been stray dogs and cats roaming the city streets, but now starving beggars had eaten them all. People were even trapping rats and eating vermin, and sifting through sewers to find any morsel that could fill their hollow bellies.

Wherever I went, Lucky followed like a protective shadow. I would never forget that it was Lucky who barked to warn us that morning when Comrade Lao and his group came to take me away. We heard that in the countryside, families were no longer allowed to have dogs. The cadres often spied by crouching outside doors and windows, listening in on conversations. With a dog in the house, the slightest sound made by an eavesdropper, or even their smell alone, would trigger barking and warn the inhabitants.

While Mom looked for work, Lan stayed with Uncle Sen, and Di and I went to the markets. We foraged through garbage and pleaded for scraps, keeping a distance from the hundreds of other children and beggars who were picking through the same alleys. Street vendors chased us away, waving ladles and spatulas threateningly, swiping if we lingered too close to their customers. It wasn't that they were coldhearted; there were just too many urchins with quick little fingers, and too few paying diners with other options.

Vicious fights broke out over literal piles of trash, and people stood guard like animals over patches of territory. "I beg from here!" a young boy shouted when I asked for spare food from a noodle stand. He stomped in my direction, and when I stood my ground, he lowered his head and charged at me like a bull. Screaming, I ran, knocking over stools and bumping a table, sending a tub of chopsticks scattering to the ground. Lucky jumped between the boy and me and snarled, then took a snap at his heel as he pivoted and ran in the opposite direction, crashing into another table before tearing through the rest of the market. The vendor grabbed a broom and tried to whack Lucky, but Lucky dodged nimbly and leaped away, padding down the alley to find me crouched in the shadows. I would never go near that stand again, and I suspected that the boy wouldn't either.

Lucky was sometimes useful in this sense, but generally he and Di were lousy foraging companions, because they gobbled down anything edible as soon as they found it. I scolded Di and reminded her that we had to save food for Mom, who was breastfeeding and needed to eat for Lan's sake as well as her own. Whenever I found any scraps of meat, or even bones, I packed them in a bag to take home. Bones could be boiled into broth, which was hearty and nutritious.

Most of the affluent had already fled, but there was still a sizable population with means that frequented the restaurants. People fought for this prime garbage, which included food discarded by people who ate so well that they could afford to throw away their excess. Di and I were no longer afraid of the crowds and stopped heeding Mom's warning about being trampled—I was small and squeezed between the hordes effectively, and could sometimes grab something really good, like a big pork bone with some meat and tendon still on it. Frequently, we got diarrhea from eating food that was dirty or spoiled, but our stomachs were hardy enough that we rarely got severely sick.

We shared with Uncle Sen everything that we brought back. He occasionally gave us items to sell or barter on the black market, which had become the main market as the city's trade slowed to a trickle. By then Uncle Sen didn't have anything in popular demand, so the revenue was negligible—no one wanted his fancy fountain pens or scrolls of antique brush painting, and they sold for the equivalent of nickels and dimes.

With some cash, Mom bought more flour and some brown sugar to make sweet breakfast buns. In the mornings, I took the wheelbarrow full of buns to a busy street and tried to sell them.

Qingdao had a hodgepodge of currencies, and on good days a mix of coins jingled in my pocket. I thought about the shiny gold and silver taels that used to be traded in imperial China, and wondered when Mom would sell the tael that she still kept in her undergarments. Though I had berated Di for criticizing Mom for holding on to the jewelry, I couldn't help but wish that Mom would just sell her gold so we could have some real food to eat.

One day, I was sitting on the corner with my wheelbarrow of buns when Mom came running toward me. "Hai," she said, excitedly. "I need the wheelbarrow. We need to take the buns out."

I helped her take a blanket and lay it on the ground, then pile the buns neatly on top and fold the blanket over so that they would remain moist and chewy. As soon as the last bun was out, Mom grabbed the handles and ran as quickly as she could on her damaged feet, the wheelbarrow creaking and rattling in protest.

She had found a job!

In the industrial area of Qingdao there was a match factory that remained open, since matches were still in high demand. People were all clamoring for jobs, and the hiring manager had decided to prioritize his family group—those who shared his surname. When Mom went to inquire about work, he told her that all positions and assignments were reserved for people from the Fa house. Without blinking, Mom said, "My last name is Fa!"

And just like that, she went from being Mrs. Ang to Ms. Fa, and received printed paperboard to fold into matchboxes. She carted the paperboard all the way back to Uncle Sen's, and Mom, Di, and I folded them—clumsily at first, but soon we could pop out boxes in our sleep. Manager Fa paid Mom in corn flour, two thousand matchboxes per one kilogram, which we then bartered or used to make corn bread for sale.

I was so happy when Mom presented me with a pair of flimsy

black cloth shoes that she had traded for at the street market. They had rubber soles, so I could finally walk with more comfort. My feet had already formed thick calluses, but it was wonderful to have an indulgence—something that wasn't scavenged, but was actually purchased for me.

14

RUBY RING

On May 25, 1949, the last remnants of the United States Navy's Seventh Fleet sailed away from the city. One week later, on June second, the tanks of the People's Liberation Army rolled into Qingdao, officially bringing it under Communist control. Rows of cadres marched through the streets singing victory songs, hailing a new era of equality and prosperity. The massive green tanks with long guns terrified us all, and within each one, I imagined Comrade Cheng or Comrade Lao crouched, ready to drag us back to hell. I tried my best to avoid the cadres, but they were numerous and sometimes tried to buy our buns. When they approached, I had to greet them with a smile, ignoring my anxiety as I tensed my legs, ready to run in case one of them recognized me.

Once again, we found ourselves poised to flee.

"We can't run from them forever," said Di while we were seated together on the living room floor folding matchboxes one evening. She folded hers hastily, and sometimes I had to redo them so that the walls lined up and the boxes could close properly. It was our only reliable source of income and I wanted to keep it.

Mom stacked another finished box in a basket that we would later transport to the wheelbarrow. "It's not just about fleeing the Communists," she said. "We also need to find our family." With each day that passed, Mom became more determined to go to Taiwan, a goal that seemed as elusive to me as traveling to the realm of the Gods. We had barely muddled our way from Zhucheng to Qingdao—how were we going to travel ten times that distance, over land and sea?

"Why are we trying to go back to them when they abandoned us?" Di asked, voicing the resentment that I also harbored. Neither Di nor I had any enthusiasm about reuniting with the Angs. I missed my cousins, but I couldn't imagine living peacefully with them, and eating dinner with Father and Nai Nai, when my knees still ached from kneeling on the ice. While my emotions simmered, Di's were at a full boil. She hated Father. She hated Nai Nai. She hated them all, even our cousins, who had done nothing more than obey. Only two subjects occupied Di's thoughts: food and vengeance.

"We do not have other options," Mom replied, exasperated, as Di looked at her with dagger eyes. "What would you have us do?"

"Stay here in Qingdao," Di answered, like it was obvious. The more agitated Di got, the more haphazard her folding became and the more lopsided the matchboxes came out. "We have a house here now, a real place to stay."

"*Uncle Sen* has a house here," Mom emphasized, noticing the pathetic quality of the matchboxes tumbling from Di's fingers. I slowly reached for Di's remaining paperboard and transferred it to my own pile. "In any case," Mom added, "we need more than a house. I don't have a steady job, and we have no money."

Di flipped her last, sloppy matchbox into the basket and said, "We do have money. We have been making money, and we have been finding food. Maybe Hai and I can also find real work. We can make a life here!"

"We are barely scraping by," Mom explained, thinking of the days when we were unlucky and came back with only a few morsels from the garbage, the times when we picked maggots out of mushy fruit. "One catastrophe, and we will be underwater. We cannot continue living like this. We will all have more means and a better life if we find your father."

With nothing more in her hands, Di sat with her shoulders tense like a cat with its back arched. "We don't even know if Father actually is in Taiwan! He could have changed his mind after sending the letter!" Her lip curled into a snarl as she said, "For all we know, he could even be dead!"

Mom rarely hit us, but she slapped Di in the face, loudly enough that it made me jump. "Watch your words!" she snapped. "The Gods are always listening, and I will not allow you to curse our own family with misfortune!"

The sound of impact seemed to echo in the room, but Di didn't even look upset. If anything, she looked proud, a red mark in the shape of a handprint beginning to form on her light skin. Di was a firecracker in a society in which restraint was a virtue. For her, making an opponent lose their temper was a conquest. She was delighted, because it meant that she had broken them. They had exploded, and suddenly the world was not such a lonely place, because underneath their skin they were firecrackers too.

Mom took a breath, her own face reddening, and said, "Our place is with our family. Uncle Sen cannot take care of us. He is sick and eventually he will have his own family to think about." Uncle Sen's first wife had passed away in childbirth a few years earlier, and the Communists took over before he could remarry. Now, even if he recovered from tuberculosis, his marriage prospects would be tepid. With the Daos' fleet gone he was a pauper, barely surviving by picking from the skeleton of their old shipping empire. It was odd that Mom credited him for taking care of us when in reality we were taking care of him. We were the ones bringing back money and food, the ones cooking and cleaning the house, all while he lay curled up in his bed.

"Even if we cannot find your father in Taiwan, we are still safer if we are under Kuomintang rule," Mom said. A piece of paperboard slid between my hands and sliced my finger—a tiny wound, but blood still bloomed. Quickly, I held it away from the matchboxes, which we couldn't stain. I wasn't eager to return to Father, but I was terrified of living under the Communists again. I already quivered when cadres walked toward me, and I anticipated the day someone from Zhucheng would see me in Qingdao. Would Comrade Lao and Comrade Cheng remember me and recognize my face among the hundreds and thousands here? I didn't know, but living with this fear was suffocating.

"The Communists don't even know that we are Angs anymore," Di countered. "For all anyone knows, we could be the fatherless family of a peasant or a Communist soldier. No one from the countryside has identification cards. If we want to change our surname, all we need to do is announce a new one! Fa—we will all be Fas!"

"You are wrong, Di, and so shortsighted," Mom answered gravely. "This revolution has only just begun. Do you really think the bloodshed will stop with the landlords? I am not a soldier, nor am I a politician, but I know in my gut that the situation here will get far worse before it gets better. You are too young to understand that. The Communists have killed a lot of wealthy people, but that means that they have also killed a lot of educated people.

What comes next? Vague promises of equality? The Communists are bandits with no concrete plan on how to govern. For the near future, they will continue doing what they know and excel at—killing people and inciting violence. Do you really think that we will be left in peace in this *liyuan* house when so many of our neighbors know that we are related to the Daos?"

Di had no rebuttal, so Mom continued. "Once the Communists get organized, they will be making lists again. The streets here are meaner than in Zhucheng, as we all know from our first days here. I don't want to be evicted a second time, because if that happens we truly will have nothing at all—no Uncle Sen and no Mr. Zhang to take us in."

"Eviction may not even be the worst thing that happens," I added quietly. Di gave me a glare, accusing me with her eyes of always siding with Mom. Silence, however, was her white flag, and she hugged her knees to her chest and watched as Mom and I folded the remaining paperboard, piling matchboxes like toy blocks in the basket.

The three of us had never left Shandong, and the journey to Taiwan would require more than a good map and a compass. Ships to Taiwan sailed only from Nationalist territory, which was rapidly shrinking. Beautiful, vibrant Shanghai had fallen in May, and the Nationalists had retreated even farther south, to Guangzhou. We were trapped behind enemy lines, and thousands of kilometers separated us from friendly ground. We could not cross the battlefields with our wheelbarrow and stacks of flatbread. There were too many checkpoints, too many risks, and there was simply too much distance to cover.

There were trains that could bring us south from Qingdao, but the stations were even more chaotic than the Catholic food dispensaries. People had been rushing to leave even before the PLA tanks arrived. Now that the Communist Party flag flew high over the city gates, the desire to escape was at a fever pitch. The passenger cars were so packed that hundreds of people climbed onto the roofs, and clutched one another to avoid falling onto the tracks below. Train tickets were impossible to buy, and the counters at the stations were almost always closed.

Even on the black market, train tickets were rare and exorbitantly priced. Real tickets were sold in a matter of seconds, while fake tickets abounded. Aggressive vendors waved them frantically to eager travelers, offering hope and selling lies. Mom ventured into the alleys, only to find more than ten types of tickets, each varying in color, texture, and design. It was impossible for us to discern which were authentic and which were scams.

We were so focused on these elusive tickets that we forgot about the risk that we assumed each time we returned to Uncle Sen's house. Back in Zhucheng, we had been stronger and had passed through quarantine with Three without so much as a cough. In Qingdao, we were weak from undernourishment and all of us succumbed to tuberculosis. For several weeks, we coughed as though there were tar in our lungs. We took turns resting but could not stay inside for long—we had to be on the streets selling or begging; otherwise we wouldn't survive. There were days when I shook with fever but still took my wheelbarrow filled with buns, a rag tied on my face to contain my illness. Since it was summer, people stared as I sat wrapped underneath a thick blanket, eyes red and miserable. "Buns," I would manage to call out when I had energy. "Sweet breakfast buns, freshly made!"

For Mom, Di, and me, the illness peaked in July. We got accustomed to the cough, the fatigue, and the pain, and worked through them. Gradually, our symptoms subsided, with Di being the first to bounce back. Mom and I followed, but Lan was too small and frail. She was just under a year old and had spent the most time enclosed with Uncle Sen.

The disease spread through her blood and attacked her bones. She couldn't verbalize how she felt, but she cried inconsolably. We didn't realize how serious the infection was until her legs started to swell. When tuberculosis affects the bones, it usually affects the spine. She had just started walking, but now she was unable to lift her legs or bend her knees. As Lan wept through the night, I couldn't help but think of Three.

I missed her so much. My ears ached for the sound of her voice, the melody of her laugh, even her obnoxious cries. In a few months, it would be the anniversary of her death. Her absence was more than a hole in our lives. Losing her had unraveled the tapestry of our family, leaving a gash in our fragile web that could never be repaired. On our most miserable days, I was grateful that she didn't have to suffer with us. Yet, selfishly, I still wished that she were here so that I could have watched her grow, one year older, one year stronger, one year wiser.

We couldn't lose Lan too. It would break Mom. Though Di and I reminded Mom that staying with Uncle Sen was a necessity, not a choice, we couldn't assuage the guilt that hung over her like a shroud. Uncle Sen felt terrible, and rummaged through the remnants of his possessions to see if anything could help pay for Lan's treatment. Mom declined, turning to the jewelry that we had smuggled from Zhucheng. After I had given Mom the ruby ring, she kept it tucked safely inside her bun, at the nape of her neck.

As Mom undid her bun and pulled the ring out, her hair fell in crinkled waves. Her hair used to be soft and shiny, as black as coal and as luminous as opals. Now it was dry and brittle, like the straw that had lined Mr. Zhang's shed. She slid the ring onto her finger and pulled her sleeves over her knuckles to hide the gleaming ruby from the sharp eyes of thieves.

Before she left, she wrapped Lan up and laid her, sleeping, in a nest of blankets. "Keep folding matchboxes," she instructed. "Carefully," she added, to Di.

Mom never told us how much money she sold the ring for, but after the sale she picked up Lan and went straight to a doctor's office. After examining Lan, the doctor told Mom what to buy and from where. There was a shortage of both medicine and medical supplies, but on Qingdao's booming black market almost anything could be purchased—anything except for the elixir of life and valid train tickets, it seemed. Mom was worried that the black-market medicine was counterfeit, since swindlers were known to bottle mixes of vinegar and sugar and sell them as remedies. However, the shelves in legitimate hospitals and pharmacies were empty. Promising that the vendors he knew were honest, the doctor gave Mom specific directions on which stalls to go to, even providing details on the vendors' appearances to avoid confusion.

Mom left the doctor's office with the name of an antibiotic written on her hand, and she returned with nearly empty pockets and two glass tubes of clear liquid. A nurse injected the contents of one of the tubes into Lan's bony butt, which lowered her fever that night.

With the remainder of the money from the ring sale, Mom bought a silkie, a black-skinned chicken, for soup that was supposed to be effective in promoting recovery. She stewed the silkie along with some goji berries, red dates, ginger, and cloves of garlic. We made Lan drink all of the soup and eat the chicken's liver and heart. Mom sliced off a portion of the chicken breast for Uncle Sen and saved the rest of the meat to feed Lan over the coming days.

Di and I both longed to grab a chicken drumstick and tear in, but our sister's life hung in a delicate balance. We fed Lan even though it was torturous not to be able to take a bite ourselves. Di licked her lips but said nothing as we watched Lan eat. Later we sniffed chicken bones as we ate our bread, imagining that we too were chewing on meat.

After a week, Mom took Lan back to the doctor's office for her second injection. Unlike Uncle Sen, Lan responded well to her treatment, and slowly the pink returned to her cheeks. She was a thin child, since Mom never had enough milk, but her face began to round out as she started eating enthusiastically again. The problem now was that Mom had lost most of her breast milk from her own battle with tuberculosis. We couldn't afford any other milk for Lan, so we had to give her warm water thickened with flour, sugar, and salt.

Each day that passed, Lan's health improved, but her legs were permanently damaged. Even with one of us supporting her, she could bear weight only on her right leg; her left leg hung limply. Lan could only crawl, pulling herself forward with her arms and kicking her right leg for support. If she was really motivated, she could flail her limbs and move faster by undulating like a snake. "She will never marry," Mom said regretfully, scrubbing the dirt stains from Lan's shirts, which wiped the floor through her motions.

Lan's condition made it even more urgent for us to find Father, not only because of the additional medical expenses that Mom anticipated, but also because she was certain that we would have to care for Lan for the rest of her life. "You and Di need to marry well," Mom said. "And then I will need to care for Lan myself. What am I going to do when I am old?"

"We will take care of Lan too," I tried telling Mom. Lan was growing out of the clothes that we had brought for her, and I was altering some of my smaller shirts by rolling up the sleeves and pinning the necks so she could wear them like dresses.

"Your husbands will not let you," Mom replied sadly. "Their families might not even accept you or Di as brides if they know you have a sister who needs long-term care. They might even think Lan was born this way and worry that you will pass the affliction on to your sons." Lan crawled over and grabbed Mom's ankles because she could tell that she was sad, but she was too young to understand why. Mom picked her up and held her close, resting her chin on Lan's little head.

So much of Mom's hope depended on finding Father, who had taken her for granted and left her behind. I wanted to point out that there was no guarantee that Father would even pay for Lan's medical care, but I didn't want to throw Three's death in her face as she mourned Lan's future. Despite Mom's complaints, we were all grateful. Just as Three's passing had shattered our world, Lan's survival allowed us to see it in a new light.

Mom had bartered that ruby ring for Lan's life. The money was in our hands for only a second before being passed to the doctor and vendors, but that sale made us feel powerful. Our bellies were never full, but we could make decisions. Our money was paltry, but we were in control of it.

In Zhucheng we lived with so many resources, yet we were impotent, pleading with and kowtowing to Father and Nai Nai for every purchase. I thought about the nights we had slept on the street and the times when Di and I vomited because we had eaten rotten food. Yet, when push came to shove, we were able to protect our own. I understood that we couldn't rely on our meager jewelry stash in the long term, but this exchange taught me more about money than any of Nai Nai's blathering about savings ever had. I learned that money is irrelevant unless it is your own.

As far as I was concerned, a job was more important than a husband. With my own income, I could care for Lan, and also for Mom in her old age. Maybe then it would be okay if we didn't find Father. It would be okay if Mom didn't have a son. It would be okay if Lan, Di, or I didn't marry. I made a promise to myself that, no matter where we ended up, I would work and earn money so that I could support Mom and my sisters.

Maybe then the four of us could be happy.

15

POLICEMAN WEI

By the end of summer, we'd started dragging Uncle Sen's furniture to the market to sell, but the demand for antique chairs and sofas was pitifully low. Most of the people who could traditionally afford to pay for them were poised to flee and did not want to accumulate anything bulky. In the end, we sold these elaborate pieces for the equivalent of a few American dollars.

Though Uncle Sen was too weak to leave Qingdao, he was willing to help us as much as he could. Mom had asked him about train tickets, and he had told her that the only way to get them was with luck on the black market, or through a connection in the government. Uncle Sen knew of an older cousin who was a Qingdao police officer and had the Ang surname. Weakly, Uncle Sen said, "The police will know someone everywhere, and if they don't, they can make a new connection pretty easily," referring to the corruption and bribery that had become characteristic of government institutions. Uncle Sen did not have this cousin's contact information, but he remembered his name: Ang Xiao-Wei. Though we had never met him, from the "Xiao" in his name we knew that he was from the same generation as Father, with his father likely being a *tang* cousin or possibly a brother of Yei Yei's.

We embarked on a grand tour of Qingdao, asking in every neighborhood for the local police station, and then going into the station and asking for Ang Xiao-Wei. Several of the stations were closed. With the Nationalist government's dire economic situation and its retreat from the North, many public officials, including police, were no longer being paid their full salaries—some even lost their jobs, while others feared persecution and fled. It was a week before we found a station in which an officer knew Ang Xiao-Wei and could give us directions to where he worked. This station turned out to be in Dabaodao, on the ground floor of a *liyuan* house on a busy commercial street not far from where Uncle Sen lived.

The first time we went there, this station was closed. Mom sent me to sell buns outside it every day so I could keep an eye on it in case it opened. It was August, and the smells of the city came alive in the heat. There were many of them: the smell of excrement from the latrines, the smell of rotting garbage from the open markets, and the smell of poverty—unbathed bodies, diseased bodies, and sometimes dead bodies. I sat outside the police station, hoping that the fragrance of sweet buns would overpower the stenches around us and draw in some customers.

On a Thursday, the station finally opened. I scrambled up with my wheelbarrow as an officer in uniform unlocked the front door. He glanced warily back at me. "Do you need help, little lady?"

"I am looking for my mother's cousin," I explained. "He is also a policeman. His name is Ang Xiao-Wei?"

The officer looked relieved to hear that I was looking for someone instead of making a complaint. Crime in Qingdao was an epidemic, and the city did not have enough resources to investigate or prosecute the majority of cases.

"Yes, he is my colleague," the officer replied. "He will be on duty here from two o'clock p.m. You can come back then." The station was now open only on Thursdays and Fridays due to the lack of funds, with only one or two staff members working at a time. Thursday mornings were the busiest time, since people had to wait all week before they could make a complaint. I thanked the officer, noticing that there were aggrieved individuals behind me waiting to enter.

Skipping and running through the alley, I almost knocked someone over with my wheelbarrow in my excitement to get home. Mrs. Ding yelled at me to be careful as I pushed the courtyard door open with such force that it hit the wall. Mom was seated outside, dutifully folding matchboxes like a human machine. "I found him!" I yelled. "I found your cousin Wei!"

Mom put aside the box that she was folding and picked up Lan and cheered, bouncing her up and down on her hip. "Let's get our nicer clothes out so we make a good impression when we meet him," she said happily.

That afternoon, the three of us washed ourselves and picked through our small stacks of clothing. We had long since traded our embroidered silk shirts for corn flour, but we had some clean blue cotton tops that made us look like civilized and polite women. Mom took all of us to the station, walking with short, quick steps that betrayed her anxiety. Would this person whom we had never met believe that we were related to him? There were so many scams now. None of us had anything to prove that we were part of the Ang family, and in the match company Mom was going by Ms. Fa.

A metal bell was tied to the door and it rang as we opened it.

The interior of the station was bare and a bit dirty, but we were lucky, because no one else was in the waiting area. At the desk there was only one officer, whom we recognized right away as Cousin Wei—his resemblance to Yei Yei was remarkable. Even in these meager times he looked healthy and strong, a typical Shandong man with broad shoulders and thick arms and legs. He even had a bit of a belly protruding from his shirt.

"Good afternoon," said Mom, her voice slightly higher than usual. "I am kindly asking for Mr. Ang Xiao-Wei. I am the wife of Ang Xiao-Long, daughter-in-law of Ang Hong-Bu."

The presumed Cousin Wei stood up and walked out from behind his desk to greet us, his arms wide in welcome. "I am Ang Xiao-Wei," he said, excited, as though he recognized us. "It is always a pleasure to meet family. I know Uncle Hong-Bu—he works at the university! Did he go to Shanghai too? How is he doing?" He frowned and added, "I hope he is not in trouble."

"No, he is safe in Taiwan," Mom assured him. "As is my husband. Quick, girls, greet your uncle Wei." She blushed, embarrassed to have forgotten this important social ritual.

"Good afternoon, Uncle Wei," Di and I said in unison. Since he was a *tang* cousin, Mom addressed him as "Older Brother," which meant he was obligated to treat us—and care for us—as though she were his sibling.

"Good afternoon," Cousin Wei replied. "What beautiful and polite girls!"

"Thank you," said Mom, continuing as though she were in a court of law and this were her only chance to tell her story. "The four of us, however, were trapped in Zhucheng. The Communists kicked us out of our home, and we only recently managed to travel here to Qingdao."

Cousin Wei's jovial expression evaporated. "So you are in trouble, then. I have had the fortune of being safe in Qingdao, but heard horrible news about our family members in the countryside. Really awful stories. Please, sit." He pulled out a chair for Mom and took two more from the empty waiting area for me and Di. Excusing himself, he went to the entrance and locked it, putting up a sign that said the station was closed. As he sat back at his desk, he reached for paper and a pencil. "A force of habit," he explained, putting them back clumsily. "I assume that what you are about to tell me is not official?"

"Yes," said Mom, sitting down with Lan in her lap. "My husband and my father-in-law fled early, luckily. They came to Qingdao first, and from here my brother-in-law was able to secure their passage to Taiwan."

"That's impressive," Cousin Wei remarked, sounding slightly jealous. "People were fighting tooth and nail to get to Taiwan. Why didn't you go with them?"

"It was my mistake," Mom explained. "I volunteered to stay home and look after the property while the family went to Qingdao. None of us thought that the land reform would be so brutal. We were unable to contact each other, and they had no choice but to go to Taiwan first."

I tried not to flinch at her explanation, but from the corner of my eye I could see that Di's face was as red as the stamp on our travel permit. I didn't dare look at her directly, fearing that one of us would blurt out the truth—that Mom was the one who had warned them and the first one who had wanted to flee! In Chinese culture, abandoning a wife was disgraceful—even if she had only daughters. Mom had modified the story to help Father save face, making it sound like it was her own stupidity that cursed us. While

I understood that she considered Father's honor to reflect on herself, a lump rose in my throat as I acquiesced to her lie through my silence.

I couldn't tell if Cousin Wei simply did not notice Di's and my expressions or if he was feigning ignorance to avoid an awkward situation. He nodded and said, "I think all of us underestimated how vicious the land reform would be. I tried to warn my family members as well, since here in Qingdao we heard news of the land reforms farther North early on. There were a few that were smart enough to leave like Uncle Hong-Bu and your husband. Some of them went south, to Nanjing and Shanghai, but I think no one expected the purge to be so quick. Many of the landlords were executed on the same day that they were evicted. My own brother and his wife were beaten to death," Cousin Wei added, wringing his hands to contain his emotions. "Not by the Communists, but by their own son."

Mom's hands covered her mouth, which had dropped open. Even Di was taken aback, her fury replaced by shock. Sordid images gathered in my head and I did not want to hear more details, but Cousin Wei continued, opening the gates to his anguish. "The Communists gathered the family and told my nephew to kill his parents, and he initially refused. My sister-in-law knew that if he disobeyed the Communists, then they would just kill them all. She told her son to comply, hoping that maybe they would let him live. The boy could at least give his parents a quick and merciful death—we had all heard about torture and long-drawn beatings. His mother asked him to kill them with a single blow. So my nephew, who isn't much older than your girls—maybe fifteen or sixteen—took a club, aimed well, and crushed their skulls with one hit. The Communists allowed him passage to Qingdao after that, so he came here to me."

Mom swallowed, and I tried to shake the image of the Zhaos' brains splattered on the ice. If only my memories could have been like the faucet in Uncle Sen's bathroom—something that I could control with the touch of a handle. Instead, they poured forth, inundating my thoughts, the screams of the Lins making it hard to focus on the present conversation. "At least the boy is safe," Mom said, sounding far away.

Cousin Wei shook his head. "No. It was horrible; the poor boy was traumatized. He wandered around my home like a living corpse. I tried my best to help him, but he took my gun and killed himself a few weeks after his arrival."

"Oh heavens," Mom whispered. *"Amituofo,"* she added, invoking the Buddhist mantra as a blessing for a peaceful rebirth. While Cousin Wei bared his scars, we kept ours hidden. Mom hadn't even told Uncle Sen about my denunciation rally, and I myself didn't want anyone to know. There was a part of me that believed that we could erase the past by pretending that it had never happened.

"I didn't know how to save him," Cousin Wei said mournfully, as though he were confessing a sin. "I don't know if my brother will ever forgive me for failing to protect his son—and letting him and his wife die for nothing."

"I'm so sorry," Mom said, trying to console him. "You did what you could, and it isn't your fault." We knew, though, from our own experiences, that there were no words that could allay his sorrow, or reassurances that could alleviate his guilt.

Cousin Wei nodded hollowly, his face ashen. "I don't know how many Angs are left now. So many of us were killed these past months."

Mom sighed in agreement. "We were on the streets when we first arrived here, looking for relatives. I asked everyone we met if they had come across other Angs, without success. I suspect that few of us from the countryside made it here. My daughters and I are lucky to be alive, and even luckier to have come this far."

"I am grateful that you made it out," said Cousin Wei, still despondent. "I only hope that there are more like you—living in the city now, so that one day I might meet them. It is lonely knowing that our roots have been erased. I can never forgive the Communist pigs for what they have done, and submitting to them as they take over my beloved Qingdao will be so hard to stomach."

Soon, Cousin Wei would have to work for the cadres, whom he hated. The Communist Party was slowly picking up the administration of Qingdao, and it had promised to resume the payment of salaries for all civil servants. Mao, through his cadres in the square, had vowed not to arrest or harm any of the Nationalist officials, including police officers, all of whom were entitled to remain in their posts. By necessity, the revolution had to have more flexibility in the cities than in the rural towns. Life in places like Zhucheng was simple and straightforward. Cities, however, were complex machines, with hundreds of thousands of cogs that could not be broken haphazardly. Without compromise, the revolution would grind to a halt.

"I feel the same way," said Mom, sensing the difficult adjustment that lay ahead. I sympathized too—my stomach turned every time I made small talk with cadres who bought our buns. I hated them, but we needed their money to survive. "I am not sure if I can ask you for this favor now," said Mom, "since I don't want to compromise your transition or cause you any trouble."

"Trouble?" Cousin Wei repeated, pulling himself away from his despair. Below the surface his grief still lingered, but he put a brave face on, his voice booming like a true Northerner's. "We are both Angs! We are *tang* cousins! We will share a family tomb! If we don't look out for each other, who else will? Please do not insult me when the same blood runs in our veins. Ask me your favor."

Mom smiled, relieved by his encouragement. "My girls and I need to buy train tickets to Guangdong Province," she said slowly, trying to gauge his reaction. "I've gone to the station several times now, but tickets are always sold out. I've even looked on the black market, but most of those tickets are fake. I need to go to Taiwan to be with my husband, and for my girls to be with their father."

Cousin Wei nodded enthusiastically. "How could you hesitate to ask me something as basic as that? Of course I will help you. There are so few of us Angs now. I want you and your husband to be safe and together, as you should be. That being said, tickets truly are hard to buy, even for us police. Too many people want to travel, and there aren't enough trains—there is a coal shortage due to the war. Many people are giving huge bribes to the ticket sellers, and even then there are not enough to go around." He paused to ask us the question that we dreaded. "How much money do you have?"

"Not much," said Mom, ashamed. I could see her toes wiggle nervously through the thin black fabric of her shoes as I thought about the millions of matchboxes that we would have to make to approach the sum for an acceptable bribe. Could we even pay in corn flour? "I also have some items that I can sell," she added hopefully.

"That's good," replied Cousin Wei. "I have some friends who can help, but even the favor of friendship cannot replace the weight of gold. I promise you I will try my best, but I cannot guarantee anything."

Mom lowered her voice, even though there wasn't anyone around us, and whispered, "I have one gold tael. Will that be enough?" That coin was the single item that Father had thought to leave us.

Anger welled in me as I imagined him enjoying the boat ride to Taiwan with meat to eat and money to spare while we were here clawing around for train tickets. That tiny golden tael was easily worth hundreds of good meals—hundreds of bowls of fish soup.

"Normally no," Cousin Wei answered bluntly. "But I will push."

"Thank you so much, Cousin Wei," Mom said, grabbing his hand with both of hers in gratitude.

"Stop thanking me," Cousin Wei insisted. "I told you: We are family. This is duty, not kindness."

"I know you are taking a risk by helping us," said Mom. "I won't take that for granted."

"Don't worry about me," Cousin Wei said, unconcerned. "I was a Nationalist official. Now I'm a Communist official. As soon as they pay me, anyway." He reached into his pocket and pulled out a few silver yuan notes. "I don't have much now, but please accept what little I can give."

Mom pushed his hand away and shook her head. "We are already in your debt. It would be undignified to take even more from you."

"I insist," Cousin Wei said, stuffing the money into Mom's hand. "If you want to thank me, don't insult me by rejecting my gift." He closed her fingers over it, and she bowed, relieved to have something that could help fill the financial void that the tael would leave. "Come here and find me again next week. Hopefully I will have some good news for you."

16

ONE-WOMAN SHOW

Every Thursday, we looked forward to visiting Cousin Wei while he was on his shift. Though each time he told us, with chagrin, that there was no progress on the tickets, we still enjoyed his company. It felt good to have social visits when my days were otherwise a series of mundane chores.

Despite having nothing concrete, Mom began preparing to leave so that we would be ready if tickets came in. The train journey to Guangdong Province would take about a week, and we could not make flatbread this time—it would be foolish to risk its spoiling. Mom decided to make hard bread, which tasted awful but had a long shelf life. We had to soak it in water to render it edible, and even then it was a chore to chew it. However, if we got train tickets two months from now, that dense, dry bread would still be safe to eat. At the end of each day, we stacked our hard bread neatly like little bricks in the kitchen, as though we were building a wall in anticipation of battle.

Meanwhile, the number of cadres in Qingdao continued to increase. They walked along every street, even venturing into private alleys, disseminating pamphlets of propaganda. Printed photos of Mao Ze-Dong were posted in stores and on walls, and given to people to wave on stakes at public events. I had heard his name so many times and endured his canon, but for the first time I stopped and scrutinized his face. I had imagined him differently—like a grand statue, an imposing giant. But here he was: slightly balding, slightly overweight, with jowls that hung down around his mouth like two little pillows—nothing remarkable or intimidating. Yet this was the man who had brought us all to our knees and held China in his fist.

There were some days when the cadres came barreling into the public squares with truckloads of coarse unrefined flour that they handed out in cloth bags. Though the flour was of low quality, it was still sustenance and people cheered joyously when they saw them arriving. Hordes of poor climbed over one another, arms outstretched toward the cadres who belted out Mao's words: "*The people's democratic dictatorship needs the leadership of the working class. For it is only the working class that is most farsighted, most selfless, and most thoroughly revolutionary. The entire history of revolution proves that without the leadership of the working class, revolution fails, and that with the leadership of the working class, revolution triumphs!*"

Mao's Communist movement had traditionally relied on rural peasants, but within the cities farmers were rare. The cadres pivoted, focusing on the urban workers instead, the ones whose sweat and blood fed the city factories. I couldn't help but be impressed at how they tailored their language to fit their audience.

Di listened to these speeches too and watched the city with her careful eyes. Absorbing the words of the cadres, she began to spit out phrases that I recognized from the public squares. She fought more with Mom and started refusing to visit Cousin Wei, who she predicted would be jailed for planning sabotage. Simultaneously, she became increasingly aggressive about staying in Qingdao, insisting that we were on the eve of a grand new era.

"I don't understand," Mom said to her as we carted several stacks of paperboard into our courtyard one afternoon. "We have such a wretched life here. Don't you want to go back to eating normal meals and sleeping in our own house?"

"Our life here will get better," Di responded confidently as she lifted Lan off of the wheelbarrow. We had to take Lan on our errands now, because Uncle Sen was too ill and she was too active. He wanted to rest peacefully, without her scrabbling through the house. "The Communists will not hurt us. We can build a new life here, without Father."

I will never again be stupid enough to believe that the Communists won't hurt me, I thought. The three of us transported the paperboard inside, grunting under its weight as we dropped it beside the door.

"We can't build a life making matchboxes," said Mom. There were paper cuts on all our fingers that lingered for days due to our poor health, but we were eager to fold more if it meant more money—there just wasn't enough work. "And what about your marriages? Do you want to marry poor men and spend the rest of your lives begging and eating scraps? Men might not even take you if they know you are from a broken family! What about Lan and her medical needs?"

"Have more faith, Mom," Di said, eyes sparkling. She had swallowed the decadent promises of Mao's cadres. "The state will provide for us. There will be cheap doctors for Lan and opportunities for us. There will be enough jobs for everyone because there will be new industries in every city, including Qingdao. Hai and I can work in a factory and we will live well off of three incomes!"

"Factory work is nothing to dream of, Di," Mom warned. "You have never done it and have no idea how grueling it is. Even if we find jobs, we cannot stay with Uncle Sen forever."

"And why not?" Di demanded. "We are the ones taking care of him. He needs us. Without us, what do you think would happen to him?"

Di and I had an unspoken consensus that Uncle Sen would likely die if we left. Each morning Mom brewed his tea and herbs, and Di and I brought meals to his bed. We even emptied his chamber pot for him and did his laundry. Without us, there would be no one to bring home scraps, make him bread, or perform domestic duties. I suspected that Di also anticipated that we could take over his house upon his passing. In her own morbid way, she was an optimist.

Mom and Uncle Sen, on the other hand, had an open consensus that he was on the mend, despite all the signs to the contrary. "When Uncle Sen recovers, he will find his own wife and start his own family," Mom replied with confidence. "We will need to leave eventually, and then we will have to pay for housing, which we cannot afford."

"Who's going to marry Uncle Sen?" Di snorted, laughing. "He has no money, and he looks like a skeleton."

"A poor girl who has no other options!" snapped Mom. "A poor girl like you and Hai! When you look at Uncle Sen, remind yourself that your husband will be in his category if we remain in this city. With our current situation you would be lucky to marry a man who owns any property at all! No matter how angry you are at your father, it is indisputable that his wealth will buy you a better husband and a better future!"

"I don't want to crawl back to someone who abandoned me!" yelled Di. "I have pride, and we don't need Father to survive!" As her voice escalated, I took Lan in my arms and rocked her, knowing that she was as sick of this fight as I was. "I refuse to return to that garbage, and you should too, Mom! Why are you such a coward?"

Di's words were brazen, but instead of exploding like Di wanted her to, Mom let out a long, tired sigh. I knew she was furious, but she didn't have the stamina to keep pace with Di's fire. Each of Mom's days was a string of exhausting and mind-numbing obligations, and she never had enough leisure time to recover. "I am not going to argue this with you anymore," she said in surrender. "If you have so much energy to fight, go make some more matchboxes and bring something useful to the table."

"You're right," Di hissed, even more agitated at Mom's refusal to engage. "I don't know why I'm wasting energy convincing you when we won't be getting train tickets anyway from useless Cousin Wei!" She stormed off, slamming the door of the apartment behind her with such force that a pile of paperboard toppled over. A few seconds later we could hear the door of the courtyard slam too, and Mrs. Ding squawking about the noise.

Mom put her hands over her face; she was as defeated as a crumpled old rag that had become threadbare from scrubbing the same stubborn stain over and over again. "I need to finish this batch of matchboxes," she said, wearily picking up the paperboard that had fallen.

I looked out the window to the courtyard, where Lucky lay sleeping in the shade of some sheets that had been hung out to dry. Di was probably several streets away by now. She had gotten accustomed to Qingdao and knew the alleys of Dabaodao like the veins on her hand.

Unbeknownst to Mom, Di had even ventured into the Villa District several times, and she had formed relationships with restaurant owners who often gave her cheap meals on the house—which she ate then and there. Di could be charming when she wanted to be and she looked older than she was. She was tall and decently pretty and had a way with words. When I asked her why she didn't bring anything back to share, she would just shrug and say that the portion she had been given was tiny. In times of hardship, Di was a one-woman show, and as a result she was not just a survivor, but a climber. Even though I detested how self-centered and selfish Di could be, I had no doubt that she could thrive in the new Qingdao; honestly, she could have thrived anywhere in the new China.

I had no idea what she was doing now, but I couldn't help but envy how easily she could slip away from responsibility. "I will make some more hard bread," I said, putting Lan down and facing our reality.

By the time Di returned, it was dark. She tiptoed in and curled up in her own corner of the room, avoiding us all. She smelled of barbecue smoke from the street markets and seemed satisfied. We were angry at her, but she didn't care. She had herself, and for her that was enough.

17

COARSE FLOUR

Perpetually, there were people waiting outside of the train station, forming a queue with their bags packed, sleeping in line night after night, hoping to snag tickets as soon as they went on sale again.

In September, Cousin Wei tipped Mom off that a new batch of tickets was about to be printed. The three of us went together to the station, a big German-style building with a tall clock tower. We were not the only ones with the early warning, and there was already a line that extended far beyond the station, at least a hundred meters into the street. Mom ended up waiting in line for three days. Di and I brought her food and occasionally switched with her so she could go home and rest. At night, she slept on the street with some blankets for padding.

On the third day, the line started to move and everyone scrambled to gather their sprawled belongings. Savage fights erupted whenever someone was accused of cutting, and there were no police on the streets to break them apart—all the available officers were inside to protect the ticket sellers, who were bracing for anarchy. Outside, people beat one another bloody while those in line watched, pressed together like matches in a box, terrified of being knocked over and losing their place. Closer to the station, a small throng took advantage of the chaos and stormed the line like a battalion, cutting in through the station doors. Within minutes, all order disintegrated as everyone in line panicked and surged forward, fearing that these newcomers were going to claim the tickets that they had waited so long for.

The tickets were sold out again before Mom could even make it inside the station. Ahead of her, there were screams as aggressive thieves mugged those who had successfully purchased them. A young woman lay on the floor, clutching her bleeding face while shrieking that her tickets had been stolen. Behind Mom, others wailed, cried, and cursed, but nothing could be done. As those remaining in line walked away empty-handed, others moved forward eagerly, determined to continue waiting until the next batch of tickets would be issued.

Mom returned home, a wad of blankets in her arms, dragging her feet and ready to collapse.

I handed her one of the sweet buns that I hadn't managed to sell that morning, and the two of us sat together in the courtyard, next to our wheelbarrow, which had begun to squeak loudly whenever we pushed it. It felt like luck was a current that we had to plow against, and after days of struggle we were exactly where we had started.

In a rare show of despair, Mom said to me, "Your sister is right. We won't be able to get these tickets." She tore the bun into two halves and handed one back to me, then shoved her half into her mouth.

I held Mom's hand, feeling the rough calluses on her palms, and leaned my head on her shoulder. She worked so hard, but we couldn't rest, or else we would end up even further behind. Maintaining our lowly status quo was itself a fight. "You always say that we will find a way, right, Mom?" I said, trying to comfort her. "And if we do not, then it is the will of the Gods." In the silence, we could hear the faint chatter of neighbors upstairs, and the autumn breeze whistling through the alley outside.

"Yes, that's true," Mom replied, and chewed absently. "What a waste of time, though. Next time at least I can bring some matchboxes to fold."

And I said, "Next time I'll walk up and down the line with our wheelbarrow and sell bread to all those hungry people who are afraid to lose their place."

Mom smiled and remarked, "What a smart daughter I have."

I tried to be optimistic, but I was also drained, knowing that we would need to repeat this charade. Perhaps we would be better off showing up late and cutting to the front like others had done—though we were neither brave enough nor stupid enough to risk getting beaten to a pulp by those whom we wronged. I wondered if any of those line cutters ended up walking away with a ticket. I hoped not, but I also knew not to expect fairness in a city where people were living in sewers and trampling one another over rice porridge.

On October 1, 1949, Mao Ze-Dong stood in Beijing's Tiananmen Square and declared victory, proclaiming himself the new chairman of the People's Republic of China. The only foreign power to recognize Mao's government was the Soviet Union, which promptly cut ties with the Nationalists. A military parade and a small air show marked this first National Day, and two hundred thousand people gathered to celebrate.

Cadres in Qingdao mounted radios on top of trucks and blasted Mao's victory speech everywhere. In the streets people screamed and set off firecrackers, waving the red and yellow flag of the new republic. "China is liberated! China is liberated!" PLA soldiers sang revolutionary songs at the tops of their lungs, tears of joy streaming down their faces. Members of the public who knew the lyrics joined in, united by these hymns that heralded the end of the war. I was with Di in Qingdao's main square, and she cheered too—it was the smart thing to do with cadres and Party supporters surrounding us, but I still felt betrayed. The party that reigned over my nightmares now ruled my country, and my sister was congratulating people as though it were New Year's Day.

Over the past weeks, I had been mentally preparing myself to face the possibility of living under the Communist government for the foreseeable future. I willed myself to focus on the positive—that finally the war would be over. Though I tried to think more like Di and believe that there would be jobs and stability, I was tumbling deeper into despair. Taiwan seemed like an impossible dream as I envisaged the avenues toward it closing.

Mao's victory declaration was followed by an expansion of the PLA's authority in Qingdao. Though this change was initially terrifying, it actually created a golden opportunity for Cousin Wei. Given the chaos at the train station, the PLA decided to deploy its soldiers to help maintain order during the next round of ticket sales. Simultaneously, they would also observe who was trying to flee and potentially catch any wanted traitors. Cousin Wei was clever, and he predicted that his superiors would also increase the police presence at the station, to demonstrate that they had everything under control. With jobs being so limited, no one wanted the PLA to start replacing any policemen, especially the high-ranking ones.

Cousin Wei embarked on a dedicated networking campaign, strategically delivering bottles of liquor and flaky golden mooncakes to key superiors at headquarters as "gifts" to celebrate the Mid-Autumn Festival in October. When assignments came out, Cousin Wei was on the list of officers who would serve as reinforcement for the ticket sellers during the next batch of sales.

Mom thanked him ecstatically, but Cousin Wei cautioned her to rein in her expectations. "There will be at least thirty more police officers in addition to me, and everyone—including the Communists' own military—will probably try to get tickets. As you know, they are worth a fortune on the black market. The next batch of sales will be at the beginning of November, for travel in December. Do you still have that golden tael?" Cousin Wei asked.

"Yes," Mom confirmed. It was actually in her undergarments, but it would have been inappropriate for her to just reach in and grab it.

"You will need to bring it to me here before I go to the station. Let's hope that it is enough." As we said goodbye, he gave us some mooncakes and wished us a happy Mid-Autumn. I ate mine as we walked home—it had my favorite lotus filling. Though I longed to eat Di's too, I restrained myself and kept it wrapped in a cloth for her.

Turning into our alley, we saw Mrs. Ding sweeping the street in front of her courtyard. Mrs. Ding had the cleanest entrance of anyone in Qingdao—she was always outside sweeping the steps, washing the doors, or hanging up her laundry with the courtyard door open. She wasn't as bad as we had first thought she was. She was nosy and pried shamelessly into everyone's business, but her gossiping nature was the result more of loneliness than of malice. We soon realized that she was very protective of her block and everyone on it. Sometimes this was annoying, since she would advise people of potential threats based on her own prejudices—the arrival of someone's bastard child ("A scam," she insisted) or someone's half-Japanese relative ("Their father is a rapist," she whispered). Generally, however, Mrs. Ding was helpful; she and a few other elderly residents were always available to assist.

With Uncle Sen's condition, Mom began to leave Lan with Mrs. Ding when neither of us could take her. Mrs. Ding had no children of her own, and she very quickly assumed the role of a volunteer grandmother. When she could afford it, she would also give us some pork fat or oranges. She had nieces and nephews who sent her money occasionally, but she made her living renting out the apartment above her, which she owned in addition to hers. That made her a landlord. A small-scale one and probably not on anyone's radar, but her anxiety and penchant for eavesdropping made her paranoid of the Communists all the same.

"I don't mean to put my nose in your business," she told Mom one day, even though that was her main hobby and pastime, "but your younger daughter is fraternizing with the Party cadres. I know she's a child and doesn't know, but someone needs to tell her that she can't be drawing their attention around here. We want to be left alone. I've been here since the Germans were here! And the Japanese! We are better off if we are left unseen and unnoticed. Trust me. I know!"

"I will speak to her," Mom agreed wearily. We weren't surprised about Di's behavior; children often flocked to cadres because they passed out candy and little drawn cards of Mao that resembled the ones that Di used to collect. Like the cadres we had met on the road, the ones in Qingdao could be exceptionally kind to street urchins, like missionaries spreading the word of a gospel. Di's favorite tunes were love songs, but in their absence, Party hymns were a welcome substitute. Day by day, week by week, Di had grown closer to the lively men and women in their four-pocket uniforms—the winners in our city of losers.

When Di started coming home with bags of coarse flour from the Communist cadres' trucks, Mom chose an opportunity to broach the subject. "Di," Mom said, "how are you getting this flour?"

"Same as everyone," Di replied. She crossed her arms and leaned against the doorframe of the kitchen. "The cadres are handing them out in the square."

Mom put the flour on the kitchen table and said, "Are you speaking with any of these cadres?"

"No," said Di flatly. She looked like a snake coiled and ready to spring. I was in the living room with Lan, who was pretending to play with some pieces of crumpled paper, the only toys that we could afford to give her.

"Mrs. Ding said she saw you talking with cadres." And just like that, Mom had pulled a pin out of a grenade.

Di erupted, her face turning red and her arms spreading wide. "Mrs. Ding is a stupid hag who is too old to even see or hear anything properly!" As she yelled this, I thought to myself that Mrs. Ding surely had her ear pressed against our courtyard door and had probably heard that. "I have to talk to people. We need food, right? How will we get anything if I just sit around with my hands in my pockets? Or do you want me to be like Uncle Sen and just lie in bed quietly?"

Di had previously insisted that she would never beg for food. I had told her that that was an unrealistic principle to adhere to, given our financial situation. I saw, however, that Di's definitions were suited to fit her ego. She never outrightly asked anyone for food, but she would strike up conversations with the right people in the right places and tell them about her situation. She would talk about how we were eating out of the garbage and how she had a "crippled baby sister" who had no milk to drink. Those with kind hearts who had taken a liking to Di would give her items voluntarily.

Mom had her head in her hands, and she said, "What are you telling them about our family? We need to be careful, Di. Don't you remember what happened to us in Zhucheng? It is best if we stay out of their line of sight."

"You are all shaking in your shoes at nothing," Di yelled back. "We aren't in Zhucheng anymore. No one here knows us. The cadres are not as bad as you think. It's all Nationalist propaganda that makes you think they are these wicked monsters."

I could not help but interject. "No," I retorted, standing up so quickly that I startled Lan. "I think they are monsters because I saw them shoot people. Mr. and Mrs. Lin were stoned to death. Our family members were buried alive and beaten. Do you remember how I looked after I came back from that rally? Or did you forget because someone waved a bag of flour in your face?"

"There are bad people in every group, but that doesn't mean the entire group is bad," Di replied with the zeal of a follower. "There are bad Nationalists too. Chiang Kai-Shek would have turned China into an American colony. At least under the Communists the foreigners have fled!"

"The Soviet Union is also foreign," I said. "Or are the cadres telling you they are Chinese now?"

Hearing us argue, Lan started to cry and crawled her way to the kitchen. "That's enough," Mom said harshly, picking up Lan and rubbing her back. "Di, you can never, ever tell any of the cadres what happened in Zhucheng. You cannot tell them anything about our family. We aren't even supposed to be in Qingdao."

"Do you both think I'm that stupid?" Di cried. Her fists were balled up in anger, knuckles white. "Do you think they would give me anything if I said who our family was? They think I am the daughter of peasants and my father died of tuberculosis—which also crippled my sister."

"Oh, by the Gods . . ." Mom gasped. "Do they know where we live? What else have you said?"

"That's it," said Di. "They don't need to know where I live. I told them we are staying with a relative. An industrial worker with no job."

"And what if someone follows you one day?" Mom asked incredulously. "You could get all of us in trouble if they learn that you lied. You could get Uncle Sen in trouble!"

"Don't be so dramatic," Di retorted. "If you are so worried about that, then the first person you should yell at is Mrs. Ding, who is the one most likely to randomly point our house out to a stranger!"

Mom took a breath and said, "I want you to stop talking to the cadres. It will only bring problems."

"It has brought us food!" Di screamed. "I'm the only one who is trying to ride this tide and raise our family up. Do you think we can avoid the cadres forever? They own this city!"

"We can avoid the cadres until we board the train and leave," Mom said firmly. "We are not staying in Qingdao."

"Speak for yourself!" Di yelled. "I'm going to join the Communist Party Youth League. When I'm old enough, I'm going to join the People's Liberation Army!" She left Mom with words that were like a slap in the face and turned on her heels, ran into the room that we all shared, and slammed the door so hard that the windows rattled.

Mom gave an exasperated sigh. "Why does it have to be so difficult with her?"

I heard Uncle Sen give a loud, wet-sounding cough in the

other room and yell feebly, "That girl is going to break my house with all her door slamming!"

"Sorry, Sen," Mom called back.

I gave Lan a piece of hard bread, which she gnawed on while still in Mom's arms. I thought about Mrs. Ding, who was probably readying herself to warn our neighbors that Di was going to lead cadres to our homes. I also thought about Di, who was probably crying in the room, feeling sorry for herself because the rest of her family didn't understand her.

Cadres occasionally wandered into our alley, which made us all nervous. They put up posters of Mao, which upset Mrs. Ding. After they left, she would wash the walls and declare that it was a pity that she had to remove the posters in order to scrub the surface beneath. These small acts of resistance gave us some comfort, but they were futile, as the Nationalists retreated farther every week. By October fifteenth, Chiang's armies had left Guangzhou and had gone west to Chongqing. I started to worry that Di was right, and we would never be able to outrun the Communists. Even if we managed to reach Taiwan, it might be only a matter of time before the People's Liberation Army gobbled up the island and the entire country was united under their red and yellow flag.

18

GOLDEN TAEL

Through careful conservation, we had built up a small fort of hard bread in preparation for the winter. The sun became lazier, hiding behind clouds and retiring earlier each day. Overnight, the cold air slunk through the Qingdao streets, and it surprised us in the morning when we opened our doors. I shivered and took out the warm coat that I had brought from Zhucheng. I desperately hoped that we would be southbound by the time winter was in full force.

Mom went back to the police station, golden tael in hand, and passed the coin to Cousin Wei the Thursday before he was scheduled for duty at the train station. "Pray," Mom commanded us. "Whenever you have time, pray. That's all we can do." Di did Mom the honor of ignoring her request instead of fighting back. I tried to obey, but it was hard for me to believe in the power of prayer anymore. Nevertheless, I went through the ritual of it, kneeling before my window and beseeching the Guang-Yin Bodhisattva to help us.

Perhaps that was enough, because a few days later, Cousin Wei came to our house with a smile on his face. Mom and I met him outside, in the courtyard, to avoid exposing him to tuberculosis. He reached into his pocket and pulled out a set of glossy printed tickets that still smelled of fresh ink. Mom screamed with joy and grabbed me in a tight hug and the two of us jumped up and down. Not only did he get us tickets to Guangdong; he got us tickets all the way to Shenzhen, a village in Bao'an County, on the border with Hong Kong. We would leave in a month, on the tenth of December.

"I cannot thank you enough for what you have done for us," Mom said to Cousin Wei. "My family will be forever grateful."

Cousin Wei waved his hand and said, "*We* are family. I don't need thanks. I just want you and your girls to be safe. Find your husband and have many sons and make sure our Ang name is passed on."

It was surreal to actually hold the tickets in our hands—a golden tael now in paper form. Cousin Wei had already left by the time Di came home with yet another bag of coarse flour from the cadres. She took off her jacket, hung it by the door, and said, "Mrs. Ding asked me why a policeman came to our house. I told her I didn't know, but it was probably Cousin Wei. She was really happy—she said it's most useful to have a relative who is a doctor, but a policeman is up there too. Was it Cousin Wei who came by, or are we in trouble?"

"It was Cousin Wei," said Mom, taking the coarse flour and putting it in the kitchen. "He came here to give us our train tickets." She said that last sentence in a neutral tone, because she wasn't sure how Di would react.

I was holding my breath, but Di's face did not even twitch, and she said, "So he wasn't so useless after all." Di walked past me and Lan and went straight into our bedroom and closed the door. Mom and I exchanged a look, both of us surprised. We were bracing for an explosion and anticipating tears, but this strangely placid Di left us both feeling uneasy.

"What if Di doesn't want to go?" I asked Mom.

Mom's eyebrows knitted together with concern, but she only said, "Let's talk about that if and when the time comes. For now, we need to prepare as much as we can. We will need money when we arrive in Shenzhen, so I will try to get more work from the match factory. Someone else can take my job after I leave, so maybe other workers would be willing to let me claim a greater share of paperboard over the next month."

I nodded. "I will try to sell more buns."

Mom didn't tell anyone except for Uncle Sen that we were leaving, and she emphasized to both Di and me that we needed to keep quiet. I had no one to tell, but I suspected that Di had developed friends and acquaintances in the city. "Above all," said Mom gravely, "you cannot talk to any of the cadres about this."

"The cadres wouldn't care anyway," said Di. "They have bigger things to worry about than a bunch of peasant women taking a train." Di's flippant attitude annoyed me. Obviously they would know we weren't simple peasant women if we managed to get our hands on these tickets. Perhaps she was right, though—they surely had greater problems to investigate than how we'd managed to crack the ticket system.

I also had another dilemma—what to do about Lucky. Mom made it clear that we could not bring him on the train.

"I don't want to give anyone any reason to refuse us entry or to kick us off after we have boarded," she said firmly.

"But don't people bring livestock on trains?" I asked.

"That was a different time," Mom answered. "These trains are going to be packed with people. The tickets that Cousin Wei got us aren't even ones that get us seats. Didn't you see people riding on the roofs?"

My heart sank as I walked out to our courtyard and Lucky greeted me with his tail wagging. "I wish we could bring you instead of Di," I said to him. He leaned his body against my leg and asked me to scratch his belly by rolling over on his back. "You're stinky," I said affectionately. "I should have given you a bath this summer to make you more appealing. How are we going to find someone to take care of you?"

One Thursday, I took Lucky with me to Cousin Wei's police station, using some rags tied together as a leash. I wanted him to make a good impression. When I opened the door, I greeted Cousin Wei, who was sitting at his desk. He responded warmly and asked me where Mom was.

"She's at home," I said. "I came here by myself."

Cousin Wei looked at Lucky and said, "Dogs are not allowed in the police station, except for police dogs."

I dropped to my knees and kowtowed to Cousin Wei as I had seen Mom do to Nai Nai so many times. "I have a favor to ask you, Uncle Wei." I felt bad knowing that Cousin Wei had already done so much for our family and we had nothing that could balance the huge debt that we owed him.

"Stop. Get up, please," Cousin Wei said, sounding embarrassed. "You know how I feel about favors between family. What is it, Hai?"

"Do you think Lucky could have a job as a police dog?" I asked.

Cousin Wei looked at Lucky, who was much smaller and squatter than the elegant German shepherds that typically assumed that role. He let out a loud, thundering laugh, and before I knew it, I'd started to cry. "He's a good dog," I said, trying my best to be an effective advocate through my tears. I wiped my face with my sleeve, which had a hole in it, and added, "He can get his own food. He can even catch rats and rabbits. He's obedient and can watch your house. He's a very good dog."

Cousin Wei forced himself to stop laughing, but occasionally a chuckle would slip out and he would try to disguise it as a cough. "I'm sorry, Hai. Please don't cry. It's just that we have specific dogs for that type of work. We can't just take any dog. Maybe I can ask around and see if I can find a home for him. What kind of dog is he?"

"The best kind of dog," I replied, starting to hiccup from my tears. Lucky licked my face, which I usually didn't let him do, because he ate so much garbage and his breath smelled bad. I pushed him off and wiped the slime from my cheek. "He's a mountain dog. A peasant dog, really—he's a true proletarian. The best type of dog to have now that the Communist Party is in power."

Cousin Wei couldn't help it and guffawed again, but he quickly regained his composure as he saw how crestfallen I was. "I'm sorry, Hai. I didn't know that you care about this dog so much. Let's see what I can do. I'll ask around. No promises, but I'll try."

I nodded and thanked him, then left the police station feeling foolish. In a time in which people were dying of starvation, my plea for my dog probably seemed to be the epitome of bourgeois. I had the fleeting thought that if Di stayed in Qingdao, perhaps she could take care of Lucky, but I knew that she would probably just sell him to a meat market if it suited her. There was also Uncle Sen, but he was struggling too much with his own health to account for any other living creature.

"Maybe we can sneak you on in a suitcase?" I said to Lucky as we walked home. We didn't even have a suitcase, though. All we had were some raggedy bags for our belongings, and there was no way we could contain him in one of those.

I turned into the alley and saw Mrs. Ding at her usual roost, bundled up in a jacket and holding her broom in her hand. She noticed that my eyes were puffy and asked, "Hai, are you all right? What happened?"

Having to answer her triggered my weeping again, and I couldn't think of what to say without letting her know that we were leaving. Mom would be furious if I told the equivalent of our neighborhood newspaper what our plans were.

"Did a cadre hurt you?" Mrs. Ding demanded, getting angry. "Tell me. I'll help you. We can figure it out together."

I wasn't as quick at spinning tales as Mom or Di, but I finally mustered, "Uncle Sen won't let us keep the dog anymore. He says that the barking disturbs him while he is trying to rest. I need to find a new home for him."

"Is that all there is?" Mrs. Ding said. "I thought someone robbed you or someone had died. You scared me with this silly drama. Your smelly dog can stay in my courtyard when your uncle is resting. Maybe it will be nice to have someone watch the doors with me."

I couldn't believe my ears. "Thank you, Mrs. Ding!" I said, throwing my arms around her and giving her a hug so tight that her old bones cracked. "Thank you, thank you, thank you!"

"Calm down," she said, pushing me away. "You all leave Lan here—what's one more little creature?"

She thought that she was agreeing to house Lucky on a temporary basis, but I was hoping that if the two of them got used to each other, maybe Lucky could move to her courtyard permanently when the time came for our departure.

I started to take Lucky to Mrs. Ding every morning. I showed her his tricks, that he could sit, lie down, and even dance on command. "He's very smart," I insisted. "If you take him to the mountains, he can even catch rabbits! He can make sure your house has no rats. He is very talented."

"Why would I take this animal to the mountains?" Mrs. Ding replied. "Silly girl. Your mutt is probably just going to take a nap. That's all I've seen him do. Rabbits indeed." She waved me off with a swish of her broom and I scampered away to sell buns, the wheelbarrow squeaking loudly.

19

STEAM TRAIN

Mom gathered some old flour sacks and sewed together some backpacks for us to carry our belongings in for the journey. She reinforced the straps, but even so she suggested that we carry them in front so that we could support the weight with our arms if we needed to—and also to prevent thieves from snatching them off our backs. We didn't have much and could wear most of our clothing in layers. The bulkiest items that we needed to pack were the hard bread and extra cloth rags for Lan, who occasionally had accidents. We no longer needed any rags for Mom, who had lost her period months ago from lack of nutrition, and Di and I still had not gotten ours—I would be turning fourteen, and Di thirteen, later in December.

Mom left a small fortress of stacked hard bread for Uncle Sen, hoping that it would get him through the winter. She purchased a bag of coal for him, at three times the usual price because of the shortage, and laid the silk blanket that we brought from Zhucheng on his bed. "Goodbye, Little Sen," she said. "Take care of yourself. I'll write to you when we arrive at Shenzhen."

Uncle Sen rarely left the bed then, and he didn't even sit up to see us off. He managed a feeble smile as I said goodbye to him. "You all take care. Write to me again when you reach Taiwan. May the wind blow swiftly along your path."

As we packed the last of our bags, which became bulky and lumpy, Mom and I both braced for the fight with Di that we were sure was coming. To our surprise, however, she stood at the door with her backpack ready—it was stuffed with hard bread like ours, and as she carried it in front of her, she could barely peek over it. Wordlessly, we locked the door behind us, Mom with Lan on her back and a giant bag strapped to her chest. In the courtyard, Lucky ran to greet us, standing on his hind legs and sniffing. I put my bag down and gave him a long hug, channeling all my energy into holding back my tears. I didn't want him to get suspicious and know that we were leaving, though perhaps our bags were warning enough. I opened the courtyard door and he bounded out, thinking that we were all going on an adventure together.

It was early in the day, but Mrs. Ding was outside, sitting on her steps in the cold, a cup in her hand and a big steel teapot next to her. She stood up and offered us tea, but we declined. Seeing our bags, she said, "I guess today is the day."

"I'm sorry we didn't tell you sooner," Mom said, bowing to Mrs. Ding for her kindness.

"Don't be," said Mrs. Ding. "I already knew."

"How?" Mom asked.

Mrs. Ding looked at me, and my stomach sank as I thought that maybe she was going to say that I had somehow given our plan away. She looked back at Mom and said, "I know everything. I've been here since the Germans first arrived!" She gestured at the door of her courtyard and said, "Send the dirty mutt in."

"Thank you, Mrs. Ding," I said, starting to bawl.

Di elbowed me. "Calm down," she whispered, though her voice wobbled too. "Don't be such a crybaby—it's embarrassing."

I gave Lucky another hug and led him into Mrs. Ding's courtyard. "You'll need to keep the door closed." I sniffed. "Because otherwise he's going to follow me."

Mrs. Ding nodded. "I know, I know. We've spent a lot of time together already—I know this animal. Not a rabbit catcher, I tell you." She gave Lan a kiss on the cheek, and Mom, Di, and me a warm embrace. "Be safe. Please write. I need to know how little Lan is doing. Now that the war is over, mail should be more reliable."

We promised to write, and Mrs. Ding waved us away, but I could see that she was getting emotional. "Hurry or you will miss your train," she said, turning to pour herself some more tea.

The walk to the station felt long, and I couldn't shake a nagging sensation that I had forgotten the wheelbarrow. I knew we couldn't take it on the train, but it was such a force of habit to be squeezing those wooden handles, listening to the creaking of the wheel and the rattle of the platform as we rolled and bumped over the road.

My heart pumped with excitement and fear as we approached the station, the giant clock tower high above and a sea of people before us. There was no line, just an amorphous crowd along the platform. Like a steel dragon, the shiny black train lay on the tracks, a bit of steam trailing from its valves. Mom told us to hold hands as we made our way through. Our tickets were under her shirt, where the gold tael used to be. She was so afraid of losing them that she didn't care who would judge her for reaching in between her breasts to take the tickets out.

The madness of the platform reminded me of the feeding frenzy when the Catholics or the cadres handed out food. Mom used her shoulder to part the crowd and the three of us clutched one another's wrists in a tight grip, fighting with all our strength to stay together as we moved forward to the entrance of the train. Over the noise of the horde, I could hear a railway officer yelling at everyone to move back. There were two armed military guards flanking each railway officer who was in charge of taking tickets. Additional railway officers were charged with sticking their arms out to form a barrier between the ticket collector and everyone else.

"One group at a time," cried an officer. "Everyone with a ticket will board. Boarding will be faster if it is done in an orderly fashion. Please step back and make a line!"

There were multiple entry points to the train, at least one for every two cars, and at some the people managed to organize themselves into short, crooked lines right before the ticket collector. At the others, however, the collectors had to randomly reach into the crowd for tickets and shout at their colleagues to let specific groups through. Nearby, a fight went off like a bomb—a collector had identified a set of tickets as fake. A man screamed profanities, insisting that he had gotten the tickets right inside the station. PLA officers seized him, but with the crowd pressed around them they could only inch back. The man kicked his legs haphazardly, knocking several others to the ground as the officers struggled to remove him like ants trying to abduct a grasshopper. As they passed us, the crowd swelled away to avoid his kicks and we almost fell over. I could see that the man was well dressed, in a clean traditional silk shirt with a high collar.

"Don't push me!" a woman roared as I lost my balance and leaned against her. She used both her hands to shove me the other way.

"I can't help it," I snapped. "I'm also being pushed!"

"Let's go," Mom yelled back to me. I tightened my grip on Di's wrist and we lunged forward again. It was like standing neck-deep in the ocean and trying to move against the tide. The nearest ticket collector was not far now, but the people in front tensed their shoulders to block us from moving any farther. Everyone in this group clutched their tickets and waved them frantically at the collector, who was anxiously checking ticket after ticket and sending people clamoring up the steel steps into the train car.

It was about half an hour before we were at the front, ready to hand our tickets over. The three of us kept our shoulders pressed against one another, a gate of bones to prevent anyone else from pushing in front of us. Mom shoved her hand into her blouse, yanked out our tickets, and stretched her arm as far as she could toward the collector, who accepted them like a deity would an offering.

I felt Di's fingers dig into my flesh as he examined each ticket. She was nervous too.

The collector nodded and handed them back to Mom. "Board," he commanded.

Joyously, we broke free from the crowd, leaping through the open train car door and up the steps. I reached back to help Mom climb up, since she had Lan's extra weight to carry.

Even though it was a cold day, the inside of the train was hot, humid, and sour from the breath and warmth of a few hundred packed bodies. The seats, available only to those with premium tickets, were made of wood and arranged in rows, all facing the same direction except a few that faced each other. Not only were all of the seats taken; people were squeezed into them so tightly that there wasn't a gap to be seen. We pushed through and found some space on the floor to settle down on. Someone had opened a window, but there were too many passengers between us and the breeze. Within minutes, we saw an arm come through it, and then a shoulder and a head—people outside were helping one another climb in.

There was shouting from the platform, and then a gunshot. Officers grabbed the climber and he yelped as they pulled him back out. The police were outnumbered, though. Here and there, someone would manage to crawl into a window successfully, laughing with relief as they landed on top of other passengers in the car, who shouted and pushed angrily at the triumphant intruder.

"Get off the roof!" an officer yelled outside. "Anyone on the roof will be shot. Only passengers with legitimate tickets may board the train. I repeat, get off the roof!" A few seconds later, shots rang out and people screamed. Mom held us close under her arms instinctively, as if her flesh could protect us from a stray bullet.

Lan started to cry. "Out!" she yelled. "Want out! Want home. Want out!" Mom tried to calm her, but Lan only swatted at her and arched her back, screaming.

"We can't get out," I tried to explain. "Please, Lan, you need to be quiet!"

Lan continued to bawl hysterically, but there was nothing we could do. No one complained, though, as everyone was focused externally on the sounds of bullets from the platform and screaming from above the train.

More and more people pushed their way into our car. I kept thinking that it was impossible to squeeze anyone else in, yet heads followed by bodies kept popping up the staircase and into the cabin. We sat with our knees against our chests and our backpacks balanced on them.

After what seemed like an eternity, the train whistle blew, loud and shrill. "We're finally going to move!" said Di. It was an old steam train, and it took several minutes for the boiler to build up enough heat for the train to slowly shift. With a clang and a shudder, the sleeping dragon awoke and began to crawl. The whistle sounded again as we pulled away, and Mom leaned her back against the train car wall, relieved. Above us there was a window that did not open, but we could see outside if we craned our necks up high. The station fell away as we rolled forward, the train building up speed.

Lan had finally hushed and fallen asleep in Mom's lap when I heard a seated passenger say to her companion, "Look at that dog by the tracks!"

"Wow, he's running so quickly," he replied.

I bolted upright. My stomach did a flip, but I reassured myself that it must have been a random stray. Lucky was safely shut in Mrs. Ding's courtyard. Peering out the window, I saw a small brown dog with pointed ears running so fast along the side of the tracks that its legs were a blur. It barked as it bounded through the yellow grass, almost catching up to our window. My heart shattered with dismay. It was Lucky! "No!" I yelled, jumping to my feet and banging my hands against the windowpane. "Lucky! Go home! Go back to Mrs. Ding! Go home!"

He couldn't hear me and probably couldn't see me either, even with my face against the glass. He must have slipped out the courtyard door when another resident opened it, and shot past Mrs. Ding into the alley. With his rabbit-hunting nose he must have tracked us to the station and figured out that we had boarded the train.

Everyone in the car was staring at me, and Mom pulled my arm so hard that I thought it would pop out of its socket. "Stop it, Hai!" she snapped. "Sit back down!"

I ignored her and clung to the window. Lucky was running as fast as he could, his tongue hanging out and his breath making little puffs in the cold air. The train was outpacing him, and he began to slow to a trot. He was such a smart dog, I thought. Could a German shepherd have tracked us through all those people to the train station? Maybe. But that just meant that Lucky was as qualified as any of them to be a police dog. Cousin Wei was so ignorant to have passed on that opportunity.

"Go home, Lucky!" I roared with the illogical hope that he could hear me. "Go to Mrs. Ding!"

"Enough, Hai! Calm yourself!" Mom used both arms now to pull me back down. Lucky had stopped and sat down in the grass, panting as our train barreled farther and farther away. "It's just a dog. He's smart and he knows the way home. He'll probably turn around and go back to Mrs. Ding's house, where she'll be waiting for him."

I couldn't break my gaze away from him as he shrank in the distance, becoming a brown dot so small that he was no longer even recognizable as a dog.

"Not if someone on the street catches him and eats him first," Di remarked.

I turned and looked at her smug face. I knew she was in a bad mood and was just trying to provoke me, but I didn't care. Screaming, I jumped on her. She was larger and stronger than me, but I had the advantage of surprise and managed to knock her back.

The people behind her yelled, but their voices sounded faint to me through the blood pounding in my ears. I sat on Di's chest and pinned her arms with my knees and started slapping her face with both of my hands. "I hate you!" I screamed. "I hate you! I hate you and I wish you had stayed in Qingdao!"

"What is wrong with all my children?" Mom bellowed. She had put down Lan, who started to cry again, and grabbed me by the collar of my shirt to pull me off Di, who had to get a few counterblows in before she was willing to sit down. Even with Mom in the middle, Di reached across to knock me in the face while I tried to bite her hand.

"Control your daughters, lady!" someone nearby shouted.

"They should throw you all off! What a way to behave!" someone else added.

Mom shoved us both against the wall of the train car and inserted herself in between us with sobbing, tired Lan in her arms. "And you've woken up your sister! Horrible girls! If we get kicked off this train, I will beat you both so hard that you won't be able to sit for weeks!"

It was rare to see Mom so angry, but I was furious too. "I wish we had never left Qingdao," I cried. "I don't want to go to Taiwan. I don't want to see Father. I just want to go back to Uncle Sen's!" Mom and I almost never fought, but the words just kept spilling out of my mouth. "Father doesn't care about us. If he did, he would have insisted that we go to Qingdao with the family. They took so much money with them that they could have paid someone to go to Zhucheng for us before they left for Taiwan—but they didn't! He was willing to sacrifice us to make his parents happy. He doesn't care! He probably has already found another wife in Taiwan and is about to have another child!"

Mom gave me a hard smack on the head with her free hand.

"Shut your mouth! I can't believe you, Hai." She looked like she was on the brink of tears too. "You, of all people!"

I didn't even feel bad for making Mom so upset. All of the suspicions and worries that I had held silently in my heart had burst forth, and I couldn't take any of the words back. Even if I could, I wouldn't have wanted to. It felt good to shout them out loud, as though doing so finally cleaned out some of the wounds that had been festering inside me.

Di crossed her arms and leaned against the wall, seeming pleased with herself. Not necessarily because her ploy to set me off had worked, or because Mom had hit me—but because I had proved that she wasn't the only one who had reservations about reuniting with our family, and therefore she wasn't alone.

The three of us were quiet as the train continued through the countryside. I looked out the window but could see only the sky, so cheerfully blue that it was hard to believe that we had had such a harried and heartbreaking morning.

20

SHENZHEN

The slow steam train stopped at every station on the line. People could descend to stretch their legs and buy food from vendors who stood on the platforms with baskets of simple meals and quick snacks. Mom was so afraid of not being able to squeeze back on the train that we never got off. She passed our canteens through the window for people to fill for us; we didn't have money to waste on snacks anyway. We stuck to our corner and ate hard bread, breaking off chunks and sucking on them until they became soft enough to chew. The bathrooms on the train were foul, and I avoided drinking too much water so that I wouldn't have to use them often.

At Jinan, and again in Beijing, we had to change trains. China's first railways were built by foreigners who had claimed various protectorates and colonies in the country. Since the overall effort had not been coordinated, the rail system was a patchwork and the tracks and trains were different gauges depending on who had built them. Many stations and segments had been damaged by Japanese bombs in World War II and strategically sabotaged by the Communists during the Civil War. The Nationalists had pulled materials from tracks on less frequented routes to repair the major lines, and by the end of the revolution fewer than half of the tracks were usable.

Although we had plenty of time to make each connection—several hours in Beijing, even—Mom was too anxious to let us linger. We went straight to the platform and scuttled onto the train as soon as we could, plopping on the floor to claim a small piece of territory for ourselves.

We rode the steam trains for eight days, sleeping sitting up or curled in balls like cats. Some people in the cars chatted with one another excitedly, some anxiously, but they almost all talked about the same thing: Hong Kong. What it was like, how to get there, and, most important, whether the border would close.

"They are only allowing Guangdong natives in," we heard someone say. "You need to have an ID card."

"No," someone else corrected. "You have to have a Hong Kong identity card."

"I heard you just need an entry visa," said a third.

"Where do you get that?" the first person asked.

"I don't know," replied the third. "We will see when we get there."

Mom, Di, and I remained silent. There was too much hurt shared between us, and not enough time for the wounds to subside. I spent my time worrying and hoping that Lucky had found his way back safely, and cursing myself for not having tied him up within the courtyard. I imagined him weaving his way through the throngs of people, and I still marveled at how he could trace our scent. At night, I envisioned him curled up and snoring softly in

Mrs. Ding's courtyard, as though picturing it in my mind had the power to make it the truth.

Only Lan could find any joy in the journey. People in the cars were kind to her and the ones in seats occasionally let her sit on their laps so she could get a better view through the window. This happened only the first few days. After that, we were so filthy from sitting on the floor that no one in the seats wanted to touch us. My clothes and the exposed skin of my wrists and hands were black, as though I had fallen into a tub of coal.

As we neared Shenzhen, the Nationalists were in the final stages of their retreat from the mainland. At every station, train passengers exchanged updates, tidbits of news picked up from vendors and station workers. Apparently, the Nationalists had been relocating their military resources to Taiwan since August. Chiang Kai-Shek had bounded back from his retirement and led the retreat, with about sixty planes flying daily between China and the island. Approximately two million Nationalist soldiers and civilians migrated by air and sea. On December tenth, the same day that we had left Qingdao, the Communists had attacked the last Nationalist-controlled city in Chengdu. After a failed defense, Chiang Kai-Shek and his son Chiang Ching-Kuo narrowly escaped via the Chengdu airport and made their final journey to Taiwan, never to return to China again.

By the time we arrived in Shenzhen, the Nationalists were gone, and all of the mainland had fallen.

21

BORDERLINE

Shenzhen's train station had been built by the British in 1911, the last stop in mainland China on their Kowloon–Hong Kong railway line. Passenger train service between Hong Kong and China had been suspended since October 14, 1949, just one day before the Communist victory in Guangdong Province.

The station itself had a long, squat main hall and a chain-link fence partially covered by wild vegetation. Our limbs were sore and tingling from lack of movement, and we braced against one another, wobbling through the train car and down the stairs to the platform. It was so warm that it felt like early spring in Shandong, except the air was moist. Around us, people spilled out chaotically in droves, as though the train cars were vomiting their contents onto the platform. Human encampments littered the station, often just blankets on the dirt ground; hundreds of refugees from the North had already settled along the sides of the tracks.

The main station building had high wooden beams, and it was flanked by rickety vendor stalls selling sugarcane, pears, peanuts, and dried oysters. Posters of Mao Ze-Dong and his premier, Zhou Enlai, were plastered on the walls, and the red flag of the Communist Party hung triumphantly at the entrance and exit. From farther away, we could hear the booming voices of Communist cadres singing victory songs in the streets to praise Mao's glory and celebrate the unification of the mainland.

We had fled from one Communist-controlled city only to land in another, now with fewer resources and no family contacts. It was December eighteenth, my birthday, but it didn't matter. We had to find shelter, and we had to find food.

Di looked at the sprawl of refugees around the train station and put down her bag, which was still partially filled with hard bread that she had carefully stacked and arranged. "Are we going to stay here?" she asked warily.

"No," answered Mom, double-knotting the cloth that held Lan on her back. "These people are probably all trying to figure out how to get permission to enter Hong Kong."

"Don't we need to do that too?" I asked.

"Maybe," said Mom. "But I suspect that it is not so strict. Look at the people who are out here—they are almost all men."

"I heard someone on the train say that the government has banned the entry of Nationalist soldiers in uniform," Di said.

"I know," Mom replied. "But we heard so many things on the train about what the rules are, who is allowed and who is not. At this point, we might as well try first and see what the authorities do. If they turn us away, at least we can ask them what the requirements actually are. Pick up your bag, Di. We've been sitting for a week, so we might as well walk now."

"Now?" Di and I cried together. Although we had been sitting, we were exhausted and covered with grime.

"Not all the way to Hong Kong Island," Mom said, exasperated. "We just need to cross the border. It's not that far." She gestured to the stream of people who had gotten off the train and were moving swiftly in unison, as though they were a school of fish, not out through the station, but along the railroad tracks. "Everyone is going to British territory. Do you think all of these people have permission to enter? What we do know for sure is that the train service has been suspended. Let's pray that the border is still open to us. If it is, it is only a matter of time before the authorities close that too. We need to be quick!"

Di and I nodded, capitulating. I didn't want to make the same mistake that we made in Zhucheng and lose an opportunity because we waited too long. With a grunt Di swung her bag back up. We flowed into the crowd and headed to the tracks, walking carefully to avoid tripping along the wooden slabs between the rails. It would be about five kilometers between the Shenzhen station in China and the Luohu station in Kowloon.

Farther away from the station, there was a group of uniformed Communist cadres, the ones whom we had heard singing earlier. Some of them looked young, perhaps even younger than me, and there was a mix of men and women. Like jubilant baboons, they jeered at us through the chain-link fence as we passed them. "Run to the white devils, you imperialist dogs!"

"Tell Chiang Kai-Shek that we're coming for him!"

"Mao Ze-Dong is going to kick out the foreigners!"

"The People's Liberation Army will lead us into Hong Kong next. See you in a few weeks!"

Beside us, everyone walked with grim faces, ignoring the cadres, who were only kicking the downtrodden. People from other parts of Guangdong had started coming to Shenzhen from the dirt roads, entering the station and going straight along the tracks to Luohu. There were even a few men in Nationalist army uniforms despite the supposed ban. They likely had been separated from the rest of the army during battle and walked here from other parts of the province.

With our movement, the sun, and the exertion of carrying the bags, we were beginning to sweat. We looked pathetic with our patchwork flour-sack bags and dirty faces, but we were in similar company. Everyone was tired, anxious, and afraid—but also determined.

As we approached the bridge connecting Shenzhen to Kowloon, there was a bottleneck because the entrance was too small, and also because people had stopped to line up at a small brick building that must have been an administrative office for the Hong Kong government. Shielding our eyes from the sun, we looked at the entrance to the bridge, which was just a brick tunnel for trains—the rest of the bridge was uncovered. Right before the overpass were six border guards. They were armed, but even with their weapons they could not hope to stem the flow of people who were passing through. Occasionally, someone would wave a piece of paper at the guards, but the majority were avoiding eye contact, walking tensely as though they expected the bridge to collapse at any second.

The border guards were observing the crowd, stopping some people and sending them to the brick office. From what we could see, every soldier in uniform was being weeded out. Soldiers behind us panicked and began shedding their uniforms, tossing them to the side of the tracks and proceeding naked toward the tunnel. I felt embarrassed for them, their skin bright and pale, dark tan lines showing where their clothing typically ended. Sometimes, the guards picked out men in civilian clothing. It was unclear what criteria the guards were following, but I noticed that they seemed to focus exclusively on male travelers.

A man dressed in a simple gray shirt and work pants approached us, a green canvas military bag on his shoulder. "Excuse me, ladies, are you all traveling alone?"

"No," Mom lied, placing her hands on our shoulders protectively. We never wanted to let people know that we were women alone. "My husband is in that brick building, waiting for our permits."

"Really?" the man asked, an awkward smile on his face as he attempted to look friendly. "I saw you all walking from the Shenzhen station." The three of us drew together like magnets before the man added quickly, "I don't mean you any harm. I was just hoping that I could escort you through the border. It's not safe for women traveling alone."

"Don't listen to him," said another man, speeding up to insert himself between the first man and us. He was well dressed, in a crisp Western suit, a briefcase in his hand. The mustache on his face was oiled and combed. "He wants to enter with you because he probably doesn't have a permit, and families have a much higher chance of passing than a man alone."

"Mind your own business, old geezer," the first man snapped, moving closer to Mom like he was claiming territory.

Unintimidated, the suited man kept pace, moving with an elegant confidence. "You should have more dignity than to try to piggyback on a mother alone with her children." He faced Mom, who was discreetly trying to steer us away from them both, and said, "Don't let anyone join your group. It's easier for a family to enter than for a soldier, but it is easiest for unaccompanied women and children. Hong Kong has a social welfare office that prioritizes protecting women and girls. If you want assured entry into Hong Kong, go alone."

"He doesn't know anything," the first man cried, lunging toward us. "Hong Kong is dangerous. There is crime everywhere and bandits are kidnapping girls left and right. Let me travel past the border with you and I promise I'll protect your family when we are in the city. Don't you want to go to Taiwan? Don't you think that will be easier if you are attached to a soldier? Vouch for me here and I'll vouch for you to Taiwan!"

Mom slowed her pace—he had uttered the magic word, "Taiwan," and from her expression I could tell that she was considering his proposal. We hadn't even thought about the restrictions or requirements for passage to the island.

"All hot air," the older man huffed. "Madam, if you want to do what is best for your girls, enter alone. Don't compromise what is ahead of you by wondering too far into the future."

Mom nodded, her initial suspicion outweighing the temptation of the soldier's promises.

"Who do you think you are, dressed like a foreigner?" the soldier sneered, his voice rising. "You think you are better than us? You probably are just trying to tag along with them yourself!"

The older man shook his head. "I have an entry permit. And I know all of this because I used to work for the Foreign Ministry in Shanghai. Starting in April this past year the Hong Kong authorities issued guidance to regulate entry, but the rules are not well enforced. Soldiers like you can take your chances going past the guards or go directly to the visa office and try your luck there. You can make multiple attempts to cross—they won't remember you. Sooner or later one of the guards will let you slip by."

"Arrogant devil," the first man spat. He left us and pushed on faster toward the entrance of the tunnel. I felt relieved as he disappeared, blending into the crowd ahead.

"Thank you for your help," said Mom to the suited man, for chasing away our unwanted companion.

"You are welcome," he replied, tipping his hat. "Good luck, and take care! See you on the other side!" He sped forward too, pulling out a piece of paper from his pocket. Farther ahead, I could see his arm as he flashed the form at the guards. I thought about how confidently Mom had shown our fake travel permit, and I couldn't help but wonder if his Western suit and his bravado had all been an act.

Mom pushed us all toward the entrance of the bridge, where the two guards had started rejecting naked soldiers too. My shoulders tensed as we approached, and I held my breath, hoping that the older gentleman was correct. The guards didn't even blink an eye as we slipped by, the darkness of the tunnel engulfing us momentarily. Past it, we saw the silvery steel frame of Luohu Bridge, a mere seventy meters between us and freedom. In later years, people would risk their lives to cross this border, many swimming across the river in desperation to escape from the Communist regime. For us, this short walk was one of the simpler parts of our journey.

Across the river at the Luohu station, the number of makeshift encampments was easily ten times that at Shenzhen. We heard that in the past two months alone, about two hundred thousand refugees had passed from China to Hong Kong. Most people would move farther toward Hong Kong Island in due course, but Luohu was the place where weary travelers, many of whom had been walking for days, could finally feel at ease and take a break.

There was a water pump nearby, and vendors were selling saltfish and rice cakes from wooden stalls. My mouth watered, but I knew better than to ask Mom for money.

We found a place to put down our bags, which had chafed badly against our shoulders, reminding me of our wheelbarrow's straps. Mom let Lan down and examined our surroundings, rubbing her sore back. The soldier who had wanted to escort us had made it through as well. He squatted in the dirt with his green bag open, eating a slice of pork jerky in big bites. I couldn't help but think that if we had allowed him to join us, maybe we would also be eating pork jerky now.

Mom surprised me by pulling me and Di in for a tight hug. "Happy birthday, Hai," she said.

I thought she had forgotten. Despite my fatigue, I smiled. "Thanks, Mom."

"Let's celebrate with some hard bread," she joked, since it was the only thing that we had to eat. We sat down on the dirt, too tired to do more than open our bags and dip our hard bread in some water. For now we were safe from Communist persecution, but the words of the heckling cadres remained in our heads. We could only hope that the People's Liberation Army wouldn't follow us across the border.

Hong Kong

22

MESSAGE IN A BOTTLE

Hong Kong was a city the likes of which I had never seen before. It was enormous, gleaming, almost alien, with massive construction and double-decker buses. The street markets were chaotic and crowded, with vendors lined up in between buildings, and walkways on both sides chock-full of shoppers. Laundry hung out of windows on wooden poles, and there were colorful posters everywhere advertising products from both the East and the West. Outside of hotels, rickshaw pullers lined up neatly like soldiers, waiting for customers. Some of the street names were strange and jarring to my ears—Victoria, Wellington, Hennessy, Pottinger. Not to mention the presence of so many European foreigners—men with shiny shoes and Western suits, and women with wide-brimmed cloth hats, belted dresses, and high heels, riding in shiny gilded rickshaws or fancy cars.

The British trod carefully with Mao's government, and they formally recognized the People's Republic of China on January 6, 1950—it was the first major Western power to do so, because of its unique position in Hong Kong and its substantial economic interests in the mainland itself.

For the first few weeks, we lived on the streets, picking through market garbage and eating the remainder of our hard bread. Mom attempted to nurse Lan, who whined because the milk came only in drops. Squatters crowded in tenements, but many others had neither family nor money and made temporary housing in alleys and under verandas. Even the rooftops had little tents now, and everywhere people were cooking, eating, and sleeping in the open.

Gangs of children roamed, gathering discarded wood for cooking, and digging in the garbage for dinner scraps. Di and I had trained well in Qingdao, and we had quick feet and even quicker fingers. A big rusty truck heavily loaded with produce hit a pothole, jostling a crate hard enough for it to crack open. Like confetti, hundreds of beans scattered onto the road, and we screamed joyously as though it were a Lunar New Year parade. Into the street we scrambled, nimble fingers snatching every bean as we dodged cars blaring their horns. "Squatter scum!" a driver yelled as his tires screeched. I almost got hit by a bicycle, its owner dinging his bell in anger as he whizzed by me. I was undeterred, though, excited because it had rained beans! We raced against other children to fill our pockets, gleefully scanning the ground for those waxy red treasures.

Every evening, we met Mom at the post office. On the street leading up to it, vendors who read and wrote letters for a living set up stalls to display their calligraphy. Mom handed a few precious coins to one of them to write a letter to Father—it was cheaper to just pay for the service than to source paper and ink. Since the charge was per word, we dictated only the basics—Father and Yei Yei's names, and a short sentence indicating that we were in Hong Kong and wanted to join them in Taiwan. The letter writer, a thin man with leathery brown skin and long, elegant fingers, assured us that many refugees sent such letters with no address, and through word of mouth they often found their destinations. I watched as his steady wrist moved the brush in expert strokes, and I marveled as the ink bloomed on the paper. It was the first time that I realized that a talent of mine, calligraphy, could be a source of income.

"Maybe I can set up a stand too," I said to Mom as she held the letter gingerly, waiting for it to dry.

"Don't be silly, Hai," Mom dismissed. "Look at all this competition. You are a girl, and a child too. No matter how great your calligraphy is, no one will think that you are a better writer than all these men here!"

Years ago, I would have agreed, and even if I hadn't, I would have deferred. Now, however, the idea remained a seed in my head. We'd made it to Hong Kong not by being demure, but by being resourceful, and any income was a rung on the ladder that would bridge the gap between our starvation and our survival.

After meeting at the post office, we looked for a place to camp for the evening. We couldn't stay anywhere for long. Squatter patrols diligently cleared street settlements, which had become niches for crime and posed fire and sanitation hazards. During the day, we kept our bags with us, which became lighter as we chipped away at the remainder of our provisions. The harsh realities of homelessness did not startle us anymore. What shocked us now was the ire of the local population.

For the first time in our lives, we were minorities. Most people in Hong Kong spoke Cantonese, the predominant language in Guangdong Province. Meanwhile, Mom, Di, and I spoke only Shandongese. We had a few basic Mandarin phrases that we could blurt out if pressed, but our thick Northern accents made us difficult to understand. Right away, people knew that we didn't belong, and the locals blamed us for bringing more poverty, disease, and crime to Hong Kong. What hurt me most was that these accusations were true. I was dirty. I was poor. I ate garbage. I didn't want to, but I couldn't help it. It was hard being akin to vermin in a glittering city.

Slowly, refugees like me began overrunning the urban area, a taint spreading like gangrene. Following World War II, the population of Hong Kong had been about six hundred thousand. By the end of 1950, it would balloon to two million. The Hong Kong authorities could no longer allow us to permeate unregulated. Police began to intercept refugees in the city center and direct them to a former battery on the west coast of the island, Mount Davis. Along the alleys and by the dumps, we heard chatter from other squatters that there was a place with food and lodging for people like us. It sounded too good to be true.

"It's probably a giant brothel," Mom said, "where lodging is a cage and women pay for rice with their bodies." She became even more suspicious when people insisted that women and girls would receive special treatment. We were too used to hustling for the bare minimum to believe anything was free. Many refugees had not entered with legal permits, and they ran in panic upon seeing a police officer. Some of them speculated that Mount Davis was a big trap, to centralize us so that the authorities could throw us in trucks and send us, shackled, back to the mainland. "Hide if you see the police," Mom warned us, certain that this was all a scheme.

While Mom took Lan to the Nationalist Liaison Office to inquire about travel to Taiwan, Di and I went back to the markets, ready to elbow our way through the throngs of shoppers. We took a detour to walk along the water, where we could see fleets of fishing boats dotting the sea far out toward the horizon. Many Chinese fishermen had fled the Communists via the ocean and were now living on their boats. *It must be nice,* I thought enviously, *to have a floating home, and fish for dinner.* In a lovely daydream, I pictured myself with a calligraphy stand, coins clinking as I churned out letters for hopeful people who gasped at the beauty of my writing. With my profits, I would buy us a boat. Mom would be at home cradled on the sea, with the breeze in our sails and with fish soup every evening.

"Maybe some sailors will have some fish scraps," I said to Di, my memory of savory fish soup so powerful that my nostrils flared, searching for its aroma.

"Old cabbage is easy to find," Di replied, adding to my imaginary stew, "and maybe even some scallions!"

A few boats were pulling in, and we ran to the docks, loosening our tongues as we prepared to beg in unfamiliar Cantonese. Behind us, we heard someone call out in Shandongese, "Hey, are you girls from the North?"

Excited to hear our language, I turned around, expecting another refugee. To my surprise, the speaker wore a gray police uniform, with tall white socks, a wide belt, and a pointed hat. He must have heard Di and me speaking to each other. He smiled at me with a set of neat white teeth, and I screamed.

"Di, run!" Throwing down our bags, the two of us sprinted away from the water toward the tangled streets, aiming to squirm into a squatter alley and lose him in the encampments.

The police officer had the height and build of a Northerner, and I could hear his big feet slapping closer and closer behind me as his long legs propelled him forward. "Stop!" he yelled. "I'm not going to hurt you!"

Lies, I thought, pumping my arms and legs harder. In the short time that we had been in Hong Kong, I had seen how police interacted with refugees. Regardless of their ethnicity—British, Chinese, or Indian—they yelled at us in languages we couldn't understand, and when we failed to comply, they only repeated their words more loudly and angrily. Along with the squatter patrols, they tore down tents, clubbed people who protested, and stormed the alleys as mothers scrambled to pick up children and pack their most precious possessions. My lungs were burning and there was a sharp pain in my knees, but I had to run faster. *I can't go back to the mainland. I can't go back to the Communists.*

The police officer's large hands grabbed the back of my shirt, the fabric tearing as he pulled me into his arms. I thrashed and squealed like a wild animal caught in a trap. Di slowed down to look over her shoulder at me, her eyes wide with dread. She had always been stronger, taller, faster. "Keep running, Di!" I bellowed. "Get as far as you can! Just run!" She let out a frightened cry, bowed her head, and sped up, her long braid trailing behind her like a kite.

"Calm down!" commanded the officer. "I said I won't hurt you, but if you keep struggling, I will have to!"

His arms were like iron, a hold that I couldn't possibly break out from. I cursed myself for my carelessness, my fish soup fantasy having cost me my freedom, and I let my limbs fall limp.

"That's better," he said, lowering his arms and stepping back, keeping a firm grip on my wrist. "I just want to talk to you. You aren't in trouble."

His tone was gentle, but I was suspicious. "How come you speak Shandongese?" I asked.

"I was recruited from Weihaiwei," he answered. Weihaiwei had been leased to the British prior to the 1930s. "There are a few hundred police officers here who were trained there to serve in Hong Kong. I'm a Northerner like you are. Where is your hometown?"

Strangely, knowing that he was from Shandong eased my fear—in a city where we felt like scum, it was encouraging to see that one of us Northerners was in a position of power. *One of us.* When I left Shandong, I hadn't realized how important my linguistic and provincial identity would become. "I am from Qingdao," I said, still wary enough to avoid disclosing that I was actually from Zhucheng. "But I've been to Weihaiwei. When the Japanese bombed Zhucheng, my family lived there for a few years. We had a house with a roof made of kelp!"

The policeman smiled. "Yes, the kelp roofs are warm in the winter and cool during the summer. Why are you in Hong Kong, then, Little Sister?" he asked. "Is your father a Nationalist soldier?"

I bit my lip, unsure of what to say. Since I'd come from the mainland, my first instinct was to deny any affiliation with the Nationalist Party. But in Hong Kong, could it be a good thing? Officials were always on one side versus another. My safety hinged on convincing him that we were on the same one.

The police officer let go of my arm. "This isn't an inquisition," he said. "I'm asking because there is help available for you if you recently came from the mainland. You must be hungry, right? I can take you somewhere with food. I can take your whole family."

Mom's voice rang loud and clear in my head. *Never go anywhere with a strange man, no matter what he promises you.* "No, thank you," I said politely, shifting away from him. "I'm fine. I just need to go find my sister."

The policeman sighed. "Okay, show me your ID card so I can make a note, and I'll let you go."

I didn't have an ID card, but I couldn't let him know that. Regardless of whether he favored the Communists or the Nationalists, he was in charge of enforcing the rules in Hong Kong—which I had broken when I crossed the border. "I have one," I said, squaring my shoulders, trying to look as confident as I imagined Mom would in this situation, "but I left it at home."

He nodded skeptically, as though this were an excuse that he had heard before. "We can go together to your home, then, so you can get it."

I swallowed. Now what? I didn't even have a home. I couldn't take him anywhere, especially not to my family. If he was going to send me back to the mainland, at least I could take comfort knowing that Mom and my sisters were safe in Hong Kong. But I was so afraid to go back to China alone. I wasn't brave enough to face it all, alone. Maybe I could return to Qingdao and stay with Uncle Sen. What if he had died already? Would Mrs. Ding adopt me?

I began to cry, glad that Di wasn't there to roll her eyes and call me a coward. "Please don't send me across the border," I said. "Please. I can't go back there."

The policeman crouched down so that he was closer to my eye level, removing his hat so I could see his face. His eyes were far apart, and he had a curve in his nose and thin pink lips. "I'm not going to deport you, Little Sister. We just can't have so many people like you out on the streets anymore. It's dangerous too—young girls are being kidnapped and sold."

Sniffling, I wiped my face with my dirty hands, still uncertain of what would happen to me. There were worse fates than deportation, such as being locked in a giant brothel. "Where are we supposed to go?" I asked.

The policeman reached into his pocket, pulled out a few pieces of dried cuttlefish, and handed them to me. "I'm going to take you to Mount Davis."

23

MOUNT DAVIS

I had been at the police station for what seemed like hours when Mom and Di burst through the doors. Jumping from my chair, I ran to them and flung my arms around my family.

"Are you hurt?" Mom asked, holding my face in her hands, her cold fingers soothing against my hot cheeks.

"I'm okay," I answered. Surprisingly, I had had a good time. The policeman, Officer Li, assured me that he was going to keep me only temporarily, and he gave me buttery maltose crackers and sweetened milk tea. There were crumbs on my shirt, and there was a cozy warm feeling in my stomach from my hot beverage.

Right away, Di noticed the crumbs and the empty cup by my chair and said, "We were worried sick about you, and you've just been sitting here having tea and eating cookies?"

It turned out that after I had been caught, Di had run all the way back to the urban center. After asking around for the Nationalist Liaison Office, she found Mom, still in line after waiting all morning. As soon as Mom heard what had happened, she broke her own rules and approached every police officer on the street, using a clumsy mix of Mandarin and invented sign language to find me. Thinking that Mom was trying to report a kidnapping, one Cantonese officer hurriedly took her to a colleague who spoke Shandongese. Relieved that it wasn't actually a kidnapping, the Shandongese officer explained what had likely happened, and he guessed which station I would be at based on the location of our encounter.

Brushing the crumbs away, I said, "I would have left, but Officer Li wouldn't let me go. He told me that I had to wait until he had time to take me to the Immigration Office for registration." The police station that we were in was far larger than Cousin Wei's in Qingdao. There was a hallway with a flickering light, which must have led to offices. A creaky door opened, and I heard Officer Li's slapping footsteps coming our way. "Here he is. You can ask him if you don't believe me!"

Officer Li waved when he saw us. "Madam, you must be Hai's mother?"

Before he could say more, Mom bowed and said, "Yes, I'm very sorry for the inconvenience that my daughter has caused you. Thank you for being kind to her."

As much as I appreciated Officer Li's delightful snacks, I resented the implication that I was an inconvenience—he was the one who abducted me and dragged me to the station! He was the one who had made us all worry.

"You are welcome," Officer Li replied, seeming pleased. "She was very good, no trouble at all." Noticing Di, he said, "I see you came back. You are a fast one!"

"Thank you," said Di, taking it as a compliment. "Can I have crackers too?" Mom glared at her, embarrassed, but Di pretended not to notice.

Officer Li laughed. "Yes, of course. I'll bring out some more crackers. But first, I need to talk with your mother. You girls can wait here. Please come with me, madam."

Di and I sat together in the chairs as Mom, Lan, and Officer Li disappeared down the hallway. Di picked up my cup and tipped it back to get the remaining drops of milk tea. "I'm exhausted," she complained. "Do you know how far the Liaison Office is from where we were? My legs are killing me. I wish you didn't tell me to run!"

"I was saving you," I said defensively. We were lucky that Officer Li turned out to be genuinely helpful—for every one of him, there were probably ten bad men who captured girls for other reasons. "I was making a sacrifice!"

"You were paranoid," she snapped. "If you didn't freak out in the first place, we could have all just come to the station together like civilized people! I should never have listened to a chicken like you." Putting her hands under her armpits, she flapped her elbows to mimic having wings.

"I'm not a chicken!" I retorted angrily. If she thought I was going to apologize for being cautious, then she was sorely mistaken. Instead, I said what I knew would upset her even more: "Also, Officer Li gave me dried cuttlefish. And I ate it all. There's none left and it was delicious!"

By the time Mom and Officer Li returned, Di and I weren't on speaking terms, and we sat fuming with our backs toward each other. Mom didn't care, because Officer Li had managed to convince her that Mount Davis was legitimate, and she was excited to go somewhere with food and housing. According to Officer Li, the British government was discreetly funding humanitarian services through charities and nongovernmental organizations that could provide relief to the incoming refugees without creating more political conflict with mainland China—Mao was already angry that Hong Kong was hosting so many Nationalist sympathizers.

As Di and Lan crunched on crackers, I boldly asked Officer Li if I could have some paper and a pencil. Mom was mortified and protested that they were unnecessary, and when he went to his office to retrieve a few sheets, she hissed, "Officer Li is not Uncle Wei. We cannot keep asking him for favors!"

Mom smiled when Officer Li returned with a small pile of scrap paper and a sharpened pencil, and she thanked him as though he had given us a sack of gold.

"Catching up with your studies?" he asked me.

I only nodded and smiled. Di and I hadn't had any teaching for at least two years now. Though I would have liked to catch up, I had no idea how. I wanted the paper so that we could save money on letters later—so that I could write to Mrs. Ding and Uncle Sen.

Together, we left the police station and went straight to the Immigration Office to apply for ID cards, which we needed in order to register with the Social Welfare Office. In the short time frame before our arrival at Mount Davis, my hopeful imagination had taken flight, fueled by the sugar from the maltose and milk tea. Officer Li had said that Mount Davis was formerly part of Britain's coastal defense, and it had barracks and an artillery depot. During World War II, the Japanese used its buildings to detain prisoners of war. It didn't sound glamorous, but from my perspective anything with four walls and a roof would be extraordinary. I didn't know much about Britain then, except that it was a wealthy country that was powerful enough to steal our land. Their former military site must have been pristine and well stocked, with pantries bursting with loaves of bread and barrels of plump sausages.

At the Immigration Office, we had met another Northerner, from Shanxi, Mr. Chong, a former soldier, who was also heading to Mount Davis. He was in his thirties, nearly bald, and he dressed in clothing that was high quality and tailored to fit, but filthy. When he heard us speak in our dialect, he asked if we had met anyone else with his surname and from his province. Months ago, he had written to his wife and daughters, instructing them to meet him in Guangzhou. Before they could reunite, the Nationalists had retreated and Mr. Chong fled across the border. Now that the border security was intensifying, he was worried that his family would be trapped in China.

"I have two daughters, younger than you two girls," he told us sadly. "Without me, my family has no income. I miss them so much, and looking at you all hurts, because I see them in your place. I can only pray that the Communists will be merciful. And if not, I just hope that someone is being kind to my wife and girls—giving them a place to stay if they are cold, and food to eat if they are hungry. I would give anything to find them."

Seeing Mr. Chong's despair when he spoke about his daughters infected me with melancholy. I couldn't help but think of Father, and I wondered if he missed us at all. In Taiwan, he was childless. Did he feel lonely without us? Did he worry? I wanted to believe that somewhere in Taipei he was having this same conversation with a set of strangers, was aching as he recounted the heartbreak of leaving us behind. More than anything else, I wanted an excuse to forgive him, to stop lamenting what he had done. Our letter to him was probably on a steamboat by now, careening away with no address, as aspirational as a message in a bottle.

With Mr. Chong, we walked toward Mount Davis, which the

government referred to as the Citizens' Village. Immigration officers had told us to register at the Mayflower Hospital, the administrative site for their services. Mom had beamed when they handed her our ID cards; knowing that we would not be punished for entering illegally lifted a hefty weight from our shoulders. As we crossed through Kennedy Town, we began to notice a distinct odor. It was common for big cities to have grungy areas here and there, but this stench was becoming increasingly powerful as we approached our destination.

I had been expecting a charming citadel overlooking the sea. Instead, we found an ugly hillside swarming with unwashed and unkempt men with hollow eyes and broken expectations. They roamed the unpaved footpaths like members of the undead, the skeletal and unsatiated remnants of Chiang Kai-Shek's army. I knew that as beggars we could not be picky, but when a ragged man dropped his pants, grunted, and defecated by a tree, I wondered if we might be better off back in the urban alleys. But we had no choice now—the police were rounding up homeless refugees and herding them here.

Every squatter camp that had been torn down seemed to have popped back up like tumors on the hillside, marring the landscape with flimsy tents and rickety mud huts. Many of these structures were just triangles made of oil paper or rattan mats braced over bamboo poles. When the wind blew toward us, the smells were a full-on assault, as though we were in a giant latrine built in a fish market's garbage dump.

"This is Mount Davis?" Di asked in disbelief.

There was a small concrete building that must have been the hospital. It was painted white, with red English lettering that we couldn't read. Chinese was written below it, but the paint was so faded and chipped that I could make out only a few characters. From the front doors extended a messy line of people, most of them with nothing more than a bag or two of their belongings in tow. "It must be," said Mom, clutching her backpack warily. "Those people must be waiting to register."

"Yikes, another long line," Mr. Chong exclaimed, wiping his forehead. "I guess we have nothing else to do, but I've done nothing but wait in lines since I got here!"

"Same with us," Mom said. "But if we can get regular meals, it will be worth the wait." After seeing the scrawny men on the hills, I had let go of any expectations regarding the quality or quantity of the food. Still, Mom was right. Even stale bread and old rice were welcome, especially if provided routinely. If we had calories to count on, Di and I could scavenge with less anxiety.

Filing into the line, Mom untied Lan to relieve herself of her weight. Most of the people ahead of us were men, sitting or lying on the ground, indicating that the line progressed slowly. "Are all of these people trying to go to Taiwan too?" I asked.

Mr. Chong put down his bags and squatted, resting his elbows on his knees. "Yes, of course. But going to Taiwan is harder than going to Britain at this point."

"I've heard that too," said Mom, sounding worried. "I was going to the Nationalist Liaison Office to understand the process, but I never ended up talking to anyone." I blushed, knowing that she had hurried away to find me at the police station.

A young man in front of us turned around, his teeth flashing as he grinned. "I'm sorry to interrupt, but I couldn't help but hear you speaking Shandongese. Are you also Northerners?" He looked like a teenager, only a few years older than me. He was well muscled, with a clean crew cut. His right leg had been amputated below the knee, and the wound was pulsing and swollen. Pus oozed from it, and parts of it had turned black. Beside him was a thick wooden stick that he must have leaned on for walking.

"Yes, we all are," answered Mr. Chong. "I am from Shanxi, and these lovely ladies are from Shandong." When he said "lovely," I knew it was just an expression, but it made me smile. On my newly minted ID card, there was a photograph of a ghastly girl with bony cheeks and limp shoulder-length hair. She wore my clothing, but her face wasn't mine. There were dark circles under her eyes, and she looked at the camera as though she were a shell with no soul. I had never been a beauty, even in Zhucheng, but I didn't think I was this ugly. Or was I? It pained me to think that I had become a girl version of the men we had seen ambling around Mount Davis. The presence of a boy close to my age made me even more self-conscious about my appearance.

The young man had a lopsided smile, and though his leg must have hurt, he seemed to be in good spirits. "We Northerners need to stick together," he said cheerfully. "I'm from Binzhou, in Shandong. My surname is Lin. Lin Biao-Wu. Don't know if you have met any Lins around here?"

"No," Mom said as she and Mr. Chong both shook their heads. "We are from Zhucheng, Shandong. My husband's surname is Ang. Have you met any Angs?"

Biao-Wu had not, nor had he met any Chongs. We were from too far apart in the province to know each other's families, though I wondered if he was related to the Lins who had been killed at the denunciation rally. In Qingdao everyone was a Northerner, but here in Hong Kong, speaking Shandongese was enough to make someone family—though not in all cases. On the streets, Northerners still stole from one another, beat one another, and in rarer instances killed one another. Generally, however, we tried much harder to get along than we had back in Shandong.

"It's been a long time since I have been home," Biao-Wu said wistfully. "I haven't seen my mom since 1948. I went south with the army as they retreated, and I wrote to my mom and siblings, telling them to meet me in Guangzhou. I've written to them five more times since then but haven't gotten anything back. It's hard for me to get mail, since I've moved around so much, but I'm hoping that since I'll be in Hong Kong for a while, I might be able to hear from them." So many soldiers had similar stories—like Biao-Wu and Mr. Chong, they had fought loyally for the Nationalists, only to realize that they should have saved their loved ones earlier. How bitter it must be to have remained a dutiful cog while the leaders above—Uncle Jian included—had known for months that this war had been lost, and rushed to evacuate their own families as the Communists advanced.

"My dad was a Nationalist soldier," Biao-Wu continued, filling our waiting time with tidbits of his life. He spoke with the assurance of a man who knew he was handsome, and was accustomed to kindness. "He was killed by the Japanese in the Second World War. It's just my mom left, and my grandparents. After my dad passed away my mom went to Jinan to work. She told me not to go to the military because she couldn't bear to lose me, but I wanted to make a name for myself so I could take better care of her when she's old."

"I hope your mother is safe and well, wherever she is," said Mom sympathetically. "You are a good son."

"Not really," said Biao-Wu, massaging his wounded leg. "I went into the army after she told me not to, and now who knows if we will ever see each other again? I was sixteen when I left. Back then, I thought the war would be over by my eighteenth birthday. I guess I wasn't wrong about the end of the war—I just joined the wrong side of it."

Mr. Chong laughed bitterly. "All of us here did," he said as he touched a leather bracelet on his wrist, which his eldest daughter had braided. "And our families are the ones who will suffer."

Every minute of Mr. Chong's life in Hong Kong was steeped in guilt. Though Mom reminded him that his own survival was essential to his family's well-being, he considered himself a coward. Mr. Chong and many others at Mount Davis refused to identify as "refugees," despite having fled from persecution. They associated the word with fear and desperation. Many of these border crossers were intellectuals, business owners, or government officials. Though destitute, they were proud, and considered themselves to be in a difficult but temporary situation—like Mom had when we were in Mr. Zhang's shed.

After three hours in line, we finally reached the registration table. A stout British man greeted us. He had a bushy beard that looked like a garden gone awry; it started under his eyes and went all the way to the middle of his neck, merging with his hair so that it looked like he wore a mask made out of an animal's pelt. When he waved to Lan she cried, clapping her hands over her eyes as though not seeing him would render her invisible. Mom frantically buried Lan's face in her chest to muffle the noise, and blurted out one of the only English words that she knew: "Sorry! Sorry!"

His name was Guh-Ling—"Colin"—and he didn't seem bothered. He spoke kindly to us in broken Mandarin as he copied the information in our ID cards. He told us that we were in luck—the former smallpox hospital had been converted to a temporary shelter, and rooms were reserved for women, children, and wounded soldiers. According to Colin, the four of us got the last open "room," which was actually a closet. There was no window or ventilation, but we felt like we had won the lottery—we would have a door, and a real roof over our heads. Biao-Wu was assigned a bed in a large shared room with other veterans in urgent need of medical treatment. Mr. Chong, meanwhile, was instructed to look for open turf along the hillside, and set up his own shelter with whatever he could find. As he left anxiously to scrounge for anything waterproof, we moved on to another line, for food vouchers.

My life in Mount Davis was a series of winding and tedious lines, as we and thousands of others waited for hours four times a day for food vouchers and then again for meal service. The daily reward for our patience was two bowls of rice porridge sparsely laced with cabbage, carrots, and rare slivers of shredded pork. Di and I still went to the markets to supplement our meals—we had to. Mount Davis had no running water, electricity, or basic sanitation facilities, but we were still grateful every time we stepped into our temporary shelter—especially when the weather was foul.

A few weeks after we were settled, Mom took us all to the Nationalist Liaison Office again after hearing about so-called Taiwanese entry permits, which everyone wanted but nobody had. The sky had been clear when we set out, but after we had waited an hour in line, dark storm clouds appeared in the distance, unfurling as rapidly as ink on wet paper. Within twenty minutes, we could no longer see the sun. Rain drizzled, and a few people at the end of the line bolted away. I didn't dare complain. We had waited so long, and we were only a few meters away from entering the building—it would be crazy to give up now! Huddled together, we protected Lan as it began to pour, water drenching our clothes and running down our backs.

"Hey!" someone in front of us shouted to the guard at the door. "Can we wait inside? It's cold and there are sick people and children out here!"

"Only thirty people are allowed inside at a time," the guard replied stoically. The first speaker groaned, and people began to shout, but the guard only added, "If I bend the rules, over a hundred of you are going to come charging through the doorway. It's a safety hazard!"

Lightning flashed above us, jagged and brilliant. Eyes on the sky, Mom picked Lan up and handed her to me. "Hai, take your sisters home. I'll keep waiting here." I could barely hear her above the sound of the water clattering on the roofs and pelting against the buildings.

"Come with us!" I shouted, uncertain how long the storm would last. "We can always come back to the office another day!"

Mom only pushed my shoulder, refusing to give up a second time. "I won't be long! Just go!" The rain was cascading in sheets, slamming on our shoulders like we were beneath a waterfall.

Nodding, I tucked Lan under me as Di and I ran from the line.

As we splashed toward Mount Davis, Lan began to scream as rain poured into her eyes and mouth. "Hush, Lan," I said. "It's only water. It can't hurt us; we just need to bear it until we get home. We'll be dry soon, I promise." I loved Lan, but she magnified every challenge tenfold.

A clap of thunder boomed like an explosion overhead and reverberated in my chest. Plowing forward, I leaped over puddles, my shoes soaked and my shoulders aching from Lan's weight. The wind had picked up and it pushed us like a bully, threatening to send us careening into the ground. "I hope Mom is inside the office now," I yelled to Di. "I hope she's okay!" Di said something back, but I couldn't hear her above the torrents of rain against my ears.

By the time we arrived at Mount Davis, rivers of muddy, putrid water were running down the hill, and tents were succumbing to the gales, flapping haphazardly before flying off their bamboo frames. Their inhabitants screamed and ran for shelter under trees or frantically charged into their neighbors' dwellings. This wasn't just a rainstorm—it was a typhoon.

Di pried at the door of our temporary shelter, and it blew open with such force that it slammed against the concrete wall. It took three people to help us pull it closed again, muffling the storm outside as it banged shut. There were hundreds of refugees crowded in the lobby and hallways, sopping wet and somber. As we wiggled our way to our closet, another clap of thunder shook the building.

"We should have never left Qingdao," Di said shakily, stepping into our closet and throwing her clothes on the floor with a wet plop.

Waiting for my eyes to adjust to the darkness, I reached blindly for a cloth that I could use to dry Lan, who was still bawling. More than ever, I missed Uncle Sen's house. Our closet was so musty and humid. With each move, we tumbled further down in the world. "I'm scared too," I admitted, wiping my face. "I don't know if we'll ever get out of this hellhole. From what everyone is saying, it sounds like going to Taiwan is impossible."

"I hope Mom at least gets some answers today," Di said. "I hope she gets home soon."

"Me too," I replied, wrapping my hair in an old shirt and pulling on some dry clothes. My life felt like the storm outside, like I was constantly battered by forces beyond my control, with no end in sight. The three of us nestled together under our thin blankets, the warmth of our bodies slowly pulling the chill from our bones. I could hear Lan sucking her thumb, and from how her head lolled against my shoulder, I knew that she was falling asleep.

We must have all drifted off, because Mom's arrival startled me awake. Some light filtered in through the windows in the hallway, illuminating the silvery pools of water that formed at Mom's feet.

"Thank the Gods you are back," I murmured, rubbing my eyes.

"Yes, it feels like a miracle," said Mom, coughing, closing the door, and shutting us once again in darkness. "Some of the streets were flooded by the time I left, and there was a mudslide on the hill. Hundreds of shelters have fallen apart, and there is no room to breathe in the lobby."

When I had told Lan that water couldn't hurt us, I was wrong. This storm would kill people. As it raged on, refugees moved farther into the shelter, so even the halls and stairways were filled. Finally, those inside bolted the front doors shut, and no one else could enter no matter how hard they pounded on the door and screamed to be let in. "Have mercy," a man in the lobby cried. "There might be children outside! We can take in a few more!"

Other people had braced themselves against the entrance. Another voice yelled back, "It won't be just a few! There are children in here too. We don't have an inch to spare and we will be crushed if people storm through the doors!" No one argued further. It was so packed that the shelter walls looked ready to buckle and collapse.

The storm didn't ease up until late morning, when the sun finally crowned through the clouds, unaware of the mayhem and suffering wreaked in its absence. Our shoes sank into the muddy ground, which was littered with tree branches and other debris. The hillside had been devastated. People searched desperately for their belongings and parts of their shelters that had blown away. Under some of the ruined huts, human limbs stuck out—an arm here, a leg there. A few bodies lay splayed in the wet grass, faces so smeared with dirt that it was impossible to recognize them.

I pitied the dead, but more than that, I felt relief that Mom wasn't among them. How close had she come to losing her life by stubbornly waiting in that line?

In chaos there was opportunity, and survivors rushed to claim anything of value. I knew it was bad karma to benefit from the misfortune of others, but poverty was its own war, and we needed all the help we could get to make it out alive. After the storm, Mr. Chong made himself a better shelter with salvaged panels of tar paper, Mom picked up a blanket, and I found a cooking pot. In a soggy tangle of clothing, Di spotted a thin, polished stick. She pulled on it, revealing fine frayed hairs at its end—a writing brush.

"Can you do anything with this?" she asked me.

I held it up in the sun, marveling at her muddy finding as though it were a gem. "Yes!" The handle was cracked and some hairs were broken or bent, but it would be functional. "This is fantastic!"

Di crossed her arms, proud and smug. "Consider it a late birthday gift."

I stroked the end, trying my best to straighten the hairs. "Thank you, Di. But now I have to find a gift for you." Her birthday had been shortly after mine.

Di just shrugged and said, "As soon as you make some money writing, buy me something nice to eat." Her reply stunned me. Not only had she paid attention when I told Mom about setting up a calligraphy stand, but she also remembered the conversation. Even more astonishing, she believed that it was actually possible—that I could compete, and maybe succeed. I carefully stowed the brush, hoping that its owner wouldn't miss it. Being poor made me a worse person, but it had also made me a braver one.

24

CLOSED DOORS

After risking her life waiting in line, Mom had met with a liaison officer who only confirmed what other refugees had told us—though the Hong Kong authorities were desperate to send us to Taiwan, the Nationalist government was hesitant to accept us. The process for getting an entry permit was convoluted, and required that an application be submitted by a sponsor already in Taiwan and vouched for by two senior military officers. For all of us at Mount Davis, it seemed like the stars and planets had to align just right for that to happen. Many of us didn't even have an address in Taiwan to write to, let alone a person willing to complete the paperwork.

In February, we said goodbye to Mr. Chong, who'd decided to return to mainland China to find his family.

"What if the Communists kill you?" I asked.

Mr. Chong replied resolutely, "There's no point in being safe here without my wife and children. I can't be happy knowing that they might be in danger. Other soldiers defected during the war. Mao can just consider me a late defector. I don't care who I swear allegiance to—I just want to go home." When he said that, I admired him and envied his girls even more. I reminded myself that Mom loved us, and that should be enough. But my stomach was in knots because I knew that while Mr. Chong would risk death for his daughters, my father might not even be willing to fill out the paperwork for our permits.

On a sunny day, the Hong Kong authorities sent trucks to take Mr. Chong and others who wanted to return to China to the border, only to have the Guangdong immigration officers send them all back. Mao's government considered these Nationalist loyalists a liability, and potential troublemakers were not welcome.

Mr. Chong returned to Mount Davis, head hanging as he shuffled back to his hut. "I spent all that effort trying to escape China, and it turns out they don't even want us. I'll have to find a way to cross the border illegally—again!"

Biao-Wu and I trailed behind him, mud squelching beneath our shoes. "I heard the Communists are much more severe about punishing illegal immigrants," Biao-Wu said. "They will probably shoot you if they catch you!"

"Immigrant!" Mr. Chong exclaimed. "I'm a Chinese man. I'm from Shanxi! Immigrant, my ass."

The next day, Mr. Chong left for Sha Tau Kok, a small town in the North with a more relaxed border—when the British demarcated their territory after the Second Opium War, they drew their line straight through Sha Tau Kok, with only a stone marking the boundary. Shoppers often wandered back and forth, and success at that crossing was relatively high. We didn't know if he made it, because we never heard from him again after his departure. However, I chose to believe—I needed to believe—that a father who loved his girls that much would succeed in reuniting with them.

Shortly after Mr. Chong left, Biao-Wu made a spectacular announcement of his own. "The Nationalists agreed to take back their veterans, so the Hong Kong authorities have commissioned a ship for nine hundred of us to go to Taiwan!" His eyes sparkled with excitement as we congratulated him, even though the news was bittersweet for us. We had a soft spot for Biao-Wu, who clicked with our family like a missing puzzle piece. When we had first arrived, we spent several days together in the hospital waiting room. Biao-Wu's leg had rotted so badly that doctors had to re-amputate it, cutting just above his knee. Lan, meanwhile, had one leg that was much shorter and thinner than the other. She could walk only by holding someone's hand for support, and anything more than a few meters caused her pain. The doctors were far more concerned about her malnutrition than about her leg, but unfortunately they could not fix either. They sent us away with nothing but a small bottle of vitamins.

As Biao-Wu prepared for his trip, I reluctantly wrote another letter to Father. Mom considered Biao-Wu's good fortune our own, and asked him to help us contact our family. When I handed him the folded paper, he enthusiastically promised to deliver it. "I will ask every soldier for that Uncle Jian of yours, find your family, and go with them to pick you up from the docks after your permits come through!"

Mom was so grateful, but I was skeptical. We'd had no answer to the letter that we had mailed over a month before. Maybe it hadn't reached Father, but I suspected that he had ignored it upon its arrival. My dark heart was in a constant battle between the child in me who wanted to believe the best of my father and the survivor in me who knew that I couldn't rely on him.

When I had the chance, I pulled Biao-Wu aside in the hallway and said, "I have another favor to ask of you when you get to

Taiwan. If my father won't sponsor our entry permits, will you do it?" Even in Hong Kong, Mom continued to tell people that our separation from our family had been a misunderstanding. As I exposed the brokenness of our family to Biao-Wu, I felt ashamed that I had yet another secret to hide from her.

Biao-Wu was confused by my request. "Hai, of course your father will sponsor your entry permits. He's your father! Although it's actually your uncle Jian who needs to complete the application, since your father isn't part of the military. But I know your family will come through for you. Have some faith!"

My lips were pressed together in a straight line. I could never explain to someone like Biao-Wu, who had had the love of his father and adulation of his grandparents, just how fragile my family ties were.

His face grew serious when I didn't reply, and he added, "But I promise you, if something goes wrong, I will personally sponsor you."

"Thank you," I said, wrapping my arms around him and squeezing my eyes shut against his chest so he couldn't see my tears. Such a hug between an unmarried, unrelated man and woman was inappropriate, but his promise was a parachute, and with it I could finally permit myself to be hopeful.

After Biao-Wu boarded the bus for the harbor, we felt his absence every day. Lan asked for him incessantly, unsatisfied with Mom's explanation that he'd gone to Taiwan and we would meet him there soon. Mom spoke about Taiwan with certainty, as though we were on a train and it was the next stop—that all we needed to do was be patient, and we would arrive.

A few days later, we went to line up for food vouchers and were startled to see Biao-Wu waiting for registration.

"I thought you went to Taiwan!" Mom exclaimed as Lan squealed with delight.

"The government wouldn't take me," Biao-Wu replied, shoulders slumped, the weight of the wasted journey having sapped his strength. "But don't worry," he added, forcing an unnatural smile. "I gave your letter to one of my friends who was admitted. He said he would deliver it on my behalf. I trust him, and he gave me his word, so I know it'll reach your family."

It turned out that the Nationalist government had accepted all of the able-bodied soldiers on that ship but refused to take any veterans with disabilities. The bed in Biao-Wu's former room had already been given to someone else, but the hospital volunteers gave him a thin pad that he could lay on the floor.

"What is most insulting," Biao-Wu told us over dinner, "is that I could have worked as a soldier. I can hold a gun. Even with my crutch, I'm still decently fast. There's also desk work that soldiers do. When I was on the battlefield, the Nationalists promised that no soldier would be left behind. After I took that long-ass boat ride to their pitiful little island, they didn't even look at me—they just turned me away."

When he joined the army, Biao-Wu had been a golden boy, strong, attractive, and charismatic. He was still all of those things— I saw all of those things, and was furious at the Nationalists for their callousness. He had given his leg for their cause, and that very sacrifice rendered him invisible. Taiwan must be the perfect place for Father, I thought—a land settled by powerful men who saved only themselves and those they deemed worthy.

By the end of February, there were too many new arrivals at Mount Davis who were in dire need of medical services. The Social Welfare Office had to make space in the temporary shelter, and Biao-Wu was considered able-bodied by their standards and sent to the hills. New squatter settlements popped up like ugly mushrooms, but hundreds of men slept on the grass with no shelter at all.

Meanwhile, our closet needed to accommodate two new women, Mrs. Tung and Mrs. Gao. Both of them were seventeen—only three years older than me—the young wives of Nationalist soldiers from Zhaoqing, in Guangdong. If it weren't for the war, my own family would have been identifying future suitors for Di and me by now, searching for potential alliances with prestigious families. Like Mom, these girls were hoping to join their husbands in Taiwan. For privacy, we put up a thin sheet to separate our spaces. We didn't talk much, because the two of them spoke only Cantonese, and the language barrier was far stronger than the fabric one.

Within a week, all of us got lice. My scalp itched so badly that I scratched open my flesh, finding little white eggs on my hands and blood beneath my fingernails. To get rid of them, we had to soak our hair in roach poison, which burned like fire. Mom gave up on Lan and shaved her head, and Lan thrashed and screamed the entire time. Looking at her patchy, blotchy scalp, Mom said only, "I suppose we aren't trying to impress anyone here."

The infestation was demoralizing, but Mom managed to cling to her optimism, certain that a letter from Father would arrive soon. Hospital volunteers distributed mail during the food voucher service, which became Mom's favorite part of the day. Her happiness while anticipating the letters was infectious, but her disappointment when the volunteers shook their heads was draining.

Unbeknownst to Mom, I had sent a letter to Mrs. Ding, telling her everything about our train journey, the border crossing, and our first few weeks in Hong Kong. I reassured her that we were well and that, for now, we were being fed and had a place to stay.

After asking her to send word about Lucky and Uncle Sen, I signed my name and borrowed postage money from Biao-Wu to mail it.

Each night, I imagined what a letter from Father, or even Uncle Jian, or Mrs. Ding, or Uncle Sen, would sound like. I spent hours in the dark composing letters to myself, even thinking about how the paper would look and feel in my hand. Sometimes the pretend news was good, and I found myself smiling in the dark. Other times the pretend news was bad, and I would cry as quietly as I could, hoping no one would hear me.

At the end of the month, an envelope arrived for Mom, who pounced on it like it was the elixir of life, expecting it to be from Father. When she unfolded the page within, however, the handwriting was not his; Nai Nai's name was at the bottom. Our hearts sank, for it could not be good news. Afraid to read its contents, Mom let the letter fall from her hands. Gently, I took it from her lap and reopened it, with Di's chin jutting out over my shoulder.

Nai Nai told us bluntly not to come to Taiwan. She said that Father had met someone else—a young nurse who had gone to Taiwan with the military. They were going to marry, and it was too late for us to change anything. She hoped that Mom could find a new husband in China and be happy.

So much power in a single piece of paper, a featherweight that felt like it could break us. I had been preparing myself for an outcome like this and shouldn't have been upset—but I was. It shouldn't have mattered—but it did. How many times did Father have to fail before I would learn? That thought triggered more distress as I realized that there would never be another time, because he was never going to see us again.

For several hours, Mom did not react. It was as though she had not heard the letter and couldn't digest its contents. Di and I, too frustrated to stay in one place, left to pick remains from the urban markets. We kicked up the dust in the road with our frantic, shuffling steps, trying to get as far away from Mount Davis as possible.

"Father is a shit," Di blurted as we passed the hospital. "He's a shit person. I hope he dies."

I should have chided her for such a horrifying wish, but instead I found her anger soothing. "I hate him too," I said, venom in my words. "This is what he wanted all along. A new family with lots of Ang sons to make up for all the Angs that the Communists killed."

"I hope he just has more daughters," Di remarked.

"Let that be a curse!" I added. The inferiority of girls had become so ingrained in our minds that comments like that slipped out without our thinking about what they meant. "I hope Nai Nai dies. I hope she gets tuberculosis and chokes on her own blood."

"That's too good for her," said Di, piling on. "I hope the Communists take over Taiwan and torture her, and Father too!"

"Yes, that's better," I agreed, admiring Di for her creativity. We were furious yet powerless. As I pored over little piles of slimy garbage, my rage built as I pictured Father's wedding, a lavish banquet that would surely have fresh crabs, fish, and meat. I hoped that he would cut his hands on crab shells and that every fish bone would lodge itself in his throat.

That evening, while we were waiting in line for food, Mom broke down like a rag doll that had lost all its stuffing. She fell to the ground and began to cry, burying her face in her hands to muffle her sobs. I looked at Di, and she understood me without any words being uttered. "I'll hold our place," Di said. "Lan can stay with me. You two go."

I held Mom by her arm and thought about all the times that I'd had to support Nai Nai, who tottered on her bound feet. It had rained briefly, and everything was wet. I led Mom to the side of the hill, took off my jacket, shuddering as the brisk, damp air hung around my shoulders, and laid it on a rock so that Mom could sit on something dry. She folded forward, placing her head in her lap, sobbing like the sky had fallen. "We should have stayed in Qingdao," she said. "Maybe I could have gotten a real job. Maybe we would have had better lives. At least we had a real home to stay in and we were making money selling bread. I dragged my girls here for what? To feed lice in this wretched hospital closet and eat slimy gruel? I'm so sorry, Hai. I'm sorry to Di. I'm sorry to Lan. I can't believe I was so stupid as to believe that your father would take us all back."

I didn't know what to say. For a child, witnessing a parent's complete and utter breakdown is a frightening sight. Mom was always the strong one in my eyes, our backbone even before we had been left behind. In the past year, throughout all the hardship, being with Mom had fueled my courage, as though she could channel her bravery to me. Seeing her so broken by despair took the breath out of my lungs, and all I could do was lean over her and hug her tightly as she cried.

I thought about our entrance to Qingdao, when I had lost all composure and had to be pushed through the city gates in a wheelbarrow. I thought of Mom then, unwavering and determined, and I drew on that version of her. I drew on me and Di wandering through the markets and selling buns in the cold, risking our lives for beans and passing corpses in the mud. I drew on holding Lan, shivering yet feverish with tuberculosis, and on the loss of Three, and on the days spent in the dirty shed, the filthy train, and the fetid alleys. I pulled threads from all of those moments when I'd had to be strong, so that I could be for Mom what she had been for me. I was no longer a child. I didn't have the luxury to be one—that had been taken by Comrade Cheng and the villagers of Zhucheng. It was taken by hunger, by exhaustion, and by the constant fight for survival.

"Don't be sorry," I said to Mom. "At the border to Hong Kong you said that we always need to try. They can turn us away if they want to, but at least we tried. And now, we figure out what to do with our lives. Even if it has to be just us, we can do it. One step at a time."

Mom looked up and wiped her eyes. "I just feel so foolish."

"Everyone is a fool in this war," I said, thinking of similar words that I had heard Mr. Chong say. "Don't you remember all of those soldiers ripping off their uniforms in Shenzhen and walking naked across the bridge?"

Mom managed a small laugh, her tears still streaming. "I've let you all down," she said, her shame underlining each word.

"No," I said firmly. "Father let us down." I almost began to cry as I emphasized that, and I stopped speaking.

Mom and I sat in silence for a few minutes, arms around each other.

"Father let us down," I repeated when I'd composed myself. "You have held this family up. You have held this family together."

Di walked over to us, Lan in her arms. "The people in line behind us said they will hold our space," she told us as the two of them reached out and hugged us too.

Mom started to cry again, and I couldn't help it this time. Di too started wiping her eyes, and only Lan looked at us solemnly, wondering why everyone was so sad.

"We will get through this," I said. "We are together and we are alive. We will find a way."

25

OPPORTUNITIES

Nai Nai's letter, as vicious as it was, gave me the gift of closure. I used to obsess about Father, wondering if he had received our letter, wondering what he might do about it. For hours, I replayed events in my past, as though analyzing those snippets of time could provide clarity on his mental state and his feelings for us. Though his definitive abandonment of us was frightening, there was also a freedom in finally burning that bridge. We began thinking of a long-term plan, and Mom began to look for work.

At the end of 1949 and in early 1950, there were several industrial strikes in Hong Kong, as workers demanded better conditions and fair pay. Many companies saw the influx of refugees as a solution to this problem, and eagerly exploited those desperate enough to work for long hours and pitiful wages. Many of the refugees who used to be lawyers, scholars, and doctors were now fighting for jobs as industrial laborers.

Biao-Wu found work at a match factory, where he easily produced tens of thousands of matches per day. Mom accompanied him one morning and told his manager that she used to work for a match factory in Qingdao, without disclosing that she only folded matchboxes. The manager hired her on the spot, relieved to have a worker who wouldn't need training. With Biao-Wu's help, Mom learned quickly and began to surpass him in production. They worked twelve-hour shifts, leaving Mount Davis before sunrise and running back home to squeeze into the dinner line before it closed. Spending the entire day on their feet was already a challenge. After the government employees learned to recognize us, Di and I convinced them to hand us Mom's and Biao-Wu's vouchers so the two of them could at least walk home at a forgiving pace.

A British social welfare officer named Anita, whom we called Ms. "Ang-Ni-Da," was especially kind to us. Ms. Anita was short, only a bit taller than Di, and had the most unique hair that I had seen—it was a light brown, and so tightly curled and voluminous that she couldn't wear a hat. She told us that it was the humidity that made it that way. Her eyes were gray, and she had freckles everywhere, even on her forearms and hands. Though she had access to an interpreter, she made a sincere effort to learn Mandarin and converse with us.

Ms. Anita occasionally brought candy for Lan, and, more important, she brought paper for me. I had told her that I was inching forward with my letter-writing service, and I was astonished by her enthusiasm. She said something in broken Mandarin about women owning businesses, and she returned the next day with a small inkstone to help get me started. "I am an investor," she said proudly, after flipping through her English–Mandarin dictionary. "Hope you make lots of money!" I was grateful for her help, and even more touched by her devotion to bridging the language gap between us.

With Lan on my back, and supplies in my hands, I marched to the post office. After selling buns in Qingdao, advertising my services felt natural. "Letter writing! Letter reading! Cheap and affordable services!" As I called out at the people passing by, I couldn't help but miss my wheelbarrow. Uncle Sen had probably sold it on the black market by now, a sad fate for an item that had acquired such sentimental value.

I had no stand, and I couldn't speak Cantonese, but I was willing to charge less. Holding the brush in my hand made me feel elegant, even with my worn clothing and dirty fingers. For so long, I had lived like an animal. Writing words, even when dictated by others, allowed me to reclaim some shreds of my humanity.

On the first day, I had so many customers that I ran out of paper. As I counted my coins, satisfied, another vendor spat on the ground and said, in Mandarin, "Don't look so smug. People are going to you because you are a charity case, like a blind masseuse. You aren't a good writer—you are only good at drawing pity."

I quickly closed my fingers, worried that he would try to snatch my bounty. Another vendor heard him and said, "Stop it, Gao-Bing. Don't be so cruel. Can't you see she's a little girl with a crippled baby?"

Gao-Bing sneered and countered, "Old Liao, she's a refugee and she's using that baby to get business, if you can even call it that. She's also charging less than we are and driving down the prices for us all!"

"Oh, come on," Old Liao replied. "She's just a beggar! Cut her some slack!"

Old Liao's pity was just as offensive as Gao-Bing's aggression. "I can speak for myself!" I snapped. The two of them thought Gao-Bing's words could hurt me, but they had no idea who I was. By now, I was accustomed to derision, disdain, and dirty looks.

With every month I spent crawling at the bottom of our society, I became a little wilder. "I'm not here to be an artist. I'm here to provide for my family. It doesn't matter why customers come to me, and I don't care what you think. Petty comments from a jealous man like you won't stop me from making money!"

Old Liao let out a hearty guffaw, smacking his table as he doubled over in laughter.

Gao-Bing fumed. "Do what you want, you urchin! But I'm warning you, you'd better stay far away from my stand. I don't want your stench to drive away my customers!"

"Don't blame me when it's your ugly samples that scare them!" I shouted back. I was glad Mom was at the factory; she would have been horrified to see me speaking this way.

"I'll take that as a compliment!" he bellowed. "They must be gorgeous if a hideous piglet with no taste dislikes them!"

I stuck my tongue out at him, my face hot. He was a jerk, but he was stronger than me and possibly vindictive. *It wouldn't hurt to set up farther away from him next time,* I thought as I slipped my brush and the coins into my pocket. With my profits, I could buy more paper. If the business pace kept steady, I could eventually buy a nicer brush. Maybe then I could set up my own calligraphy samples, which would blow Gao-Bing's out of the water.

True to my word, I found Di and the three of us went to buy springy fish meatballs and dragon beard candy with the money I had earned. Lan watched in awe as the hawker pulled maltose coated in powdered sugar until it became wispy like silk, and folded the fine strands around crushed peanut and shredded coconut. The candy was a whirlwind of textures, melting in our mouths, becoming chewy, then crunchy, a sugar bomb with a hint of salt. Food was joy. Food was love. As we sat on the street laughing and licking our sticky fingers, I felt proud that I could buy us a fragment of happiness. Finally, there was a light in this abyss that surrounded us.

While Mom was in the factory and I wrote letters, Di the diplomat began learning Cantonese and English, befriending restaurant owners who paid her a few cents to wash dishes and mop floors. In Qingdao, Mom and I had worried that Di was a bag of flour away from hopping into a tank and joining the Communist Party. Now that we were in Hong Kong, she had forgotten about Mao and had become fascinated by the British monarchy. Di at her core was a survivor, not a loyalist. Yet again, she had adapted.

Together, Mom, Di, and I hustled, with the goal of moving into a real apartment with Biao-Wu and our Cantonese roommates. No one at Mount Davis could afford to leave on their own—but a collective could squeeze into a tiny tenement apartment and make it work. Maybe we could even have electricity and running water again.

By the end of March, there were about five thousand refugees at Mount Davis as the battle for Hainan Island, one of the last Nationalist strongholds, raged on. More Nationalist soldiers arrived by boat and swarmed around the hospital's administrative office and the hillsides. Nearby, the wealthy families in Victoria Peak were becoming increasingly infuriated by the reek of poverty wafting toward them. Many of the rich were also foreigners and had been pressuring the government to relocate us since the beginning of the year.

The Hong Kong authorities sent another ship of nearly nine hundred Nationalist veterans to Taiwan. This time, Chiang's government accepted only those with entry permits. Thirty-five men disembarked in Taipei; everyone else returned to Mount Davis.

"This is outrageous," Biao-Wu exclaimed as he, Di, and I watched them line up to reregister at the hospital. We were with another Northerner, Han Ming-Zhu, a man in his late forties who had become our new Mr. Chong. "These are all able-bodied men. What is their excuse now?"

Mr. Han was originally from Hebei Province, and he had worked for the Ministry of Justice in Beijing. He was one of the first refugees to settle at Mount Davis, and he had made a sturdy wooden shelter with actual furniture inside it. Everyone knew Mr. Han, who made it his personal mission to meet all new arrivals. In response to Biao-Wu's question, he replied, "The government is afraid that Communist spies are hiding among us."

"So eight hundred worthy citizens are sent back to rot in Hong Kong because of the possibility of a single Communist among them?" Biao-Wu asked incredulously.

"Of course," Mr. Han said. "How can you be so naïve, Biao-Wu? National security is of the utmost importance. What do we know about anyone here really? Some of us arrived with documentation, but many only have their Hong Kong ID cards. A Communist intelligence officer could easily sneak past the border, go to the Immigration Office, and make up a fake name and a fake life." Leaning forward like he was telling a ghost story, he lowered his voice and said, "And just like that, Communists infiltrate our community, waiting for the first opportunity to go to Taiwan and destroy us from within!"

Biao-Wu crossed his arms. Because of this paranoia, thousands of soldiers stagnated in Hong Kong in miserable conditions. "I get your point," he said. "But still—with the right questioning, it would be pretty easy to figure out who is really one of our soldiers and who is an impostor."

"Of course not!" Mr. Han cried in disbelief. "So many of our soldiers defected during the war. They could easily come back as spies, or train others to pass our screenings. Think, Biao-Wu! You aren't fit for manual labor anymore, so you need to train your brain! If you can hone your intelligence, doors will open for you when you get to Taiwan."

"I already told you," Biao-Wu said, annoyed, "I don't want to go to Taiwan anymore."

Beside me, Di also spoke up. "I don't want to go to Taiwan either. I heard there are too many newcomers, and the government can't handle the resettlement."

Mr. Han was the most patriotic person I had ever met, and any criticism of the Nationalists, no matter how slight, triggered a robust defense. "Preposterous!" he said, indignant. "Resettlement takes time. It can't happen overnight! It's not like the British are doing a better job resettling anyone here. You two are being pigheaded. Both of you will have more opportunities in Taiwan than in Hong Kong. Here, we are in a colony ruled by foreigners. In Taiwan, we will be governed by our own people!"

Though Mr. Han had never been to Taiwan, he spoke about it like it was our homeland. Since I'd read Nai Nai's letter, however, thinking of the island only reminded me that Mom had been betrayed, and that my sisters and I were unwanted. I didn't want to be anywhere near the Ang family, and I was grateful that the sea stood between us. "How can you be so optimistic," I asked, "when your own entry permit hasn't even arrived?"

Mr. Han's elusive entry permit was a sore point. Huffing in anger, he said, "I'm not going to waste my time arguing with you children when you can't even understand that I'm giving you advice for your own good. My entry permit will come through, and when it does, I'll be laughing at you from my mansion in Taipei!" He waved us off, and since he was our elder we obeyed, slinking away as he continued to watch the miserable men in the registration line.

Di, Biao-Wu, and I all had different theories about Mr. Han. A man like him, with a prestigious position in Beijing, should have moved to Taipei long ago. Given his connections, his entry permit should have been expedited. Di disliked Mr. Han and thought he was a liar who had never actually worked for the Ministry of Justice. Biao-Wu, meanwhile, insisted that Mr. Han must have offended a senior officer, who was now blocking the approval of his application. Both of them thought I was crazy, but I was convinced that he was a spy and that he was here intentionally. There were rumors that the Nationalists had intelligence officers in Hong Kong dedicated to recruiting refugees for guerrilla attacks across the border. It would explain his suspicious nature, and his efforts to keep track of everyone at Mount Davis.

Mr. Han ignored us at dinner that evening, still upset about our earlier conversation. Along with Biao-Wu, the four of us sat on the ground to eat with some Northern veterans, all of us carefully balancing our bowls to avoid spilling any of our precious meal. Biao-Wu and his friends slurped loudly. Occasionally, one made a lewd joke and another scowled and pointed out that there were "ladies" around. There was nothing traditional about how we lived in Hong Kong. Our world had been broken by the war, but perhaps that meant that we could piece it together in a different way. Maybe here, we could finally live—not as we ought to, but as we wanted to.

26

THE LETTER

At the end of April another letter arrived. Mom was at the factory, and Ms. Anita handed the envelope to me as I was preparing to head to the post office. "For your mom," she said.

At first, I was excited, thinking that it was from Mrs. Ding or possibly Uncle Sen. When Ms. Anita was out of sight, I shredded the envelope and opened the letter, hoping to hear about Lucky. Goose bumps rose along my arms when I realized that it was from Uncle Jian.

I read the letter three times, not believing my eyes. Uncle Jian said that he was writing to us again, since he hadn't heard back from us and was worried that his previous letter had gotten lost. A repatriated soldier had given him our letter from Mount Davis, and Yei Yei wanted us to go to Taiwan. Uncle Jian would get our entry permits. Did we have any form of identification? If we did, he needed copies. If we did not, we had to get them as soon as possible. There was going to be another ship to Taiwan at the end of May. If the entry permits arrived on time, we might be able to go. We should write back to him as soon as possible—he listed an address in Taipei, written clearly so we couldn't mistake any of the characters.

I refolded the letter and held it in my hand as though it were a bomb. Weeks ago, I would have rejoiced at this news. Nai Nai, however, had shattered our world, and here came Uncle Jian with a tiny bandage that couldn't salvage the wreckage. I had made my peace with the Ang family's rejection, and instead of relief, I felt anger that my foundation was breaking again. Uncle Jian's letter raised more questions than it answered. Did Father remarry? Did he even want us back? It seemed like it was Yei Yei's decision to bring us to Taiwan—did Father support it? He had the greatest obligation to us, but the letter wasn't even from him—did he not have any opinions, or was he expecting us to interpret his thoughts through Nai Nai and his younger brother? I shoved the letter in my pocket, tied Lan on my back, and went trotting as quickly as I could to look for Di in the city center.

I found her seated outside one of the restaurants that she cleaned for, a bowl of dumplings in her hand. When she saw me, I could tell that she was debating whether or not it was too late for her to hide her bowl, but I wasn't there to reprimand her for eating food without us. There were some things that I had simply grown to accept, and Di's individualistic survival instinct was one of them. "We got a letter from Uncle Jian," I said.

Her mouth was full of dumpling, but she reacted with her eyes, which widened so much that I thought they might fall out of their sockets. She reached her hand out, and I gave her the letter to read as she swallowed her food, a chunk so large that I could see it move down her throat. As she unfolded the paper, I seized her bowl. There were only two dumplings left; with the deftness of a kung fu master, I stuffed one into my mouth and the other behind my shoulder straight into Lan's mouth. Lan squawked at first but then started chewing with delight, dumpling juice dribbling onto my shoulder. I couldn't fight Di's gluttony, but I had at least learned to play by her rules, or lack thereof, when food was around.

"I don't understand," Di exclaimed. "Nai Nai told us not to come!"

"Uncle Jian said there was another letter that he sent," I said. "Do you think that old witch intercepted it and sent her own?"

"Probably," Di said angrily. "She's a devious old bat. Do you think she invented the nurse too?"

"I have no idea what is real and what is a lie in Nai Nai's letter," I replied. "But we know Uncle Jian wouldn't lie. What Yei Yei wants ranks higher than what either Nai Nai or Father wants, so I guess that's why he's working on the permits."

Di's eyes darted to her empty bowl, but she said nothing. Under normal circumstances eating those dumplings would have been a declaration of war and Di would have tackled me and pummeled me until I cried. Uncle Jian's letter was a fragile peace treaty between us, reminding us that the grievances that we had against each other were nothing compared to the rage that we harbored against Nai Nai and Father.

Without warning, Di began to tear the letter.

"What are you doing?" I shrieked, grabbing the paper from her hands. Lan also screamed, unhappy at my sudden lurch forward—her head bonked against my neck as she tried to adjust herself.

"We can't give this to Mom!" Di yelled. "She's going to drag us to Taiwan!"

"But we want to go to Taiwan!" I yelled back.

"No," retorted Di, "Mom wanted to go to Taiwan, but that was before they told us they didn't want us."

"Nai Nai doesn't want us," I said, clutching Di's hands for dear life while Lan began pulling my hair in protest. "The rest of the family doesn't feel that way!"

The restaurant owner, a plump Chinese woman with short, curly hair and dressed in a Western-style flowered dress, heard our skirmish and came charging outside. "What is all this commotion?" she yelled in thick-accented Mandarin. "You two are going to disturb my customers!"

"Sorry, Mrs. Siew," Di said in Cantonese. Seizing that opportunity, I kicked Di in the stomach and wrenched the letter from her hands. Lan bobbed up and down on my back as I ran as quickly as I could, expecting Di to tackle me with a vengeance. However, she was too preoccupied with repairing her relationship with Mrs. Siew, who was a source of both food and income. Breathless and with lungs burning, I kept my pace all the way to Mount Davis with the letter squeezed tightly in my hand, ignoring the ache in my back from Lan's weight and the pinching from her fingers digging into my shoulders.

I had sweat so much that the ink had begun to bleed. Some of the beginning was blurred, but the address remained clear. Focusing, I committed it to memory, just in case Di managed to get her hands on the letter again.

That evening, Di did not come back for dinner. Lan and I waited alone for the vouchers, with Lan babbling about dumplings the entire time. Mom and Biao-Wu came back fatigued, reeking of sawdust and sulfur, their hands stained with red phosphorus. Over porridge, I told Mom about the letter, showing her the two ripped pieces. "It was an accident," I lied. "Di wanted to read it too and grabbed it quickly from my hand." I didn't feel like explaining our fight, and deep inside I didn't fault Di for her emotions.

Mom held the letter together like the two halves of a friendship necklace. "Neither of you should have read this without me," she admonished, but she wasn't angry. Her eyes had lit up, and her hands began to tremble. "Our family wants us," she whispered. "They are going to sponsor our entry permits. They want us to go to Taiwan!" A wide smile radiated from her face, as though we had witnessed a miracle. For her, the dead had risen.

"Wow, that's wonderful!" Biao-Wu exclaimed, clapping Mom on her shoulder. "I'm so happy for you! Your husband is a good man after all! I guess he ended up calling off the marriage?"

"We don't know," I said, interrupting. "The letter is from our uncle Jian, and it says nothing about my father."

Mom scowled at me. Now that the Angs were back, she wanted to save Father's face and avoid discussing family business in front of Biao-Wu. "He must have," she said. "He can't possibly have two wives." Her spoon sank into her porridge as she folded the letter back up. Polygamy was illegal, but not long ago it had been common for rich men to have concubines. Were the laws different in Taiwan?

"Do you think Nai Nai just lied, then?" I asked, pressing on. As far as I was concerned, Biao-Wu was our family more than any of the Angs were. "Or did Yei Yei intervene to stop the marriage?"

Holding up her hand, Mom said, "That's enough, Hai." Her voice was stern, but she was too happy to be annoyed by my questions. "It doesn't matter. I don't know what your father is doing, but at least in Taiwan we have family. We can build a better life. I trust Uncle Jian. As long as we can get those permits, my prayers will be answered!"

Biao-Wu looked at me and was confused by my dour expression. Part of me felt bad for ruining Mom's moment, but another part begged for restraint. Nothing had actually been done—no paperwork had been filed; no application had been approved—and we had no idea what kind of welcome awaited us. Uncle Jian's letter seemed to have erased Mom's grief, as though her weeks of anguish had never happened. Was I crazy for doubting our good fortune? Was I small hearted for holding a grudge?

The sun was setting when Di slunk back, and deliberately refrained from making eye contact with me as she grabbed her porridge, which I had saved for her. She was so entitled. I should have just eaten her share, which was what she would have done. Here Mom was, wiggling with joy, and I was mad at everyone except Lan.

"Finally, you're back," Mom said jubilantly, still unaware that Di had torn the letter. "We have some money saved. Let's all go to the night market and get some snacks to celebrate!"

Di had arrived with her shields up, and she launched right into her attack. "I don't want to go to Taiwan. I want to stay in Hong Kong!"

Mom's face reddened, and Biao-Wu cleared his throat and graciously made up an excuse to give us some privacy. "I have to go to bed early tonight," he said, grabbing his empty bowl. "I'll see you for dinner tomorrow. In the meantime, you two girls be kind to your mom—you only have one, and she loves you more than anyone." I found his words condescending, but they succeeded in triggering my guilt. I knew Mom's factory work was debilitating, and each day she spent sweating in that poorly ventilated factory chipped away at her. Biao-Wu tucked his crutch under his arm and hurried toward the hillside, the tension between Mom and Di mounting.

As soon as he was out of earshot, Mom said, "We shouldn't air our grievances in front of others. I don't want you two arguing in front of Biao-Wu or anyone else at Mount Davis. We are beyond lucky to have family to sponsor us. Do you know how many people here long for that privilege?"

"That family abandoned us!" Di cried. "We are doing better in Hong Kong, and we don't need them anymore! Soon we will have enough money to move out of Mount Davis, and we can rebuild our lives without them!"

Mom sighed. "Di, why must you make everything so difficult? Are we going to repeat every argument that we had in Qingdao now?"

"And what about the Communists?" Di asked, remembering her old friends. "They have been planning and training to capture Taiwan for months. Is it even safe for us to go there if war is going to break out?"

"Who says Hong Kong is safer?" Mom shot back, her voice escalating.

"An attack against Britain is not the same as an attack against the Republic of China," said Di, sounding proud. "Ms. Anita says that Mao is still afraid of the West and Britain is powerful."

"Di, we are not British!" Mom yelled, sounding like Mr. Han.

"We don't have to be British to live well here!" Di yelled back. "There are opportunities for us to improve our lives!" The two of them had become so loud that people were staring, but there was nowhere else for us to go—it would have been even more awkward fighting in the closet, with Mrs. Gao and Mrs. Tung inches away.

"Di, are we living in the same Hong Kong? Do you not realize how little money I make? What opportunities do you see for yourself? I've been looking around, and all I see are low-paying jobs and backbreaking labor. Do you want to spend the rest of your life cleaning kitchens?"

"I won't spend the rest of my life cleaning kitchens," Di

snapped back. "I'm going to become a waitress. And then maybe a cook. And then one day, I will own a restaurant. Whatever happens, I want to do it on my own, not through the Angs' charity!"

"Our lives here are sustained by charity!" Mom exploded, too angry to care about saving face. "At least in Taiwan, we will receive help from our own family. That's not charity—it's obligation." Before Di could retort, Mom continued. "You are a child, so you can still dream. I am a mother, so I must plan for your future as well as my own. Here we must simply survive. In Taiwan, we can hope for more. I also have pride, but I will gladly swallow it to give you girls a better life."

Di's eyes flashed angrily. "Don't use us as an excuse. You are a coward, and you are running back to Father because you are afraid to fail."

"Don't talk to Mom like that," I interjected, Di's harsh words having crossed the line. She glared back, and I could tell that she was blaming this fight on me, for being a mama's baby and opening this letter full of worms.

"I have to be afraid!" Mom shouted. "I have you three girls to think of. What would you do in my shoes? Turn down a safe home for your children? Say no to money, to security, to food—real food?"

"I would rather make matchboxes and eat garbage for the rest of my life than live with Father and Nai Nai again!" Di yelled back. "At least then I would have my dignity!"

"Oh please, Di," I said. "You're the one who went cavorting with the Communists for flour, and now you're glorifying colonizers because of porridge."

"That's different!" Di exclaimed. "That's adapting!"

"Well, why can't you just adapt to the Angs in the same way?" Mom asked, frustrated.

"Yeah, Di," I added, "you can't just slap a different label on what you're doing and claim that you are better than everyone else. This is just like how you claim you don't beg, while telling sob stories to anyone with food. You're just as much of a beggar as we are!"

Tears bloomed in Di's eyes and slid in drops from their corners. "I hate you both!" she bellowed. "The two of you are always ganging up on me. Why don't you all go to Taiwan and kiss Nai Nai's ugly little feet? I'm going to stay here with Biao-Wu." Flipping her braid as she turned, she ran toward the hillside.

"Di, come back! Come back right now!" Mom cried after her. "It's getting dark and it's dangerous!"

Mom started to chase after Di, but I held her back. "It's okay, Mom. I'll get her." As the ocean swallowed the sun, the sky became a deep shade of sapphire. Was Di really going to knock on Biao-Wu's ramshackle hut, which he shared with six other soldiers? "You go inside with Lan; Di and I will be back soon." I was tired and didn't want to trudge up through that foul grass, but Mom would be on her feet all day tomorrow and needed a break. As Mom took sleepy Lan in her arms, I headed after Di.

I regretted yelling at Di, even though I was still angry. Though I wouldn't admit it, I understood what she had meant. To us, the government was as far removed as heaven. Nationalist, Communist, British—we had no choice but to accept the regime in power and move forward. It was like learning to carry an umbrella and smile through the rain. What Father had done, on the other hand, was personal. No matter how bad the storm, Di was unwilling to return to his shelter. Was I also that proud? I too imagined a life in Hong Kong beyond the rubble of Mount Davis. I had an expansive catalog of dreams, because where we were, everything was aspirational, and anything was worth fantasizing about. But I sympathized with Mom too. It's one thing to brave a storm yourself. It's another to watch your children suffer through it.

I had long lost sight of Di, and I realized that I didn't actually know where Biao-Wu's hut was. It was getting harder to see. Little campfires burned for those lucky enough to have spare wood, but their flickering light only made it more difficult to discern the path ahead of me, which was black by comparison.

"Hi, pretty girl," said a man who raised a glass in my direction as he squatted in a circle with his friends. The smell of liquor was potent, and they cackled as I quickened my pace.

"Aw, so shy!" another one commented. "What's your name?"

"We aren't going to hurt you!" said a third. "Come on—hang out for a while!"

I broke into a run, frightened by their forwardness and embarrassed by their laughter. To them, my fear was a joke, but I had heard too many stories about atrocities suffered by girls on the streets to feel anything but afraid. "Biao-Wu!" I called out, letting my anxiety get the best of me. "Di? Biao-Wu! Di! Where are you?"

I would be safer if I headed back home, but I couldn't leave Di behind. What if she was lost too, wandering past these patches of sniggering drunks? There were thousands of tents and huts, and I wasn't even sure that I had headed in the right direction. I chided myself for believing that we could make it in Hong Kong when I couldn't even make it on this hillside.

"Hai!"

Biao-Wu's voice rang out, loud and clear. I charged toward him, and saw his figure outlined in golden light from the fire that burned behind him. His waving arm was like a flag, signaling friendly territory.

As I approached the fire, I saw Di standing in front of Biao-Wu's hut, with six other men and their bedding out in the grass. "You have some nerve," I said to her, out of breath. "I almost got lost trying to find you! Do you know how dangerous it is for you to wander off alone?"

"Go away!" Di yelled. "I'm staying here tonight. Biao-Wu and his friends are letting me sleep in their hut."

My jaw dropped, and Biao-Wu quickly added, "Not all together, of course. My friends and I will stay out here; Di will be in the hut alone."

"I'm not concerned about that," I snapped. I had been flabbergasted because I had already noticed that the men were prepared to sleep outdoors. "Did my sister convince you all to give her your shelter when she has a real concrete room waiting for her?"

"They offered," answered Di icily. She looked indignant, but I knew how she worked. With her silver tongue she had spun them around her finger, and seven soldiers gladly placated this damsel in distress. *Absurd!* I mused to myself that Di's kidnapping should be the least of Mom's concerns.

"Come on, Di," I said tersely, not caring if I came across as a bully. "Mom is worried. We need to go home."

"No!" she cried, ducking into the hut and closing the threadbare rattan mat that was its door.

"Di!" I yelled through the mat. "Biao-Wu has to wake up early to work at the factory! And maybe his friends have jobs too! Stop being so selfish!"

One of the soldiers in the grass said, "Calm down, Big Sister. It's not worth being so upset. Just let her stay for the evening. We will take care of her, we promise."

Turning on him, I said, "If I go home and tell our mother that I let my younger sister stay out all night with seven men, she's going to make *me* sleep out in the grass." I charged into the hut and grabbed Di's ear as she shrieked and pulled my hair. I screamed and the two of us clung on to each other, clawing and kicking. In the scuffle, something fell from Di's pocket, drifting and twirling before landing face up by the fire.

It was a trading card.

The sight of it hit me like a bucket of ice water, pulling me from the heat of our fight. Though the light was dim and the paper too faded for me to recognize whom it was of, I knew it was one of Di's treasured singers. Before this moment, I hadn't seen her with any cards, and I assumed that she had left them all behind. I was wrong. I was stupid. All this time in our journey, I'd thought my sister was loud. I'd thought she was a shouter, a yeller, a troublemaker. How could I have failed to realize that my sister was actually silent? Since we'd left our *siheyuan*, Di never sang a single song—not a word, not a note, not even a hummed melody. In that small, crinkled card, I now saw a face, one of a young girl from Zhucheng who had ceased to exist—and her loss hurt me more than any physical blow could.

Distracted, I forgot about our fight until Di grabbed the collar of my shirt.

"Okay, okay," Biao-Wu yelled as he stepped between us, taking a kick to the chest that was meant for me. "Enough fighting! There are those of us here who might never see our siblings again, and meanwhile, the two of you are trying to kill each other!" Smoothing his shirt, he gestured for us to follow him. "I'm going to walk both of you back now. Maybe you can use this time to make up and think about how lucky you are to have each other!"

Biao-Wu was older than us, so I deferred, despite being sick of his high horse. We followed him down the path, staying on opposite sides. As if by a magic trick, Di's card had disappeared—I hadn't even seen her pick it up. Had I imagined it?

Twice in Hong Kong, I had risked my own safety to save Di, but she had never actually needed my help. While I had been terrified searching in the dark, she had somehow found Biao-Wu's hut and made herself its queen. I used to think she was manipulative and shameless, but now I saw her for what she truly was—a girl who had been forced to grow up too rapidly and mercilessly. Where others might have crumbled under the pressure, Di had become an iron rod, trading her soulful voice for a suit of armor. I was wrong to doubt our survival in Hong Kong. Maybe Mom and I would struggle, but given enough time, the warrior girl who'd replaced my songbird sister could rule this city.

27

HANGING NECK

Di and Mom barely spoke for weeks, until I managed to convince Di that it was premature to be so angry. With Ms. Anita's help, we had gotten copies of our Hong Kong identification cards and mailed them to Uncle Jian's address, but there were still many pieces that would have to fall into place before leaving Hong Kong was a possibility. Mom and Di were both optimistic, but for opposite outcomes, and as long as we did not discuss the topic, our dinners were civil. That brief stability, however, was quickly shattered.

It started as a whisper, and spread from one dirty ear to another until all of us had heard that Mount Davis was going to be shut down. The Hong Kong authorities were going to relocate us to Rennie's Mill, on Junk Bay. None of us had been there, but Mr. Han told us that it was so remote that it would take over three hours to travel back to Hong Kong Island from there. Mrs. Gao told us that its Cantonese name, Tiu Keng Leng, meant "Hanging Neck Ridge," and that it was haunted by foreign ghosts. In the darkness of our closet, she told us the local legend. Canadian businessman Alfred Rennie had tried to start a milling company there, and he hanged himself after it failed. Since then, the site remained abandoned, and only ghosts dared to go there. Unsettled by her story, I asked Mr. Han if what she'd said was true.

He replied, "No, it isn't." I sighed with relief, but then he continued. "Rennie's suicide was from drowning, not hanging. But other than that detail, yes, it's all true."

Shuddering, I prayed for protection against angry spirits, and for the swift arrival of our entry permits.

Mr. Han was vocal against the relocation and held meetings by the hillsides to organize protests. "We need to be united," Mr. Han said to a crowd one day. "No more affiliations based on our provinces or our surnames. We must identify together as the Mount Davis community, as a whole, or we have no hope of fighting this!"

On a Saturday, the four of us and Biao-Wu all went marching throughout Central at Mr. Han's behest, a protest that was quickly broken up by armed policemen. As we ran back from the city center toward Mount Davis, locals dumped buckets of water and garbage on us from their balconies, shouting in Cantonese. "They are calling us dirty parasites," Di seethed. "They say we are ruining Hong Kong, eating and living for free, and driving down wages. They want us to get out of their city!"

"Many of us want to leave," I said, slime on my shoulders and rotten food in my hair. "But look what happened to Mr. Chong, and all the people who can't get permits. We're stuck here!"

There were a few smaller protests outside of the hospital's administrative office, but the voices of thousands of raggedy refugees were faint compared to the amplified cries of the privileged few on Victoria Peak, who had been pushing for relocation.

The Social Welfare Office began conducting surveys in order to assign spots, hoping that most people would opt to find their own housing. Since Biao-Wu had a job, he decided to pool resources with some others and rent a room in the city. Most refugees, however, did not have enough income to support themselves. As terrible as Rennie's Mill sounded, so many signed up that there wouldn't be enough space for them all.

Women and children were in the first-priority group, so we were guaranteed places. Mom was relieved, because all of the services for repatriation would be coordinated from there. Di, however, was apoplectic. "What about my jobs cleaning restaurants? What am I going to do for money?" she cried. "How are we going to get market scraps in the middle of nowhere?"

"You are a child, Di. You shouldn't even be working," Mom replied wearily. "We won't be here in Hong Kong much longer, so we don't need to keep making money. At Rennie's Mill we will still have government food."

"You mean the same rice porridge that has been getting more and more watery each month?" said Di, tipping her empty bowl forward to show us how easily the remnants trickled. "It's just rice and cabbage soup at this point. We can't live off of that!"

"We have lived off far worse," Mom countered. "And again, it is temporary. It'll probably just be a few weeks until we get our entry permits for Taiwan." I couldn't help but cringe at the word "temporary"—whenever Mom said it, she seemed to jinx us to an even longer period of suffering than we had originally anticipated.

"I'm tired of always starting over!" Di shouted.

Mom stood up, taking Lan. "I'm done, Di. Be angry if you want, but I won't sit here and let you yell at me. Complain to someone who cares. I'm going to get water." Lan waved as Mom stormed away, and tears streamed down Di's cheeks, her fury turning into grief.

"Why don't you say anything?" Di asked me, crying. "Why aren't you fighting?"

I didn't fault Mom for leaving, but I was annoyed that I had to deal with Di in her place. How did she have so much energy to argue? The thought of abandoning my letter-writing business was depressing—I had just bought a silky new brush and better paper, and was preparing to set up my own samples. Sometimes I felt like I had no space to think about my own feelings because I was always managing fights between Mom and Di.

"I hate Father too," I said, "but Mom is right. Our lives here are hard, even harder than in Qingdao. We struggle for everything, even daily necessities. Though I don't like it, it's obvious that life will be easier in Taiwan."

"So you want to go back to the Angs, then?"

Sighing, I answered with the first thought that came to my mind. "I want to go to school." Di raised her eyebrows, and I knew she thought I was being a goody-goody, but it was true. The callus on my finger had faded, but the memory of learning had not. "I want to write again," I continued. "I want to have my own paper, my own pens, a desk, and ink. I want to have books, and a clean place to read them in. I want all of these little things that used to seem like nothing but are now beyond our reach." Was I weak for feeling this way? Or even selfish?

"So you will forgive Father in return for some paper and ink?" Di sniffed. "You and Mom are made of the same material. I don't understand either of you."

And I don't understand you, I thought, fatigued by her recalcitrance. Interpreting Di was like looking at ripples in the water and trying to see an image. I saw her in fragments and could not put the pieces together to comprehend her as a whole.

"You've always been Mom's favorite," Di continued bitterly. "It's easier for you to side with her because she loves you so much."

"Mom loves you too," I said, leaping to her defense as well as my own. "Mom loves us all."

"She does," Di acknowledged, "but there is a clear order. There always has been. You are special because you are the first. Lan is special because she is the baby. And I'm in the middle. I'm the most disposable of all the girls."

"Why do you need to think like that?" I asked, frustrated by this debate. "None of us are disposable."

Di looked me in the eye and said, "All girls are disposable, and you know it."

And there it was, as clear as day, the real reason behind Di's hesitance to leave Hong Kong. Of all people, she could never forget that truth—it was in her name, "Brother," which marked what Father had wished for most, and constantly reminded us of what we could never be. When we were on our own, Di was an essential, irreplaceable part of our family. All of us needed to work together to survive. Upon our return to the Angs, however, we would once again be useless mouths to feed.

"We are not disposable just because Father and Nai Nai think we are," I said, though I wavered because of my own insecurity. "No matter what happens in Taiwan, you, Lan, Mom, and I will always be a family. We are our own family, and that will never change."

"You are as optimistic as Mom is" was all Di said, unmollified. With tears on her shirt and her hands clasped together, she looked lonely, as though she was in a place that none of us could reach.

Di's independence was her strength, but it also created distance between us. I didn't know what had come first, the love that Mom and I shared or the consideration that we exhibited for each other, but each nurtured the other. No matter how tired I was, I helped Mom with Lan and chores. No matter how hungry she was, Mom made sure that we ate first. Our relationship was constantly reinforced by mutual care and sacrifice. I wondered if Di believed that it was not possible for her to foster such trust and dependence or if she simply didn't want to. Love binds you to people, and if there was anything that Di truly needed, it was freedom—a freedom that I had envied, without understanding until now that it also came at a cost.

When Mom came back Di slipped away, muttering that she was going to Central to do some cleaning.

"Be safe," Mom called after her, but I could tell she was relieved by her departure. She handed me a heavy, wet canteen. "I don't know what to do about Di."

"She will come around," I said, doing my best to sound confident. "She has a loud mouth, but in the end we are a family and she will stay with us." I wasn't sure about that at all, but I knew that was what Mom needed to hear.

"You don't think she will try to persuade a restaurant owner to adopt her?" Mom asked with a smile. She knew that a joke was what I needed to lighten my heart.

I laughed. "No restaurant owner can adopt Di. She will eat their entire menu and they'll be out of business in a day!" As the two of us and Lan sat together, I knew that this camaraderie was exactly what Di was referring to. I tried to shake this unpleasant feeling, but it only dug its nails in and dredged up insecurities. In a world in which girls were a gift for other people's sons, how could I be confident that Father would send me to school? Mrs. Wu's forced marriage in Zhucheng had frightened me, but a similar fate could await me in Taipei. Why give me books when it was easier to just hand me and all these expenses to another family?

Later that afternoon, our third letter arrived. Di was still gone, so Mom and I read it together. It was a short note from Uncle Jian saying that he had submitted applications for our entry permits. He hoped that it would take only a few weeks, but the government was backed up. The Liaison Office would notify the Social Welfare Office when the permits were ready.

Mom folded the letter and held it against her chest as though it could sustain her heartbeat with its proximity. "I feel like I've finally done something good," she said, eyes distant. "When Father left Zhucheng, I should have made him take you and Di. I'm sorry that I didn't fight harder then. At least now I know you are on your way back to the life that you deserve—the life that I want you to have."

Her words hung heavy, but her apology was unnecessary. "It doesn't matter," I said, thinking back to how I had felt the night that the family chose to leave us behind. Safety to me was Mom. *It always was, and always will be.* "I would have stayed anyway, Mom. Without any hesitation, I would have chosen to be with you." With Di, I was so confident that Taiwan was the right path. With Mom, however, I wavered. The life that I "deserved"—that I wanted—was a life in which my mother and sisters were happy. I just wasn't sure which city would offer that outcome.

28

REFUGEE GOVERNMENT

By June 1950, there were approximately seven thousand residents in Mount Davis, which by then was widely known as a pro-Nationalist enclave. One Sunday, the eighteenth of June, we gathered by the hospital to celebrate the Dragon Boat Festival, a holiday with grim origins. A great patriot, Qu Yuan, drowned himself after his wrongful exile, and his anguished friends threw sticky rice into the river to distract the fish from nibbling on his body. To honor him, Chinese people ate *zhongzhi* and watched dragon boat races on the anniversary of his death.

Back in Zhucheng, Mom used to make fantastic *zhongzhi*, which she stuffed with plump mushrooms, pork belly, and dried shrimp. At Mount Davis, we eagerly stood in line, salivating as hospital volunteers carried out trays of *zhongzhi* that had been gifted by a philanthropist. I knew that we wouldn't be getting anything luxurious, but even some sugar or a few peanuts would be divine.

From far away, a drumbeat rattled and cymbals rang. Lan

started to bob her head and clap her hands, and we cheered when we saw a group of dancing singers coming from Victoria Peak; we thought that the hospital had arranged a surprise performance. As they got closer, however, we began to recognize the tune and make out the words—they were singing the "March of the Volunteers," the anthem of the People's Republic of China.

"Arise, ye who refuse to be slaves! With our flesh and blood, let us build a new Great Wall!" It was a pro-Communist workers' union, waving red-and-yellow flags and performing a rice-planting folk dance, their faces smug as they carried portraits of Mao. *"March on! March on! March, march, march on!"*

Beside us, Biao-Wu yelled a string of profanities and charged forward. Within seconds, hundreds of other veterans had lunged from the line as volunteers called for order, in vain.

"Get inside the shelter!" Mom screamed as livid men pushed past us, teeth bared and fists up. I threw Lan on my shoulder and linked arms with Di as the table of *zhongzhi* crashed to the ground, green triangles scattering in the grass. People dove on their hands and knees, collecting as many as they could in their arms. Di and I angled our elbows, prepared to tackle our way through and claim our share. As if reading our minds, Mom cried, "Ignore the *zhongzhi*! Just get inside!" Mount Davis had turned into a battleground as refugees collided with the singers, tearing their flags and breaking their signs, wrestling the bearers to the ground and pelting them mercilessly.

The workers' union was outnumbered. There were only fifty of them, and there were thousands of us—thousands of former soldiers still stinging from defeat and embittered by the hard life in Citizens' Village. Mr. Han had grabbed a broken table leg, and he held it high in the air like a sword, yelling at everyone to continue the advance. Wailing, the pro-Communist marchers turned to retreat, and the refugees ran after them, screaming savagely like warriors.

Inside the shelter, we stood with our hands and faces pressed to one of the windows, watching as the police arrived to break up the fight. Clubs in hand, they arrested dozens of individuals and herded the rest up the hill, threatening to deport anyone who disobeyed. It was a toothless threat—we all knew China wouldn't accept any of us—but the refugees obeyed because they were afraid of losing their food rations. Bamboo leaves and shredded posters of Mao littered the ground, and anything edible had been grabbed during the melee. Biao-Wu came back with a torn shirt and a bloody nose. He had clubbed people with his crutch, and there was blood along its sides and bottom. "It went well," he said cheerfully when he saw our shocked faces. "First Nationalist victory in a long time!"

If the Hong Kong government had had any doubts about relocating us to Rennie's Mill, they would have dissipated after this Dragon Boat brawl, which made headlines in several local and international newspapers, bringing unwanted attention to an already delicate political situation.

A few days later, social welfare officers instructed us to collect our belongings and go to the pier early in the morning on June twenty-sixth. We had even less now than we did when we left Qingdao, so it took us only a few minutes to pack and say goodbye to our two roommates. Neither Mrs. Tung nor Mrs. Gao was going to Rennie's Mill. Cantonese-speaking soldiers were in the last-priority group because the government assumed that they could adapt easier to life in Hong Kong, so the new site would be overwhelmingly Mandarin. Mrs. Gao decided to look for an apartment with Biao-Wu and other refugees. Mrs. Tung, meanwhile, had started dating another man and planned to remarry.

Neither of them had children, and whatever love they had for their husbands in Taiwan was too weak to tether them. I wondered what Mom would have done if she didn't have us. Mom had more white hairs and worry lines than a typical woman in her thirties, but she was still beautiful and could have easily found another partner—maybe one without a nasty mother like Nai Nai. In my heart, I knew that Mom's love for us chained her to her past. That knowledge settled within me like bricks of guilt, building a house of remorse that held the memories of Mom's hard life. Di, however, thought Mom was weak and refused to believe that every move she made was motivated by sacrifice—that her willingness to go back to the Angs was a testament to her love, not for our father, but for us. I wished that Di could see Mom's courage and altruism, but I was at a loss as to how to open her eyes.

Over the course of a day, about five thousand people and their baggage were transported from Mount Davis to Rennie's Mill. To assuage the superstitious people who hated the macabre Chinese name, the government changed the Mandarin version to Tiao Jing Ling, which meant "Smooth View Ridge." Unlike with Citizens' Village, the government called our enclave at Rennie's Mill what it was: a refugee camp.

As we waited to board the ferry to Rennie's Mill, police officers sprayed us front and back with DDT to kill any lice that might have remained on our bodies. "Arms out, legs wide," an officer yelled. Mom clapped a hand over Lan's nose and mouth and we squeezed our eyes and lips shut as the spray guns blasted us with a thick chemical cloud. I accidentally inhaled some and coughed so hard that my eyes watered. Our clothes were damp, but we were presumably pest free. Di fanned her face to try to clear the toxic air and looked mournfully toward the city center.

Mom had taken all of the money that she made in the past few months and stuffed it in her favorite hiding spot, her undershirt. Now that we were going to Taiwan, we didn't need to be so tightfisted. I fantasized about us taking that money and going on a spending spree in the city center, coming out of restaurants so full that we would have to loosen our pants and waddle home with our bellies hanging out like pregnant women's. But I knew what Mom was saving for. She couldn't trust that those entry permits would come through. It was the same reason that she still hadn't sold the jade bangle. We had been through so many ups and downs, and we didn't know what else would be thrown our way.

The ride from the dock in Kowloon was long and bumpy and our heads bobbed and swayed as our truck veered sharply along the curving mountain roads. As we rumbled closer to Rennie's Mill, there were only uncultivated expanses of land, without a single store in sight. Even if we'd wanted to spend our money, there were no places for us to spend it. I couldn't help but think of Lucky, who might have been able to catch rabbits in this wild landscape. I never heard from Mrs. Ding, and I wondered if she had received my letter—maybe she had, and her reply never made its way to me. Like Di, I too was tired of moving—tired of breaking bridges each time and leaving pieces of my heart with people whom I would never see again.

As we descended from the truck, we heard hammering as construction workers set up additional tents, designed by the Social Welfare Office and made of wood and tar paper. The government had originally planned for housing one thousand refugees, but about five times that number would arrive. "There's nothing here but dirt," I said out loud. The tents were small, gray, and uniform, lined up in neat rows like tombstones.

"Can you believe that it will take three hours for us to walk back to the dock?" Di asked, with melancholy. The auto path led to Lei Yue Mun, a small town from which we could take a boat to Shau Kei Wan, on Hong Kong Island. "What are we going to do here? Turn into rabbits and live off the land?"

Mom shushed Di, but others around us were also muttering, unnerved by our sparse surroundings. There were more women and children around us, and the little ones were cranky. If we needed provisions, it would easily take half a day to get them from Hong Kong's city center.

Ms. Anita greeted us all. She was more nervous than usual, her hair pulled back and an interpreter beside her. It hadn't been her decision to move us here, but she represented the government that did. Through the interpreter, she informed us that each tent would hold four people, and that each person would get a monthly ration card that could be stamped twice a day for rice and vegetables at the canteen. Everyone needed to bring their own bowls and do their own cooking, which triggered grumbling. It wasn't that people were unwilling to cook, but many of them lacked pots and pans, or money with which to buy them.

Mom leaned closer to Di and me and said, "We will need to go to Central and buy some supplies. Good thing we have money saved!"

"If you are going to the city center, you should buy extra and resell here for double the price you paid," Di remarked.

Mom scowled and said, "It's bad karma to take advantage of people's desperation."

"I'm just trying to be resourceful," Di said haughtily.

We turned our attention back to Ms. Anita, who was giving a presentation about water, which we had to get from a stream. "If you are thirsty, it may be tempting to drink directly from the nice, cool river. Do not do this! Always boil your water before drinking it." She went on to list the various types of waterborne parasites that could make us sick and took out a folder of photographs to illustrate her points. People gasped in horror as she flipped each one out—there were ghastly photos of worms crawling out of people's anuses, mouths, and even eyes.

"Gods, we really came to a hellhole," Di whispered as Ms. Anita distributed the photos so everyone could get a good look. When they came to us, we passed them on quickly with disgust. I already had too many unpleasant dreams to add man-eating parasites to the mix.

Ms. Anita concluded her presentation by informing us that there would be staff from the Social Welfare Office in the canteen every day, in case there were serious medical emergencies. She wished us well and directed us to check in with her colleagues.

The Social Welfare Office assigned the four of us to a single tent—number 68. Mom crouched and lifted the flap gingerly. We squeezed in behind her, but there was barely enough room for us all. It was hard to imagine four big men like Mr. Han sharing the same space. There was no floor, just the dirt ground, and once the flap was closed, the darkness mixed with the smell of fresh soil made me feel like I was in a crypt. Di sensed my fear and put a hand on my shoulder. "Hey, Sis," she said, "I heard that the locals buried Alfred Rennie in an unmarked grave. What if his body is underneath one of these tents?"

With a shriek I dove back into the sunlight, and Di's delighted cackles rang out through the tar paper.

"You two, stop it," Mom snapped, rolling up the flap and tucking it over the frame. "There are worse dangers here than that foreigner's ghost. Those parasites, for example." We all shuddered, thinking back to those gruesome photos.

"I wonder what type of apartment Biao-Wu found," Di said

wistfully, sitting along the side of the tent and hugging her knees. "He probably has electricity, and maybe even running water. I bet he is living above a bunch of restaurants and a market!"

"I hope he's doing well," I said, eyeing a crawling millipede. With the flap open, flies buzzed and meandered into the tent, flitting in and out of our hair. I had thought Mount Davis was our rock bottom, and now here we were.

That first night, we folded our backpacks and used them as pillows, with only thin wool blankets donated by missionaries to separate us from the rocky soil. Lan slept sprawled on Mom's chest, but Di and I spent the night tossing and turning, finding something sharp no matter how we arranged our bodies.

The next day, Mom set out for Hong Kong Island, and returned late in the evening with some thick padding and tar paper, a roll of twine, a large kitchen knife, and a teakettle in her backpack. "That hike is more than three hours!" she huffed as she set down the heavier items. "It's probably two and a half for fit people like Biao-Wu and his friends, but it's a long road and very bumpy!" As she sat on the ground I rubbed Mom's feet, noticing that both of her heels were bleeding from her shoes chafing against them.

"I'll boil some water and see what we can use for a bandage," I said, imagining worms crawling into these open sores. "We can't let these wounds get infected!"

Mom nodded, fanning herself after the exertion.

Over the next few days, additional refugees floated into the camp on foot. Some brought their own building materials and set up shelters, while others slept in the open air. Many of them were unregistered, which meant they had no rations. They picked grains of rice and beans from the canteen floor and begged from other refugees. Daily life was so difficult that hundreds of unregistered former soldiers volunteered to fight for the Republic of Korea in the Korean War, which had broken out in June. Sadly, the South Koreans didn't want them, and they sent them all back to Rennie's Mill.

Our rations were paltry, but Mom would never say no if someone asked for help—usually we could spare only a few spoonfuls of rice, but she made sure that we always gave something. Watching her at the camp reminded me of her kindness to the workers back in Zhucheng, which Nai Nai had seen not only as a weakness, but as a betrayal of the family—a loss of resources that could otherwise have benefited our own kin. All of that extra rice that we gave away could have been stored and sold on Hong Kong Island—but that was not Mom's nature.

Mom's generosity, however, was reciprocated in various ways, as those who benefited helped us where they could. One man reinforced our tent with wood that he found, so that our walls shook less when the wind blew. Another built us some shelves so we could store our belongings, and a platform so we had a place for our bedding at night. The most precious payment, however, was from Mr. Tai, who could kill rabbits with a slingshot. Once he was settled, he gave us chunks of meat for stew, and taught Di and me how to set up rabbit traps. Though we were rarely successful, it gave us something to occupy our time—spreading apart the underbrush and searching for brown balls of rabbit dung at least staved off boredom, if not hunger.

Mrs. Ying, a doctor's wife, taught us how to identify fever vine, a medicinal plant used to treat inflammation that also had edible leaves. It smelled foul, but we were so hungry that we held our noses and ate the leaves raw whenever we found them. There were also a few types of grasses and seeds that we could eat or boil into tea, which Di and I spent our days foraging for.

"Be careful out there," we heard a woman say to her children. "Your uncle says he saw a wild boar!"

I should have been more afraid of the boars than of ghosts, but her warning only made me excited. "Di, imagine if we could kill one! We could eat for months, I bet!" Building our pathetic rabbit trap seemed like a waste of time now as my mind swirled with visions of roast pork, meatballs, blood cakes, and rib soup.

"Let's be extra nice to Mr. Tai," Di said, her eyes shining with ambition. "I can't even remember the last time I had a pork hock! If anyone can catch a boar, it's him!" Later, we saved some fever vine leaves and went searching for Mr. Tai. There was a meeting by the canteen, and Mr. Han and a few other men were addressing a small crowd.

"Unity is strength!" Mr. Han said. "Rennie's Mill is our hometown now, and we need to work hand in hand to make it livable!"

The residents, led by Mr. Han, had petitioned the Hong Kong authorities for permission to form a refugee government. They were going to set up a police force, composed of former soldiers, to protect the area from Communist infiltration. There were going to be rules to promote sanitation and hygiene, including regulations on when and how the river could be used, and designated areas to serve as latrines. A dedicated team of volunteers would liaise with charities to fund major projects, like a dock, and smaller necessities, like medical supplies.

After the meeting, we found Mr. Tai, gifted him with our crumpled leaves, and asked him if he could help us kill a boar. "Are you crazy?" he asked, shocked by our request. "That would be suicide. I don't have the tools to take down a boar. They are strong and violent. If either of you ever see one, back away slowly and get as far away as possible!"

Disgruntled, Di and I retreated to our tent, our culinary dreams dashed as we chewed on stinky herbs with sides of rice and salty vegetables.

In August, Biao-Wu arrived at the camp, embarrassed that his foray into independence had not succeeded. "I know what everyone is thinking," he said preemptively when he saw us. "I was too proud and I overestimated myself. I wasted my time and what little money I had, only to come here anyway."

"What nonsense," Mom said, giving him a hard clap on the back. "We are just happy you are here!" We invited him to eat with us until his ration card came in. After that Mom cooked his portion along with ours and we ate together daily, just like at Mount Davis.

"My Cantonese is not good enough," he explained to us one evening. "It's difficult to really live in the city center without it. I know some basics and I can get by, but I took for granted how comforting it was to go back to Mount Davis every evening and just understand and be understood. It was lonely, and that is what drove me crazy." Between bites of rice, he continued. "My wages at the factory were barely enough to cover food and rent. You know how little they pay. I figured that if I'm going to be scraping by, I might as well do it here, with my friends and fellow soldiers."

Mr. Han and some veterans from Shandong greeted Biao-Wu enthusiastically. "Prepare to work, young man!" Mr. Han commanded. "We have several projects lined up. As long as you can hold a hammer you can serve."

The most ambitious project that fall was a road—*the* road. Our refugee government had decided to build a shorter, better road that would allow us to travel to Lei Yue Mun in only thirty minutes. If it was successful, many of us could work on Hong Kong Island again. The government provided building supplies, and every ablebodied man had to build at least three hundred feet of road. Those who could not contribute to the labor helped by cooking rations so that our workers could return to a prepared meal.

There were aspirations everywhere, and there was construction everywhere. A group of missionaries agreed to fund the purchase of materials for a health clinic. The hospital agreed to fund the latrines. Every day, people were working on huts with thatched roofs, paper windows, and wooden doors. Little by little, Rennie's Mill was becoming a rudimentary town.

"I'm surprised you all are still here," Biao-Wu said to me one day as I sat outside, using his knife to sharpen a branch into a point. If refugees could build a giant road, surely we could also build a boar trap. Another child had described one that he had seen in his village, and against Mr. Tai's advice, I had enlisted Biao-Wu's help to construct it. "I thought you would be in Taiwan by now."

I touched my finger to the tip of my makeshift spear, wondering if it would be sharp enough to pierce a boar's wiry hide. "The process is so slow. I imagine we will catch a boar before our permits come through, if they ever do."

Biao-Wu and I had made seven of these spears, and we were planning to dig a trench in the ground and cover it with branches and leaves. Ideally, a boar would wander across it and fall onto these wooden stakes, and then we would have a feast.

Before we could ask for a shovel, however, Mr. Han brought the entire project to a screeching halt. "Reckless!" he admonished as he confiscated our spears. "Do you know how many children are running around this camp? Do you know how much easier it is to kill a human child than a wild boar? The greatest enemy of humanity is stupidity! If you have spare energy, carry water to the men who are working on the road!"

My hands were sore from whittling, and I winced as Mr. Han trundled away with the spears that I had worked on so diligently.

"Sorry, Hai," said Biao-Wu. "I guess if they finish that road, you can take up your letter-writing business and just buy some pork with your profits."

"When do you think that will be?" I asked, dreading the answer. "Months? Half a year?"

Biao-Wu wiped his knife with his shirt and carefully stowed it in its sheath. "Mr. Han says they'll be done by spring."

Would we still be here at Rennie's Mill then? We were approaching the end of summer. This winter, I would turn fifteen. Now it had been months since we had last heard from Uncle Jian, and the taste of grass and herbs made me nauseous. My breath smelled sulfuric, like the fever vine, and I had lost more weight. Even though it wasn't yet fall, I was freezing from anemia and didn't have enough clothing to keep me warm. Around us, our camp was improving, yet the changes came too slowly for me. I hadn't needed the boar hunt for the meat; I needed it so I had something to work toward, something that I could control. More than anything else, I needed a distraction from the entry permits that seemed less likely to materialize with each day that passed.

When Biao-Wu and I returned, disconsolate, to the tent area, we found Mom clapping her hands, whistling her praise. Lan was standing by the tree line, slightly bent, small arms out like airplane wings. Upon seeing us, she waved and took a few steps forward. Leaving Biao-Wu, I ran to take her hand, expecting her knees to buckle and for her to scrape her palms on the twigs and gravel. As she smiled and wobbled, however, I froze. She was limping, clumsily and carefully, like a younger child would, but she was moving on her own.

Even in a place like this, Lan had grown—slower than expected, but still, she sprouted. As Biao-Wu cheered and knelt down with open arms to encourage her, I realized that she was stronger than

I thought. She was the wheat that burst through Shandong soil, and the Northern flowers that bloomed in snow. I took comfort then, because maybe I too was stronger than I thought. We all were. Heads high, fists clenched, we could endure yet another winter together—and months from now, when the cold winds finally wavered, our new road would welcome spring.

29

GOLDEN TICKETS

Once a week, a social welfare officer came to the camp with updates on entry permits from the Liaison Office. In early September 1950, the Hong Kong authorities successfully negotiated permits for hundreds of veterans with disabilities. Ms. Anita excitedly offered Biao-Wu a spot, and was confused when he declined.

"You . . . don't want to go?" she repeated, wondering if she'd made an error in translation.

"I want to stay here," Biao-Wu confirmed.

Later, over dinner, he told us, "What I said the first time remains the same. I am not interested in returning to the Nationalists. Just because I didn't make it my first try on my own doesn't mean that I won't succeed in the future. Hong Kong is going to be my home. I'll learn Cantonese in time. And maybe, once things are better in the mainland, I can go back and find my mom."

Mr. Han scolded Biao-Wu when he heard this. "Stubborn! Stupid! Biao-Wu, someone offered you a golden ticket and you said no. Do you know how many thousands of people would kill to be in your position?"

Biao-Wu shrugged. "They don't need to kill anyone to be in my position. They just need to cut off their own leg."

Offended by his tone, Mr. Han picked up his bowl and left to eat with one of his many other friends. "I can't stomach my food with such idiocy for company. Fortune is wasted on the foolish. Youth is wasted on the young!" He stomped away, muttering about second chances and lost opportunities.

It was almost Mid-Autumn Festival again, and a charity funded by the Nationalist government had sent us hundreds of red paper lanterns printed with the flag of the Republic of China and the words *Long live President Chiang Kai-Shek*. Mr. Han had given Di and me a box of lanterns to fold and distribute, promising mooncake as a reward. That same charity was going to send crates of these golden treasures, and rumor had it that they would have whole yolks inside them! I hadn't eaten eggs in months, and it was wonderful to have something tangible to look forward to.

I had just finished folding the last of our lanterns, heeding Mr. Han's warning to avoid creasing or wrinkling Chiang Kai-Shek's name, and was rushing to gather our laundry—washing hours at the stream would end soon. In the distance, I heard Mom yelling our names from the canteen.

"Hai! Di! Hai!" She was sprinting as quickly as she could, pumping her arms like a madwoman, nearly tripping on a rock when she saw me by the tent. Something horrible must have happened. Did she lose one of our ration cards? Did someone get gored by a boar? Did the government decide to shut down Rennie's Mill too?

I dropped everything in my arms and ran to her. "What is it, Mom?" I asked anxiously. "What's wrong?"

Mom threw her arms around me and hugged me so hard that

I almost fell over. "Our entry permits came through! Our entry permits came through!" She shook my shoulders and jumped up and down in excitement. "We are going to Taiwan!"

I screamed and hugged Mom back, burying my face in her shoulder, but inside I felt hollow and numb. Despite all of the time spent obsessing about Taiwan, I had never actually expected this day to come. I thought that we would be like Mr. Han, perpetually talking about our entry permits without ever receiving them.

"Ms. Anita will let me know when the next boat leaves," Mom said, still panting from having run all the way from the canteen. "Once there are enough passengers with permits, the government will charter a ship. We might be gone before winter!"

When Di returned, Mom grabbed her hands with such force that Di's fingers turned white as she jubilantly told her the news. Di's hands flew over her mouth as she laughed ecstatically, hugging us both. "Finally, we can leave this muddy mess," Di exclaimed. "I thought for sure we were all going to grow old and die in this tent." Conditions at Rennie's Mill were so terrible that even Di was eager for a change. She was unable to supplement her diet with restaurant scraps, and stewed grass and herb salad had broken her resolve.

On the day of the Mid-Autumn Festival, Di and I received our mooncakes, which were filled with red bean. There was no egg yolk, but we didn't mind. In Taiwan, surely we would be able to eat eggs and have real mooncake again. The two of us sat together outside our tent, hands cupped around our cakes like they were precious baby birds.

"Do you think Yei Yei still has money?" Di asked, finishing her cake in two gulps.

"They packed everything when they went to Qingdao," I replied, savoring mine in small bites, letting the grainy red bean spread on my tongue. "They must have arrived with a fortune. Maybe they spent it all. Or maybe Father has a nice job in Taiwan and they are earning even more. I hope that's the case." I kept half of my mooncake and wrapped it carefully in a cloth so that I could enjoy another euphoric tasting later.

"How do you feel about seeing Father again?" Di asked.

"I haven't thought about it," I answered. "I don't think it will feel real to me until we are on that boat." By now, Father was a nebulous entity, more of a concept than an actual person. I defined him by his absence, and couldn't even imagine seeing him in the flesh.

Di eyed the remaining portion of mooncake in my pocket enviously. "I can never forgive him for leaving us behind."

"I don't think we have to," I said. "We only need to coexist with him. We don't need to like him." We had never had much interaction with Father anyway, and he probably wouldn't even notice if two of his daughters gave him the silent treatment.

Di leaned her head on my shoulder, its weight heavier than I expected. "Will you miss this place when we leave?"

The idea that I could miss the foul dirt of Rennie's Mill was so preposterous that I snorted and giggled. Di started chuckling, and before we knew it, our vibrating laughter had amplified, shaking through our bodies with such force that we tumbled backward, eyes up at the sky. Above, the windswept clouds were wispy like beard candy, and I started to cry, the white and blue light blurring together. My tears ran freely, dripping from my face and trickling down like rain, my secret thoughts seeping into the raw earth. Leaving was going to break my heart, but I didn't need to admit it—my sister already knew.

Later that evening, we gathered with some of our friends and climbed up to the highest point to watch the swollen full moon, a luminous golden orb. With no electricity or other human development in the area, the night sky was a pitch-black blanket scattered with glittering silver stars. As we put our arms around one another, I thought of the people whom we had met since we left Zhucheng. Perhaps they were looking at this same moon, which also shone above Mr. Zhang, Mrs. Ding, and Uncle Sen. Miles away in Taiwan, maybe Father too had his head toward the sky. Lan sat curled in Mom's lap, the lunar light reflected in her little black eyes. At this point, she had spent the majority of her life as a refugee.

It was a cool October morning when we climbed into the military trucks that the government sent to collect the few hundred refugees going to Taiwan. Biao-Wu could have been seated next to us, but instead he stood outside with Mr. Han, waving. Mom left him our teakettle and reminded him to boil water before drinking it. He hadn't seen Ms. Anita's traumatizing parasite presentation, and Mom was certain he would get lazy and drink from the stream. "Other soldiers drink from the river and they are fine," he told us. "Foreigners need to boil the water because their stomachs are weak, but those of us who have grown up here are used to it!"

"Just boil the water," Mom pleaded. "It's so easy and only takes a few minutes."

"Not when you have to wait all that time for it to cool down," he replied. "But I'll do it just to give you peace of mind." I was pretty sure that he wouldn't, but that was out of our control. We were better off just praying that his stomach was as powerful as he seemed to think it was.

Lan was cranky and exceptionally uncooperative, crying that she wanted to go back to bed as she slipped from Mom's arms and tried to scrabble out of the truck. Nothing could dampen Mom's spirits, though, and she just remarked cheerfully to Di and me, "I suppose you two are behaving so well that it's Lan's turn to fight me." Lan was small, and Mom picked her up easily and used her strong legs to grip her while Lan sobbed and pushed to no avail. Unlike on the train, now we were surrounded by people whom we had known for several months. They were patient and took turns saying kind words to console Lan, who only threw her head back and wailed.

As the truck started, Lan looked up and calmed down, suddenly interested in looking out the window to see the scenery move. She pulled herself onto Mom's lap, her face red from crying, and waved back toward Biao-Wu and our friends as we drove down toward the mountain path. Lan was too young to understand that this was a real goodbye, and it was unlikely that we would see any of them ever again. Just as her tears stopped, mine started to fall, since I knew that Biao-Wu and others we cared for were now just names on my list of people to write to. Hopefully I would have better luck receiving replies once we had a fixed address in Taiwan—I was losing these people in the flesh and couldn't bear losing them in written form too.

When we arrived at the harbor, the sky was gray and the sea reflected its muted tones. I had never ridden on a steamship before and was impressed by its size—it was larger than many houses were. Ms. Anita smiled when she saw us and called out, "Today is the big day!" I ran from the truck and gave her a tight hug, which seemed to surprise and please her as she wrapped her long arms around me. I realized that I would also miss this enthusiastic and quirky foreigner who had given me paper all of these months.

"I'll miss you, Hai," she said. "I hope you can finally go back to school when you are in Taiwan. Maybe when you are older, you can be a famous calligrapher, and I'll read about you in the newspaper!" I blushed at her high hopes for me when just going to school seemed to be a far reach, given that I had missed so much already.

After so many goodbyes I wished that I would be numb to them, but with each one I was still inundated by grief. Mom thanked Ms. Anita for everything that she had done for us, while Di whispered to me, "It is her job. She gets paid to do this. It's not charity." I pinched Di, who squawked and stomped on my toes with her heel. Though I yelped, Mom ignored us both. She had checked our paperwork multiple times already, but she checked once again before handing it to Ms. Anita, who also reviewed the documents.

"You're all set," she said. "I hope you send word when you can so that I can see that you girls are doing well!"

"I will," I promised. The remaining paper that she had given me was carefully stowed in Mom's backpack, wrapped up with clothing to protect it from getting dirty. We had less to carry now, since we hadn't packed any provisions except our canteens and a few strips of pork jerky that Biao-Wu bought for us with his savings. "Not as good as wild boar, but maybe you'll still remember us at Rennie's Mill when you eat it!" he had said.

Our feet made hollow sounds as we stomped up the gangway. The ship's horn blasted loudly, and I instinctively covered my ears, my backpack slipping forward. We found a row of seats in the cabin and settled comfortably. What luxury it was to sail on such a ship and sit in chairs again!

Another deafening toot signaled our departure, and the ship began to budge hesitantly, as though it were pushing through mud instead of water. Then, smoothly and surely, it moved with finesse, gliding away from the pier. Mom stayed seated with Lan while Di and I ran out onto the deck to look at the city.

As towering Hong Kong diminished in the distance, I couldn't help but feel fear and sorrow. Back at our seats Mom smiled from ear to ear, and Lan laughed, but I couldn't shake the weight from my chest. We had been living in squalid and unhygienic conditions, with barely enough food, and finally we were on our way out. Yet we were also leaving a community where we had strong bonds—where we felt cared for and loved. Now we were heading to an unknown in every aspect. I focused on Chiao, my cousin whom I had missed so much years ago. Would our friendship still be the same?

Toward Taiwan there was hope, but all the emotions that I had buried deep within me were beginning to bubble to the surface. How would it be to see Father again? And Nai Nai?

I ached. I reached my hand out to the only other person whose feelings I knew matched my own. Di's fingers closed around mine, and she held on to me tightly. The wind blew around us and ruffled our clothing and hair, but the warmth from her hand made me feel grounded and safe, at least for a brief moment. Both of us knew that in more ways than one, we could never return home again.

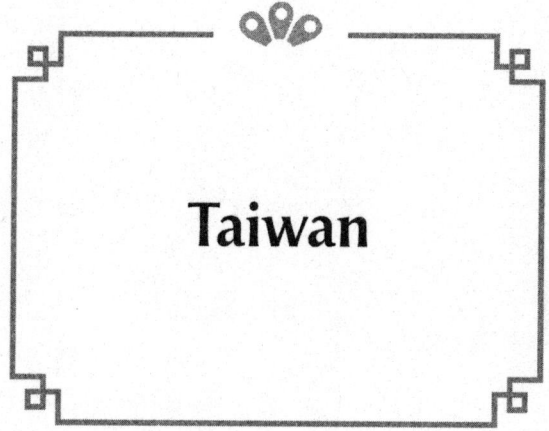

Taiwan

30

REUNIFICATION

When our ship dropped anchor, Mom put her hand on her chest, where our precious travel documents were. To an outsider, she looked like a patriot, pledging allegiance to the island as the gangway lowered. Dozens of flags lined the port—blue sky, white sun, and red all over, the proud flag of the Republic of China. Watching them flapping defiantly was surreal—almost as though the revolution had not happened. The country that we had mourned these past years was still alive, still holding on.

We filed into line at the customs and immigration office, which had a giant framed photograph of Chiang Kai-Shek in the main hall. Chiang had declared martial law on the island shortly before his arrival in 1949, beginning a period of authoritarian rule that would last nearly fifty years. His eyes burned with an intense sense of purpose, as though he were scanning us all to determine if any spies lurked in our midst.

Mom held my hand, but my fingers almost slipped because she

was sweating so much. When it was our turn to speak with an immigration officer, Mom rushed forward to the booth and presented our papers with shaking hands.

I felt like I had when we were at the final checkpoint in Qingdao, even though all of our documents were legitimate this time. There was still a part of me that didn't believe it would work out—that we would be sent away on the next ship to Hong Kong and have to trudge back to Rennie's Mill and beg for our tent back.

The immigration officer flipped through our documents so quickly that I wondered if he had even read our names. He held up each of our ID cards and looked at our faces. Then he grabbed a large seal and stamped our entry forms with beautiful red ink and signed his name below it. "Welcome to the Republic of China," he said, handing everything back to us.

Mom bowed quickly and thanked him as she snatched the papers. She scurried down the hall, pulling us along as though she was afraid that he would change his mind.

There was a long glass window that separated us from the people waiting in the arrival hall. Everyone was looking for someone, their eyes eagerly scanning each person who came out. Shouts of joy erupted as people reunited. Ahead of us, a man and woman ran toward each other and embraced as though they were two halves of a magnet. Beside us, a man with tears in his eyes knocked on the window and waved frantically to his wife and son, who had just rounded the corner. A young soldier shouted, "Mama!" as he barreled his way forward, leaping to grab an elderly woman's bag as she covered her face and sobbed. The cacophony of laughter was disorienting as groups of soldiers welcomed their stranded comrades, jumping on one another like children. Love permeated the air as people knitted back together, beginning to heal the anguish of months or even years of separation.

I wanted to be happy for them all, but envy overwhelmed me as we waited awkwardly by the door, unable to identify anyone we knew in the crowd. Where was my father?

Then we heard a voice to the side call hesitantly, "Sister-in-law?"

Turning, we saw a man in his thirties with a long face, thick eyebrows and lips, and ears that stuck out slightly. Mom's eyes widened. "Jian!" she called back, relieved.

"By the heavens, you all look terrible!" he exclaimed, still blunt and careless with his words. "I thought it was you—there can't be many women with three girls on the ship." Uncle Jian hadn't changed much since we last saw him, which had been shortly before Lan's birth. He looked distinguished in his green uniform, which was neatly ironed, and his shoes were polished. Our clothing was a mix of donations from charities and a few items that had survived from Zhucheng, and it hung loosely like sails on our bodies. Our shoulders were doorknobs, and our collarbones jutted out like chicken wings. It had been a long time since we interacted with someone who was neither a refugee nor a person who regularly worked with refugees. The sight of us must have been a shock indeed.

"Thank you for coming to pick us up," said Mom. Her posture was stiff and formal, as though she were making small talk with a stranger instead of reuniting with a family member.

"Don't thank me—it's what ought to be," Uncle Jian replied, reaching for my backpack. "Give me your bag." It looked pathetic and lumpy and I felt embarrassed, as if I were handing him garbage. "You didn't bring much," he commented. "I can't imagine what you have been through. Let's get you home—you must be exhausted. Have you eaten yet?"

"No," Mom said honestly. *We haven't really eaten in a long time,* I thought.

"I'm sorry—what a stupid question. I shouldn't have asked—it's a habit," Uncle Jian said, and cleared his throat. "You must be starving. The girls are like skeletons!" He led us out to a parking lot full of military vehicles. After depositing our bags in the trunk of an army jeep, he opened the doors for Di and me to climb into the back, while Mom took Lan with her to the front. "It will take about forty minutes to get home, so try to get comfortable," he told us, starting the car.

I leaned against the cloth seats, feeling the hum of the motor through the fabric. The auto road hugged the coast and waves washed against the rocky shore, flooding tide pools with alabaster sea-foam. Farther out, fishing boats cast wide nets like spiderwebs over the water. As Uncle Jian drove, we sat in a brooding, tense silence. Mom stared quietly out the window, but I could tell from the furrow of her brow that her mind was a thunderstorm.

Suddenly, without anyone prompting, Di piped up, "Why didn't Father come to pick us up?"

Uncle Jian kept his eyes on the road and answered, "This area is restricted for military personnel to collect their relatives or colleagues. Remember, only families of soldiers or civil servants can enter Taiwan now. I had trouble sponsoring your entry permits, since you aren't my direct relatives, but I was able to call in some favors in the end. I'm sorry about the delay; it took a long time to get everything in order."

Indeed, it had been almost half a year since we received his first letter. "Thank you, Jian," Mom said sincerely. "We are so grateful."

"What are you talking about?" Uncle Jian replied as we cruised by a crumbling shrine. "We are family. It's my duty, nothing more. No more gratitude, please. I only wish that the process had been faster."

We had turned away from the coast and were passing agricultural land, the plots demarcated with neat straight lines. It reminded me of farms in Zhucheng because of the fieldworkers wearing broad straw hats to keep the sun out of their faces—except that by October Zhucheng was cold and most of the crops would have been harvested already.

The question that we were all itching to ask was about the nurse whom Nai Nai had mentioned in her letter. I darted my eyes to Di, hoping that she would be brazen enough to raise it. She looked back at me, her lips pressed shut, conveying that she had already asked about Father's presence. It was my turn.

I took a breath and blurted, "Nai Nai said that Father was going to marry a nurse. Is it true?"

"Hai!" Mom exclaimed. "We will talk to Father when we see him." Her indignation was feigned, and she looked at Uncle Jian, wondering how he would reply.

Uncle Jian's thick eyebrows arched like caterpillars rearing. "When did you hear from Mother?" he asked. "Did she write to you?"

"Yes," Mom answered tensely. "The first reply that we received was from her. She told us not to come because your brother was about to marry a nurse."

Uncle Jian laughed. "Ah, Mother. She's so sneaky." Nai Nai was truly blessed with two filial sons—Father, who obeyed her every word, and Uncle Jian, who found her capriciousness endearing. Neither of them registered her malevolence, and they dismissed her malicious acts as antics, without understanding the extent of their impact. For us, Father's possible remarriage was no laughing matter—it had racked Mom with anxiety and pulled her into depression for the past months. "I knew she was up to no good,"

Uncle Jian continued, sounding only slightly exasperated. "She offered to mail my letter to you. When I never heard back, I suspected that she might have done something, but I didn't want to accuse her in case it just got lost in the mail. She's very sensitive, you know. So I wrote my second letter and mailed it myself, and had you send your replies to my military address."

Di leaned and whispered to me, "We were right. That nasty old witch!"

I only half paid attention to her because I was so focused on what Uncle Jian would say next.

"So, what about this nurse?" Mom prompted, hoping that he would tell us that she was a figment of Nai Nai's fantasy.

"Oh, Yan-Fei?" asked Uncle Jian, without realizing that the ease with which the name rolled off his tongue betrayed the severity of this dalliance. "My brother was dating her, and she is a nurse—that is true. But in his defense, we weren't sure if you were even alive. We had heard such gruesome stories about the Communists killing people in the countryside!"

It seemed that they had assumed we were dead—or hoped it? At the denunciation rally, I had come close. Had the Angs been worried when they heard those stories? If I had indeed died, would Father have mourned me? Would he have lit incense and prayed at the temple? Would any of the Angs, for that matter? I thought of Mom, Di, and myself alone at Three's funeral and answered my own question: *Of course not.*

"How long were they dating for?" Mom asked, the quiet tone of her voice chilling.

Beads of sweat formed on Uncle Jian's forehead, which I could see in the rearview mirror. Deflecting, he said, "As soon as we got your letter, Father told him to end it. It was a matter of honor. Once we knew you were alive and it was possible for you to join us, we couldn't just—" He stopped abruptly, and though his sentence broke off, we heard the words just the same: *replace you*. Like old clothes, or broken bowls, a lost woman could be replaced with a new womb or, worse, a new love.

I wanted to hold Mom's hand, but I was too far away in the back seat. Anguish emanated from her as she sat, shoulders hunched, fists clenched, wondering how close Father had come to marrying again. My own anger was building; I was furious that it was Yei Yei who'd ended the affair, not Father himself. It hadn't even been a full two years since our separation. How could Father have given up on us so quickly? How could he have lined this woman up to replace Mom, hoping that she would have children to replace us? I thought I had stopped caring about Father and his opinions, but my armor had cracked and here I was, as hurt as Mom, as Uncle Jian reminded us how little we mattered.

While the three of us seethed in our own thoughts, Uncle Jian tried to alleviate the awkwardness by rambling onward. "Mother wanted him to marry the nurse. I know you never got along with her, but you know how she is. The rest of us were against it once we knew you were coming back, and now we never see Yan-Fei anymore. No harm done. You and my brother can be together again. It's like it never even happened now. Lucky that you wrote to us when you did. Otherwise we would really have had an embarrassing situation." He forced himself to laugh, but it came out in a stuttering, artificial way. Beside me, Di looked ready to tear someone apart with her bare hands.

"Maybe I shouldn't have said anything," Uncle Jian said, capitulating. "I feel bad for upsetting you all. It isn't as bad as it sounds—I'm just not a man who is good with words. That's why I became a soldier—I'm not made for university like my brother."

"No," Mom said, stiffly. It was probably best to hear it from

Jian, since even his attempts to sugarcoat the past were more honest than anything Father would say. "I'm glad you told me. I was wondering this whole time whether there would be a second wife waiting. At least now I can enter the house a bit easier."

"Don't be crazy. Second wife? Polygamy was banned ages ago. What do you take us for, backward barbarians?" Uncle Jian exclaimed. "No, it's just you. And we are so thankful that you are alive. I didn't know that you weren't in Qingdao when the family left for Taiwan, and when I found them in Taipei, I felt awful because I was the one who pushed them to leave. I'm so sorry for what you went through—had I known you were in Zhucheng I would have asked them to wait and take the next boat so that they would have time to go back for you."

"You don't need to be sorry," said Mom, softening. "You are why we are here now. And we are not your responsibility. My husband could also have decided to take a later boat and wait for us."

Uncle Jian sighed, moving to defend his brother. "He didn't think it would be so difficult to go back to the mainland. He didn't want to leave you behind."

"Really?" Mom asked dubiously.

"Of course!" Uncle Jian said. "He felt even worse than I did about what happened, naturally. He wanted to go back for you all, but the exit regulations prevented him from returning to the mainland."

I leaned over to Di and whispered, "I wonder when he went from feeling awful to going on the prowl for his new wife."

"Exactly," she whispered back. "How convenient these exit regulations are."

Perhaps we had been too loud, because Mom turned her head and gave us both an intense disapproving glare. We zipped our lips shut and folded our hands together in our laps, restraining the turmoil within. The exit regulations weren't a lie. While they were strict, I had no doubt that the strings that Uncle Jian pulled to get us our entry permits were likely the same strings that could have been pulled if Father had really wanted to find us. I thought about Mr. Chong at Mount Davis, when he'd snuck across the border, braving persecution to find his wife and daughters, and about that father we had seen at the airport who cried when he was reunited with his family. Whatever love those men had for their wives and children was simply missing between Father and us. Even without the exit regulations in place, there would have been another excuse—boat tickets were too hard to find; the journey was too dangerous; Nai Nai needed her son . . . For that, I hated him even more.

Uncle Jian turned off the main road, and we started to make our way through smaller, winding streets. Though Taipei was still mostly rural, there were urban areas cropping up to accommodate the sudden increase in population density. We passed people who were wearing jackets even though it was warm. Their faces and hands were tan, and though it was early in the day, there was movement on every street. Children dressed in school uniforms clutched books in their arms, and pedicabs picked up passengers. Bicycles were everywhere, easily outnumbering any other form of transportation.

We passed a market, and vendors were setting up their tables and stalls. One lady untied what looked like a large bedsheet that she was using as a sack. Like a magician, she laid it over her table with the flick of her wrists, and the sheet draped over the edges like a tablecloth. The clothing inside it remained folded in neat piles, so all she had to do was reposition it and she was ready to start her day.

Uncle Jian's jeep rolled to a stop in front of a small, old *shiheyuan*. It was dilapidated but still one of the nicer homes in a neighborhood composed of chalky-looking buildings. The walls were made of gray concrete smoothed over with plaster, and the windows and doors were painted vermilion. Instead of stone lions, there was a young mango tree by the entrance. Without the foreboding statues, Nai Nai had to supplement the home's protection. Like locks of hair, red scrolls, with phrases in gold lettering to ward off evil and misfortune, hung on both sides of an iron security gate. I felt like we were ghouls and those warnings were meant for us. Despite Nai Nai's efforts, her hungry ghosts had arrived.

"Welcome home," Uncle Jian said as we descended from the jeep. "We've already prepared a space for you. We don't have as much money as we used to, but we were able to buy this *shiheyuan* and set up a life here. Just don't expect it to be as nice as in Zhucheng." He stopped, catching himself, and apologized again. "I'm sorry. I'm an idiot. I know you must have seen so much worse on your journey here. I'm glad we are back so I can just shut up and stop spitting out the wrong thing."

Uncle Jian was remorseful, but I had already forgiven him when we received his first letter, and, like Mom, I credited him for securing our entry permits. I also decided to forgive Yei Yei, who had forced Father to dump his new girlfriend and also instructed Uncle Jian to ensure our passage.

My stomach ached and my palms sweat as I thought about how we would be facing Father and Nai Nai soon. I knew too that no matter what we wanted to say, the first words had to come from Mom. How would she react when she saw Father? Would Di be able to hold her explosive mouth shut? Would I be able to contain myself if Mom stayed silent?

The courtyard doors swung open before we approached them,

and Father stepped out, the sun behind him like a halo. Like Uncle Jian, he hadn't changed. His hair was jet-black, while Mom's had threads of gray, and he was dressed in a crisp white short-sleeved shirt and navy pants. He had always had a young face, and now he looked more like our brother than like Mom's husband. "Thank the Gods, you are all here and you are alive! I'm so grateful to the deities who watched over you and brought you all to our doorstep." He held the courtyard gate and door open for us as we stepped inside.

Mom moved stiffly, self-consciously, making me cringe. I wished that she had charged past that threshold with her head high and her chin up, but instead she looked like a beggar approaching a rich man's home.

"Mom is the one who brought us to this doorstep," I said resolutely. "We did pray along the way, but we did not pray our way here." We walked, we crawled, and we traveled by rail and sea to reach this destination.

Father looked at me and blinked and said, "Yes, of course. We make our own fortune, after all."

I managed to pull my face up in a smile, while Di didn't even bother. She glared at Father with eyes like daggers, which made me feel like a traitor for attempting to be polite.

"Is this Lan?" Father asked as Lan shrank in Mom's arms, tired from the journey and intimidated by these men whom she had completely forgotten.

Mom nodded. "She is two now. She's changed so much, hasn't she?" Lan had gone from a chubby baby with folds on her arms and legs to a child with frail limbs and a belly that protruded, not from fat but likely from intestinal parasites. She tucked her head under Mom's chin and looked at Di and me, unsettled by the intensity of the anger that radiated from our rigid bodies.

Nai Nai and Yei Yei came into the courtyard, along with Aunt Ji and Pei. I recognized all of their faces and, surprisingly, it did not feel like so much time had passed—it was as though we had finally woken up from our extended nightmare and it was only yesterday that we had lived and eaten together in the same complex. Nai Nai leaned on Yei Yei's arm for support, but she also carried a wooden cane carved with a simple lotus flower.

"Hai?" called the deep voice of a man.

It took me a minute to realize that this man was Chiao! He had lost his baby fat and grown at least thirty centimeters. My mischievous cousin had disappeared, and a sophisticated young man stood in his place, wearing a school uniform. "Chiao!" I exclaimed, waving at him.

"By the heavens, you look horrible," said Chiao, blunt like his father. "I mean, just awful. What happened to you? It must have been terrible, since you just look so bad."

"You've changed too," I said. "Though I guess for the better. You look like a soldier!"

Chiao shook his head. "We should have never left you in Zhucheng. You look like refugees!"

"We *were* refugees," I replied. I wondered to myself, *Are we still refugees? Is that a status that goes away?*

Nai Nai, like Di, did not bother to mask her feelings. She didn't pretend to be happy to see us or concerned about our well-being. Her expression made her look like she was both severely constipated and indignant at the same time—as though we had interrupted her while she was on the toilet. Eyeing Lan's shriveled leg, she grimaced and said, "What happened to Three's leg?"

Mom's scathing expression would have flayed a normal person's flesh, but an old dragon like Nai Nai didn't even shiver. I wanted to stomp on her delicate feet and send her crumbling to the ground in agony. How I longed to see that disgruntled scowl transform to anguish! Mom, however, quickly replaced her placid mask and said, "Lan got tuberculosis in Qingdao. It infected her legs, but we took her to a doctor and she survived."

Nai Nai raised her brows, weighing the financial cost of raising Lan versus how useful she could be to the household. *Medical bills? Surgery?* Then she wrinkled her nose. "What a smell," she said, disgusted. "All of you need to wash up in the yard. Those squatter camps in Hong Kong are riddled with disease. We certainly don't want you all bringing tuberculosis or any other sickness to this home. Or lice! Do you know how hard it is to get rid of lice?"

My scalp burned as I recalled the pungent odor of insecticide, but Mom only bowed her head and said, "Of course, Mother. We will wash now."

"Come on, Mother—let them eat first," Uncle Jian said, reaching for the door to the house. "They must be starving."

"Don't be ridiculous, Jian," Nai Nai snapped. "It will only be a few minutes for them to wash, and then they can enjoy their food like civilized people instead of refugees." She said the word "refugee" as though it were an insult, like "barbarian" or, even worse, "Communist."

"I'll pull water from the bathroom," said Father, thinking he was being helpful. I winced and thought of how Di always called me a "mama's baby" for being so obedient. Did I come off to Di like Father came off to me? I hoped not.

While our relatives went back inside, Nai Nai made us strip and wash ourselves in the courtyard because she didn't want us trailing in our filth. "Make sure to rinse the courtyard floor so that dirty water doesn't just pool here," Nai Nai called from over her shoulder. If it weren't for the neighbors, she would have sent us to roll outside in a trough like animals.

The well water was cold, and Mom had to pin Lan down to lather her. Quickly, however, Lan became too slippery and darted away, scrambling on her hands and knees through the courtyard yelling, "No bath, no bath!" Mom and I chased her, all of us nude, Lan's spindly, soapy arms sliding like eels through our desperate fingers. When Di finally managed to tackle her, Lan sank her jagged teeth into Di's shoulder, prompting Di to slap her on her bottom. Both of them screamed, an embarrassing spectacle made worse by the fact that we hadn't been that dirty to begin with. We had bathed with frequency in the streams at Rennie's Mill!

"Lather your hair well," Mom commanded us as she seized Lan and scoured her mercilessly. I hoped that none of our relatives witnessed this circus, which only made us look more uncouth.

To avoid Nai Nai's disgust, Di and I washed so well that layers of gray rolled off our bodies and our skin was pink and raw. I supposed that it was unfair to expect Mom to do anything but obey, but there was a torrent of emotions that she was suppressing—not just in herself, but in all of us. *When will these rich pigs finally learn the meaning of justice? There must be accountability for their crimes.* Though I was trying to resist, my brain kept regurgitating Communist phrases, which lingered on my tongue, prickling against my lips. I swallowed them and helped Mom rinse off the courtyard as Nai Nai had requested.

After wiping our feet carefully with some towels, we put on clean clothing from Aunt Ji and headed to the kitchen. Our new home was plain, with simple wooden furniture and few decorations. There were a porcelain urn and an antique painting of the Guang-Yin Bodhisattva that I remembered from Zhucheng, but it seemed that the family had left most of their belongings in Qingdao. Uncle Jian seemed to think that in a few years the Nationalists would attack the mainland again, and we could return and retrieve any belongings that remained. According to him, the Americans' Seventh Fleet—our old Qingdao acquaintances—were blockading the strait because of the Korean War, which had broken out shortly before our relocation to Rennie's Mill. The People's Liberation Army had been poised to invade Taiwan, and Mao had been livid about the interference. In retaliation, he sent the troops destined for the island to the Korean border instead, buying Chiang time and further cementing the Nationalists' alliance with the United States.

In the kitchen, Aunt Ji had prepared a platter of buns and fruit, including pineapples, bananas, papayas, and slices of watermelon, as well as some fruits that we had never seen before—Taiwanese mountain apples with waxy red skin, and green guavas with pink, seeded flesh. The rainbow before me was as surreal as a mirage. I couldn't even remember what fresh fruit tasted like. Di seized a banana, and I started shoving the soft papaya into my mouth, barely swallowing before chasing it down with bites of tart pineapple. The crisp, ripe watermelon exploded on my tongue as I chomped my way down to its rind, swallowing the seeds in my haste. Lan had planted her face straight in the platter, a chunk of papaya hanging from her nose when she rose for air.

"Did the Communists ban chopsticks too?" Nai Nai snapped disdainfully as we licked our fingers. "And table manners?" If looks could kill, we would all have choked and keeled over in a puddle of fruit juice, but we were too hungry to care. We devoured everything on the table, but we were still ravenous. The fruit slaked our thirst but did not keep us full, and the few buns could not make up for years of rationing. I felt like an ungrateful guest, longing for more but not feeling familiar or comfortable enough with my hosts to ask for it.

31

SAVAGE WOMEN

Both Yei Yei and Father were working as teachers in Taipei and relied on modest government salaries, without land or businesses to supplement their income. Though Yei Yei had brought money from the mainland, it was not enough to sustain the lifestyle that they had been accustomed to in Zhucheng. It was astonishing to hear Nai Nai complain about the hardship she'd endured since moving to Taiwan. She lamented having to use a cane because there were fewer people in the house to help her walk around. She was despondent that meat was a limited commodity and that she had to eat rice. She was devastated that her home was smaller, and that her furniture was plain, and that she hadn't had new clothing recently.

Despite the downgrades, Nai Nai still retained a few of her Zhucheng habits. Every week, she ate a whole pork kidney because a traditional doctor told her to. Every morning, she had two eggs poached in chicken soup, which she thought would preserve her youth and vitality. She rarely performed house chores, and she still spent most of her day lounging like royalty and barking commands at the other women.

Soon after we arrived, Mom washed all of the bedding and linens and cleaned the entire house, hoping to please Nai Nai and ease our transition. Each day, Mom rose early to make breakfast, and went to bed only after every surface gleamed. Still, Nai Nai grumbled that she served no purpose now that we had no workers to cook for, and gave her any additional assignments that she could think of—like polishing her cane and all of Yei Yei's and Father's shoes.

Despite the years that had passed, Nai Nai still remembered the fortune-teller's words. Reminding Mom that she was only thirty-three years old, Nai Nai arranged for the four of us to share a bedroom while Father slept in the living room alone. "Four more mouths to feed," Nai Nai muttered. "And one of them a cripple. We can't afford any more!"

Occasionally, if Nai Nai was in a really foul mood, she would bring up the nurse her son had almost married and say, "Yan-Fei was such a smart girl. So useful too. She could bring in an income. What a pity." In Zhucheng, Nai Nai would have spat if a nurse had come near her son, but in Taiwan's hard times, she welcomed any additional salary to the family coffers.

Mom ignored her, head bowed as usual, and went about her chores while Di and I gritted our teeth.

One morning, I was sweeping the kitchen when Di had taken Lan outside to play. Nai Nai sat at the dining table, drinking the last drops of her daily eggs and soup while Mom cleared Father's and Yei Yei's dishes. As Mom walked to the sink, a bowl slipped from her hand, shattering loudly against the floor.

Nai Nai cried out as though someone had dropped her firstborn child. Face scrunched in fury, she yelled, "Careless! So careless!" Frazzled, Mom dove to pick up the broken pieces of ceramic, cutting her thumb in her haste. "You think now that you are back here you can be absent-minded because we are made of money? Go kneel!"

"I'm sorry, Mother," Mom replied automatically, like a machine instead of a person. She dumped the shards into the garbage, dried her hands, and accepted her punishment, kneeling obediently in the corner of the kitchen.

"Don't yell at my mom!" I found myself screaming, my errant words like angry birds breaking free from their cage. Years ago, I would have never dared to raise my voice at Nai Nai. However, seeing my brave mother, who had led us through the darkness of war, cowed before this ignorant queen was too much to bear. I couldn't grit my teeth anymore. I couldn't keep silent anymore. "It was an accident!" I shouted, meeting Nai Nai's piercing obsidian eyes. "She's the one working all day while you sit and do nothing. You are the one who is a useless mouth to feed!"

Face red, Nai Nai hobbled over to the table so that she could grip onto it, and then in one swift motion she whacked me across the face with her cane. As blood flowed from my split lip, its metallic taste flipped a switch in me and my vision blurred. Memories resurfaced, and I found myself on my knees at Wildflower Field, my hands tied and my heart pounding with terror. I was small, impotent, as I fought with my mind to stay in the present. *I am in Taiwan. I am in the Ang family home.* The ground beneath me had turned to sand and I was sinking, the words "snakelike scoundrel" echoing in my ears.

Mom screamed and ran to me, her strong arms wrapping around my torso like a tourniquet. Her touch and her voice pulled me trembling back to reality, the kitchen solidifying again before my eyes, which watered as I blinked. Rennie's Mill had turned us into savage women—I had yelled at an elder and Mom had risen without permission.

Wielding her cane like a sword, Nai Nai smacked Mom on the back as though she were trying to slice her in two. "Terrible mother, terrible child! I wish the Communists had killed you all so you ungrateful, nasty women wouldn't be in my household! Both of you, go kneel!" Still shaken, I took a deep breath as Mom took my hand and the two of us went to kneel in the corner of the kitchen.

I wiped my lips, leaving a bright crimson trail of blood on my palm, while Mom kept pressure on her bleeding thumb. After Nai Nai stumbled away, Mom said quietly, "Hai, you need to respect your elders." These were the words that she was supposed to say, and she echoed this traditional mantra like the cadres repeated Mao's speeches. We could still hear Nai Nai's cane clicking sharply against the floor like a ticking clock.

My heart rate finally began to slow, and I replied, "Respecting elders means standing up if they are being bullied."

Mom smiled, but my words seemed to have cracked her shell. "Don't worry about me, Hai," she said, voice wavering. "I'm used to her. It's been some time, but I know this life. It's my life." She paused, then added, "And I don't want yours to be anything like it." Tears began to fall from Mom's eyes, but she wiped them away quickly and said, "I want you to marry well, but I want you to be like that nurse, so no one will look down on you. Have a job, so that you can support yourself."

I think what she meant was, *so you can leave if you want to.* "No one should look down on you, Mom," I said angrily. "You work harder than anyone else in this house."

"But I cannot bring money to the table," Mom explained. "My work doesn't count."

I fumed, thinking of how diligently Mom fulfilled her domestic duties, and of the labor she put into raising all of us. Nai Nai considered the expense of hiring house help to be too high yet still did not credit Mom's contributions as savings, and in that sense earnings, for the family.

As I knelt by Mom's side, I made a promise to both of us that I would study rigorously when I got back in the classroom. If I did well enough, maybe I could get a job with a good wage, and Mom, Di, and I could do what we had planned to in Hong Kong—make our own living.

"Please don't cry, Mom," I said, trying to assuage her. "I'll work hard. I'll make sure Di does too. We will both go back to school now. You don't need to worry."

Mom nodded and said, "If you go to school and do well, then this journey will have been worth it. Living with Nai Nai will have been worth it."

Later, in our bedroom, Di saw my split lip and asked what had happened. I told her about my fight with Nai Nai, expecting praise. Instead, she said in an accusatory tone, "You had a fight with that old witch, and you didn't call me?"

I was confused. Di was always telling me I was a goody-goody, and I had finally spoken up and she was upset. "Are you angry at me?" I asked in disbelief.

"Yes!" Di yelled, stomping her foot. "I've been wanting to scream at that wicked bat since the moment we got here, but I've been holding it in so much that my stomach probably has an ulcer. Because you and Mom are always telling me to be good and control myself! And now you two hypocrites go and have a delightful telling off and I didn't get to say my piece?"

"I wouldn't exactly call it delightful," I said, pointing to my lip, annoyed that Di had the gall to scold me. "How could we call you when we were too busy being hit with Nai Nai's cane?"

Di crossed her arms, still looking agitated. "Do you think it's too late for me to go yell at her too?"

"Yes!" I exclaimed. "Don't make it worse. Mom and I had to kneel all day until I went to ask Yei Yei if we could get up." I didn't tell Yei Yei that I had yelled at Nai Nai; I said just that we were made to kneel because Mom had broken a bowl. He only rolled his eyes and sighed and told me Nai Nai had been anxious lately and cautioned us to try to stay out of her sight—which was impossible considering she had a never-ending list of tasks for Mom to do.

I wished that I had just told Di that I had tripped and fallen, because over the next days she was itching for a confrontation, waiting for Nai Nai to say something mean so she could hurl back a litany of insults. Stressed, I tiptoed on eggshells, anticipating the explosion of Di's fury, which inevitably would cause more trouble for Mom.

That time came one evening after Father returned from work. "Quick, quick," Nai Nai called to Mom. "Get your husband some tea! He's spent the entire day working hard, and he needs to be able to relax when he comes home." With a soft groan, Mom rose to her feet—I knew they throbbed, because she had spent the entire day carrying buckets of water around the courtyard. She had scrubbed and rinsed the walls of the *shiheyuan* until they looked several shades whiter than before, and her hands were chapped and her arms were sore.

"I'll get the tea, Mom," I offered, jumping up and running to the kitchen.

"A well-taught lady doesn't run like a little boy!" Nai Nai scolded behind me. I slowed my pace, taking deliberate and dainty steps like I was practicing a dance, until I was out of her sight. The home was small enough that I could still hear her while I was in the kitchen. She added, "Speaking of well-taught ladies, how is Yan-Fei? Does she still come around the school?"

I stopped midpour, frozen, holding the teakettle. This was the first time that Nai Nai had mentioned the nurse since our fight in the kitchen. I braced myself, certain that this would be the provocation that Di would pounce on.

Silence.

"Not really," I heard Father reply.

Before he could say more, I slammed the teakettle down and ran back into the living room, not like a little boy this time but like a hurricane. "Yan-Fei?" I repeated, my courage bolstered by the rage swirling through my blood. "Yan-Fei? How can you continue to talk about this woman like she's still a part of our family? Hasn't my mother been through enough?"

I didn't know what had caught Di's tongue, but my outburst was the catalyst that she needed to go ballistic.

"You are a horrible, miserable, evil hag!" Di yelled, leaping to her feet.

"Di!" Mom and Father exclaimed together.

"You will not speak to your grandmother like that," Father scolded, his anger a rising wave. When we were younger, we had been terrified of making Father mad. Now, however, we were no longer little girls—and we were no longer afraid.

Pivoting, Di faced him and shouted, "And you are a pathetic coward!"

"You are not too old for a spanking," Father barked back, raising his fist.

Mom held up her hands and cried, "Both of you girls need to stop now!"

Ignoring Mom, I joined Di, our two storms merging into one as I shouted, "You, Father, are the one we blame most. You were supposed to protect us, but you ran away to save yourself!"

Father moved to strike me, but I easily dodged and slipped to the other side of the room. Pointing my finger at Nai Nai, I said, "You sit here complaining incessantly, when you have no idea what we had to live through after you abandoned us in Zhucheng. We had to stay with animals in a shed!" Father clumsily chased me, but I was too quick for him. As a child, I used to hold still and take his beatings. His bumping into furniture as he tried to catch me showed me just how weak he was when we stopped complying with his rules. "We walked until our feet bled to go to Qingdao, only to be told that you all fled to Taiwan without us! We crawled into city drains to pick out chicken bones because we were so hungry!"

"We got lice!" Di cried. Father panted with exhaustion, his hand having fallen to his side. This was the first time that any of us had spoken about what we had endured. Di eyed him venomously and said, "Because of what you did, Hai was tortured by the Communists. Did you know? Did Mom tell you?"

Father's mouth fell open, but he didn't answer. I knew Mom hadn't told him. That type of secret was reserved for family, but the chasm between us had grown so wide that our shared blood couldn't bridge it. I wasn't ashamed, though. He needed to know.

Di's face was crimson as she continued. "Because of your profits and the wealth of the Ang family, Hai had to kneel on the ice while people screamed at her and threw dirt and snow in her face. They blamed her for your escape! The cadres beat her so badly that she almost died. She almost froze!"

"It should have been you," I said, meeting Father's solemn eyes, holding his gaze until he looked away. My words were brazen, but they were true, and no harsher than what he deserved to hear.

"While you were all here eating fruit and chicken soup, I took your punishment. We survived the people who scared you so much that you ran across the sea. We have faced worse than you, and we will not allow any of you to insult our mother again." To Nai Nai, I shouted, "If you ever—*ever*—mention this nurse again, whatever her name is, I will grab your cane and make you kneel!"

"I'll beat you like the Communists beat my sister, so you can get a taste!" Di shrieked, hitting an octave so high that glass could have shattered.

Frightened by the shouting, Lan began to cry. Father stood paralyzed, brow scrunched and eyes downcast. Was this what guilt looked like? Did he feel responsible, remorseful?

Nai Nai trembled, not with fear, but from her own fury. She lifted her cane and tried to rise, but her foot slipped and she fell back into her chair with a pathetic clump. Though Mom had done nothing, she looked terrified, bracing for the wrath that she knew was coming. With a frantic hand, she motioned for Di and me to get behind her, but we didn't need to. As Nai Nai struggled to rise, I saw her for what she was—the most feeble of us all, unable to even stand on her own, dependent on our obedience to reign.

The front door clicked open and Yei Yei entered, unaware that he was sailing into the eye of a storm. Confused, he glanced from one face to the next and settled on his shaking wife's. "What is going on?" he asked.

"Out of my house!" Nai Nai screamed, gripping the armrests of her chair. A vein on the side of her head was pulsing and blue. "This heathen woman and her barbarian children are a plague on our household. Never in my life have I witnessed such shameful behavior! I want them out. I want them out!"

Yei Yei put his head in his hands and said, "It can't have been that bad. Did they break more dishes?"

"I want them *out!*" Nai Nai shrieked, barely coherent, spittle dripping from her mouth.

"Everyone, go to your room!" Yei Yei commanded, exasperated. He looked at Father and said, "Not you, Xiao-Long. You stay here and tell me what happened. All the women, to your room!"

Nai Nai began to cry and said, "After everything I have done for them, they mistreat me. My ungrateful daughter-in-law comes into my home and eats my food and sleeps under my roof and insults me and no one defends me. My own son, whom I raised from a baby, only watches while they bully me."

"To your room, now!" Yei Yei bellowed.

Nai Nai took her cane and hobbled toward her bedroom, wailing loudly, like a train pulling away from a station. "Why did I even bother having children?" she uttered in between dramatic heaves of air.

I grabbed Mom's arm while Di grabbed Lan, and the four of us retreated to our shared room, which had a Japanese shoji door. We sat on our sleeping mats, trying to listen to Yei Yei and Father's conversation, but their voices were too low for us to distinguish their words.

Mom nervously smoothed the wrinkles on her pants. She said, voice hoarse, "You girls have really done it now. I've never seen Nai Nai so angry."

"It needed to be said," Di huffed, unapologetic.

"We cannot keep living with her rubbing her fantasy life for Father in our faces," I added indignantly.

Mom shook her head. "You still cannot speak to Nai Nai that way. She is your grandmother. She raised your father. Without her, there would be no you."

"She intercepted Uncle Jian's letter to try to stop us from coming here," I argued. "She preferred that the Communists kill us, or that we starve to death!"

"Living under Nai Nai is not worse than living at Rennie's Mill," Mom emphasized. "At least here it is clean, we are safe, and we have some real food to eat. Now I'm worried the Ang family is going to throw us out on the streets!"

"You are the one who said that they wouldn't go to all the effort to get us our entry permits just to have us starve, Mom," retorted Di.

"That was before we provoked Nai Nai!" Mom cried. "They will all say I am a bad mother and that we are bad influences on the rest of the family. Both of you need to stop talking back to your elders, including me!"

We heard Father's heavy footsteps and hushed quickly as he slid open the door. He was pale and looked shaken. "All of you need to apologize to Nai Nai," he said somberly. "A flower which neglects its roots can never bloom. Nai Nai can be difficult, but she is still the eldest woman of the household and entitled to your respect."

"Of course," Mom answered, before Di or I could respond. "I am sorry about our daughters. We have had a difficult journey and they are under stress. It is my fault for not controlling the situation." She grabbed Lan, and Di and I trailed behind her like ducklings, ignoring Father, who stepped aside to let us pass.

Mom slid Nai Nai's door open, and we found her lying on her bed, the back of her hand over her eyes, her tiny bound feet propped up on a pillow. They looked like children's toys. We were in Taiwan, a new place in a new era, but here Nai Nai was, keeping her little lotuses neatly wrapped like we still lived in imperial China. The pain of maintenance must have been excruciating, but I was too furious to pity her.

Yei Yei sat at the foot of the bed, glasses in his lap, looking more annoyed than angry.

Mom got on her knees, and Di and I did the same. The three of us kowtowed in unison. "I am sorry, Mother," Mom said on our behalf. "My daughters spoke out of turn. I will make sure to teach them better over the next years."

"Sorry," Di and I repeated, like we were echoing a new vocabulary word. Maybe we should have tried harder to sound sincere, but admitting defeat was difficult enough as it was.

Nai Nai sat up, scowling. "You are only apologizing because my son forced you. I mean what I said. I don't want you in my home. You can stay here for tonight, but I want you out by tomorrow evening!"

"Let's discuss in the morning," Yei Yei said. "You are tired. Why don't you just rest?"

"Not a chance," Nai Nai seethed. "I refuse to have these barbarians influencing the other children, passing on the nasty attitudes and trashy habits that they've picked up from the Communists. They need to leave!"

"I understand, Mother," Father said, standing behind us. He too knelt and kowtowed to Nai Nai. "They are my family. I am responsible for them. I want you to live a long, happy life free from stress, and if the presence of my wife and children brings you such trauma, then they cannot live here."

Mom gasped and clasped her hands together, prepared to grovel for forgiveness. Regret washed over me as I saw her distress—but only briefly. I did feel remorseful for burning the bridge that Mom had tended to so carefully, but I wasn't afraid. We knew street life. As hard as it had been, I disagreed with Mom. This *shiheyuan* was worse than Rennie's Mill. Even there I had seen her smile more than I had these past few weeks. Piles of fruit were not worth the cost of her laughter. She wanted to come to Taipei for us. We had to leave this house for her.

I opened my mouth, ready to launch, but Father preempted my attack and said, "I will move out with them."

It took me a long moment to register his words, but even then I couldn't believe them. *He's coming with us?* I looked at Di, who was equally confused. Father rarely took a stand for anything; he was like a jellyfish, floating along with whatever current captured him. We were so accustomed to disappointment that we didn't know how to react. *He chose us?*

Nai Nai covered her eyes with her hands and wailed as though he had announced a terminal illness. "No!" she cried. "It's not your fault, Xiao-Long. You couldn't possibly have controlled them while they were all the way across the sea. Their behavior is entirely their own. Seek a divorce—no one would blame you!"

"A man does not abandon his wife," Yei Yei growled at Nai Nai. "I wanted to discuss this tomorrow, but if you must hear it now, Xiao-Long has a responsibility to his family. The middle school in Douliu is looking for teachers. It is a step up from Xiao-Long's current position as an elementary school teacher. The location is not as desirable as Taipei, but it is still a good opportunity!"

Nai Nai began to cry again, curling up into a ball like a wounded animal. "My son! How can you support sending my son away?" she sniffled at Yei Yei. "My eldest son! Who is going to take care of us?" Father's leaving would break tradition, a veritable slap in the face for someone like Nai Nai, who clung to Confucian values.

Yei Yei replied, firmly, "We have others living here with us, and you and I are not so old. We will manage."

"I won't be far," Father said, reaching out to hold Nai Nai's hand, which was slick with tears. "We can visit frequently. Chiang-Yue and I will teach our girls well, and then perhaps we will come back one day. But for now, the distance is for the best."

Still on her knees, Mom looked hesitant, as though it were all too good to be true. I also wondered why Father had made such a bold move. Was it guilt? Was it obligation? Was it possibly love? Whatever the reason, it made me feel vindicated. Silence was not the virtue that we had always been taught it was. In all these years, it had been the enemy of change. With this small step, I hoped that my mother was on her way to the life that she deserved—the one that I wanted for her.

32

HERITAGE

In Douliu we lived in a small row house—simple, bare, but clean. It was amazing, not only because it was an actual home with glass windows, plumbing, and electricity, but also because it was *ours*. We didn't need to share it with another family, and we didn't need to share it with members of our extended family. In the back, there was a small yard that Mom used to raise chickens. She was determined to help bring in an income, and every day she made flatbread and sweet buns and sold them out in the street, along with hard-boiled eggs.

As Northerners we had been dismayed when we passed only rice paddies on the road and suspected that wheat could not grow in such a hot and humid climate. Though Taiwanese people traditionally relied on rice as their staple, the Americans had introduced wheat flour through aid programs and charities. We were thrilled to be able to make our bread and noodles, which the Taiwanese also began to incorporate into their cuisine. Mom used empty cotton flour sacks to sew clothing for Lan, who became a walking advertisement for the United States, their Stars and Stripes on every outfit.

Christian charities gave away milk powder and cooking oil to anyone who attended church services and studied the Bible. Mom was a devout Buddhist, but she was also practical. She went to St. John's Church, a few streets from the main market, and even got baptized in exchange for these essential items. "You need to wear these," she told us excitedly one Sunday, draping wooden cross necklaces over our heads. "The Americans are giving out Spam!" Together we raced to the church, crosses jangling. Usually, lunch meat was distributed only after tropical storms or other humanitarian disasters. Was there a holiday? An American celebration, perhaps? It didn't matter. We loved Spam and eagerly stood in line outside St. John's stained-glass doors whenever it was distributed.

Meanwhile, Father began his new job at the middle school. As a courtesy the administrator waived our school fees, but we still had to pay for the expensive uniforms. All of Mom's egg and bread money went into two white shirts and blue skirts, one set each for Di and me. "Don't get them dirty," Mom cautioned as I twirled, excited to have a new outfit. "You'll have to wash them on the weekend."

School had occupied my thoughts since Mom and I had knelt on the floor together in Nai Nai's kitchen. After scrabbling in the mainland, I figured learning would be easy—all I had to do was sit, listen, and remember. I was fifteen and had never been in a classroom, but I expected it to be similar to having our tutor in Zhucheng.

Father had warned us that public school classes were taught exclusively in Mandarin, which Di and I barely spoke. Under Chiang Kai-Shek, it was illegal to speak any language but Mandarin in public, a policy intended to promote nationalism and unity. However, none of the islanders had spoken it before 1945—most of them spoke Fujianese, Hakka, or aboriginal languages, while the elite used Japanese. Still, islander children were punished in school if teachers caught them chattering in their native tongues.

"You cannot speak Shandongese in class," Father emphasized. "I know Mandarin is a struggle for you, but when in doubt, remember that silence is a wise man's friend." Despite his concern, I wasn't intimidated. After all, we had survived in Hong Kong without Cantonese. I shrugged him off, skipping to school with a backpack full of self-assurance.

On the first day of class, however, after the teacher introduced me, there were only a few sentences that I fully understood. In the mainland, I could follow Mandarin well enough if I focused, but I had never had to concentrate on it for hours at a time. The administrators had put me a few years behind because of the gap in my education, but even so, I was lost. Math contained symbols that I had never seen, and literature was a mystery. School might as well have been full of witches casting spells. Every day, I sat with my lips pressed together and hands folded, nodding occasionally to pretend that I was following the lesson. One afternoon, however, the teacher called on me in history class. At the chalkboard, he pointed to a map of China and said, "Ang Li-Hai, what happened in the *blah* century when *blah blah*? The *blah blah* struggled—how did they *blah* Germany?" I should have understood these sentences, but it was the last class of the day, and my tired brain was in a fog.

Father said to be silent, but when I failed to respond, the teacher only walked closer to my desk and repeated himself. My faulty mind still refused to translate. I knew the word "parasite" in Mandarin. I had spoken with government officials and I knew other tough words, like "reactionary" and "deportation." Why wasn't I getting this? *Don't speak Shandongese, or everyone will think you're a bumpkin!* In my distress I couldn't even remember how to say "I don't know" in Mandarin, a simple phrase that I had uttered countless times. The teacher cocked his head and held his hands up. "Li-Hai, this should be an easy question, since you came from Qingdao."

My classmates were staring at me, expecting a reply. Something about Germany, but all I could think of was Mrs. Ding and her constant assertion that she had been around since German rule. *Silence is a wise man's friend.* "Sorry!" I yelled in Cantonese. Then in Mandarin I blurted, "Answer don't have!" Everyone laughed and hooted while the teacher called for order and I shrank in my seat, wishing for the hands on the clock to fly so I could go home.

It was mortifying. I wasn't the only one who struggled with our national language, but I was the only one who was a freak about it. Most of the children in my class had Fujianese roots and had been learning Mandarin for only a few years. Together, however, they at least could whisper in their native tongues and find camaraderie outside of the classroom.

Dejected, I met Di at the end of the day. She leaned against the chain-link fence of the schoolyard, her short hair neat and tidy—school regulations prohibited long hair, so Mom had given us matching bobs. Her mouth moved in an exaggerated way as she practiced her Mandarin tones, which flowed like a musical wave. "You are so good with languages," I said, frustrated by my earlier embarrassment. "I wish I could pick them up as easily as you do."

Di shrugged. "You probably could if you tried to learn, instead of just clinging to your Shandongese mommy."

"Shut up," I snapped, irritated that she had to flip my compliment into an insult. "I just don't have as good an ear as you do!" The ease with which she had conversed in Cantonese with the restaurant owners in Hong Kong had been amazing.

As we walked home, however, I knew that Di was right. I never pushed myself linguistically because I always had Mom to converse with, and I'd had our Northerner bubble at Mount Davis. My classmates today had pointed at me and mocked me in Fujianese, and I'd had no retort. *Maybe they weren't even talking about me*, I thought hopefully, dreading having to return the next day. *Maybe I can skip school and go sell eggs with Mom at the market.*

Di's voice, however, rang in my head. *Mama's baby!*

And then Mom's voice followed. *If you go to school and do well, then this journey will have been worth it.*

They were both right. Not only did I have to go back to school, but I had to improve. Over the next months, I practiced my Mandarin, repeating the tones everywhere I could—while walking to class, while cleaning the house, even while playing with Lan. After school, I went to the market with Mom and became like Mrs. Ding, chatting with everyone to practice my vocabulary and conversation skills. I even learned some Fujianese as Taiwanese customers spoke their own mix of languages back to me.

Within a few months, I understood what the bullies in school had been saying when they sneered at me: *garbage princess, beggar girl.* I thought I had left that all behind when we crossed the sea. Did these children know what I had done in the mainland? Was there a smell that lingered, or something else that marked me?

Apparently, there were refugees in Taiwan who had arrived with nothing and lived in military dependents' villages. Even with the meagerness of Father's salary, we were still in a better position than many of them. These starving mainlanders often stole fruit from Taiwanese farms. I learned this because a group of my classmates brought a bucket of peach pits one day and ambushed me after school, pelting me with them and calling me a thief. Blocking my face with my arms, I ran to the market, two of the kids hot on my heels. An older Taiwanese lady who sold dried squid, Mrs. Chen, saw me zigzagging between the stalls and intercepted my aggressors, smacking them with a rolling pin and sending them home. She told me in Mandarin that she knew their parents and would make sure they were punished if they bothered me again.

After that incident, all of my classmates left me alone—literally. I wished that I had someone like Biao-Wu, a friend whom I could talk to, but the only other student who spoke my language was Di—who was not my friend. With Nai Nai gone, the two of us lacked a common enemy. Father, whom we once both hated, now became a source of conflict between us.

Father never apologized for leaving us in Zhucheng, and after our cataclysmic fight with Nai Nai we simply didn't talk about what had happened. I didn't know if my parents discussed any of it with each other, but in Chinese culture it was inappropriate for a child to air such grievances to a parent and uncommon for a family to discuss trauma. That being said, I accepted Father's departure from the Ang family *shiheyuan* as his attempt to make amends. Away from Nai Nai, Mom could finally be comfortable in her own home, and live as a family member instead of a servant. I can't say that I forgave Father, but I understood that he had made a difficult decision in our favor and I could move forward.

Di, on the other hand, could not let go. We had countless arguments over this subject. One Saturday, we were going to wash our uniforms and I grabbed Father's white shirts too. Eyeing the bundle in my arms, Di said, "He didn't tell us to wash his shirts."

"I know," I replied. "But it would be nice for him to have clean clothes to wear to school on Monday too." It was midspring and the sun already shone vigorously. We sweat so much that we had to wash our uniforms during the week as well as on the weekends, but they dried quickly in the blazing heat. I rinsed out our kitchen sink, plugged it, and filled it with soapy water.

"Why are you being so kind to him?" Di asked. "In Hong Kong you were the one who said that we only had to live with him, and that we didn't have to like him."

I plunged the clothing into the sink to let it soak, gossamer bubbles floating into the air. "You don't have to like Father," I said. "But I think you would be happier if you stopped dwelling on the past and focused on moving forward."

"I don't just dislike him. I despise him," Di said firmly. I knew she meant it. She was able to be polite and interact with Father, but she would never care for him again.

Reluctantly, I put the kettle on the stove. It was hot enough outside that I didn't want the additional heat from the fire, but we still needed to sterilize our water before we could drink it. "We are living under his roof and eating food that he paid for," I pointed out. "We need to be grateful for that at least." Confucian tradition insisted that gratitude was the foundation of filial piety—parents were credited with giving children life, a debt that could be repaid only with a lifetime of obedience and dedication.

"I'm sick of always being told to be grateful!" Di exclaimed. "It's not like we do nothing in return. We have chores at home, and we also help at the market."

With the kettle on, I turned back to the clothing and started scrubbing each item one by one, and Di then wrung them out by hand. "Di, if you want to continue detesting Father, you can. None of us can stop you. I wish you could understand that I want you to put your anger to rest not for him but for you. Isn't it exhausting reckoning with this hatred every day and every night?"

"No," Di replied, twisting Father's shirt with such force that a small waterfall gushed from the fabric, splashing into the sink. "Hatred is easy. Forgiveness is hard, and I don't think Father is worth that effort."

"You're wrong," I said. "Forgiveness is hard in the short term, but it is easier in the long run."

Maybe there was no right or wrong in this case, and our answers were due once again to our personalities. I rarely held grudges because of the mental energy required to recall who had wronged me and how. Di, on the other hand, kept an internal blacklist and remembered details with an uncanny accuracy. It was possible that for her, hating Father was no more difficult than inhaling and exhaling. For me, such hatred would have fostered a toxic and unbearable living environment.

Mom's chickens clucked as we carried the laundry to the yard. Di passed me pieces of clothing and I clipped them onto the clothesline. As the bright sun shone through it, the laundry gave off a light floral scent from the detergent. The fragrance also lingered on our hands and arms, a perfume for poor girls.

A week later, Mom surprised us all by announcing that she was pregnant again.

"Do you think it's a boy this time?" I asked as Mom took out her sewing box one morning and sorted through Lan's old clothes. She was already making tiny outfits out of flour sacks and collecting donations from the church.

"By the Gods, I hope so," Mom said, pausing to put a hand on her stomach as if willing the baby to develop the correct genitalia.

"But you aren't thirty-six yet," said Di. "So it's probably another girl."

"Don't be like Nai Nai," I chided as I folded a pair of pajamas that Lan had outgrown; it had the words *America and Republic of China Cooperation* in red, white, and blue along the leg. "Father said we make our own fortune!"

"Exactly," Mom agreed, cutting another flour sack into pieces. "Don't be so pessimistic, Di."

Eight months later, Mom gave birth to her fifth daughter, whom she named Li-Hua, *hua* meaning "Chinese heritage," reminiscent of the home that we had left behind. Nai Nai wrote a letter that was a tirade of *I told you so* and *How could you not listen to me?* but she was in Taipei, so her vitriol, reduced to lines of ink on paper, was easily ripped up and discarded. Without family nearby, Mom had to skip her confinement period. She took a week of rest, and then was back in the market selling what she could with both Lan and Hua, in matching flour sack outfits.

33

JADE BANGLE

The year that Hua was born was the same year that Di finally got her period. Though I was turning seventeen, my body still had not recovered from malnutrition. I didn't mind, because it meant that no one would broach the subject of marriage, and I could focus entirely on my studies. After each major test, everyone's scores were posted outside the school, ranked from highest to lowest. The top three names were always written larger than the rest. If a student did well, the entire town would know, and their parents would be proud. If a student did badly, the entire town would also know, and it often resulted in bullying.

One of my peach pit throwers, a lanky boy with poor eyesight but no money for glasses named Kwan, was often in the bottom ten. Once, his mother sent him to buy dried cuttlefish from Mrs. Chen, who shook her head when she saw him and said, "I see you had a tough time with the test. You need to study harder and do better. Otherwise you'll be cannon fodder for the Communists!" She threw some extra pieces of dried fish in the bag and said, "Fish makes you smart. Maybe this will help you do better next time."

"It doesn't matter, Auntie Chen," he replied. "I'm just going to take over my father's farm. I don't need school."

Mrs. Chen pinched his arm and said, "Everyone needs school. Did you know educated farmers have better crop yields than poor farmers? Maybe if you paid better attention in class, you would know, and I wouldn't have to tell you."

When I first started school, I was also toward the bottom of the class, along with Kwan. As my Mandarin improved, I began to climb up the list of names. After test results came out, I ran to the board to find my name, and soon noticed that the top ten students were almost always students who went to cram class. My family could barely afford our uniforms and now there was Baby Hua to consider—the tuition was out of the question.

After class, the students who paid filed into the cram classroom, with their leather bags, shiny shoes, and pristine, fitted uniforms. As I watched the door close, I thought of Mom's words at the Hong Kong border. In my life going forward, I no longer wanted to regret failing to fight. One day, I followed the high rankers to the cram class and lingered outside, trying my best to look nonchalant when the teacher, Mrs. Lu, passed me. Teacher Lu was a young woman, not much older than I was, with cropped hair like a student. Once class began, I crouched by the door and listened to her lesson, writing with my notebook balanced on my knees. Maybe she would yell at me and send me home, but at least I would know that I had done everything I could.

After weeks of walking past me, Teacher Lu finally confronted me as she was about to start her lesson. "I've seen you here every day. Do you want to take this class or not?"

My face flushed in embarrassment. "Yes," I said hesitantly, ashamed. I was a thief who had stolen her wisdom, and now she had caught me. "I'm sorry that I didn't pay you. My family doesn't have the money."

Her hand was on the door as she said, "That's unfortunate." I braced myself for recrimination, expecting her to slam the door in my face. "I don't want you standing so awkwardly outside," she continued. "I have a few extra seats—just come in and sit down. I won't tell the administrators if you won't."

I couldn't believe my ears as she stepped back and held the door open for me to enter. "Thank you!" I exclaimed, gratefully gathering my belongings and claiming one of the empty desks.

From that point, instead of going to the market in the afternoon I went to cram school, soaking up every lesson like a sponge thirsty for water. My grades continued to rise, and in the final year of middle school I was consistently in the top ten. The gift of a stranger can make the difference of a lifetime.

Most of my cram school classmates planned to go to high school. Though I yearned to go too, the associated fees combined with the loss of potential income made it unrealistic for my family. The cultural favoritism for male children meant that families with limited means would send only their boys to high school. Meanwhile, there were two popular options for girls: teaching school and nursing school—specialty schools that had no fees and provided housing, meals, and stipends.

Each June, teaching school entrance exams were held on the same day at campuses in every major city. Given my good grades, I felt confident enough to aspire for the one with the best reputation—Shi Fan School in Taipei. However, I still needed to pay an exam application fee and purchase textbooks and practice books. Timidly, I asked Father if we could spare the money to cover these costs. Though I knew what the answer would be, I had to try.

As I expected, Father said, "No, it's too expensive." Hua was still young, and Mom's milk supply was so limited that we had to supplement it with formula. Lan's leg was often inflamed, and she needed pain medication just to walk. There were too many other priorities for the family. I could tell Father felt bad, and he added, "Let's save and see where we are next year."

Even though I had expected a negative response, my disappointment was a weight that dragged my shoulders down everywhere I went. Had I been a son, Father would have scrambled for the funds, or Yei Yei and Nai Nai would have paid. On the way to school, during school, and with Teacher Lu in cram school, there was a shadow on my face. Why did I bother working so hard? I might as well have been relaxed like Kwan; neither of us was going to take exams, so despite my efforts, the two of us would end up in the same place, except I didn't even have a farm to inherit. How would I help Mom now?

One afternoon, I decided to skip cram school and went to find Mom at the market. I pondered quitting altogether, though I liked Teacher Lu enough that I didn't want to disappoint her. The street that Mom was on was comfortable and cool, shaded by buildings in the afternoon. Some grannies had set up a mahjong table, and the bamboo tiles clattered together as they shuffled them in sweeping motions. Baby Hua slept soundly tied on Mom's back, while Lan played paper dolls with the daughter of another market vendor. Mom looked up, surprised to see me. "I thought you were in cram school," she said.

"There was no class today," I lied. I didn't want to tell her how discouraged I was, because it would only make her feel bad. "I might as well come help you here."

Mrs. Chen saw me and waved and said, "I saw your name at the top of the test-result list again. Excellent job! Your parents are so lucky to have such a diligent daughter!" She bundled up a small package of dried fish and gave it to me. "A small gift to help keep that brain of yours strong."

"Thank you, Mrs. Chen," Mom replied on my behalf. "You are too kind."

I accepted the fish with a smile, even though I wanted to throw my head in my hands and cry. I put the package in my backpack and then gathered some buns in a tray so that I could walk around and peddle them.

Mom stopped me and said in a low voice, "I was going to tell you this evening, but since you are here now, I want you to know—I have the money for your books and application fee."

"Really?" I asked, putting the buns down in disbelief. "From where?"

Looking around to make sure no one was paying attention, she unbuttoned the collar of her shirt and showed me the jade bangle that hung on a cord around her neck. Mom believed in jade's protective properties and wore the bangle all the time, though not on her wrist, because she was so afraid that thieves would see it and try to rob her. Even in the shade, that jade managed to catch light and emit a warm green glow. "We're going to sell the bangle," she said.

My heart swelled as I remembered this bangle passing all the way from Zhucheng to Taiwan with us. Its green reminded me of the bundles of fresh *jicai* that we picked in the mountains, evoking memories of hope. "This is all that you have left from Lao Lao," I protested. The Chinese believe that, over time, jade absorbs the aura of its bearer, and its color will change to reflect that energy. In this case, this stone was not only a gift from my Lao Lao; it also held her essence, because she had worn it for many years. "It's precious to you," I insisted. "I can't let you give it up."

Mom shook her head and said, "I treasure this bangle because it is a way for me to hold on to my past. But my past is not nearly as important as your future."

"But we need to save it for emergencies," I said, thinking of Lan's tuberculosis treatment and the train tickets. "What if the Communists invade and we need to escape again?"

Mom understood my apprehension but replied, "We cannot put the present on hold because of fears of what might lie ahead. We ate hard bread and slept on floors, saving this bangle for an important cause—and this is it. This is an opportunity with a limited window. I do not want to risk waiting a year, when Di may need money for her education too. This time next year, I want to be sending you off to school—not sitting here counting coins and hoping the numbers add up."

Mom and I both knew, though she did not say, that there was a strong possibility that I would end up married within the next year. Given the financial strain on the family, Father was incentivized to have Di and me out of the house sooner rather than later. If I were wed before the next exam period was announced, the decision to support my education would be my husband's, and not my father's. In all likelihood, my future husband would prefer that I focused on raising our children as opposed to investing in my career.

"This has to happen now," Mom reiterated. "We don't need to tell your father until after it is sold and your fees are paid for." It would be a secret sale, a small act of rebellion to open the gates that Father had deemed closed.

I looked at my mother, who sat on a crate with little piles of buns, flatbread, and eggs laid neatly on dishes around her, a worn cloth purse holding the coins that she had collected from her sales throughout the day. *This has to happen now, or you might end up like me* was the full meaning behind her words.

I threw my arms around Mom, and also Hua, who was tied to her. "Thank you, Mom. I promise you, I will study hard, and I will pass." Silently, I also made a promise to myself: *I will get a job, and I will make money to support Mom.*

That spring, while other people my age were socializing and even dating, I spent every free hour committing my textbooks to memory, aiming for Taipei Shi Fan. I practiced writing essays and continued to focus on Mandarin. I read as much as I could and took notes on everything. The callus on my finger from holding a pencil had faded while we were trying to escape the mainland, but now it had re-formed. During those weeks of constant study, my hand ached from writing. The stress that weighed on me was not only the fear of failing the exam, but also the fear of failing my family. Mom announced that she was pregnant again, increasing my sense of responsibility because another sibling was forthcoming. I had to stop being a burden on my parents and get that stipend.

34

FISH BRAIN

June arrived, and it was scorching hot every single day. I thought back to Zhucheng, when the summer would occasionally bring a blistering heat wave, but nothing like the ruthless island sun and suffocating humidity. Mom said, "Our blood is not meant for these temperatures. We are Shandong people, with ice in our veins. We are built to endure the rage of winter, not the wrath of summer."

The day before my exam, Father accompanied me to Taipei. We would be there for only two nights, but Mom had stuffed my bag anxiously, as though I'd be gone for weeks. "Mom," I said as she carefully folded a *qipao* and tucked it under a floppy hat. "You know we lived for months in Hong Kong on half as much as this, right?"

She grabbed a belt and a full skirt and looked for space to jam them in. "You are not going to Taipei to beg in the markets. You are going to meet your future classmates! You need to look nice. Try to see what young girls are wearing in the city these days. I don't know if it's Western style or traditional, but I want you to have both."

"I'm not going to wear a dress to the exam," I said, trying to take out the ill-fitting formal wear that she had picked from the church donation bins. "I need to be comfortable. I'm just going to wear my school uniform."

Mom's eyes widened in horror. "Your middle school uniform? You can't wear that!" She fumbled through my bag and yanked out my uniform and replaced it with a hideous blouse from the church that had a ruffled collar and tacky orange flowers embroidered on the sleeves.

In a separate bag, she had packed buns and fruit for several days.

"There will be food at the *shiheyuan*," I told her as she counted out twenty vegetable dumplings and threw in another bunch of bananas. "Father said Yei Yei is preparing a big feast for Chiao, since he will be taking high school exams."

"You never know," said Mom. "Nai Nai is so stingy—she might not let you eat with them! In any case, I want you to have snacks to take with you on exam day. How can you do well on your test if you get hungry?"

"Okay, thank you, Mom," I said, surrendering. The bags were heavy, but packing was Mom's way of showing her love, so I had no choice but to bend at the knees and sling them over my shoulders. It would be a long, sweaty walk to and from the bus station.

That evening, when we arrived at the *shiheyuan*, everyone was in a great mood except for Chiao, who clenched his hands nervously whenever anyone asked him if he felt prepared. Yei Yei was beaming. He wanted to make sure his only grandson ate well, so he had bought meat as if it were Lunar New Year's Eve. In the courtyard Aunt Ji had set up a long table, with plates of steamed whole fish, stewed meatballs, tender bok choy, and some Taiwanese specialties—fresh shrimp cooked with garlic and tomatoes, and pork kidney sautéed with chives. I rubbed my hands together, excited that I too would benefit from the goodwill intended for Chiao.

Nai Nai sat several seats away from me, but as I loaded my bowl she still eyed me with disdain, and mentally tallied the cost of everything that went into my mouth. "Ladies shouldn't eat too much meat and fat," she remarked. "It's bad for the skin. No one wants a wife with a blotchy face and greasy hair. Have some cucumbers and fruit."

"Thank you for the advice, Nai Nai," I said, and took a single cucumber slice with my chopsticks before tearing into the fluffy meatballs drenched in fragrant brown sauce. Nai Nai frowned but said nothing more. Yei Yei did not want any arguments bringing bad energy that could potentially stress Chiao and affect his performance. He pulled out the skull from the fish and placed it in Chiao's bowl, believing the Chinese superstition that eating fish brain could make a person smarter. Chiao gagged but ate obediently. He had never liked fish, and I could tell from his watering eyes that the goopy brain was close to making him vomit. Apparently, he had to endure this ritual every time the family had whole fish.

"Are you excited for tomorrow?" Chiao asked me, after gulping tea to wash away the remnants of brain from his mouth and shaking his head as if that could dislodge the flavor.

"I don't know if 'excited' is the right word," I replied. Tomorrow was the day that I had been thinking about ever since Mom sold her jade bangle months ago. It was the single day that would determine whether my daily labor from then until now had been worth it or had been a colossal waste of time and money.

"I am looking forward to it being over," lamented Chiao. "Then I can live my life again. For the past few months I couldn't even take a piss without having a textbook in my hand, or else Mom would yell at me for being lazy!"

"It's so much pressure." I empathized, even though my parents had not pushed me at all. They both knew that I was pushing myself harder than they ever could. Plus, Mom didn't have time to monitor me—Hua and Lan needed attention, and she was often nauseous from her pregnancy. Chiao's mother had only him and Pei to focus on, which was easier but not a blessing—Aunt Ji longed for additional children, but after Pei she had only miscarriages and a heartbreaking stillbirth.

"At least you're a girl," Chiao remarked. "You can just get married if you don't want to study, and someone will take care of you. I have to study and get a job."

I rarely got annoyed with Chiao, but I snapped, "It's not as easy as you say. I would happily trade with you and go to university."

Chiao shrugged. "Too bad we can't. I want to join the military, but Dad insists that I be like Yei Yei, even though he himself didn't take that path! Dad says that he saw too many young boys die in the mainland and doesn't want me to gamble with my life. Especially since the American blockade in the strait is the only reason the war is paused. Once they leave, bombs will fly."

Though we had left the mainland long ago, the war remained a constant backdrop in our lives. Even if Chiao went to university, he would still have to complete the two years of military service that were compulsory for all men. Women were exempt but were required to take several hours of arms training each week. At Shi Fan, target practice was included in the curriculum, and I learned to handle a range of weapons. Taiwan's population was comparatively small, and when the People's Liberation Army landed on our shores, men and women alike would have to defend our home.

At the end of the evening, Chiao gave me an affectionate slap on my shoulder. "Good luck, Big Sister," he said. "I know you'll smash that exam to smithereens!"

"Thank you, Chiao," I said. As he stood up, I found myself still disbelieving that this tall, handsome man was the same butterball who used to run through the fields with me and break watermelons back in Zhucheng. "Good luck to you too—make us proud!"

"I'll try," Chiao sighed as Yei Yei pointed at his watch, insisting that Chiao go to bed so his brain could rest. Nai Nai gave me a dirty look before taking her husband's arm so she could hobble back to her room. I stayed behind to help Aunt Ji clean up after dinner, then returned to the living room to set up some pillows and a blanket. Father, however, surprised me and said, "Hai, I want you to have a good night of sleep before the exam, so you take the bedroom. I will sleep on the sofa."

"It's okay," I protested. "I'm fine on the sofa." I had slept on much worse, and was so tired that I could pass out anywhere.

Father insisted. "Tomorrow is an important day for you too, and you also need to rest. I can always sleep on the bus if I'm tired. You are a smart girl and you worked hard for this." That was the nicest thing that Father had ever said to me, and I tucked those words into my memory. His consideration was unexpected, and after an evening of listening to Yei Yei boast about Chiao, I didn't think anyone else, even my own father, remembered why I had come to Taipei. I didn't need the bed, but I had been starved for Father's encouragement for so long that the simple gesture moved me.

The next morning, I walked onto the campus at Shi Fan, along with hundreds of other students from all over Taiwan, bleary-eyed but so pumped with anxiety that my mind was alert. Despite Father's goodwill, I had slept horribly, and spent the night sweating as potential exam questions popped into my head. I even had a nightmare in which I opened the exam only to find that it was in a foreign language—the characters looked like scribbles, and all around me everyone was writing up a storm while I was left struggling to read.

The campus grounds were beautifully manicured, and the buildings were modern and clean. There were girls in high heels and silk blouses, pencils tucked behind their ears, smiling and chatting with one another as they lined up for registration. Though I had studied hard, I felt as out of place as I did when I had sat on the ground by Gao-Bing's stand and started hawking my letter-writing services. Could my fellow applicants tell that I used to be a beggar? I smoothed the ruffles on my shirt, embarrassed, as I filed into the line with my cloth shoes and my bag of dumplings and bananas. *I should have left these at home,* I thought. I had brought them for good luck, as a token of Mom's support, but the lumpy bag smelled like cabbage and made me look even more like a street urchin.

With my heart beating and adrenaline rushing, I found my room and sat at an open desk, as tense as a racehorse waiting for the starting gunshot to sound. A school administrator read out instructions while an assistant walked up and down the aisles, placing an exam packet facedown in front of each applicant. Back at the chalkboard, the administrator watched the clock, and everyone had their eyes pinned to its second hand. As soon as it hit twelve, he said, "You may begin." Paper rustled collectively as everyone flipped their exam over, followed by the sound of furious scribbling.

I saw the questions, and sighed with relief. They were easy because I had prepared so much. I could recite the answers to several of them from memory, and I knew exactly what the exam graders wanted to see. It was going to be all right; my family was going to be all right. When I entered that classroom, I had my shoulders slumped and my head low. When I walked out, forty-five minutes before the time limit, I did so with confidence.

Back at the *shiheyuan*, Father asked me how it went. I told him the questions and what my answers were. He listened attentively and eagerly, offering his own suggestions and praising some of my responses. It was like I was recapping a sports game to a person who was both a player and a fanatic. The two of us rarely had common interests to converse about, and when we took the bus from Douliu to Taipei we had ridden in silence. On the bus ride back home, however, we talked about teaching, and I enjoyed it. For most of my life, I had seen him as an aloof authority figure who was an ally of Nai Nai, Mom's tormentor. Now I got a glimpse of my father as an individual—as a human whom I could relate to.

The specialty schools posted exam results outside their campuses, and successful candidates would also receive letters by mail. We got a letter from Uncle Jian first—Chiao had gone to the Shi Fan campus to check the results on my behalf. "Hai, your name was posted on the class list for Shi Fan!" Father exclaimed when he read Uncle Jian's letter. "Chiao saw it with his own eyes!"

Mom screamed and jumped up and down the way she had when we got our entry permits for Taiwan. "I knew it! I knew you could do it!" she cried, while Father admonished her to be careful because of the baby in her womb.

"Congratulations, Big Sister," said Di enthusiastically. "We knew you would make it!"

"I hope he read the names correctly. This better not be a joke," I said, thinking of Chiao's childhood pranks.

"Don't be ridiculous," Mom said dismissively. "Chiao would never do that! We need to buy you new clothes. If you are going to study in Taipei, we can't send you looking like a country bumpkin!"

Mom rattled on about the various items that I needed, almost like she was preparing a trousseau for marriage. "You need a nice dress for formal occasions—nothing too flashy, just something classic. Not the church donation dress—a proper, tailored dress. You need to look respectable—you're going to be a teacher, after all. Nothing too short, but we also don't want you to look like an old maid."

I trusted Chiao not to joke about such an important matter, but I also knew he could be careless. What if the name he saw was actually Ang Li-Wai? Or Ang Lao-Hai? I remained cautiously optimistic until a few days later, when the formal letter from Taipei Shi Fan arrived. When I opened it, I broke the dam that restrained my happiness and it burst forth with such intensity that I screamed and ran through the house. "I got in, I got in, I got in!"

Mom only looked at me confused and said, "Yes, we know. We found out days ago."

I waved the letter in her face and said, "It is official now!"

Later that night, I took my acceptance letter and slept with it under my pillow. I finally felt as though I had some measure of control over my own destiny. In a few months I would be in Taipei, earning a stipend and bringing additional income home. Nai Nai was wrong. I wasn't just a useless mouth to feed—none of us girls were. There was enough money from the sale of the jade bangle for Di to take her exam the next year. By the time Lan and Hua were older, I would be working as a teacher and could save my salary to pay for their school and exam fees too. Eventually, all of us would have jobs, and Mom would no longer need to worry.

35

GOLDEN CHILD

In the winter of 1953, Mom gave birth to her sixth and last child—a baby boy, whom Yei Yei named Li-Ming, *ming* meaning "intelligence." She had just turned thirty-six years old. This tiny, wrinkly creature displaced Chiao, who was in high school, as the next heir of the Ang family. Mom was relieved to have finally given birth to a son, elevating her status in the eyes of the family elders. However, being irrelevant had afforded her the luxury of a quiet life in Douliu. After Ming's birth, Yei Yei insisted that Father transfer back to Taipei because the future heir had to live in the Ang family *shiheyuan*.

At that time, I was finishing my first semester at Shi Fan and earning awards for my calligraphy, ranking first in my school. I couldn't help but think of my letter-writing service in Hong Kong. It would be petty to write to Gao-Bing to brag, but on occasion I fantasized about his reaction if he learned that the piglet of Mount Davis had her calligraphy on display at Taipei's art center—multiple times! Though I had wonderful teachers, the school cafeteria was a major factor in the improvement of my skills. There was always meat or fish, and I ate so well that I finally recovered from the years of undernourishment; I was eighteen when I got my period.

Mom was right. If I had waited a year to take that entrance exam, I wouldn't have had the opportunity at all. With Ming's arrival, Father would have put every cent we had into a savings fund for his education. I finally understood the gendered aspect of free will and fate. Father believed in making his own fortune because he was a man with choices laid out before him. Nai Nai and Mom believed in fate because they generally had to rely on the decisions of others. From my own experiences, I learned that our lives are a mixture of both. I had worked hard for my place at Shi Fan, but it would all have been irrelevant had my brother been born a year earlier.

As children, Di and I occasionally resented Chiao, who was heavily favored by our grandparents. Ming, however, loomed so large in our house that every other child was in his shadow. I pitied Lan and Hua, because at least Di and I had grown up with Mom's unwavering and steadfast love. With a baby brother absorbing every ray of Mom's affection, my two youngest sisters were completely in the cold.

When Ming was only six months old, Mom and I had the worst fight that we ever had. It was a typical Friday evening. After class, I hopped on the public bus toward the *shiheyuan*, clinging to the exterior rail along with other hitchhikers so I could save the fare. Each month, I gave Mom my stipend, forgoing luxuries because I couldn't enjoy them when I knew that she was still selling eggs at the market. Mom complained to me about the price of formula, which had increased in the past year. She had boiled water and prepared a bottle of milk for Ming, who cooed happily and reached out with his chubby hands. Hua was only a year old, and crawled on the kitchen floor. When she saw the bottle, she started to cry. Handing Ming to me, Mom stood up to prepare another bottle. Instead of formula, however, she reached for a pitcher of cloudy gray liquid. I recognized it immediately—rice water.

Mom handed the pathetic gray bottle to Hua, who shook her head and continued to cry. In response, Mom set it on the floor and took Ming back into her arms, leaving Hua to wail.

I couldn't believe it. "Mom, why are you giving her rice water when there is so much formula?"

"Don't worry," said Mom. "She's upset now, but she will calm down eventually and drink it."

Hua's face was scarlet as she screamed, and a lump rose in my throat as I thought of Three. "That's not what I'm worried about," I cried. "Hua must be hungry. How often does she get milk?"

Unconcerned, Mom replied, "Hua is a year old. She doesn't need milk anymore. Formula is so expensive, and we can't afford it for two babies. She'll be fine. Lan survived off of flour and rice water for over a year, and she's a healthy girl now."

"Lan had severe malnutrition!" I exclaimed, disturbed by her nonchalance. "The doctors at Mount Davis said so! Her arms were like rails! It was abnormal!" Hua cried often since Ming's birth, and I had assumed it was just jealousy. I was horrified to learn that it was likely due to hunger. "I know money is tight, but we have enough for her to have formula too!"

Mom started getting angry. "Why are you yelling? Just look at Hua. She's plump. She's old enough to eat rice, and gets as much as she wants from the table. She's not starving!"

I opened my mouth, but my disappointment was so heavy that it weighed down my words. Hua was plump compared to Baby

Lan, but she was thin compared to our brother. As for Lan, she wasn't healthy either. Though it had been years since we had left Hong Kong, Lan had problems with her liver and bones from the hunger that had plagued us. Even in Taiwan, we rarely ate meat at home. I knew that Father expected everyone to make sacrifices so that Ming could live well, but I felt betrayed by Mom's outrageous behavior.

Beside me, Hua stopped wailing. She crawled toward the bottle of rice milk and began to drink it just as her brother finished the last few drops of his milk. At this tender age, she was already learning how our world worked. One day she would stop fighting it and, when handed gray rice water, she would drink without complaint.

I squeezed my fists together. "No!" I yanked the bottle from Hua's hands. With her mouth free, Hua began to scream anew, with even more force, furious that even her watery meal had been confiscated.

"What are you doing?" cried Mom, leaping to her feet. With Ming in her arms, she couldn't stop me as I dumped the rice water in the sink and scooped a heaping spoonful of formula into the bottle. "Hai, are you crazy? I told you, she doesn't need it!"

Ignoring Mom, I shook the bottle after filling it with boiled water, and I handed it to Hua, who grabbed it eagerly and started sucking and drinking it in gulps as though she was afraid that someone would take it away. "You should be ashamed!" I yelled at Mom, so loudly that Ming began to cry. "I am ashamed! I'm ashamed to see you act this way, when you know how much we suffered because we weren't sons!"

Mom rocked Ming, and glared at me furiously. "Hua is *my* daughter. I am doing my best to take care of them both, but we have to cut corners. You know nothing about running a household and raising children!"

"I helped raise Lan!" I shouted. "I helped raise Three! I helped with Hua too! I know how much milk a baby needs, and Ming is drinking so much that I assumed that there were two babies guzzling through the formula in this house! And now I see that none of it is going to Hua? They might be your children, but you are all using my stipend!" I felt bad for dangling the money in Mom's face, but it was the only way to assert that I had a say in the house—without my contribution, I was only a daughter who would marry away. "I don't care how you spend my stipend, and I trust you to make the right decisions—but it's unacceptable to claim you are doing your best when one of your children is eating like a prince and the other is eating like a refugee!"

Ming settled down, but Mom began to weep. "Hai, Ming is the only one who will support us when we are old. The only one who can care for us in the afterlife. I love Hua and all my other daughters, but I have a duty, as a wife, to make sure Ming grows up well. When you have your own son, you will understand."

She cried because she thought I was judging her unfairly, without realizing that her words had cut me deep. Mom hadn't said it explicitly, but I heard it loud and clear: All of us girls were worth less than Ming. She loved us less than Ming. Yet Mom was confused by my anger, and oblivious to my pain. To her, the ancient traditions centering the son were our pillar, entwined in our religion, inseparable from our existence on this earth. Telling her I was hurt would be like saying I was offended by the typhoon that had torn through Mount Davis. In her mind, these injustices were part of being a woman, and bearing them was simply our fate. Men made the rules in our society, but women often enforced them.

Was there something about having a son that transformed us?

Was that why Nai Nai was so wretched? Was that going to be me as a mother? I didn't want it to be. After what I had been through, how could I fall into that same pattern?

When I had first aimed for teaching school, I thought of it primarily as a means to support my family, to make Mom proud, and to have the freedom to leave a miserable home. I didn't realize that having my own money would also allow me to push against the destiny and beliefs that others tried to impose on me. I was frustrated by the extent to which Mom had internalized the inferiority of girls, but I also understood her. She was the person I loved most for my entire life. I knew her strengths, and I knew her weaknesses. How could I stay angry at Mom when she was the reason that I had my stipend? How could I look down on her when she hadn't had the choices that I had? I couldn't change Mom's beliefs any more than I could tear Nai Nai away from fortune-tellers, but I also couldn't resent Mom any more than I could resent Hua for giving in and drinking the rice water.

I returned to campus early that weekend, and decided that going forward, I would buy Hua's formula before giving Mom the stipend. I couldn't make Mom love Hua and Ming equally, but I could at least mitigate the consequences. This was my way of adapting, of finding a path around obstacles that wouldn't budge, and people who wouldn't change. Maybe, at the very least, I could interrupt the inheritance of our own inferiority from generation to generation, and break this damaging cycle.

36

ACCIDENTAL LOVE

When I told Di about the fight we had over formula, she was neither shocked nor upset. "Mom is a coward. I keep telling you that, but you still keep acting surprised when she does something cowardly." Di was in nursing school now, having passed the entrance exam, and no longer considered the problems in the Ang *shiheyuan* her own. Like a bird, she had left our nest, and she reacted with indifference to my complaints.

In early 1955, with the end of the First Taiwan Strait Crisis as her romantic backdrop, Di announced that she was dating someone, a mainlander whom she had met while in school. She had kept the relationship secret for a long time because his name was Ang Li-Tang, which meant there was a strong possibility that he was a *tang* cousin of ours. We had never met him, but Yei Yei knew of his father, and we were indeed related. Di's lover was further removed from her than our parents were from each other bloodline-wise, but since he was also an Ang, the families considered the relationship incestuous. Father ordered Di to end it, but Di ignored him. She was no longer living in his house and she had her own income, so he had no leverage against her. The pair continued to date for almost a year.

Determined to break them up, Yei Yei tried to kindle a romance between Di and a customs officer who was a friend of a friend. Yei Yei set up a date for Di and Mr. Yuan Jia-Shen, which I was supposed to attend as a chaperone. The three of us were to meet for lunch at one of Yei Yei's favorite seafood restaurants. I dressed plainly, in a white shirt and pants, since I would be there only to preserve modesty. Di cared nothing for the date, but I pushed her into wearing a dress and a hairpin with red glass beads—at least out of politeness to this young man who was about to treat us to a fine meal.

"He's so old," Di complained. "Did you know he's twenty-six? Six years older than me?"

"That's not such a big age gap," I said. "There are many couples who are further apart than that."

"It doesn't matter anyway," Di said. "My boyfriend and I are going to get married even if the elders oppose it. I'm waiting so we can do it on Yei Yei's birthday and then surprise them at the dinner celebration." She cackled as she applied a thin layer of lipstick and snapped her purse shut. Her high heels clacked on the tile in the hallway as she made her way out the door.

I rolled my eyes. Di's sense of humor had only gotten darker over the past years. As a nurse, she had anatomy lessons using cadavers. One Friday, she had cut off a piece of flesh from one of them and brought it back to the *shiheyuan* in the evening. I was outside with Chiao, and she told us it was delicious beef jerky. I took it with my fingers and thought the smell and texture were strange, so I refused. Chiao grabbed it from me and examined it curiously, and then took a bite. "It's awful," he said. "It tastes fermented." Di then burst out laughing and called him a cannibal and told him what the meat really was. She laughed so hard that tears streamed from her eyes, while Chiao kept spitting on the ground and rubbing his tongue. I shuddered as I recalled that horrific prank, even though Chiao later told me that taste-wise it was not as bad as the fish brain that Yei Yei regularly made him choke down.

As Di and I walked to the restaurant, she stepped lightly, almost skipping in the street. I was surprised to see her so happy, given that she had vehemently opposed this date. Her lipstick was a nice touch, the bright red contrasting against her pale skin and matching the beads on the hairpin. When we approached the main street, we saw a man standing outside of the restaurant who must have been Jia-Shen. He wore a Western-style suit with a silk tie and freshly polished shoes. His hair was neatly combed, and he had a thin face with a high nose and eyes that slanted downward at the corners. From all of Di's griping, I had expected him to look like a stale office worker, but he was handsome. I had never met Li-Tang, but surely she couldn't call Jia-Shen old after seeing him now—he had a youthful face and easily looked our age.

We introduced ourselves, and he opened the door of the restaurant for us. I noticed Di looking with a smile at a black car that was parked on the opposite side of the street. I didn't think much of it as we took our seats and Jia-Shen handed us menus and asked what we liked to eat.

"Anything you order is fine," I said, which was what I had been taught to say. Many Chinese social interactions followed a script—an open-ended question was posed by one party, but culturally speaking there was only one acceptable way to answer it. Since we knew Jia-Shen would be paying and he was still a stranger, it would have been impolite of us to suggest dishes.

"Let's order a few different items, then," he said, scanning the menu. Now, if he was polite, he would proceed to order an abundance of food that we would struggle to finish. This was a date, after all. I smiled to myself, thinking that once again I would benefit from the goodwill meant for another. Hopefully he would order shrimp with honey and walnuts—my favorite dish. Crispy duck with taro would be nice too, but this was a seafood restaurant, so it would be foolish not to order fish.

Jia-Shen called the waiter over and ordered steamed whole fish, clams sautéed with basil, sea cucumber stewed with mushrooms, and shrimp with honey and walnuts. "Wow, that sounds wonderful," I said, thrilled that my shrimp dish made it. Under the table I nudged Di with my foot.

"Thank you," she said quickly. "I am so excited to try everything! Let me just go to the water closet to wash my hands." With a smile, she rose and went toward the back of the restaurant.

The waitress placed a pot of jasmine tea on the table, steam curling up from the spout. "So, are you a nurse too?" Jia-Shen asked me.

"No," I replied, opening the teapot to check if the tea was already steeped. The water was pale and the tea leaves were shriveled, so I replaced the lid. "I am a teacher."

"That's an excellent job," he said warmly. "Your parents must be so proud to have both a teacher and a nurse in the family!"

"No, no," I said, "you are too kind." Another social concept—when one was complimented, it was polite to be modest. Bragging about oneself was frowned upon, which was also why I was supposed to attend this date—I could brag about Di while she sat beside me and said *No, no* and *Not at all* so that she could appear modest while all of her strengths and virtues were highlighted.

"I was told that you are also from Zhucheng?"

"Yes," I replied. "You said 'also'—does that mean that you are from Zhucheng too?"

"Yes!" he answered enthusiastically. "How nice it is to meet others from Zhucheng."

No wonder Yei Yei liked him. It was hard enough to find people from Shandong here in Taiwan, let alone from Zhucheng! I was tempted to switch to Shandongese but remembered that we were in public and had to speak in Mandarin—especially since both of us were government employees.

I poured tea and we spoke about our families for several minutes before I realized that Di still had not come back from washing her hands. "I'm very sorry," I said, blushing. "Please excuse me while I go check on her."

Trying my best to combine speed with grace, I walked to the back of the restaurant, where the sinks were, but saw only kitchen staff. There was a back door for deliveries, and it had been propped open to let in fresh air. *No way*, I thought. Anger rose in me as I realized that Di must have slipped out. How could she leave me in such an awkward situation? How could she be so selfish? Part of me was also shocked that Di could love someone so much that food became secondary. She too had heard the mouthwatering medley that Jia-Shen had ordered. How could anyone say no to that?

I took a few minutes to calm myself so that Jia-Shen wouldn't see how furious I was. When I went back to the table, some of the dishes had already arrived and he was patiently waiting with his chopsticks on the table. He looked at me inquisitively. With my best calm voice I said, "I am so very sorry. This is embarrassing, but my sister seems to have left."

To my surprise, Jia-Shen laughed, a hearty, warm chuckle that reminded me of boiling soup on a cold winter day. "Wow, that may be my worst date ever. My friends are going to have a field day when

I tell them the lady ran away before the date even started! They will say it's my face that scared her, and I guess that must be it."

"No, of course that's not why!" I exclaimed, aghast, while trying to think of a good excuse for Di that wouldn't betray that there was another man in the picture. "She gets very nervous about dating, and I think she lost her composure and ran back home. I'm sure she's probably with my grandparents, who are scolding her for being so ridiculous. I'm just so sorry to have wasted your time."

"Not at all," he replied. "I am having a great time." Now, social norms didn't force him to say that—he was well within his right to suggest that we postpone.

"Really?" I asked, trying to analyze his expression to see if he was being honest.

"Yes," he said. "Please sit and eat before the food gets cold. Or were you planning to run away too?"

"No, of course not," I said, pulling my chair out and sitting so quickly that I almost slipped off the edge. "The food looks delicious. My sister is missing out."

"She really is," he said. As if reading my mind, he added, "The shrimp with walnuts here is amazing. It's my favorite dish."

And just like that, I was on a date.

Jia-Shen's father had been a prominent herbal doctor back in Zhucheng—for a while he had been the only doctor in Zhucheng, and one of the few health care workers in the entire rural area. Though he cured many people and saved lives, his children kept dying young. Jia-Shen's mother gave birth at least seven times, and in the end only Jia-Shen and his sister survived past infancy. Dr. Yuan said to his wife, "How can I heal so many people, yet cannot save my own babies?" He concluded that he must have committed some sin in either this life or a past life, which in turn cursed his children.

He dedicated himself to doing good deeds, hoping to counter

the bad karma that he must have collected. In addition to practicing medicine, Dr. Yuan was a landowner with many tenants on his property. He decided to stop collecting rent and asked the tenants to give him only what they wished to, and no more than they could afford. Every Lunar New Year, tenants brought barrels full of marinated pork belly and pork hock to his house as gifts to show their gratitude. Jia-Shen told me that he could not look at pork hock now because he was so sick of eating it. Dr. Yuan's kindness padded Jia-Shen's life with goodwill. As he was growing up, everyone took extra care of him, knowing that he was Dr. Yuan's heir and one of only two surviving children.

When the Communists invaded Shandong, the principal of Jia-Shen's boarding school moved all of the students and teachers to Taiwan. All of them had assumed that hostilities would cease and they could return home in a few years, but soon they realized they would have to rebuild their lives on the island. Jia-Shen and his classmates became as tight-knit as family and helped one another find good jobs in the early stages of the Nationalist government's regrouping.

Back in the mainland, the Communists came for the Yuans. The peasants, however, refused to turn on them. Later, as higher-ranking Communist officials came to Zhucheng, cadres dragged Dr. Yuan into the street. No one from the village participated in his denunciation rally. Dissatisfied, the cadres beat Dr. Yuan to death with their fists and sticks, and then forbade the people of Zhucheng from burying his body. "He is to rot on the street and be eaten by stray animals," a cadre declared.

One peasant in the village defied this order and gave Dr. Yuan a burial. When the Communists found out, they killed him too. Other peasants helped Mrs. Yuan and Jia-Shen's sister escape to Qingdao, where they continued to live with extended family. Jia-

Shen wrote to them every week, and sent money each month to help make ends meet.

After only three months of dating, Jia-Shen proposed to me. Father and Yei Yei were even more excited than I was and invited him out for drinks before I had even agreed.

Di snorted when Yei Yei emphasized the renown of Dr. Yuan. "We are in Taiwan, and Dr. Yuan is dead. No one here remembers things like that," she scoffed. Di was wrong, and perhaps it was her forbidden infatuation that made her so naïve. Though we were in Taiwan, due to Chiang's discriminatory hiring, the government was largely controlled by mainlanders—people like Yei Yei, who were always thinking back to their roots. Jia-Shen's career would later shoot up like a rocket. Everywhere he turned, someone was willing to help him because of who he was and who he was related to.

Father glared at her and said, "Be glad your sister recognized a big fish when she saw it! Imagine the scandal we would have had if Jia-Shen went around telling people how rude you were to him. Do you know how well connected he is? If he trashed our reputation, no one else would date my daughters, and your younger sisters would end up as spinsters!"

Di laughed flippantly. "He was so dorky-looking, with his hair parted like a schoolboy's. But Sis is dorky too. They will have a wonderful future together."

"At least our relationship isn't incestuous," I countered as Di made a face at me.

Mom was also eager for the union, but for another reason. "His father is dead, so you don't need to worry about him. And his mother is in the mainland! Maybe she'll die before China is reunified, so you'll never have to live with her!" Mom pointed out these somber facts with such glee that I muttered a Buddhist prayer under my breath to apologize to the deceased Dr. Yuan.

After considering the proposal, I gave Jia-Shen my terms. "I will marry you," I said, "but I will not leave my own family. I want to take care of my parents. I want to keep my job and decide what to do with my wages, even if that means supporting them." I had already graduated by then, and I was earning a salary as an elementary school teacher in Taipei. For the past half year, I had been putting money aside for a large purchase: Lan's new legs. There was an eight-hour surgical procedure that could straighten them, reducing her limp and eliminating her pain. As much as I loved Jia-Shen, I would never be his wife if that meant that I'd have to ask his permission to cover this expense—or any others.

Jia-Shen not only agreed to my terms, but he also gave me the rest of the money to pay for Lan's surgery from his own savings. That was how I knew that I had found my life partner. We celebrated our engagement at the same restaurant where we had had our accidental first date, and now that we were engaged I didn't have to hold back—I ordered my favorite dishes, and an extra helping of shrimp with walnuts. Three months later, we were married in a small ceremony with only my family and Jia-Shen's boarding school friends in attendance.

Di and her lover did not follow in our footsteps. Though they had pledged to ignore family pressure and elope, in the end Li-Tang caved and broke up with her. Yei Yei and Father were relieved when they saw Di's puffy eyes, because that meant that it was really over. The two men invited Uncle Jian, Jia-Shen, and Chiao to celebrate with several rounds of fiery rice liquor. Jia-Shen and Chiao didn't care about Di's relationship, but they were happy to have any excuse to party. While they were out drinking, Mom and I tried our best to console Di, who was curled up in her bed, sobbing into her pillow as though she had received a death sentence.

Within a few weeks, we found out that Di was pregnant. Di

had always been private about the relationship, so I didn't know much about her discussions with Li-Tang, except that she had made a last, tearful attempt to convince him to go through with the marriage. Not only did he refuse, but he also denied any responsibility for the child she carried.

Father was furious. Ming was only a toddler and unable to fight, so Father contemplated sending Chiao to beat up Li-Tang on Di's behalf. Yei Yei, however, forbade it. Li-Tang was still an heir of the Ang family—his descendants would sweep the Ang tomb and pay respects to the Ang ancestors. "It is your fault for not controlling your daughter," Yei Yei told Father. "Li-Tang claims the baby isn't his, and now everyone thinks Di is a whore!"

Mom took a sullen and listless Di to get an abortion. "Thank the Gods we have your marriage settled," Mom said to me after they returned. "I don't know what we will do about Di. The community is small, and people will know. They will consider her damaged goods." Father's goal was to marry Di off as quickly as possible, before people gossiped about the "incestuous" relationship, the possibility of multiple partners, and the abortion. The abortion itself was not taboo, but the premarital sex was.

There was a teacher whose father was a family friend and who had been infatuated with Di on first sight and pursued her for several years despite her persistent rejections. Like me, he had never gone to high school or university. Specialty school was acceptable for a woman, but for the Ang family, a proper man should be a university graduate. Given Di's scandal, however, the family's requirements became more flexible. This suitor was similar in age to Di, employed by the government, and also a mainlander—and, perhaps more important, he knew about Di's prior relationship and abortion and was willing to accept her. When he broached the possibility of marriage to Father, Father immediately agreed.

I expected Di to raise hell, to unleash a fury so frightening that the island of Taiwan would tremble and the deceased would turn in their graves.

Instead, Di acquiesced to the arrangement without so much as a whimper.

It was then that I realized how heartbroken she was. She didn't care about life. She didn't care about her future. She had lost her will to fight, which for someone like Di meant that she had lost her sense of self. I wished that I had been nosy enough to follow Di around like I had done when we were younger and figure out where Li-Tang lived or worked. If I could, I would have taken a cleaver and chopped off his testicles despite Yei Yei's insistence that he needed to produce Ang sons.

One morning, I was walking with Di to buy bedsheets, which would be part of her trousseau, when she gasped and hid behind me. "What is it?" I asked.

"Let's turn back and walk the other way," Di said quietly.

There was a shiny black car parked in front of us. I thought back to my first date with Jia-Shen and the car that Di's eyes had lingered on. Was it the same car? Since I couldn't remember, I asked, "Is that Li-Tang's?"

"Stop it, Sis," she hissed. "Let's just go."

"It's empty," I said, looking through the window. On the passenger seat, there were a stack of papers, an umbrella, and a small tube of lipstick. If Li-Tang had a car, he must be very wealthy. Or he was a chauffeur. Di was so in love with this person, yet none of us knew anything about him except that he had been a university student when they met and that his surname was Ang.

"He might come back soon," Di said anxiously. "I don't want to see him."

"Fine," I said. "You go around the corner and wait for me there."

"What are you going to do?" Di asked, her voice getting shrill despite her trying to keep it to a whisper.

"You'll see in a few minutes," I said, shooing her away. Di didn't leave, though. She just watched as I took out my keys. In a swift motion, I dug in as hard as I could and wrote *ASSHOLE* and *COWARD* on the hood of the car. I climbed up and scratched long, messy lines like a child's scribbles all over the roof, and then climbed down and wrote on the trunk *UNMANLY ASSHOLE DESERVING OF DEATH!*

Di watched me, her mouth agape. I grabbed her arm. "Now let's run!" We dashed through an alley like we were running from the Hong Kong police. We linked arms as though we had to push our way through the train station in Qingdao. We took a tight turn into another alley, just like we used to when we raced other street children for scraps. So many times Di and I had fled together hand in hand, and this felt no different. Di was the only other person in my life whose adolescence had been interrupted by trauma, who would always carry those memories from the mainland as we became adults in Taiwan. Together, we slowed down as we reached a busy street, and caught our breath in the shade of an apartment building.

"He's going to know it was me!" Di wailed, burying her face in her hands.

"But it wasn't you," I said, fanning my face as sweat dripped down my forehead. "It was me. If he tries to bother you about it, just compare your handwriting. I'm sure you two sent each other a lot of letters."

Di started bawling. "I can't believe that I was stupid enough to waste my life on this asshole." She had cried so much over the past weeks that it was hard to believe that she had any tears left, but they gushed from her eyes and ran down her cheeks.

Gently, I dabbed her face and eyes with my handkerchief and said, "Let's go get some oyster omelets and rice noodles. My treat." I knew those were two of her favorite street food specialties. Di sniffed, nodded, and let me lead her toward one of the best outdoor markets, a narrow alley that was packed with food stands. The pungent and delicious smell of fermented tofu wafted through the air, even though that vendor was on the third street away from us. There would always be a special place in my heart for these little restaurant stands. I seated Di on a red plastic stool in front of the oyster omelet chef, and I sat on the opposite side after placing our order.

"You made a mistake, yes, but you didn't waste your life," I said. Though Di and I had our differences, I was proud of her. "You are graduating this year and you are going to be a nurse. You will have a job and your own income. If you don't want to get married, then don't get married. Who cares if Father gets angry? You of all people shouldn't care, since you hate Father anyway." It was surprising advice coming from me, who usually tried to bridge the gap between Di and my parents.

"You don't understand," Di said, sniffing and blotting her eyes with my handkerchief. "You found your dorky soul mate. You have the perfect marriage."

"No one has a perfect marriage," I replied, ignoring the insult that she had slipped in. "But you can still have a very happy one. A blissful one, if you find the right person."

As Di sobbed more loudly, I felt like Uncle Jian, attempting to make her feel better yet seeming to only tear at her wounds. "I did find the right person," she cried. "But our family ruined it. I've been abandoned again, and now no one else will want me."

My heart split as I watched her put her head on her arms and cry. "The right person would never have put you in this position," I said. The way she had used the word "abandoned" struck me painfully. "Li-Tang is a coward. The two of you faced the same pressure. You held on, and he buckled. How could a chicken like him be a good match for a brave woman like you?"

Di looked up, her eyes swollen. "I just don't want to be alone anymore. I've always been alone. I'm tired of being alone."

When we were children, Di had always played by herself. She had been independent, fearless, shameless. We had spent our whole lives together, but she was still a mystery to me. She had been so angry at Father for abandoning us. Why wasn't she angry at Li-Tang? She was so quick to label Mom a coward. Why not Li-Tang? And here I was, sitting before her. Did I not count as a person? Did my presence make her feel lonely?

The chef called me to pick up our plates of oyster omelets, and when I'd returned with them Di ate silently and without expression—as though she couldn't taste the silky oysters enrobed in tapioca flour, the egg batter that was crispy on the outside and chewy on the inside. She might as well have been gnawing on hard bread. Undeterred, I took Di on a tour of the food alley, stopping by several stands and presenting her with beef noodle soup, grilled chicken skewers, and grape tomatoes dipped in candy syrup, to dampen her despair.

"Thank you, Sis," she said quietly as she finished her last tomato. "You are the only one in the family who has ever cared about me. If I miss anyone when I leave, it will be you."

Her words stunned me. As she threw her skewer into the garbage, I felt like I was looking at a ghost. Whatever fire had burned in her had been extinguished. The Di I had grown up with was a girl who was scrappy and clever enough to flourish in the harsh conditions of the mainland. A girl who made connections everywhere and anywhere and fought for what she wanted. "You have survived far worse than heartbreak," I finally said. "You don't need to give up, Di."

Di sighed and said, "You will never understand me, and I will never understand you. You've never truly had your heart broken, Big Sister. I hope you never will."

Despite my advice, Di went through with the marriage that Father had approved. She moved out of the family *shibeyuan* with her new husband and never looked back. I thought back to years before, when Di told me that she couldn't wait to marry and leave the Ang family. Perhaps her haste to agree to the marriage was just that—so that she could finally sever ties with us. After her wedding, Di was true to the words of her young self; she became like a bucket of water that had been thrown out the door. Try as we might, we could never bring her back again.

37

BIRTH

I was twenty-three when I became pregnant, and it was late June 1960 when I went into labor. Every summer in Taiwan I thought my blood would boil, and now that I was pregnant the heat seemed to seep into my skin and burn me from the inside. Lying on my side in the hospital, I felt like a whale that had been stranded on the shore of a terribly hot beach. Mom was in the room with me, fanning me while Jia-Shen waited outside. A few of his close friends from school came to the hospital, lugging cases of beer and a large bottle of fine liquor. The beer was for passing the time, and if the baby was born healthy, they would celebrate with several rounds of shots.

We were technically on the fifth floor, but in reality it was the fourth floor. Chinese people consider four to be an unlucky number because it sounds like the Mandarin word for "death." Most hospitals in Taiwan avoided having a fourth floor because no one wanted to be on it, and in the elevator the numbers went straight from three to five. Even with our floor labeled as five, Mom muttered that it was unfortunate and hung Buddhist beads on my bed for good luck, and a Christian cross just in case.

My labor lasted for two days, and after the first twelve hours my husband and his friends were so drunk off of beer that they had to go home to recuperate. By the time Jia-Shen was sober enough to stagger back to the hospital waiting room, I was in the final stages of labor.

I made a vow to never have children again as the waves of pain felt like they would inundate me. I didn't know about Jia-Shen's drinking until after the fact; otherwise I might have summoned the strength to haul myself out of bed and stab him with a scalpel. Mom had lied to keep me calm and insisted that he was devotedly pacing back and forth outside the hospital.

Time was a strange thing. I was certain that I had been pushing forever and that winter must have been upon us. As I clutched the bedsheets in agony, I began to believe that the baby would never come out and I would die pregnant. Then suddenly it was all over. I heard crying and felt a euphoric sense of relief. It was a familiar sound, as I had heard it several times, when my siblings were born. Then it had been Mom who was sweating and exhausted—and now it was me, with Mom sitting anxiously by my side.

"It's a girl!" the doctor announced as a nurse toweled my baby off and handed her to me.

Beside me, Mom wailed and began to cry.

I was weary, and light-headed from the endorphins racing through my body. At first, I thought I was hallucinating. "Mom?"

"I was hoping it would be a boy." She sobbed, her thin shoulders shaking as she wiped her eyes with the back of her hand. Mom had given birth to five girls, and despite the disappointment that she might have felt, she had never cried when the baby's sex was announced.

"Stop it, Mom. You are being so dramatic," I said hoarsely, holding the baby up to my breast to latch on. Though this was my first infant, I had watched Mom so many times that I knew what to do.

Mom's tears continued to fall as she said, "I just don't want you to end up like me." She sniffed. "I want you to have a son, so your position is assured."

I reached out with my free hand and placed it on Mom's, giving hers a squeeze. "My position is assured because you sold your bangle so that I could go to school."

As I lay alone with my daughter later that night, I thought of everything that Mom had done—that we had done together—to bring us to this point in time. Mom could never forget the years of anguish she had suffered hoping and praying for a son while internalizing the belief that she was not worthy of decent, human treatment if she did not bear one. Though my parents remained together, Mom would never recover from the trauma of being left behind with her daughters, of being treated like she was disposable because her children were the wrong sex. In that hospital room, I made a promise to my daughter. "I will make sure that you grow up well. I will make sure that things are different."

After my daughter, I had two sons. Even though my children had enough food, I could never let go of the experience of starvation, or the lingering fear that in a day, everything that we had built could crumble. I fed my children with the goal of keeping them fat, not only because I associated plumpness with health, but also so they could have some cushion in case disaster struck. When I cooked chicken from the market, I peeled off the skin and cut it into strips to feed to them like noodles. They were enormous babies, with sausage arms and drooping jowls, but I still worried that they weren't eating enough. For the rest of my life, I would never feel completely safe; even in our best moments, there was a voice within me that questioned when we might be forced to flee again.

With Di and me married and out of the house, Nai Nai resumed her nasty attitude toward Mom. Even though Mom had finally produced an heir, Nai Nai was so accustomed to abusing her that it was easy to slip back into old habits. Initially, Nai Nai tried to behave better when I visited, but with time she grew audacious. When I took my children to the Ang family *shiheyuan*, Nai Nai would make Mom kneel in front of us all for absurd reasons, like overcooking an egg. In her old age, she clung to power like a mad queen, exercising her authority simply to reassure herself that it was still there. I had grown up watching Mom kneel. I didn't want my daughter to do so too.

I pulled Mom aside and asked, "How long has this been going on?"

Mom looked at me quizzically and said, "What do you mean?"

"The kneeling," I said, upset. "Obviously!"

"Oh, Hai," said Mom, not even ruffled. "That's been going on forever. You know that." Mom had never complained to me, so for years I assumed that Nai Nai had stopped this deplorable practice. The only time Mom complained about the Angs was when Lao Lao passed away. Like many mainlanders in Taiwan, she was waiting for the day when the borders would open and she could visit the Daos. She was devastated when she learned that she would never see her mother again, and she asked Father if she could light some incense for her on Lunar New Year. Not only did Father say no; he was offended that she would even ask. It was bad fortune to pray to another family's ancestors; Mom's parents were the Dao men's responsibility, and incense for them had no place on the Ang family altar.

My own life was so different from my mother's that I sometimes forgot the traditions that she was still entrenched in—having to ask her husband for permission to light incense for her own mother, and then abiding by his decision. I tried to convince Mom to separate from the Angs and come live with me, but she refused to leave Ming. For years I saved money to buy her a small apartment in our building, so she could have her own space. "It's yours, Mom," I told her when I handed her the keys. "Whenever you want to move in, I'll help you."

Mom was elated, but not for the reason that I had hoped. "This is wonderful," she said. "We've been saving so Ming can have his own home when he is older. Please put the apartment in his name. I want him to have it." Mom existed for my brother. She didn't think about how frugally I had lived just so I could gift her with a space where she could be happy, where she could be safe.

There were so many aspects of my parents and their relationships that I wished would change. Yet, year after year, they repeated the same behaviors, as though they were in a purgatory of their own making. Despite my frustration, I didn't always speak up when I should have. In my moments of weakness, I always thought of Di, whom we had seen only a few times since her marriage, even though she lived in the same city as us. Di was never afraid to break the silence, and if she was, then I would have been compelled to. Somehow, in her I found courage. Though Di and I had fought so often in our youth, I realized that when she left, I had lost a part of myself.

When Mom was fifty-eight, Nai Nai commanded her to kneel for the last time. For the first time in her life, Mom said, "No."

"What do you mean, no? I told you to kneel and you will do as I say!" Nai Nai hissed.

"No." Mom repeated it, firmly. Since Mom was fifty-eight, Ming was twenty-two. He had graduated from university already, and earned his first paycheck. With tears streaming down her face, Mom said, "I don't have to obey you anymore. My son is earning money now, and he will take care of me. I won't rely on you—or your son—any longer."

When Mom told me this story, I was crushed. Not because of her defiance—for that I was grateful, proud that she had finally stood up to Nai Nai. What broke my heart was that Mom felt that she had had to wait for Ming to grow up before she could do it. While Ming was still in diapers, I had been giving Mom my salary. I had paid for her apartment. I was more than happy to care for her in her old age; in fact, I had budgeted for it. It pained me that despite my love and support for her, in her mind it was still her son who made the difference between her servitude and her freedom. Taiwan itself had evolved around her, but she continued to see our world as it had been before World War II—as a world in which men operated, and women were significant only insofar as they could perpetuate this way of life through the births of heirs.

I frequently thought back to our journey through China, and of the resilient, intelligent, and resourceful woman who was my mother. She was talented in so many ways, yet the bulk of her life had been within the family walls, working harder than anyone else around her without acknowledgment or gratitude. I often wondered how our lives would have been if we had stayed in Hong Kong. Perhaps Di would have blossomed, and there wouldn't have been this distance between us. Perhaps Mom still would have found a way to get us through school, while building a life of her own.

Mom never said that she regretted going to Taiwan, and if anything, my and Di's success validated her decision. Many nights, however, I felt regret on her behalf. I wished that she had taken the dedication and determination that she had put into reunification with the Angs and put it into any other plan. Realistically, I knew too that our resources had been so limited that it would not have been possible for her to get an education for herself, and starting a business would have been a struggle. Sometimes, though, I saw people selling dumplings and buns in the night markets with lines so long that they wound around into the alley, and I wondered if that could have been Mom. I saw restaurant owners with gold wristwatches and shiny cars, and I wondered if that could have been Di. We will never know.

38

HEIRESS

It wasn't until my own daughter turned twenty-two that I was able to stop dwelling on alternate lives for Mom and Di and let that anguish go.

My greatest challenges as a mother were identifying the values that I wished to pass to my children and finding the courage to break with tradition when I needed to. It was often difficult to contradict what I myself had been taught, and deviate from what others around me continued to uphold—but I knew my children's future depended on it. There are ways in which I have failed, but there are also ways in which I have succeeded.

Despite the social pressure, I refused to perpetuate the Confucian focus on sons and the antiquated belief that only men can worship their ancestors. While I couldn't shield my daughter from discrimination, I could at least emphasize the importance of her independence—the sanctity of choice. Regardless of what she wanted to do with her life, I wanted her to be brave enough to open any door, confident enough to pursue any path.

Because of my own experience, I encouraged all three of my children to value their education, which should never be taken for granted. Of all of them, it was my daughter, Yun-Mei, who listened to me most. She took so many notes at school that she ended up with a finger callus like mine, and stayed up late reading anything and everything. I set money aside so that after she left middle school, I could send her to take high school entrance exams. I wanted her, like Chiao and my brother, Ming, to have a shot at university.

Yun-Mei scored so well on her exams that she placed at First Girls' High School. As the name implies, it was the best high school for young women in the nation and the most difficult to enter. The school was known for its signature green uniform. When I purchased that uniform, it was like I had stepped out of the store with the world's finest, most beautiful dress—I danced home with my bag as though it contained a million-dollar outfit. After carefully ironing out every crease and wrinkle, I asked her to wear it and come with me to run errands.

Since Chinese culture requires modesty, it would have been rude of me to run through the streets shouting to my neighbors that my daughter was going to First Girls' High School. So instead we went to buy flour. We went to the butcher. We took the long way to the post office to mail a letter. We took the bus back home and got off a stop early so that we could walk back through the market. I beamed as she strode beside me in her green uniform, a silent announcement to everyone looking our way that my daughter was not only going to high school—she was going to the best high school.

Four years after that, it was June again and she took her college entrance exams. I knew she was smart, so I didn't worry about her placement—she would definitely be accepted at one of the public universities, which were subsidized, and also ranked higher than any of the private schools. I was just giddy that my daughter would be the first girl in our family to attend university at all.

When the results came back, we saw that she, as Chiao would say, had crushed that exam into smithereens. She was accepted at National Taiwan University, the best and most competitive university in the entire nation. My aspirations for my daughter had been modest, I realized. I had wanted her to reach the same targets that the men did. As the first in our family to be admitted to National Taiwan University, she was on track not only to reach those targets—but to surpass them.

My daughter was twenty-two when she graduated, and was admitted on a scholarship to a master's program—not in Taiwan, but in the United States of America. It was hard for non-Americans to enter these programs, and even harder for them to get any financial support. Not only was Yun-Mei going to be the first among our relatives to pursue a master's degree; she was also going to be the first to travel abroad.

At her graduation ceremony, I soaked in the moment, and came to the epiphany that a story does not need to end with a single person. Sometimes, success is something that happens over the course of generations, something that is built upon life after life, each one opening a path so that those coming after can walk easier, farther, like the refugees who made the road at Rennie's Mill. My mother had limited education and sold eggs in the market. I had a specialty degree, but university was out of my reach. My daughter was going to have a master's degree, and she was going to be a scientist. A scientist!

That August, my husband and I stood together at Chiang Kai-Shek International Airport as my daughter waited in line for security. I had done her hair that morning, even though she kept telling me it was unnecessary since she would just be confined on planes for the next twenty-four hours. She looked elegant with her leather suitcase and with her shoulder-length hair in curls—she resembled Mom, with her large eyes and pronounced cheekbones. I had picked out a cream-colored silk shirt and a knee-length tweed skirt for her. I bought her high heels, even though she told me she wasn't going to wear them, since heels were the new foot-binding. I made her take some dumplings and bananas, even though she said food wasn't allowed past customs. Inside her bag were her lab coats, which I had carefully washed, starched, and ironed, even though she said that they were essentially aprons and didn't need such rigorous upkeep. She didn't understand that I treated these items with reverence because of what they symbolized, as opposed to what they actually were.

To say that I am proud is an understatement.

When I think of my mother, I will always remember her as the person who walked through the gates of Qingdao on disfigured feet, a child on her back, another beside her, while pushing me in a wheelbarrow. Through her strength, I became who I was, and through that, I cannot help but feel that my daughter's success is also hers to rejoice in.

At that airport, I felt as though every harsh and terrible hurdle in my life had been worth enduring so that I could bask in the glory of that moment. My heart beat loudly as my daughter crossed the security line. She turned and waved to us and blew a final kiss before fading among the crowd that was hurrying toward the gates. After she was gone, I told my husband that I wanted to stay for a little bit longer.

I blinked and tears fell, but it was a mix of emotions. Sadness that she would be so far away from me, and happiness that she had come so far. I closed my eyes and imagined her in her lab coat in this foreign land, breaking the barriers that neither Mom nor I could have crossed. Mom had opened doors for me, so that I in turn could open them for my daughter. Through that work, my daughter earned her independence, and with that, her freedom to find happiness.

I wiped my eyes and smiled to myself. I knew then and there that my daughter would never kneel to anyone. I slipped my arm around my husband's and we walked away from the security line, toward the airport's main exit. We passed through the shadow of the double doors, and then the bright sunlight shone against our faces.

I stood tall and thought of Mom. I glowed. We were victorious.

AUTHOR'S NOTE

I spent the first years of my life in Taiwan with my grandmother, my Puo Puo, on the fourth floor of a building that often flooded during typhoon season. Four is an unlucky number for Chinese people, but in this case, my grandmother considered it good fortune—we never got water damage. On the downside, there was no elevator and she had to lug me, a forty-pound two-year-old, up three flights of stairs. She was strong, physically and mentally, and crazy in the best possible way.

After my parents finished their studies, I moved back to the United States to live with them. They were shocked by my size. Apparently, I had been drinking a gallon of whole milk every two days, and my grandmother fed me chicken skin. In almost every home video she is chasing me, diligently shoving food into my mouth with chopsticks. As a child, I assumed that her aggressive force-feeding was just a quirk. It wasn't until I was an adult that I understood that it was a consequence of trauma.

AUTHOR'S NOTE

The few years that she spent as a refugee in mainland China marked her for the rest of her life. In Taiwan, I knew her as a woman who laughed easily and smiled often. She never spoke to me about what happened during the Communist Revolution, but I understood that she had suffered. Every evening, she used a heat lamp on her knees because she had spent hours kneeling on the ice. My mom told me that Puo Puo used to forage for edible plants and beg for scraps in markets, until she managed to reunite with her father in Taiwan. I knew only bits and pieces of her story and did not realize how incredible her journey was until after she had passed.

I started writing this book in March 2022, shortly after my daughter's first birthday. I was in Seattle visiting my mom, and we started planning a trip to Taiwan. I still have not returned to the island since my grandmother's death in 2013. To me, Taiwan and Puo Puo were one and the same, and the idea of being there without her filled me with regret. I hated that my children would never get to meet her, and I wished that I had taken the time to ask her more questions while she was alive.

During that Seattle visit, I interviewed my mom about my grandmother's journey to Taiwan, with the goal of recording a family history. It became apparent, however, that there were too many gaps for the story to truly be a biography. There was too much that I didn't know, and couldn't know, too many chunks of time having disappeared with my grandmother's passing. As a result, I pivoted to writing a work of fiction, inspired by her true story, which became a dream in and of itself.

This book consumed me. I had little time to write because I was working a full-time job as an international human rights lawyer, and also had an infant and a toddler. Every spare moment I had was devoted to this story. At least half of this manuscript was

AUTHOR'S NOTE

written on my cell phone, whenever I found a pocket of time—on the subway to my office, in the elevator up and down to the lobby, and while walking to pick up my son and daughter. Several chapters were written in the dark as I waited for my kids to fall asleep, sometimes with my daughter clinging to my chest. I was determined to finish this book because I was afraid of what would be lost if I didn't.

Line by line, I strung together paragraphs that morphed into scenes—collections of snippets that I had taken from my mom and interviews with other relatives. Still, many gaps remained. I turned to academic research, reading everything I could about Qingdao and Hong Kong during 1949 and 1950. I already had a background in modern Chinese history, and I reached out to professors specializing in topics that could be pertinent to my book.

My greatest challenge was finding first-person sources in English. Though I am fluent in spoken Chinese, my reading level is elementary at best. Qingdao in particular was a murky abyss. Though I have several relatives who live there, none of them were willing to speak about the past. They said it was a dark period, and that was all I needed to know. I couldn't accept that answer, so I delved deeper and discovered that the US Marines and the Navy's Seventh Fleet had been stationed there following World War II. Through them, I found old pictures and maps of Qingdao and China's fractured railway system. The diaries and memoirs of soldiers ended up being my most valuable resource for piecing together the city.

While there was more English material available about 1950s Hong Kong, as well as photographs, there was little information about Rennie's Mill, which quickly became my obsession. I knew that my grandmother had lived there, but I struggled to find

AUTHOR'S NOTE

details. When I contacted scholars specializing in British–Hong Kong relations, I was told that there were no refugee camps in Hong Kong at that time. Yet I also knew that from November 1949 to December 1949 alone, about two hundred thousand people crossed into the colony from China. My research process here was slow and halting, but as I chipped away, it all became clear.

Through academic journals and books, I learned that the Hong Kong government avoided referring to the newcomers as "refugees," due to political sensitivities. Though Mao Ze-Dong's government ruled China, Chiang Kai-Shek's government still held China's seat at the United Nations. Drawing attention to the refugee crisis could have prompted international support, and any intervention would have included Nationalist representatives. To avoid this diplomatic powder keg, the Hong Kong government initially referred to Mount Davis as the "Citizens' Village" instead of as a refugee enclave. In 1954, Edvard Hambro submitted a report to the UN High Commissioner for Refugees entitled "The Problem of Chinese Refugees in Hong Kong," which provided more detailed information about the crisis. By then, Mount Davis had already been shut down, and most Nationalist sympathizers were in Rennie's Mill.

Since Rennie's Mill was closed to journalists, there was little information in Western news about the conditions there. My most comprehensive source ended up being a PhD thesis by Kenneth On Wai Lan, submitted to the University of Hong Kong, titled "Rennie's Mill: The Origin and Evolution of a Special Enclave in Hong Kong." I was, and still am, in awe of the refugees of Rennie's Mill, who not only survived but blossomed in such a harsh landscape. Against all odds, they turned Hanging Neck Ridge into a village that would eventually be known as Little Taiwan. Contrary

AUTHOR'S NOTE

to everyone's expectations, it endured until 1997—when the authorities bulldozed it to the ground, shortly before Hong Kong returned to the People's Republic of China.

Though I have tried to be as historically accurate as possible, I have taken creative license, and I wish to emphasize that this book is fiction and should not be relied on as a historical text. There are characters and events that came entirely from my imagination, and scenes that have been dramatized. Nevertheless, at its core, this book tells a family story, one that is dear and personal to both my mom and me.

Writing this book was a work of passion, but it was also a work of grief. I grew up with parents who loved me, and I had a close relationship with my family. Nevertheless, the difference between boys and girls was still obvious in our society and traditions, and reiterated on a constant basis. Chinese people have a saying, *Zhong nan qing nu*, which means "Value men; belittle women." Sexism was, and still is, so ingrained in our culture that many women consider it part of fate. As many fables around the world illustrate, a person cannot fight fate.

Since my great-grandmother's time, however, each generation has come closer to eradicating the harms instilled by our ancestors. I credit that to our increasing access to education. My schooling not only taught me about how the world is, but gave me the tools to think about how the world should be, could be. As a child, I thought the disparities between boys and girls were unfair, and as an adult, I wanted change. Those feelings led me to become a women's human rights lawyer and eventually to work for both nongovernmental and international organizations.

Achieving gender equality requires our society to transform itself in several interrelated ways. Education, while only one facet,

AUTHOR'S NOTE

creates a foundation for working toward other goals. It can lift people out of poverty and break harmful cycles that have endured for centuries. In my mind, there is no greater tool for empowering children than good teachers and parents. For my family, the freedom to learn and study has led to a dismantling of sexist traditions, and I hope that my son and daughter will grow up in a more just world as a result. In the end, they are the ones who inspire me to continue fighting for change.

This book is a tribute to my grandmother, but it is dedicated to my children, who are part of her legacy. While I did not need to write this story in order to remember my Puo Puo, through it I feel as though I have kept her memory alive. My mom and I are honored to share her journey and celebrate her strength and determination. I will always miss her, and am grateful to have had her fierce, crazy love. Wherever she is, I hope she is happy—and I hope she is proud.

ACKNOWLEDGMENTS

First and foremost, I'd like to thank my parents. They have made countless sacrifices for me, and I am privileged to have their love and support. With regard to my writing, there are two particular moments that shine. First, when I was in middle school, my dad gifted me a collection of Sherlock Holmes stories—his favorite when he was growing up. Inside, he wrote a dedication, wishing that one day my own stories would blossom. Though I lost that book, I held on to that memory. Second, when I was thirty-five and had long forgotten about childhood dreams, I had to log in to an old account that my dad had opened for me. One of the security questions was "What did you want to be when you grew up?" To my surprise, my dad had put "writer" as the answer. It helped me remember who I was, and dared me to dream again.

With regard to this particular book, it is my mom who carried it. She pulled the meat of this story from her memories, and helped

ACKNOWLEDGMENTS

me interview relatives and translate Chinese articles. Most important, I was able to write about the selfless love that mothers have for their daughters, because it is something I have received plentifully. No matter how old I am, my mom still tries to take care of me. It is a kindness that I no longer take for granted, and one that I cherish even more as time goes by. Without my mom, *Daughters of Shandong* would not exist. She is, after all, this story's happy ending.

I am beyond grateful to the amazing women who helped transform this book from a dream into a reality: my spectacular agent, Alexa Stark, and brilliant editor, Amanda Bergeron. It has been a privilege to work with Berkley, and in this regard, I'd like to thank Ivan Held, Christine Ball, Jeanne-Marie Hudson, Craig Burke, Claire Zion, Sareer Khader, Lauren Burnstein, Tina Joell, Jin Yu, Jessica Mangicaro, Kim-Salina I, Vi-An Nguyen, Anthony Ramondo, Christine Legon, and Dan Walsh.

I would also like to acknowledge my friends, who graciously served as my beta readers—especially those who slogged through my first draft and gave kind encouragement: Katarína Medľová, Cynthia L. Winfield, Karan Lee, Zakiya R. Adair, Norine Groden, Lan Shiow Tsai, and Dorothy Du LeRay. In addition to them, there were countless people who provided much-needed emotional support during the writing process: my husband, David; my brother, Jesse; my knitting club (especially Anne Chubbuck, Anna Gulko, Johanna Li, Joyce McKenney, and Suzanne Lorang); my AAPI writing group; and my friend Sylvia Hordosch.

In particular, I am lucky to have David's steadfast love.

Finally, I'd like to express my gratitude to my children, Calvin and Katrina. You are the reason I keep going. Whenever I have a setback or a bad day, you are the ones who give me hope. For you, I can endure anything. I love you both, forever and always—with all my heart, all my soul, and everything in between.